I0654877

The Commandment Trilogy Part 3:

The City and the Desert

Derek Bickerton

Aignos Publishing
an imprint of Savant Books and Publications
Honolulu, HI, USA
2020

Published in the USA by Aignos Publishing LLC
An imprint of Savant Books and Publications LLC
2630 Kapiolani Blvd #1601
Honolulu, HI 96826
http://www.aignospublishing.com

Printed in the USA

Edited by Zachary M. Oliver
Image "desert-dune-arid-africa-hot-984081" from Free Photos by
Pixabay
Cover by Daniel S. Janik

Copyright 2019 by Derek Bickerton. All rights reserved. No part of this
work may be reproduced without the prior written permission of the
author.

13 digit ISBN: 978-0-9996938-0-3

All names, characters, places and incidents are fictitious or used
fictitiously. Any resemblance to actual persons, living or dead, and any
places or events is purely coincidental.

First Edition: August 2020
Library of Congress Control Number: 2020943995

Dedication
To Yvonne

Acknowledgements

Post-humous thanks to Derek and Yvonne's friend Dr. Zachary M. Oliver and family for believing in the overarching importance of this work. With their help and assistance, Dr. Bickerton's timeless voice and humanitarian message will continue to be available to future generations.

Foreword

This last of the books in Derek Bickerton's The Commandment Trilogy was a labor of love, Mr. Bickerton having passed prior to its release. An academic giant in the field of linguistics, he was an equally talented humanistic author and speaker. Having met and discussed a variety of topics several times during the early preparation of this third and final work in the trilogy, I have had the opportunity to read and reread not only the first two books but to do the same with this third work prior to its release. I can say with authority that for those seeking wisdom in life, as with his prior two works, this one will not disappoint.

- Daniel S. Janik MD PhD

Derek Bickerton

Chapter 1

They had held prayers in the Caesarium prior to sailing. They had prayed again on the quayside, the delegation flanked by hordes of acolytes, parabolani and urban monks. Then, Theophilus had blessed the ship—Cygnus, the Swan, by name—with all the more sincerity since he himself was going to be on it. Only then could they go aboard, the archiepiscopal delegation first, of course, followed by cohorts of slaves and servants bearing mattresses, bedding, cooking utensils, food and drink—everything they might need on a voyage that, if the winds proved contrary, could take three weeks or longer. The ordinary passengers, with their permits to leave Egypt clutched in their hands, waited their turn on the quay, marveling at the richness and variety of the wares required for the functioning of an archbishop and his entourage.

It was late to be traveling—late October, almost the end of the sailing season. This could well be the last boat out of Alexandria for Constantinople or any other far destination that year, barring emergencies or urgent state business. From November through March, the Mediterranean might be struck at any time by savage storms, and cloudy nights made it impossible to steer by the stars, even a late October sailing was dangerous. Plenty of ships never made it, and the captain, watching the strange ceremonies on the quayside, regretted the old days when you slaughtered a bull before leaving and could at least learn your chance of survival from a diligent inspection of its innards. As the secular passengers, many of them Christians, filed aboard, they crossed themselves, a precaution which the sharp-eyed captain noted, had been neglected by the clergy, who must think their superior status gave them a lock on providence. *Dream on*, the captain thought. *The sea neither knows nor cares who or what you are.*

Not that Theophilus was unworried. Too much turned on this voyage to take it lightly. He briefly inspected his cabin near the stern of the ship; it was the best, of course, but since the ship had very few cabins—even a lot of the clergy would have to sleep in tents on the deck—that really wasn't saying much. Then, he left his servants to arrange it for him and went back on deck to observe the departure.

For a long time, nothing much seemed to be happening. The sailors had loosed the mooring ropes but still kept a turn or two around the bollards. Nobody seemed in a hurry to raise the sails. Theophilus recognized the reason for the delay: a sleek single-tier galley manned by a couple of dozen oarsmen were heading in their direction. A stiff north wind, blowing out of a cloudy afternoon sky, made it impossible for them to exit the crowded harbor under sail. The galley turned and backed up, someone threw a line to its steersman, the steersman made fast the line, and then, straining at their oars, the galley's crew slowly got the Cygnus under way. The captain of the Cygnus had already waited days for a favorable wind, and had decided he dare not take the chance of waiting any longer.

The oarsmen were into their rhythm now and the Cygnus clipped along, meeting already the sharp chop of the winter Mediterranean as the wind pushed the waters through the harbor entrance. Theophilus felt the first faint stirrings of queasiness in his bowels. In an hour or two, he knew from bitter experience, he would be prostrated by seasickness—in a contrary sea, these broad-beamed, deep-bellied ships rolled uncontrollably. He could delay things only a little by remaining on deck, but he did so, even though a line of horizon squalls promised rain soon. The huge tower of the Pharos slid by on his left, he could see the daylight-dulled glow of its perpetual furnace dimly reflected in the vast bronze mirror high overhead. As always, the sight cheered him.

"There's Alexandria for you," he said to the deacon standing with obsequious unobtrusiveness at his side. "Nothing like that in the entire world."

"That's very true, your Reverence."

"Where's Father Isidore, do you know?"

"In his cabin, I think, your Reverence."

"Not surprised." Theophilus grunted. Isidore was a worse sailor than he was, if that were possible. He waited while the big square mainsail and the more flexible foresail went up, while the galley cast off and headed for home. When the Cygnus started to tack into the rising seas, he went below.

Isidore, as he had expected, was stretched out on his mattress, his head in his hands. "Feeling it already?" his superior asked. Isidore groaned for an answer.

"Don't worry," Theophilus said. "This is your last voyage."

That got Isidore's attention. He looked up, his face green. "You think we're going down?"

Theophilus laughed. "Not yet, anyway. I mean, when you're in charge in Constantinople, you won't have to go anywhere any more. If you need to see anyone, they'll come to you."

"You're very confident," Isidore muttered.

"So I should be. I've been working on this for years. The synod is fixed, I can promise you that. We'll have a clear majority. Nobody else can pick up more than a handful of votes. You're a shoo-in, Isidore."

And, don't ever forget who put you there, he added to himself, or you'll

4

regret it.

"But...the Emperor..."

Theodosius had died; Arcadius had succeeded him. None of this worried Theophilus. "Arcadius is a good Christian, he'll do what his spiritual advisors tell him to. And they're in my pocket." Theophilus turned to leave; he could feel his own nausea rising fast. "Hold on," he reassured his candidate. "Just a few more days."

He went to his cabin, told his servants to leave and laid down. He would have traveled by land, but it would have taken too long. The passes over the Isaurian Mountains would have been closed for the winter by the time he reached them; he would have had to take the long way round, by the coast. He'd never have arrived in time. That was funny, though, when you thought about it. Obviously they didn't want to waste time appointing a new Archbishop, but was it possible—was it even remotely conceivable—that the date had been deliberately set so as to make it difficult or impossible for him to attend?

He dismissed the idea. He had kept, he flattered himself, a low profile in the capital, working always through intermediaries, he had no enemies there that he knew of, unless maybe the anti-Origenists? No, that storm in a teacup certainly hadn't spread beyond Palestine yet. Besides, what difference would it make, even if he didn't attend in person? His creatures knew who they had to count on for favors, support, patronage. No, the only person to blame was the old Archbishop, Nectarius himself, for having had the lack of consideration to die in early September, thus obliging the authorities either to leave the Eastern Church without a leader for the best part of a year, or convene a synod with what might look like indecent haste. If only the old fool had waited until next March!

The ship ploughed on. The wind shifted to the east, and they sighted the southern tip of Rhodes on the seventh day. As the captain, steering between Rhodes and Karpathos, headed into the island-studded Aegean, the seas subsided and, after a week of misery, Theophilus was able to come on deck again. The fresh sea breezes soon revived him. His only worry now was that something might go wrong back home during his absence. Alexandria was so volatile, you could never tell what trouble the Jews or the heretics or even the remaining pagans might stir up. Luckily he had strengthened the administration of the Church. Always suspicious of Timothy, who knew too much about him to be trusted, he had brought in champions of unimpeachable orthodoxy, stout anti-anthropomorphites like the two Tall Brothers, Eusebios and Euthymios, to make sure the books balanced, deal with his less sensitive correspondence, and see that none of the vast and ever-growing army of monks, hermits and other religious strayed from the paths he approved of.

The Cygnus would have finished by making quite good time, but for a storm in the Sea of Marmara that held them back for three days when they were almost in sight of their destination. Early in the morning of the eighteenth day, Theophilus, woken by the bustle of men lowering sail and getting ready to dock, came cautiously on deck to see a misty sun drawing gleams of gold from the spires and domes and statues of the Imperial city.

They docked at Phosphorianos, the harbor at the junction of the Bosphorus and the Golden Horn. Theophilus' servants hurried to hire litters, and soon the party was on its way south, alongside the old, original wall of Byzantium, now deep within the great city. *How it has swollen,* Theophilus thought, *in a single lifetime!* Towards the episcopal palace, vacant now Nectarius was gone, and placed at the disposal of the more illustrious in the synodal gathering. Soon the cupola of Constantinople's cathedral—the Great Church, Hagia Sophia, or Divine Wisdom—loomed over the crowded roofs, and then the litter-bearers burst out into the Augustaion, a broad piazza surrounded by roofed colonnades and ornamented with towering statues appropriated by the blessed Constantine from sites all over the Mediterranean.

It was, Theophilus had reluctantly to admit, fully as spectacular as anything in his own city. Over to the right of the piazza rose the walls of the Hippodrome. He reckoned it stood near enough to the cathedral for worshipers to have their ears assailed by the bestial roaring of the Green and Blue factions, if chariot races and divine service had the bad luck to coincide. At least in Alexandria, he consoled himself, we don't have to put up with that sort of thing. Straight ahead soared the basilica of the Senate House, imposing enough on the outside, but a mere shell, host to a body of silk-clad parasites whose sole function, apart from ceremonies, was to rubber-stamp imperial decrees. Between Senate House and Hippodrome lay the entrance to the Imperial Palace, a vast labyrinth of buildings and inner courtyards that extended from the Agustaion to the shores of the Sea of Marmara, so that if the populace rose in revolt or barbarians stormed the city, the Emperor and his court could always escape by boat.

Theophilus' litter turned left and entered the courtyard of the episcopal palace. He descended from it next to the covered walkway that linked palace and cathedral. Making his way around scaffolding and between heaps of building material—the palace had been burned down by rioting Arians a few years earlier, and torpid old Nectarius hadn't managed to get all of it rebuilt— he was greeted by a bowing and smiling chamberlain who escorted him and the rest of the Alexandrians to the rooms prepared for them. As soon as his bags had been unpacked and his possessions arranged, he set out to make contact with his friends and supporters. The date of the synod had been postponed for several days, he soon learned, so as to accommodate himself and other clergy coming from remote dioceses. He need not have worried—he was not being excluded, and he had all the more time to cement his alliances and ensure that Isidore had a truly impressive majority.

Then, on the third morning, a messenger came for him.

The liveried official, his bureaucratic rank indicated by the lozenges sewn into his uniform, bowed low and addressed Theophilus with elaborate rhetoric and florid courtesies, but the message was unmistakable. His presence was requested by the Imperial Lord Chamberlain and Superintendent of the Sacred Bedchamber, Eutropius.

And, it was requested now.

Theophilus was none too pleased. He presumed the interview was merely to arrange some formality, but he had hoped to escape meeting Eutropius except on formal occasions. He had met him once before, when the latter came to Egypt on a secret mission for the Emperor Theodosius. And he had unpleasant memories of the evening when, on the express instructions of the Emperor, he had wined and dined Eutropius, and, Eutropius, as repellant morally as he was physically, had held forth with a blatant cynicism and a ruthless self-regard that deeply shocked even Theophilus.

But, Eutropius was far too powerful a figure to offend. And, so, Theophilus readied himself. In the corridor outside, Theophilus signaled to one of his deacons to accompany him.

"No, no!" the official cried urgently. "Just you! Alone! Those were my strict instructions!"

Theophilus was puzzled. Surely Eutropius did not intend to have him assassinated? Although such things had been known to happen, the idea was laughable. What would be the point? Besides, not even the most powerful minister could kill a Patriarch, the ranking third (even though he bought by rights to be second) in the entire Christian hierarchy, and hope to get away with it. *Perhaps he wants to confess to me*, he thought, the very idea forcing him to stifle a giggle of irreverent mirth. God knows he had sins enough.

He accompanied the official across the great piazza and through the immense bronze doors of the Imperial Palace, while its uniformed guards clicked their heels and stood stiff as pokers. Through innumerable halls and corridors they proceeded, past curtained alcoves and dripping fountains, until the official handed Theophilus over to an official with even more lozenges, who conducted him through further halls, exchanging passwords now as they negotiated guarded doors, and finally up a marble staircase that narrowed sharply in its last flight, forcing them into single file. At its top, a last pair of guards vetted them. Theophilus was forced to wait while one of them entered the room beyond and spoke softly with the person within. Then a curtain was lifted aside; he was ushered in.

He stared about him with unconcealed curiosity. Unlike the vast halls through which he had come, this was a relatively small room, almost feminine in its appearance—its walls hung with heavy drapes and tapestries, the furniture light and exquisitely made, vases, statuettes and bric-a-brac of every kind scattered all over it. Its window faced south, and through it he caught a dazzling glimpse of sunlight on water. The one businesslike item in it, a massive desk with tiers of drawers and pigeonholes, stood in shadow, well to one side; a young clerk sitting at it seemed absorbed in his figures. Eutropius was seated by the window, gazing out, apparently unoccupied, although Theophilus was willing to bet that, moments before, he had been hunched over the clerk's shoulder, directing operations which, if half the rumors were true, involved his own enrichment much more than the Emperor's.

As soon as he entered, Eutropius, sitting by the window, signaled for the clerk to leave and for Theophilus to seat himself in a chair arranged so that he could not look at Eutropius without the low but bright morning sun almost blinding him. Squinting into its light, he saw again that grotesque figure, bloated, swathed like a woman in saffron silk robes, with its great, completely hairless head and its face rouged and painted like a whore's, although even the layers of make-up could not conceal the fact that the skin beneath it was lined with a thousand tiny cracks, like a piece of very old and dried-out silk. He smelled a revolting perfume that could surely only be there to disguise yet more disgusting odors from the crevices of the obese body. The small, pouting mouth opened and Eutropius said, in his lisping, fluty voice, "I trust you had a pleasant voyage from Egypt."

"Not too bad, Excellency," Theophilus said airily. It was essential, before people like this, to show, without loss of respect, a perfect confidence and ease of manner; they would sense the least trace of weakness or fear, and pounce like jackals. "I'm afraid I'm not the best of sailors—the ascetic life leaves me with a touchy stomach."

Eutropius nodded sympathetically. "All that fasting," he said, without even a smile, knowing they both remembered how unashamedly they had stuffed themselves that night in Alexandria. Theophilus prayed his disgust did not show. He knew Eutropius' whole history. He knew Eutropius had been born a barbarian on the Assyrian frontier, had been castrated as a child and then sold as a slave to an army farrier who alternately beat and buggered him until, tiring of him, he sold him to another soldier. When he grew too old and ugly to be a catamite any more, he had worked as a pimp for his latest owner, a rich, depraved merchant, until, judged too worn-out even for that trade, he was given his freedom and thrown onto the street.

What most men would have seen as his greatest defect was in fact his greatest strength. Eunuchs were rare and in great demand. They were rare because castration was forbidden throughout the Empire. They were in demand because they did not, and could not, have children.

Nepotism was the terror of the imperial bureaucracy. There were no lengths to which an official would not go to advance the career of his son. At the very highest level, he might even overthrow or assassinate the Emperor himself, if there was the remotest chance that by doing so he might seat his own son on the Imperial throne. Even if you appointed an elderly, childless bachelor, there was no guarantee that he wouldn't sire some by-blow somewhere, for whose future he would work as assiduously as any other father. At best, then, you got incompetent officials appointed way over their merits; at worst, mayhem and revolution. With a eunuch, you could be reasonably sure of undivided loyalty, and you could be sure, too, that if you needed to kill him, no son would loom, seeking vengeance.

So, Eutropius had joined the court staff.

His rise had been meteoric. Hidden all along under the slave's gear he had kept a photographic memory and a rat-trap brain, quick as an abacus. That, linked to the skills learned in a lifetime of providing pleasure for others, had given him the edge even in a school of shark-like competitors, which the Imperial court surely was. In no time, it seemed, he had obtained the confidence of Emperor Theodosius, and simultaneously, by a subtle and traceless series of harassments directed at Arsenius, the Imperial tutor, he had caused the latter to flee to Egypt and become a hermit. That put Arcadius, heir to the Eastern throne, a listless, lackadaisical and none-too-bright lad of sixteen, firmly into the eunuch's hands.

No sooner was Theodosius dead and Arcadius acclaimed as his successor than Eutropius, putting his old pimp skills to work, had inflamed Arcadius' lust and turned it, by a display of pictures and lyrical descriptions, towards someone else in his power—the beautiful, voluptuous, and insanely ambitious Eudoxia. Within just a few months, he had had them, both in his debt, safely married to one another. And in a few more, he had arranged for his only serious rival, the prefect Rufinus, to be cut to pieces on a parade-ground by Gothic legionaries while the Emperor watched, horror-struck but powerless. Now, Eutropius was without question the most powerful man in the Empire.

All this was all too vividly in Theophilus' mind as he struggled to make polite conversation. He was unnerved, too, by a discovery. A movement by Eutropius had disclosed, in the eunuch's left hand but half-hidden by his robe, a carefully-rolled document, tied with a ribbon. At first, the Archbishop had thought nothing of it—probably something Eutropius had been reading before his arrival. Then, as if accidentally, Eutropius moved his hand so as to bring the document into the light, and to the Archbishop's amazement he recognized his own seal on it, broken. What on earth...? Though he could give neither name nor reason for it, he felt deep in his bowels the first cold, leaden touch of fear.

"Now, as for this consecration," Eutropius said, "I'm sure everything's going to go off smoothly, isn't it?"

"I don't see why not," Theophilus countered. "But before that, of course, a small chore has to be performed."

Eutropius raised a pair of all-but-nonexistent eyebrows.

"I mean, of course, we have to select who we're going to consecrate. "

"Oh, really?"

The walls of Theophilus" stomach contracted. "I'm sorry, Excellency, I was under the impression that that was what we'd all been called here for."

He paused. "Go on," Eutropius said, in a mincing tone that somehow conveyed an undercurrent of warning.

"Of course, I realize," Theophilus went on, 'that several candidates may be put forward—naturally, anyone would covet such a position. I have to say, though, in my own humble judgement, that the best is Isidore, former priest of Scetis, an ascetic of blameless life, more recently a distinguished peacemaker within our flock, who, I am given to understand, has been offered massive support from a very wide range of..."

"That boring old fart," Eutropius cut across him. "I wouldn't give you two drachmas for him. I'm sorry, Archbishop. I'm afraid that part of it's been decided already."

Theophilus' face flamed, anger made him reckless. "How can it have been? This synod has not yet been convened..."

"It's been convened," Eutropius said patiently, "to put its seal of ecclesiastical approval on what's already been decided. By us."

He did not bother to say who "us" meant. "You really can't be so naive as to suppose we would allow an appointment of this importance, the Archbishop of the Imperial City, to be decided by a bunch of bishops? They can't even agree about what kind of God they have, so why should they be able to agree about an Archbishop, let alone pick the best one? No, we've already chosen our man. Indeed, he's already been informed. He should be here in a few days."

"Who?" Theophilus asked, dreading the answer.

"John of Antioch, the one they call Goldenmouth."

Theophilus was consumed by fury. "That...that obnoxious little...the one who's always whining about the poor, telling the church to give away all its...? No. I won't stand for it."

"You will stand for it," Eutropius said, and now there was a cold, iron resolve under the fluty tones. "What is more, you will help to convince your fellow-bishops of the rightness of our choice. And when all the other formalities are completed, you personally will consecrate him in Hagia Sophia, and you will give him the Kiss of Peace before the Imperial family and the assembled congregation."

"No!" Theophilus cried in a voice that must have been fully audible to the guards outside the door. "No! I will die first!"

A slow smile spread over the great, creased, painted face. "Indeed," Eutropius said softly. "You very well may."

With deliberate slowness, still smiling malignly, he began to untie the pink silk ribbon that bound the document. The room was warm, overheated, even, but Theophilus felt his bowels turn to ice,

"Cast your mind back," Eutropius said, in a leisurely voice, as he unrolled the document, "oh, say ten, a dozen years or so. To the days when the usurper Maximus had seized half of the Empire and was threatening to take over the other half...Does that ring a bell?"

A cold sweat was pouring down Theophilus' back. "Your Excellence, I really don't know what..."

"You wrote a letter," Eutropius said. "This is that letter."

"I write many letters; you can't expect me to..."

"I shall read it," Eutropius said. "It begins, 'to the most excellent and illustrious Emperor, Maximus" Ah, now I can tell from your face that you do remember it. In that case I won't embarrass you by reading the rest of it, I'm sure you remember vividly how you offered the usurper your most complete loyalty and allegiance in return for his protection of the Alexandrian church and his support for the orthodox faith against the Arian heresy. There's a word for that, isn't there?"

Theophilus, rigid with shock, could not speak.

"The word is treason."

"I never meant it," Theophilus blurted out. "It was an act of policy, I had just been consecrated Archbishop, the Arians were still threatening us, I had to protect my church at all costs, and for a few months it looked as if..."

"As if Maximus would win?"

Theophilus gulped.

"You must understand my position!"

"Oh I do, I do," Eutropius said soothingly. "I understand it perfectly. I also understand why you sent the exact same letter to the real Emperor. A man who bets on both the Green and the Blue can hardly lose, can he? Unless, of course, someone finds out."

Now that the worst was out on the table, Theophilus felt his indomitable spirit rallying.

"How did you get hold of it?" he demanded.

Eutropius laughed. "You of all people to ask that? I know you have an excellent intelligence service. Mine is better, that's all."

"And in any case," Theophilus protested. "You can't accuse me now. It's too late. Theodosius is dead."

"But his son is very much alive." The eunuch's hooded eyes almost twinkled with self-satisfaction. "I don't think Arcadius would be very pleased to hear about an act of treachery against his father, do you? You know perfectly well what his answer would be." And Eutropius, raising a long-nailed finger, drew it across the bulbous folds of his neck. "Archbishop or no Archbishop."

Wild thoughts chased one another through Theophilus' brain. They were alone. No witnesses. Physically he was younger, stronger, fitter than the eunuch. He could overpower him in seconds, tear the letter from his hand, suffocate him with an embroidered cushion. And then simply walk out of there, bowing and smiling over his shoulder as if to a living Eutropius. The cathedral was only ten minutes away, he would throw himself down before the high altar and claim sanctuary and no one, not even the Emperor's guards, would dare to touch him there. Eutropius was loathed as much as feared. He need only claim that the eunuch had made some vile proposition to him—he could concoct something–and that in a fit of pure moral outrage he had struck down the indecent beast. And his conscience would not trouble him for an instant, for it was clearly God's will that Isidore should reign in Constantinople rather than some fancy orator or whining liberal.

Within seconds, he knew this was sheer fantasy. Anyone as devious as Eutropius would be bound to have given copies of the letter to a trusted crony, together with appropriate instructions. In all probability, too, the clerk who had been dismissed on his arrival would return as soon as he had left and discover the body. Theophilus would never leave the palace alive.

"But to look on the brighter side," Eutropius went on, blithely unconscious of how narrowly he had escaped. "If you do exactly as I tell you, then as soon as John is consecrated, this," he raised the letter, "goes into the fire."

"How can I trust you?" Theophilus asked bitterly.

"You have to. You have no option."

"John will turn on you, you know," Theophilus said. "He's a viper. You'd be safer with Isidore."

Eutropius giggled. "I'm not worried. If I make 'em, I can break 'em—right, Archbishop?" He paused, but Theophilus made no comment. "Well," he said after a moment, "Which will it be?"

"I'll do it," Theophilus said in a choked voice.

"Good." Eutropius rolled up the letter, retied the ribbon. "I knew you would. You see, Archbishop, I've always known that you were a sensible man."

Derek Bickerton

Chapter 2

Leila could not believe what was happening to her. She had always tried, insofar as she could, to avoid even thinking about the curse of Eve, the emissions of blood that had come regularly, every month, since she ceased to be a girl. These rude reminders of her carnal nature had always appeared to her as gross impositions, punishments for the first woman's disobedience, causes of shame to be hidden from the eyes of others and never, ever, admitted in conversation. But last month, and now again this month, no blood had flowed.

She remembered enough from the time before the White Monastery to know what this meant.

When for the second time the flow failed, and she knew for sure, she was filled with a mixture of joy and fear. She had not, God be thanked, gotten pregnant from the rape, and she had lain with Zachary for nearly two years now without conceiving. She had come to believe she was barren—either by nature, or from the abuse inflicted on her, or perhaps, as she sometimes feared in her darker moments, through God's curse on her for her disobedience to Shenoute.

But why did she feel so disturbed, so insecure? She had longed for this to happen. She had longed for it so many months, ever since, in one of those moments of reckless honesty that periodically broke through her usual modest reticence, she had offered herself as his companion in the flesh. Or, even before that, yes, perhaps even before, when love for him had first stirred in her frozen heart.

Now, as she struggled to cope with her altered state, she clutched that love to her, like a charm or a talisman that would preserve her through all that was to come. It was a strange and precarious flower, that love, existing like a plant on the desert's rim that grows where the least accidental presence of moisture permits it to grow. She had never expected to love any man in that way. Left cold, indifferent if not actively repelled by the yokels she had known as a girl, she had seen herself as giving all her love to Christ, of being His spiritual bride, as some clerics fulsomely described it. But, neither the pale, anguished figure on the cross nor the Redeemer descending (someday) in all His Glory had come to preserve her in her hour of need. Only Zachary had done that—Zachary and the nameless bandit who had protected her on an earlier occasion. All-too-human men, indistinguishable to outward appearance from those who would savagely exploit you for their own selfish pleasure and then cast you carelessly aside—yet touched and transfigured by the inward flame of compassion.

She had loved him, she knew now, from that first moment in the harvest, when the mad boy was harassing her, and she had seen him striding past her with his friend, so handsome, so serious-looking, with something in his face that reminded her of her earlier protector, and she had thought, if only, if only someone like that would notice her…And at that instant, as if obedient to her thoughts, he had turned, seen her and gone into action, fearlessly, indifferent to his own safety. She had been so confused and terrified, in those days, so convinced of her own worthlessness she could hardly bring herself to believe that anyone could care enough for her to put her well-being before his own. She imagined he must be like those mule-drivers and camel-drivers who had pushed weaker men out of the way, usurping their places in the line of panting beasts waiting their turn with her. She feared he had driven off the mad boy only so that later he could ravish her himself, at his leisure.

How ridiculous those fears seemed to her now! Yet they had remained very real to her, for days after their first meeting, when he had followed her throughout the day and lurked outside her secret retreat all night. How could anyone worthy really care for her, after what she had become? And if she risked leaving her shell of isolation, how could she prevent herself from being hurt again?

It was not until the day of the Nile Festival, when he first spoke to her and she could see he meant her no harm, that she had been ready even to speak to him, and then he had taken the flowers she herself had woven and placed them around her head. And at this gesture, at once so trivial and so touching, she had felt the warmth and kindness within him and immediately, without warning, her heart opened to him—all her carapace of silence and forced indifference melted like wax in a candle-flame and she was soft and helpless before him. If he had tried to take her, that first night they shared a shelter together, she would have fought, she would have protested, but something deep within her would have yielded and rejoiced.

But, he had not even tried.

She did not know then whether to be glad or sorry. Because she did not know, then, whether his continence sprang from principle, or concern for her, or whether he simply found her too plain and uninteresting to serve his pleasures. Only gradually she had learned that it was neither the first nor the third of these. If he had once abstained from things of the flesh on principle, that principle no longer held, and the realization of this had filled her with fear for him, for the peril in which it might place his soul. And she had learned over the months, from the way he sometimes looked at her, that he did not find her uncomely. So her love for him, at first an irrational impulse, had broadened and deepened, taking root in the knowledge of how he felt towards her.

For she had realized, in those first months, that if he abstained from the least touch, or profane word, or even a suggestive smile, this was because he believed either that she remained committed to her vow of chastity or that she had been so broken by her experiences that even the thought of physical contact with a male horrified her. And indeed, for a long time, the second of these was true. But as time passed and the tenderness of his presence soothed her fears, that horror had gradually begun to recede. As for the rest of their life together, she had regretted that their different jobs had kept them, for so long, so often apart. She would have liked to spend more time in his company, merely from the pleasure of feeling him near her.

Then, on that evening when she first confessed to him what had happened to her after leaving the White Monastery, he held and comforted her, as a lover might whose love had been purged of all impurities. It was then that she finally, thoroughly gave him all her trust. She felt certain now that it was not in his nature ever to abuse her. And this knowledge allowed her desire for him, which had smoldered, unacknowledged, fiercely suppressed, ever since that first moment in the harvest fields, to redden like a blown coal, threatening to inflame the hard-won peace of her new life.

Then, there came that week of chill, wintry rain, and his outburst at her for something that was not her fault, and the depression, darker than a starless night, that had then fallen upon her. He had told her he wanted to leave her. To her own shocked and shamed amazement, she had heard herself shamelessly telling him that she would, if he wanted it, become a real wife to him.

She knew, the moment the words were out, how he might misinterpret them. As a cheap trick, a woman's blackmailing device to hold him to her at all costs. No such intention had ever crossed her mind. All she had wanted to do was show him that she knew and understood and wanted to acknowledge all he had done for her with the only gift it lay in her power to give. And she tried to tell him this, or at least to convince him she had had no base motive, fearing even as she did so that if he suspected this, her denial would only serve to confirm his suspicions. But he had not suspected her. Simple and open as he was, he had accepted her, as he had always accepted her, for what she seemed to be, or chose to present herself as. And she knew at that moment that she would yield her body to his, even if he told her that the very next morning he would leave her forever.

Then, as if divine providence itself had smiled on their union, there had come the news that had changed their lives. And their first night of love. She had readied herself for the worst, knowing he would wish to be gentle but believing that no man in the grip of passion could restrain himself, that even the best were brutes, in those moments.

She was amazed at his gentleness, his patience. As amazed as she was grateful. And when, suddenly, a memory of that terrible first night after the monastery flashed across her brain, and she cried out, before she could control herself, that he must stop...He stopped. She could not believe it. She had been taught that it was impossible for a man to do that. The vision passed. Overcome with remorse for letting things that had nothing to do with him spoil his pleasure, she cuddled down silently close to him, and instead of trying to take her immediately he stroked and comforted her until she grew warm and open to him, and only then began, with infinite care and slowness, to enter her.

All that night she had clung to him, sleeping only in snatches, consumed by a love in which gratitude played a greater part than desire. And for days afterwards she moved in a dream of rapture, half-stupefied, more in touch with those hours of delight than with any of the mundane things that were happening around her.

Of course, you couldn't remain indefinitely at that level. Life went on. She came gradually to earth, engaged inevitably in problems of finding a better house, furnishing it, giving up her job (for Zachary now earned more than enough for the two of them) and ensuring that everything he might want was made available to him as soon as he wanted it, if not before.

And she went to church, now, too—a church which was by this time no longer a mere room in somebody's house, but a solid stone building of its own, thanks to the generosity of the holy Archbishop Theophilus. She had gone there, after that first night, to pray God for forgiveness for having slept with Zachary out of wedlock. She stood at the back of the church, among the catechumens, and nobody spoke to her or paid any attention to her, beyond giving her looks of disapproval. She did not attempt to take Holy Communion. But she went back. She could endure the frosty stares, raised up as she was on the buoyant stream of their love. She regarded them as a form of penance—or, more superstitiously, as a balance to her good luck, insuring that she would not tempt the anger of fate by an excess of happiness.

One day, curious, the priest spoke to her, and she told him that she had been baptized. Unbelieving at first, he had questioned her on the faith, found to his surprise that her knowledge was thorough and her beliefs orthodox, and promised to speak for her to the elders of the church—they still did not have so large a congregation that they could afford to be picky. The text for his sermon the following week was John 8.1-11, and he pointed out that if even adultery could be forgiven, then Christian charity should certainly be extended to those who, while joined in marriage or at worst stable concubinage with pagans, Jews, heretics or other unbelievers, expressed sincere belief and strove to the best of their ability to bring their recalcitrant spouses within the fold.

After that, she was allowed to stand among the baptized laity (but of course behind the widows and virgins) and to take the sacrament with them. And some of these now began to treat her with greater respect, even some friendliness, although a minority, headed by Sophia, Didymos' wife—who felt that the sermon had lowered her to the same level as Leila—still held themselves aloof.

She tried to get Zachary to come to church with her, but he would not. His resistance surprised her, because in other ways he always tried to please her. But it was as if, whenever she mentioned church, or religion, or any topic of that nature, he closed his mind to her. He did not become angry, or resentful. He simply did not hear her. And his resistance filled her with fear for him. "I don't care, for myself," she would tell him. "This isn't something I want you to do for me. It's for you. I'm afraid, Zachary, I'm so afraid of what's going to happen to you. When you die. I can't bear to think of you burning forever in hell-fire. I just can't bear it."

"Why should I?"

"Because you won't go to church."

He would sigh and gaze at her patiently and say, "show me where it says I'll be damned if I don't go to church."

She could not.

"Don't you believe any more?"

"Of course I believe." She was never sure whether he was telling the truth or not.

"In God?"

"Naturally."

"In Jesus and the Resurrection?"

"Of course. What is this, a catechism?"

When this happened, she would clench her hands until the nails bit into her palms, but she tried never to show him her frustration. "If you believe, why won't you come to church with me?"

"Because I don't have to. To love is to obey the whole Law, Romans 13. 10."

"But if you won't come to church we can't get married!"

"We are married."

"We're not!"

"We're married in the sight of God," he always insisted. "What difference do you suppose it makes to go into a church with a whole lot of strangers staring at you and have a priest mumble some formula or other? What is it, have I been unfaithful to you? You know I haven't. Do I want to be? You know I don't."

She would desist, for a time at least, for fear of angering or alienating him, trying to repress the fears, forget sadness. And, she would succeed in this, for a time, but it would come back; it always came back.

Then, she had found that she was pregnant.

She wanted his child, wanted it with all her heart. Whatever might happen afterwards, that child would be an enduring expression of the love they now shared, a blending of her seed with his. And more than that, the act of bringing a new life into the world would somehow help to annul the shame through which she had passed. Did he want it, though? When she told him, when she knew for sure, he had seemed genuinely pleased. But, afterwards, when she needed reassurance, she couldn't be so certain. He told her he wanted a child. But did she merely imagine it, or was his voice the same voice with which he reaffirmed his religious faith? Could he merely be saying it in order to pacify her? Or, was it merely in her own mind, because she was so afraid of childbirth, of the pain, of the risk of death, of the sheer strangeness of it all, alone as she was without a single female relative to help her. She feared what the child might do to their relationship, and she feared, too, that the priest might not baptize it. Infant baptism was still the exception rather than the rule, and many held that it was absurd to baptize creatures who could have no conception of what baptism meant. But her fear for her baby's soul exceeded even her fear for Zachary's.

All right, he told her, he would come with her, he would agree to marriage. When? Well, soon. In a week or two. But, he always had some excuse to put her off.

Then, in the third month, she felt the pain.

It was nothing much at first. She ignored it as she went about preparing their evening meal. When it came again, it was like a hand gripping her bowels. Fear invaded her mind. Her legs felt weak. The iron pan she was holding grew suddenly too heavy to hold and fell to the floor, spilling its contents. Normally such an accident would have filled her with shame and confusion but now she hardly noticed it. It's just something I ate, she told herself frantically, I'll lie down, and it'll go away in a minute. She struggled towards her bed, but the journey of a few yards had suddenly become an infinity of space. She clutched a door-jamb for support. Oh God, don't let it be the baby, she prayed. Just me. I don't care how bad the pain gets as long as the baby is all right.

The pain was coming in waves, each wave higher than the last. *I've got to lie down. I've got to!,* was the only thought in her brain. She launched herself across the room, but although she herself seemed to remain still and upright the room began to revolve around her, crazily, out of control. Suddenly, she found herself on the floor and somebody, somewhere, was screaming.

Vaguely, as if from a great distance, she recognized the voice. It was her own.

She might have passed out then. She had no consciousness of time. All she knew was that Zachary was coming. She heard his step, quick and eager, as it always was if he had something to tell her about. She heard him call her name, heard the note of fear and uncertainty already in his voice. She cried out to him, but this time no sound came.

When he saw her, lying on the floor a few feet from their bed, she was curled in a fetal position and blood was running out from between her legs. He turned immediately, ran to their neighbors' house and beat on the door, shouting for help. As soon as he had explained the emergency the wife came running. "Help me lift her," was all she said, and then, "Clear out, there's nothing you can do." He sat miserably in the kitchen until she reappeared with something wrapped in a bloody cloth in her hand. He did not have to ask what it was.

"She's sleeping," the neighbor said. "Don't disturb her, let her have her sleep."

"She lost it," he said.

It was a statement, not a question.

The neighbor nodded. "Sorry. Afraid so. Be careful with her. She's going to be…well, a bit strange for a while, until she gets over it."

She left. Zachary went in and gazed down at Leila. She lay on her back, unconscious, hardly breathing. He felt overwhelmed by his love for her. He wanted to reach out and protect her, as he had always done, but against this he was powerless, and the powerlessness tore at his heart. He bent, lifted and replaced a sweaty lock of hair that had fallen over her brow. She stirred, and he did not kiss her, as he had meant to do, for fear of waking her. He stood over her, staring down, for a long time.

His mind went back to the interview he had had only an hour or two before. To the complete surprise of it, and then the excitement, and then, the profound uneasiness, the fear. He had come in flushed with the news, hardly able to wait until he could tell her, anxious to know what her reaction would be.

But, he could not tell her now.
Least of all, now.

Chapter 3

Eusebius, one of the Tall Brothers, was hard at work in his office in the Caesarium. It was late, long past dark, but he worked on in the flickering lamplight with the heavy drapes drawn so that nobody would know he was working so late. He did not want anyone to know because what he was doing was not really part of the job Theophilus had left him to do. Indeed, if Theophilus had known what his deputy was up to, he would have been far more than displeased. And Eusebius had learned by now that the vast ecclesiastical complex of the Caesarium was packed with Theophilus' spies.

Just in case of trouble he kept close to him on the desk a roll of papyrus on which he had been calculating the dates of Easter and other church festivals for the year 399. If anyone other than Euthymius entered the office, he would simply slide this over the documents he was examining and pretend to be working on it. He hoped his nervousness would not show. What I'm doing is quite legitimate, he told himself, and indeed very necessary if the Church is even to keep people's respect, let alone fulfil the goals of its Founder. I must hew to the line, letting the chips fall where they may. But, it didn't sit well with him that he was, as others might see it, conspiring against his employer and benefactor.

There came a knock on the door. At least it wasn't Archdeacon Timothy, who would just have walked in as if he owned the place. Hastily, Eusebius slid his camouflage over the work and called out, "Who is it?"

"Me, Euthymius."

"Come in, brother." The second of the Tall Brothers entered and closed the door carefully behind him.

"You don't have to knock, you know," Eusebius told him.

"Didn't want to alarm you."

"But, now you're in; maybe you should shoot the bolt."

Euthymius hesitated. "Then, if anyone else tries to come in, that would make them even more suspicious."

Eusebius thought about that, then shrugged. "You're right. Leave it. Do you think we're becoming a little...?" he added, twisting his index finger against his forehead.

"No," Euthymius said flatly, and sat down on the other side of the desk. "Not given the nature of the man we're dealing with." He gazed at Eusebius over the desk with a wry look that was almost, but not quite, a smile of distaste. "He's done what he had to do, by the way."

"The mail from Constantinople is in?"

Euthymius nodded.

"He's consecrated John Chrysostom, Goldenmouth. Everything went smoothly, by all accounts. The Emperor nodded off in the middle, apparently. These things don't have quite the appeal of a chariot race. But, our man put a good face on it, managed to preach a sermon without mentioning hell, fire and brimstone more than twice, and everyone went away highly edified."

"He must have been seething inside," Eusebius said.

"He must indeed."

"And what's happened with Isidore?"

"No idea." Euthymius dismissed the former candidate for the archiepiscopal throne of Constantinople with a casual wave of his hand. "He'd better look out, though. The Sly Fox never blames himself for his failures. He's going to need a scapegoat."

"Do we know what the Superintendent of the Royal Bedchamber had on him?" Eusebius asked.

Euthymius shook his head. "Nothing's come down so far, but it must have been pretty terrible for Theophilus to knuckle under like that. Something political, I would imagine. The kind of stuff we're looking at...Well, I mean, that's chickenfeed so far as they're concerned."

"They'd probably approve of it."

"They probably would, too."

"Which makes it all the stranger that they chose a man like Chrysostom for Archbishop."

Euthymius tilted back his chair, rocked on it for a moment, returning it to the vertical with a sharp click. Chairs! They took some getting used to. After squatting for years on a roll of papyrus that also served you as a pillow, he felt almost guilty in a chair. There was something unduly regal about it that tempted you to pride, when so many had nowhere to set their rear ends but the floor.

"You're right," he said. "I've thought about that, too."

"The eunuch...I mean he's known for his wickedness...What could have prompted him to pick someone as holy as..."

"He's known for being a eunuch," Euthymius cut in. "And we of all people shouldn't hold that against him. I mean some are born so, some are made so, and some become so for the Kingdom of Heaven's sake... Matthew 19.12, I shouldn't have to remind you of that."

"But everybody says..."

"I don't care what everybody says." Euthymius spoke as usual in his flat, no-nonsense, take-it-or-leave-it voice. "Everybody, and when I say everybody I mean people in the World, not us, despises eunuchs because they don't have all their masculine equipment. And only men with all their masculine equipment are supposed to run things. Eunuchs are supposed to shut up and say yes sir, no sir. And if one of them is more cunning and knowledgeable than the so-called real

men, then the real men start yelling and screaming about it...I'm not apologizing for Eutropius. I just don't want to judge him, that's all. He's a child of God, just as we are, testes or no testes. And doubtless as proud, vindictive, avaricious as the next. But in there, somewhere, there's a spark. And, just once in a while, divine grace blows that spark into a flame. He knows John personally, were you aware of that?"

Eusebius confessed that he wasn't.

"Oh yes. The eunuch went to Antioch, couple of years back. Some government business. And was impressed, or so they say."

Eusebius thought about it. "But, you know...if it's true what they all say about him, Chrysostom I mean—there's going to be trouble. A real Christian for once, running the Church in a city like that...Can you begin to imagine it? Denouncing the greed, the injustice, the corruption..."

"That was my other idea," Euthymius said with a snort of amusement.

Eusebius looked at him inquiringly.

"Well, just imagine everything Eutropius had to put up with, on his way to the top. Snubs. Insults. Contempt. All those fancy aristocrats sneering at him. And he had to swallow it all and smile. For us, of course, it would have been the perfect exercise, wouldn't it? A continuous lesson in humility. But for a man like that...Don't you think he'd want to get his own back on them? My second theory is that he brought in John Chrysostom for revenge...If you'll excuse the vulgarity, to kick some upper-class butt."

"And you think John will do that?"

"I know it," Euthymius said with absolute confidence. "He'll go for the Imperial family itself if he has to. He can't be flattered; he can't be bought; he can't be scared..."

"A dangerous man, then."

"Of course, but also one who delights the heart of the Lord...How did the research go today?"

Eusebius shuffled his documents. He was the slowest of the Tall Brothers, lacking the razor-sharp intellects of the other three, but he was conscientious and could be trusted absolutely. "I've found another three, I think. Two, for certain. Look at this one. Particularly blatant case. See, here's a bequest of one thousand, one hundred and forty-seven solidi specifically for the relief of widows and virgins in the parish of St. Theonas, testator, Hierax son of Hilarion, deceased last June...So I checked the files. No record of disbursements. No list of beneficiaries. A dead end. But here, in the Ecclesiastical Building Fund, for that same month, June, there's a credit entry of one thousand, one hundred and forty-seven solidi."

Euthymius, who had come round the desk, was craning his neck over the other's shoulder, the better to see the evidence. "You'd think," he said, "he'd at least feel ashamed enough to fudge the figures a bit."

"He thinks he's invulnerable."

"Right. A bad case of lithomania."

"I beg your pardon?"

"Lithomania," Euthymius explained. "That's what Isidore of Pelusium called it. Theophilus is crazy for stone. Let the widows and orphans starve, let him rob them of everything so long as there's double the number of churches, three times as big as is needed, with a fat priest in every one of them to pray for the Sly Fox's soul." He turned sharply to Eusebius and asked, "Why are we doing this?"

Eusebius was thrown off balance by the question. "Well...I mean... somebody has to find the truth about what's happening..."

"Yes, but now that we know for sure, what are we going to do about it?"

They stared at each other, blankly. They were neither of them worldly men. They had wanted to make sure that the archdiocese with whose management they had been entrusted was doing what it was supposed to do. Now that they knew it wasn't, they felt lost. "I suppose," Eusebius said, "we could make out a list of these. With all the facts and figures. Lay it before a church council and let them..."

"You think they'd do anything? Against their own archbishop?"

"Well...in that case we could take it to Rome."

"To the Pope!" Euthymius snorted. "Brother, you think these people are religious? They're politicians! No Pope is going to risk a schism with the East for a little pious fraud here and there. It's not as if he'd spent it on whores, and I doubt the Pope would lose much sleep over it even if he had." He shook his head darkly. "It's none of our business, really."

"What, swindling the poor?"

"No. Judgement."

A long silence fell, broken by the sound of Eusebius nervously cracking his knuckles. "You think we should go back to the desert, then," he said at last.

"Indeed I do. I'm not going to go on working for an administration once I know it's corrupt."

For Eusebius, that wasn't enough. Not after all those hours of patient toil in which he had pieced together the pattern of Theophilus' infamy. "Surely we should disclose it...somehow."

"Eusebius, my friend." A hand fell on his shoulder. "Let me tell you a story. I heard this the other day, from a hermit from Scetis. Seems somebody had taken a mad boy out there to try and get him cured. He just left the boy hanging around the cells while he scoured the place for some miracle-worker. Now this kid's helpless; can't speak properly; can't defend himself. And some so-called hermit, just the kind they're starting to get out there now, comes out of a cell, grabs him and starts sodomizing him. You couldn't get anything much viler than that, could you? So this other hermit was just about to hit him when he thought, 'Hey, if God doesn't send fire from heaven to devour this creature, who am I to do anything?' In other words, who am I to judge? So he didn't do anything."

"You're trying to say we must accept injustice?"

"'Justice is mine, said the Lord.' Let Him deal with Theophilus. Not us."

Eusebius shook his head sadly. "It's hard."

"I know it is. But when did Christ ever say it would be easy?"

Derek Bickerton

Chapter 4

Darion and the woman were making their way towards Darion's cave. Darion went first, partly because he knew the way and she didn't, partly so his resolve might not be weakened by having to watch the sway of her hips as she walked. The movement of a well-built woman's hips had a powerful effect on him at the best of times, and a malicious whisper in one corner of his mind still kept telling him what a fool he was, not taking advantage of this situation.

And indeed the landscape around him might have been purposefully created for taking advantage. At this place an escarpment separating the Nile valley from the interior desert had been cracked and broken by the rare storms—rare in a man's lifetime, numerous over the vastness of eons—that had brought flood-water downslope. Those storms had created gullies, isolated headlands of rock, twisting ravines overhung by gloomy precipices. No longer could one see for miles—sight was bounded by a limit of a few yards, and any act, however bestial, could be committed in the certainty that it would have no witnesses. He could not help turning to her and asking her, "Are you afraid?"

"No," she lied bravely.

"Alone with a desperate character?"

"I trust you."

The simplicity and straightforwardness of this cut to Darion's heart—unworthy of it though he might be, how could he turn around now and betray that trust? "Well, I still think you should wait out here for me," he said. "I'm about to enter the underworld."

She looked around her. In the wall of rock to their right, a narrow fissure opened into a depthless blackness. "If you don't mind," she said, "I think I'd rather come with you. I'd be more afraid alone out here."

"Suit yourself. Makes no difference to me." From his bag, Darion took flint, tinder and a small stub of candle. He chipped at the flint with his dagger until a spark that fell on the tinder began to smolder, then blew on the thin thread of smoke until there sprang up a tiny flame.

"You're prepared for everything," she said, watching him.

"Have to be, in this life. Here, let's go." He took her hand and, holding the candle in front of him, drew her into the cave. "Keep your head down," he said. "The roof's very low and there are bumps in it. Oh, and if something flies at you screeching, don't worry, it's only a bat."

"It'll get in my hair," she complained.

"No it won't. That's just an old wives' tale."

They made slow progress. The floor of the cave was uneven and she held back, afraid of falling, he almost had to drag her along. "Did you ever rob a tomb?" she asked when they paused for a moment to rest.

"Uh-huh. Several times."

"That used to fascinate me when I was a kid. Tomb robbers. All those wonderful old jewels and things. Scary, though, all those spirits and demons. Weren't you afraid?"

"Little bit, first time out." Darion began to pull her along again. "Afterwards, nothing. It's all in the imagination, if you ask me. As for the game itself, it's overrated. Practically everywhere is cleaned out by now. Just once in a while you get lucky."

"You didn't worry in case their ghosts came after you?"

"Whose ghosts?"

"The ones who were buried there."

Darion laughed. "When you're dead, you're dead," he said. "You don't come back. Ever hear of anyone who came back?"

"Our Lord Jesus Christ came back."

"Oh-oh." He stopped. "So, you're a Christian.

Thanks you."

"Thanks for what?"

"…For not beating my ear off about it, first thing when we met, like most of 'em do. Hope you're not going to start now." Just then the warm and constant pressure of her hand was reminding him of her sex, of the darkness, of the absolute power he had over her, if he chose to exercise it.

"I won't if you don't want me to," she said submissively. "I just mentioned it because He did come back. Not as a ghost, either, as flesh and blood, just the same as us."

"I don't know about that," Darion grumbled. "Always sounds like Isis and Osiris to me—sons of gods, dead bodies coming to life…Anyway there's not much point talking about it. Nobody really knows. If they're honest about it…Well, here we are. The bandit's treasure-chest. At least, this is real." He had stopped, at a point where the narrow passage they were following widened out into a chamber several feet in diameter. Prying loose a rock from its wall, Darion revealed a cavity, reached in and opened the leather sack inside it, and she saw the candle-flame reflected in a dim glimmer of gold. He heard the sharp intake of her breath, and knew she had not completely believed him until now. *But still, she trusts me*, he thought. *True, she didn't had much choice. But, she didn't needed to give her trust.*

"I shouldn't," she said.

30

"Why not? Because it's stolen?"

"Because there's no way I can repay you."

"Do you want to count it?" Darion realized he had never counted the money since the gang divided it up in the first place. Strange! He knew people who would have been counting it every five minutes. Did it really mean so little to him?

"Of course. I mean, I really wish...if I didn't need it so badly, or if it was just for myself. I would never...I wouldn't dream of taking more than I needed." *She's lovely*, he thought, *in her confusion. Wants to and doesn't want to. Wonder if she feels the same way about...*

He recoiled from the temptation. *The forces of law and order, respectability and good government have treated her like a piece of shit*, he thought. *Let's see if the thieves can do a little better.* "Go on," he said, ashamed of himself, and disgusted, too, by the image of them squatting on the cave floor and squalidly counting out gold pieces—it didn't quite fit with an act of reckless generosity such as this. "Why don't you just take the lot?"

"I couldn't," she cried.

"Give me one good reason."

"It's all you've got."

Darion tapped the dagger at his side. "Plenty more where that came from," he said with grim humor.

"Then, I'd be the cause of you sinning! I don't want that!"

"No you wouldn't. I'd do it anyway, whether you took it or not."

"But, I only need three hundred," she protested.

"No you don't. If you're as flat broke as you say you are, you'll need start-up money. I know there's over three hundred here, I just don't know exactly how much...If it makes you feel better, I'll just take a bit to keep me going." And he picked up a handful of coins and concealed them about his person. He handed her the bag. "The rest's yours."

In the flickering flame of the candle, he saw to his surprise that she was crying—not passionately as before, but softly, inaudibly, the tears welling slowly out of her eyes and trickling down her cheeks. She tried to speak, but could not.

"Move," he said. "This candle won't last much longer." He drew her out of the chamber and back along the passageway.

"I don't know how to thank you," she said.

"Then don't," he replied gruffly. They did not speak again until they came out into the open air.

It was late in the afternoon when they reached the small town where her husband was imprisoned. Darion had passed by it several times but never stayed there, a fact that relieved him as they entered its narrow streets—it would be doubly absurd to do a good deed and get arrested as a result of it. They stopped outside a low square building constructed, unlike the others, of hewn stone rather than mud bricks. She turned to face him.

"That's where they're holding him."

"Will they turn him over to you, just like that?"

"If the magistrate's in. His office is in there, and the court, too."

Darion handed her the bag, which he had been carrying because it was heavy. "Best of luck, anyway," he said.

She took the bag, hesitated a moment, and then, stepping lightly forward on her toes, flung her arms around him and kissed him. He smelled her hair, felt the tremor in her flesh. He knew women. He knew, husband or no, with just a push or two she would have yielded to him. Idiot, he told himself, you should have grabbed her back there. More roughly than he had meant to, because he felt awkward and confused, he broke away from her. She smiled up at him in gratitude, tears forming again in the corners of her eyes.

"You're a good man," she said. "May God guide you and guard you." Then, she turned and entered the building.

Darion began to walk away. Then, on a sudden impulse, he turned, crossed the street, and sat down in the angle of a wall. After a few minutes, he began to play his flute. To his surprise, when he had been playing for a while, somebody dropped him a coin. Then someone else. They were copper coins, practically worthless, given the current inflation, but he smiled politely at them each time.

"Thank you, sir… thank you, ma'am…Thanks, little boy." *I suppose one could live this way*, he thought, *though it would be a pretty poor living, and what if someone who knew me saw me?*

As he played, he reviewed his actions over the last few hours. Crazy, anyone who knew him would think. And his loins still smoldered dully with desire for her. Yet despite the physical ache, he could not bring himself to regret what he had done, or not done. He would never have taken her against her will. And though he knew from that momentary embrace that she was attracted to him, he knew too that if she had yielded it would have been mostly out of a sense of obligation. And that she would have felt guilty and ashamed afterwards, either hiding the festering little secret or confessing, perhaps to the ruin of her marriage. Whereas his own pleasure would have dissolved the moment the act was over. No, instead of regret or bitterness, he felt a mild, warm glow of satisfaction.

It was nearly dark before the woman emerged. This time she was not alone. A man was with her, a tall man, a little older than she was, with a bruised and swollen face, who walked with a limp. As they came down the two shallow steps from the doorway, they turned towards one another and embraced. Their faces were aflame with happiness. Darion felt a pang of jealousy so sharp it was like a physical pain. *Asshole*, he thought. *You don't deserve her, and you don't know how lucky you are, either.* They were so absorbed in one another that neither noticed him, even though they passed within feet of him. He watched while they walked away down the street, their arms round one another, stopping to kiss again every few yards. He saw the tenderness with which she touched his bruised face. Then they turned a corner and disappeared.

Darion remained where he was. An idea had come into his mind. He had been virtuous enough for one day, it was time to even the score.

Soon, it was completely dark. And soon after that, a well-dressed man came out of the building opposite. Greek, by the look of him, and someone of importance too, for he was accompanied by a slave with a stout club. Could be just someone there on business, but probably not.

Darion rose and followed them at a leisurely pace. The slave, for all his stout club, didn't look much use as a bodyguard. He just trudged along, glancing neither to right nor to left of him, answering monosyllabically the few words his master threw at him. As they crossed a dark, deserted square Darion picked up speed. Running now lightly and noiselessly on the balls of his feet, he caught up with them as they entered the street on the far side of the plaza and twisted the club out the slave's hands. Almost before the slave knew what was happening, just as his mouth opened for a shout, Darion spun, still under the impetus of his own motion, and hit the slave with the club, hard, on the side of the head. The impact made a dead, hollow sound—Darion hoped the slave had a thick skull, he didn't want to kill him, but the slave dropped anyway, like a stone. His master just stood there, one of those who, in an emergency, simply freeze, the jaw down a little, the eyes glassy with shock.

Darion swung in behind him, locked off his air supply with an arm tight around his throat, thrust the tip of his dagger about an inch into the flesh below his ribs, and with quick, shuffling steps shunted him into the mouth of an alley hardly wider than a man's shoulders He heard the sobbing, whistling sound of the man's breath, smelt the sweat of fear and a richer, more fetid smell that quickly overpowered it. *Damn him*, Darion thought, *he's shat himself*, and spun the man round, quickly, to avoid getting it on his own clothes, moving the dagger-point from ribs to throat and staring directly into the man's eyes.

"Are you the magistrate here?" he asked.

The man nodded dumbly. Then he found his tongue. "Don't kill me! Don't kill me!"

Darion wasn't surprised. There were a few hard cases, but mostly those who wielded power just collapsed when power was taken from them. Fine brave fellows at the right end of a whip or with burly subordinates at hand. Yet all you had to do was put the steel to their throats and see them turn to mush.

And this was the man by whose orders the faithful couple he had just seen had been cruelly and savagely mistreated. Darion had planned on cutting a number of pieces, some of them rather essential, from his living flesh. But now all he felt was disgust, sickness of spirit, a desire to be out of there as soon as he could. Turning the man and quickly letting go of him, he swung a single, savage punch to the nape of his neck. The magistrate staggered drunkenly and collapsed. Darion went through his clothes, pleased to find quite a bit of money there, and then set off, walking fast, not quite running, through the outskirts of town and away through the fields beyond, towards the desert.

How he longed for the desert, its cleanness, its emptiness, its pure, dry air, the endless vistas of its vast solitude!

Maybe, he thought, *I'm really not cut out for this life after all.*

Chapter 5

Leila recovered slowly from her miscarriage. It had taken place in the spring, but the heat of summer had come and the earliest crops were being harvested before she was able to function normally again. Normally, as far as her body was concerned, that is. Her mind was another matter.

She refused to believe, as Zachary tried to explain to her, that the miscarriage could have resulted from any of a dozen natural causes, that women had miscarriages all the time without it meaning anything, that instead of letting herself fall into a morass of guilt and depression she should thank God that the event had not been fatal, as happened all too often. None of this would she accept. She had become convinced that the miscarriage was God's punishment for the breaking of her vow of celibacy. What explanation could be more natural and logical than that? She had been destined for a life of chastity, so a just God would aim the punishment right at that point, right where she had so willfully frustrated His designs, by killing the child in her womb. "If you won't be a nun I won't let you be anything else," Zachary had parodied this argument. "Do you really believe God acts like a spoiled three-year-old?"

But, she insisted that his words were blasphemous, even though he explained he had only been trying to preserve respect for God's dignity, a respect her own attitude certainly didn't show. Zachary went wild with frustration. He did not understand what was happening to them. Always they had been able to talk to one another. They had disagreed sometimes, over his lack of religious feeling for the most part, but things had always been straightened out or smoothed over; there had never been this wall of blank incomprehension that had risen mysteriously between them. He felt lost, betrayed. Being a man, the trauma that the loss of a child can cause, especially when the mother has both longed for it and feared it would never come, left him simply uncomprehending. His own attitude seemed to him the only realistic one: all right, it's gone, I'm sorry, let's make another.

On top of which, his own loss of faith made it hard for him to see how, given her beliefs, the depression that such a trauma can bring in its wake would almost inevitably be compounded, intensified. What concerned him more than that was the fact that she would no longer let him make love to her. He had understood that at first, naturally—she had something physically wrong with her, her intimate parts had been bruised and battered, he had expected several weeks to pass before they could resume normal relations. But the weeks grew into months, and still she turned away from him, turned him away with what he took, mistakenly perhaps, to be an expression of distaste. Why had he become repulsive to her, he asked? He felt she must be punishing him for something, some crime he had never consciously committed.

The news that he had for her, that night he came home and found her unconscious, had had to wait—wait until it was news no longer, until the opportunity that had been offered him had passed. Perhaps he had made a mistake, telling her. Perhaps, but he had never previously felt the need to censor his speech to her. So it seemed natural for him to say, one evening when she had begun to recover, "You know, I had something to tell you, just before it happened."

"Yes?" She seemed listless, remote from him, not really interested, but he ploughed on anyway.

"They offered me a job. In Alexandria."

"Really?"

"He's got a business there, apparently. My boss." Export and import, the same as his own father's. "And he needed someone to manage it for him, the guy quit that was running it, he said."

"You're going to leave me, aren't you?" she said in that new voice she had acquired somehow, that voice of toneless indifference, resignation. "I always knew you would, one day."

"No I'm not going to leave you," Zachary said, his voice angrier than he had intended. "It's too late now, anyway. They got someone else for the job."

"You should have taken it," she said in the same lifeless voice.

"How could I? You couldn't have come with me, and I couldn't have left you here alone, not in that condition."

She turned away from him. She was trying to hide it from him, but he heard a harsh, dry sob that she could not suppress. He put his arm around her shoulders and gently turned her towards him.

"What's the matter?"

"Nothing."

"I'm not stupid."

"No, really it's nothing." She rubbed at the corner of her eye. "Just …just a woman's foolishness."

"Go on," Zachary insisted. "I won't let up until you tell me."

"It's just that…that I'm afraid you're going to resent me. For holding you back."

"No, of course not!" His answer was all the more vehement because, if he was honest with himself, he would have had to admit that there was a grain of resentment there. He was ashamed of it, tried to ignore it or make it go away, but it was there. He had wanted to go to Alexandria.

When he began working in the estate office, he had found it interesting, at first, learning how a large estate was run. After a year, he could have run it himself. He was quick; he was honest; he didn't make mistakes. The steward delegated more and more work to him until, in effect, he was indeed running the estate himself, but without either the pay or the respect that this should have earned him. So when the chance of travel and promotion was offered him, he wanted immediately to seize it. He had been coming home, full of excitement, anxious to tell Leila about it, how this time he really would go through with the marriage ceremony, how he would send for her as soon as he had established himself in the city, and what a wonderful life they would have there, together—and then he had found her lying there unconscious, and knew at once that he could not accept the offer. If only she'd waited another few days! He knew how childish and illogical that thought was, but he couldn't help having it. As the days passed, as spring turned into summer, he grew more and more bored and restless. The atmosphere at home had grown so tense that he took to going off drinking with Didymos and Didymos' friends, not every evening, at first around once a week, then twice, then more frequently still. It had not occurred to him, before the miscarriage, what a risk he had taken, building a relationship with someone who had no family and no real friends where they lived. He had blundered into his life with her like a sleepwalker. He realized quite early on that she depended on him entirely; he had not realized, until the miscarriage, how draining of energy such a dependence could be.

It was not that he had ceased to love her—if he had, there would have been no problem. Rather, though still loving her, he was beginning to find that love a trial to him. When he was with her, he wanted to get away from her. When he was away from her, he missed her and worried about her. Had he kept his faith he could have welcomed such a trial as a test of his patience, his forbearance. Now he was finding, as many had before him, that a life without faith, though it does not incur more hazards, makes the hazards that do occur more irksome, and exposes the soul to the buffeting of fate.

Then, one hot and windless morning, the steward said, "Boss wants to see you."

"Remember a few months back I offered you a job in Alexandria?" the owner started off without any preamble. "Seems the fellow I put in there isn't working out. The job's still open if you want it."

Zachary did not know whether to be glad or sorry. He had spent months getting used to the idea that he had sacrificed his chance. Hearing the contrary was almost like reopening an old wound. His answer, "I'm glad you have so much confidence in me, sir," was carefully calculated to supply the minimum of information.

The owner did not welcome prevarication. "Well," he said brusquely, "do you want it?"

"Can I have till next week to think about it?" Zachary asked. The owner sighed. For a moment it seemed he was on the point of saying, "No." Then, he hesitated and said, "You can have a day and a night. If you haven't told me you want it by this time tomorrow, forget it. I'll find someone else."

And that was that. Zachary wondered what it would feel like to be able to change someone's life with a couple of words. If he accepted, he might one day find out. If he did not, he would remain mired in rural Egypt, indefinitely. Had he been alone, he would have accepted immediately. But he was not alone. He had Leila.

It never occurred to him to conceal the news from her. Afterwards, he might wish he had, might have wondered why he had not had the sense to foresee the possible consequences. But he had always told her everything; he did so this time too.

The moment he saw the stricken look on her face he realized his mistake. "But, you're better now," he said. "You're well enough to travel, anyway. What's the matter?"

"I've never lived in a city."

"Cities are just the same as anywhere else." Zachary's regard for the truth was tempered a little by his eagerness to convince her. "There's nothing to be afraid of. You'll soon get used to it. There's so many things to do there…"

"Sinful things," she said stubbornly. "Temptations."

"You've been talking to the priest."

"No. It's what everybody says."

"That's not the real reason, is it?"

When she did not answer, he knew that he had guessed right. "So, what's the real reason?" he persisted.

"I don't know."

"You don't know, then you're admitting there is one, right?"

"I never said there was. Why can't you just leave me be?"

"Because I still care for…" Zachary began, then he stopped. She had run into the bedroom. Through the half-open door he could see her lying face-down on the bed. He went in and lay down beside her, on his back, staring up at the cracked ceiling.

After a while he said, "Aren't you going to tell me?"

"You wouldn't understand."

"You can't know that."

"It's different for a man!" she burst out. "You can go anywhere, make friends...When I came here I didn't have a friend."

"You had me," Zachary objected.

"That's not what I meant! Nobody liked me, nobody would speak to me." She continued to lie there face down, not looking at him. Zachary leaned over to touch her, but she shook him off.

"Only now, when I've been here almost three years, people are just starting to treat me as if I was a person. Three years, Zachary! I don't want to go through that again."

"It's different in cities."

"Yes, I'm sure it is. It's worse!"

"No it's not," Zachary said, still trusting in the power of rational argument, despite so much experience to the contrary. "In cities there are people from all over. They come and go, all the time. Because half of them are strangers anyway they don't care who they talk to. It's not like here, where a stranger stands out like a sore thumb."

She was silent again. He suspected that, though what she had said might be a genuine reason, it still wasn't the real one. "You hadn't finished eating," he said at last.

"I'm not hungry."

They lay there for some time in silence. Zachary did not know how to deal with her when she was like this. His only strategy was to wait her out, let her mood pass, whatever it was, hope it would not last too long. *The ceiling needs re-plastering*, he thought absently. *If I were going away I wouldn't need to think about that.*

"I'm not going," he said at last.

Did he mean it, or was he saying it just to see what response he would get? He himself wasn't entirely sure. She rolled over abruptly, raised herself on one elbow and said, "No. You want to go. I know you do. You should go."

"How can I?" he asked, thinking, I can't cope with this. "How can I go if it means leaving you?"

"We're not married. "

"What difference does that make? We're married in the eyes of God, and I've told you I'm going to do it anyway, we'll have a proper wedding, just as soon as we get to Alexandria, with my family and everything. It'll be..."

"You just said you weren't going!"

"I meant if we did go!" he snapped, furious that she, the illogical one, should have caught him out. "If we'd gone, I mean. Why do you twist everything I say?"

"How do you suppose you could have taken me to your family?" she demanded, ignoring his complaint. "Just a little country girl! You know how they'd have treated me, rich city people like that. And they'd have thought you were a fool too, to want to marry someone like me, instead of some rich city woman."

"They wouldn't," he insisted loyally, 'they're not like that," knowing in his heart that they probably would have and were. That had been a bridge which, when he thought of taking her with him, he had always carefully refrained from crossing—it would all work out somehow, he had assured himself. But there was enough truth in what she said to convince him that if he tried to rebut her, he would lose the argument.

Argument? Why were they arguing, what were they arguing about? Hadn't he told her that for a second time, if less willingly than the first, he was renouncing his hope of a fuller life, for her sake? So what was she complaining for, trying to catch him out, making him look ridiculous? He could see no point in going on like this, so he sprang from the bed and returned to the kitchen. But the food they had been eating had gone cold, and now looked stale and unappetizing. *If I go out for a while*, he thought, *she may calm down a little*. He called, but she did not answer. He left, slamming the door.

For a while he searched for Didymos, but Didymos was not in any of his usual haunts. Indeed, he saw few people about; most of the villagers had been working frantically to clear the harvest before the Nile overflowed its banks, starting at first light and finishing only when dusk made the fields invisible, then going to bed early so as to start work before sunrise. Rather than drink alone or in company he did not care for, he decided to return home.

He asked himself often, afterwards, at what point in the evening he began to have a presentiment that things were badly amiss. Was it in the village itself, making him hurry home earlier than he had intended? Was it when he saw the door of the house left slightly ajar, though he knew he had shut it? Or was it not until his voice went unanswered, and he felt that indefinable sense— a lack rather than a presence, a sense of thought-waves passing through space without meeting a mind they could rebound from—that is given off by a vacant house?

Certainly it was not until then, or a few moments later, that the image sprang fully formed into his mind, as clear and sharp as if it had been telepathically transmitted...

The river!

The Nile had been rising fast for days, its torrent was already crumbling the rims of its banks. Without knowing why, without—yet!—even wondering what the sudden thought of it might portend, he had already begun to run towards it. In the darkness, he heard it before he saw it, a dull rushing rumble that first revealed itself to the eye in irregular flickers of white, wherever the foam of its rapids and whirlpools reflected fitfully and feebly the light of a waning moon. The flickers were almost on a level with his feet—tonight perhaps, certainly the next day, the inundation would begin.

He hesitated on the bank, looked right, looked left, and then, on an inward instruction which, though wordless, came as clearly as if a voice had spoken to him, turned left, downstream. Running along the bank, he saw her, in the moonlight, hurrying ahead of him. He shouted, but if she heard him, over the noise of the river, she gave no sign.

She had left the house only a few minutes before his return. She had as yet no very clearly formed conception of what she meant to do, beyond the driving need to make herself absent from their house, the village, his life.

It was not because she had ceased to love him. Rather it was because she loved him so much that her failure to be what he wanted had become intolerable to her.

All her life had been failure, no matter how you looked at it. She had failed as a dutiful daughter, and as a cloistered celibate; she had failed as a wife; she had failed as a mother–she had failed even to become a mother. And now, instead of being a helpmate to Zachary, father of his children, obedient spouse, support of his career. She was holding him back. She knew that only his concern for her kept him here in Tebtynnis. She knew that his soul, made for finer things, longed to be released into a wider sphere. She would have traveled with him, into that sphere, gladly. But, she had learned in time that she would always bring him misfortune, that she was doomed here and throughout eternity for the breaking of the solemn vow she had made in the White Monastery.

That left only one thing she could do, only one way in which she could serve him—by getting out of his life altogether. Then he would go on to achieve the destiny he deserved. But she could never tell him the real reason for what she was doing, for the mere telling of it would make her own goal impossible to achieve. He was too kind, too generous ever to allow her to sacrifice herself for him. If she told him, he would insist on staying with double the determination. They would be linked like two people, one of whom can swim while one cannot, who are roped to one another and then hurled into a raging torrent...

Like this one.

When she left the house she had had no definite plan. She did not even stop to consider where she might go—it was enough that she should get away from there, go anywhere where she could no longer intervene between Zachary and what she saw as his proper destiny. So final a destination as now coursed turbulently beside her had never occurred to her. But now, as her eye was caught by the glint of moonlight on the roiling water, she was seized by a sudden visceral desire to fling herself into it. The desire came first, no doubt about that, long before tardy logic came to back it. Even as she ran her eyes, fascinated, followed the swirling, speeding vortices, whirlpools that even as they spun by her seemed to collapse inwards on themselves, dragging the light down after them. It was a desire like you had sometimes, on top of a cliff, to hurl yourself into space. Space was there, water was there. Come to me, they cried, lose yourself in me, I am vast and all-embracing and deep within me there is rest, silence, peace.

If she threw herself into the river, her problems would all be solved, she reasoned. Zachary would be free of her, and she would be free of her own sorry tale of failures. It would take no more than a second...

Terrified, she pulled her mind back from the thought. That was forbidden. To take her own life was a sin that would fling her into an eternity of hell-fire. Her problems would be far from over—rather, they would be just beginning. But to her horror, her mind could not break free. The dull roar of the river, the dark swirling mass of it, the fugitive gleams coming and going on its surface, had invaded her whole consciousness, filling her with an image so powerful that her conscience shrank to a screeching, whimpering little voice somewhere down and away on the periphery of it all. She hung in the balance, her flying feet trampling the edges of a bank which, section by section, was already crumbling under the pressure of the water, falling off in miniature landslides the dull splashes of whose falls were barely audible above the clamor of the flood.

Then, close behind her she heard footsteps, their speed as urgent as her own.

She turned, losing a precious second, saw Zachary, and ran on, straining her limbs to the uttermost. It was hopeless. Within seconds he had caught her by the arm and tried immediately to stop, but their joint impetus was so great that, staggering, they both lost balance and fell headlong, he on top of her, both of them on the lip of the collapsing bank.

"Leila! Are you mad? What do you think you..."?

"Let go of me! Let me go!"

Writhing, she twisted from under him. A crack ripped through the caked mud of the bank, passing directly under Zachary's right side. His words broke off into a yell of shock and sudden panic, he rolled leftwards, clawed at grass, held on while behind him a house-sized slab of ground gently subsided and dissolved. Leila, scrambling to her feet just clear of the crack, seemed wholly unaware of how near both of them had come to death. She had already begun to run when Zachary, lurching to his feet, started out again in pursuit of her.

"Leila! Look out, it's going to..."

He would never know whether she had hurled herself deliberately into the void that opened before her or whether, unable to stop in time, her own reckless speed had swept her into it. He saw her hands fly up, her legs and the lower part of her body vanish as if sucked downwards by some irresistible force. He heard her scream of pure animal terror, and then he was braking violently, throwing his whole weight backwards in an attempt to avoid the same fate. He was only half-successful—one foot went over the edge, he had to twist his body around and throw himself face-down to keep from following her. When he lurched to his feet, the current had seized her and was sweeping her away from him.

Zachary did not think. He did not reason out the best strategy, nor wonder whether the chance of saving her outweighed the risk to his own life. Immediately, instinctively, he hurled himself into the water. He felt it seize him, stronger by far than any human in its grasp, and sweep him along, but he felt no fear at all, only a terrible anguish and an iron intention to save her at whatever cost.

For a moment he could not see her anywhere, and he was gripped by a blind panic. Then he briefly glimpsed her head lifted above the waters, only a few yards away from him. He thanked God for those hours spent as a child with children he was supposed not to play with, flinging himself into the Mediterranean not just when it was flat calm and blue but also when it was turgid with storm and brown like this with Nile water hurled back upon the land. He could swim as strongly as almost anyone, almost as strongly as Moses, perhaps, when with sword between teeth the old bandit had crossed this river bank to bank. He drove himself to the limit of his strength, using his energy recklessly, certain that in this way, in a few moments, he could reach her and drag her to safety.

Indeed, the gap closed between them, but it closed slowly. The turbulence threw Zachary from side to side, it cost him precious effort merely to hold a straight course in that confusion of waters. Her head bobbed up, now to his left, now to his right—at one moment, she seemed no more than a couple of arm's lengths away. *Now's the time! Now!* the thought blazed through his mind, and gathering the last of his strength, he launched himself towards her.

Her face was turned towards his at that moment, and he saw the lost, wild, desperately pleading look on her face. Whatever had been her intention when she fled from him, he knew from that look that she did not now wish to destroy herself, that with her whole heart she was imploring him to save her. He reached out to her.

At that moment, a whirlpool in the current, gliding past them, silently spinning its sinister brown disc, drew her head under, and his hands met vacancy. She did not cry out, but he did, a cry of loss and desolation that the roar of the waters swallowed without trace. With the last of his failing strength he forged on in the direction she had seemed to take, and after what seemed to him an eternity—although it was no more than a few seconds—her head did indeed re-emerge but further away from him.

A cold despair entered his heart. He forced his body to go on, but he knew already that it was useless. The sea at its roughest didn't have the demented energy of a great river in flood. He felt the strength pouring out of him like water from a sieve. The distance between them no longer shrank. Instead, it increased rapidly. He knew that he no longer had any chance of reaching her, that his own life would be in peril if he did not turn immediately and try to reach the bank.

The bank! With the cruel clarity of hindsight, he knew instantly what he ought to have done. Instead of flinging himself after her, he should have run down the bank as fast and as far as he could, until he was ahead of her, then dived in and swum against the current—not that he would have made progress, of course he too would have been swept downstream, but at a slower rate than her. And then the current would have carried her into his arms. It might still not be too late for that, he told himself, knowing it was a lie, struggling to stifle the awful sense of guilt that welled up inside him, illogical but none the weaker for that, at the thought that he was abandoning her.

He angled towards the bank.

But the current, without his noticing it, had swept them both out towards the middle of the stream. The bank was now barely visible in the darkness. Gripped by a sudden, animal fear he inched his way towards it, knowing it was futile to spend what little energy remained by heading for it directly, shorter though the distance might then be. By now he had lost sight of her completely. He flailed on blindly, not daring to think any more, concentrating every fiber of his being on his own survival.

By the time his feet hit bottom and his hands, clutching convulsively, scrabbled for purchase on a slope of slippery mud, he was almost unconscious.

He lay for several seconds, spread-eagled on the bank, unable to rise. Sheer willpower forced him to his feet and drove his wilting legs, on the brink of collapse, to the top of the bank. He gazed wildly out over the whirling torrent. Gleams of light, spinning vortices, flecks of foam that vanished as swiftly as they appeared—that was all he could see. An entire palm-tree, roots and all, swept by him like a battering ram driven at the wall of a besieged city. He began to move downstream at a stumbling run, then realized to his horror that the palm-tree was outdistancing him, pulling away from him with every second. And he knew then, finally, that Leila had gone forever.

He staggered to a halt, bent over against the sudden pain in his side. Over him and around him arched the impassive night, lit dimly from the west by its low, shrunken moon. The stars glittered with an icy indifference. Half a mile downstream, a cluster of lights marked where some boat, or perhaps several, had managed to find a safe anchorage at which those aboard could ride out the initial fury of the flood. But nothing either of man or nature moved, changed, acknowledged in any way that a life had ended, that a living soul had passed from the earth.

Zachary flung himself to the ground, consumed in an agony of grief and shame.

Derek Bickerton

Chapter 6

Veiled, voluptuous, opulently dressed, the widow Eugenia sat facing the priest Isidore, ex-pastor of Scetis, ex-diplomat, ex-candidate for the throne of Hagia Sophia. Isidore was easily the more restless and ill-at-ease of the two—still close enough to the desert to feel acutely uncomfortable in the presence of an attractive woman, especially a woman aware of her own attraction, like this one. Past the full flush of youth, true, and her manner, Isidore had to admit, seemed unexceptionable so far; her gaze serene and open, her tongue discreet, nothing you could fault there. But why did she think it necessary to dress up for an audience with a priest as if she were attending an imperial reception, or the theater, even? Why couldn't she just wear shapeless shifts, or even rags, as poor widows did? It wasn't that Isidore, too old now to be troubled by lust (though the memory of it still occasionally flickered through his mind), felt personally tempted. Simply, his sensibilities were offended.

However, he kept all of this from his face as he listened intently to the woman saying, "...and naturally my husband regretted that he had not been more...generous during his lifetime, but you know how men are, Father, he would keep putting things off..."

"And how much did you say this legacy was?" Isidore asked.

"Ten thousand gold pieces."

Isidore looked suitably impressed. Not a king's ransom, perhaps, no more than you'd expect from one of the richest merchants in Alexandria, but a solid sum nonetheless. "But, Father..." she was saying hesitantly.

"Yes, my child?" Child didn't sound quite right for this substantial female, but 'madam" was too formal and her given name too intimate. He was almost old enough to be her grandfather, anyway.

"My husband was most particular—and I agreed with him entirely—that this money should be devoted to the upkeep of the poor."

"Naturally."

What was so remarkable about that? But Isidore felt himself reacting to something in the woman's tone—something more urgent than the occasion seemed to warrant, tinged even with a trace of suspicion. He remained warily on guard.

"You see," Eugenia went on, "one hears...I really don't quite know how to put it..."

"You may speak in absolute confidence."

"Well...stories..."

"Stories about what, madam?" The more formal expression slipped out easily now, helped by a cooling of Isidore's tone that was automatic when anything smacking of gossip loomed on his horizon.

Her large, expressive eyes rolled at him, a touch fearful. "That may be all they are, Father, and I don't want to get anyone into trouble..."

"No need to fear that," Isidore said flatly.

"Well then," she said in a rush, "stories that money given to the church doesn't, how shall I put it, always end up being spent for the things it was intended for."

"The church in general, or this church in particular?"

"The Alexandrian church, Father."

Isidore was silent for a moment. He had made the connection—this must be what Euthymius had been darkly hinting at, the last time they spoke together. Almost the only time, actually, since Isidore's return from Constantinople. Indeed, both the Tall Brothers had seemed edgy, uncomfortable, unwilling to open up to him, ever since his return.

"You mean," he said at last, "you wouldn't—I mean your husband wouldn't have wanted this money spent on, oh, say the addition of a new chapel to the Caesarium, or the provision of new silk curtains for..."

"Decidedly not, Father," Eugenia said with an intensity that overrode her normal politeness.

"I see." Isidore forced his frown of concentration into a warm, reassuring smile. "Please take it as given that I personally will see to the disposition of these funds. They will be distributed among the poor of Alexandria exactly as your husband wished. If you would like me to send you an itemized account..."

"That won't be necessary, Father. I know I can rely on you."

As she rose to take her leave, her perfume hit him like a wave. *I'll never understand these women*, he thought. *Coming on like virgins and scenting themselves like harlots, what kind of mixed messages do they think they're sending? Or don't they think?* If only Theophilus would get onto them the way John Chrysostom did, invoking God's wrath on those so-called Christians who walked the streets with a fortune in jewels while the poor begged for scraps at their feet. But when he'd merely mentioned this to the Archbishop, Theophilus had flown into a rage, and Isidore couldn't be sure whether it was just the mention of Goldenmouth's name or the fear of alienating rich parishioners that had most provoked his anger.

When Eugenia had gone, Isidore sat for a while in silence, thinking. Then he rose, walked down a corridor and across a paved courtyard, and knocked on a massive, worm-eaten door.

"Come in. It's not locked."

Isidore entered, opened his mouth to utter a routine greeting, then stopped. Euthymius was packing books and rolls of papyrus into large leather bags.

"What's up?" Isidore asked.

"We're leaving. Resigning, that is."

"Who's we?" Isidore asked automatically, though he already knew the answer.

"Me and Eusebius."

"Why?"

Euthymius looked uncomfortable. "We'd rather not say."

"Does the Archbishop know?"

"Not yet." Isidore somehow understood from the other's tone that the Tall Brothers were not exactly looking forward to their interview with Theophilus, and were postponing it to the last moment, perhaps merely because of its inherent unpleasantness, perhaps so they could escape as soon as it was over.

"I'll be sorry to see you go," Isidore said sincerely. The three of them had always thought alike, about the eremitic life, the Divine nature, Origen's books. He would have counted them as friends, but Euthymius merely shrugged and went on with his packing.

"You know," Isidore went on, trying not to feel hurt by this rejection, "I was going to tell you about something that happened to me just now, but I suppose if you're leaving it's no longer any concern of yours."

He had now got Euthymius' attention. The Tall Brother stopped dead, a book in his hand, staring fixedly at him.

"A woman came to me about a legacy her husband had left. To us. The Church, that is."

He paused. Euthymius quietly laid the book down on the table in front of him and said, "Go on."

"She seemed worried that it might not go where it was intended to. That it might be used for something else, you know, building, maintenance, new ornaments for..."

Isidore was not prepared for the look of anxiety that suddenly appeared on Euthymius' face. "Why did she think that? Did she mention any names?"

Isidore, surprised, said, "No. She wouldn't say where she'd got it from. Just, you know, gossip..."

Euthymius relaxed.

"Just gossip," he repeated.

"And so I immediately thought about what you were trying to say last time…I didn't understand what you were getting at, not then. But now, putting two and two together…" Isidore hesitated, trying to read the other's face; then he decided to take the plunge. "Frankly, I've suspected for quite some time now that those in charge here were not always, well, to be absolutely frank about it, that they were diverting charitable…"

He got no further. Euthymius stepped forward and threw an arm around his shoulder.

"I'm sorry, old friend."

"Sorry? What for?"

"For suspecting you. Eusebius is always telling me I get irrational about this. I can't help it, though, so much spying and tale-bearing's going on."

"I don't understand," Isidore protested. "Suspecting me of what?"

"Well, it wasn't just me, we both figured you for one of Theophilus' creatures. I mean it looked obvious to us, sending you on all those missions, backing you for Constantinople…"

"I've always admired him," Isidore admitted. "As a highly intelligent man, a leader—and of course, simply as our Archbishop, I owe him my loyalty. But frankly, the way I've been treated since," he waved his hand vaguely northwards, "what happened up there, I have to confess he's stretched that loyalty pretty thin. Treats me as if it was all my fault. Though quite apart from that," he added quickly, anxious lest the Tall Brothers think his position the result of mere personal feeling, "I would never let loyalty blind me to, to anything really reprehensible that was going on."

He stopped abruptly. Euthymius, nodding, seemed satisfied with his words. "Well, something reprehensible is going on."

"You have proof?"

"Absolute proof."

"But you don't want to take any action."

Euthymius gave him a piercing look. "Do you?"

"No. Not really." How much of our reluctance is a genuine refusal to judge, Isidore wondered, and how much is cowardice? We both know the power Theophilus wields, we both know how vindictive he is; we both know he believes that he and the Egyptian Church are one and that therefore anything he does must be right. Lucky for us Ammonias isn't involved, the Earless One would just plough ahead regardless.

"So that's why you're leaving," he said. "Then I suppose I'm in charge now."

Theophilus had carefully left their roles vague.

Euthymius shrugged. "Good luck, in that case."

Isidore had a sudden inspiration.

"You know; I don't have to tell him about this legacy."

"What about the paperwork?" Euthymius objected.

"I'll destroy it. All of it, if I can get hold of it."

Euthymius gave a short, harsh bark of laughter, with no humor at all in it. "You're really serious, aren't you?"

"Better believe it."

"He's sure to find out, you know him."

"I'll take my chance on that," Isidore said, scared himself by the rebellious feelings that had suddenly been roused in him, worried lest he had committed himself to too much. *I'm too old for this kind of thing*, he thought, but once he had confided in the Tall Brothers, he feared their quiet disapproval, should he back down, even more than he feared Theophilus' rages. "What's he doing now, do you know?" he asked nervously.

Again that bark of a laugh. "Oh, he won't bother you for the next day or two. He's closeted with Timothy, working on his festal letter for next year. Guess what the theme is."

Isidore shook his head.

"He's going to get down on the Anthropomorphites. He's still so mad about Constantinople he had to find someone to take it out on. Turns out they're no better than pagans, which is ridiculous, really. Still, it's in a good cause, I suppose."

"God is a spirit," Isidore said automatically.

"God is a spirit," Euthymius echoed him. "Not a blown-up man. But incidentally," and he leaned confidential lips towards Isidore's ear. "I really would try and make sure he doesn't find out what you're up to. Because if he does…Well, I wouldn't be in your shoes, that's all."

Derek Bickerton

Chapter 7

Another morning was breaking over Scetis, a serene, clear morning, with a sparkle of chill in the air, for it was once more the winter season, and for the last several days a wind out of central Asia had brought down a breath of that country's implacable snows. Now the wind had dropped, and the slim plume of smoke from the bakery, where that week's shift of hermits was already at work preparing the agape and the weekly bread ration, rose vertically, unbroken, into the blue air.

And the other hermits? John the Dwarf was weaving baskets for a hermit too sick to do it himself. Papnoute was praying that his admirable self-restraint in the matter of Mother Theodora would be rewarded by a third angelic visit. Theodora was praying for Papnoute, whose strained politeness hadn't fooled her for a moment. Please God, she prayed, grant him the humility to just one day ask someone, preferably not me, but yes, even me, should You will it, for advice. Serapion, awake since the ninth hour of the night, was praying that God would take him before he became a burden to others, and God, benignly smiling on him, had seemed, he thought, to give his assent. Or perhaps he had just dreamed it. Certainly Benjamin, still dozing, albeit in a kneeling position, dreamed he was at Heaven's gate and St. Peter obligingly offered him a drink. He accepted. "That's vinegar!" he exclaimed indignantly. "Exactly," St. Peter remarked in an enigmatic tone. Then, he woke up.

Arsenius was reading the Life of the Blessed Anthony and wondering two things: one, should there really have been quite so much emphasis on the miraculous, and two, would he not be following the saint more faithfully by selling the book and giving the proceeds to the poor, rather than just reading about him? And Moses, his herbs still unwatered, was reading too, stubbornly, determinedly, not liking at all the content of what he read (and not overly impressed by its style, either, if it came to that) but persevering out of a sense of duty, for it would indeed be his duty to read it aloud, in public, at synaxis, later that day, and to try, if possible, to make its words palatable to his audience.

The document he was reading was the Archbishop of Alexandria's festal letter for the year 399. The overt purpose of the festal letter was to announce the date that had been calculated for Easter that year, and hence those of all the other holy days that used Easter as their reference point. But by tradition, the Archbishop always took the opportunity to include in his letter a homily directed towards what, in his opinion, was the most crucial religious issue of the day.

Normally this was innocuous enough—some well-established theological doctrine would be reinforced, or some currently popular sin assailed. This time, however...Moses' displeasure expressed itself in a series of grunts and quite unconscious cracking of his knuckles as he read doggedly on.

And Poemen? Poemen the Shepherd was trying to rid his mind of a cluster of thoughts that had suddenly congealed, sometime in the night, into a small but ominous cloud.

He was remembering a prophecy that the Great Macarius had made before he died. "When you see a cell built close to the marsh," the old man had said, "know that the devastation of Scetis is near, when you see trees, know that it is at the door; and when you see young children, take up your sheepskins and flee." No one had taken much notice of this at the time—the old man had already begun to show signs of senility, and it wasn't as if he was John of Lycopolis, who had successfully predicted every major event in twenty years, including his own death. To the contrary, Macarius had never predicted anything else in his life, at least not that anyone remembered. But...

Well, for two or three years now, as more and more hermits arrived, new cells had been built closer to the marsh: one of them was the one Arsenius had turned down. And then, just a few days previously, a child had appeared in Scetis.

It was a strange story. Carion, an Egyptian peasant with a wife and two children, had left his family to become a hermit. His wife, furious at being abandoned, followed him to the desert with the children, a girl and a boy, told him that they were starving and demanded that he take them. And Carion, torn with compassion, had called the children to him. Both of them came running, but as they approached him the little girl turned suddenly and ran back to her mother. "All right," Carion said. "You can take the girl. I'll take the boy and look after him." And he had done just that.

Well, that left only the trees, and the trees should have come before the child. Were the trees there already, in some form not easily recognized? Poemen thought of the stumpy, scruffy palms that grew by the marshes, that supplied raw materials for mats and baskets, but they'd always been there. The trees of the prophecy had to be growing in the dry dusty heart of Scetis itself. Would any of Moses' herbs qualify? Some had gotten to be rather enormous lately. And the scriptures spoke of the mustard plant as a tree, something that had always puzzled Poemen, who knew it was just a bush.

But why should he let some senile maundering spoil so lovely a morning? Most people who knew him would have counted Poemen among the least superstitious of hermits. Asking himself this question, he realized that his memory of Macarius' words had tapped into a deeper disquiet that had been building within him for quite a while now, a disquiet that had to do with the way Scetis seemed to be changing.

What had finally brought that disquiet to the surface was the incident of the mad boy who had come for a cure and instead had been sodomized by a hermit. Such an incident would have been unthinkable ten or even five years previously. But the hermits coming into Scetis now were not all of the kind that had come before. Poemen fought against admitting this for as long as he reasonably could. Everyone knew how old people always complained that the world was falling to bits all around them, that people were no longer what they had been in the speaker's youth. But this, as well as the frailty of age, bespoke a lack of charity. Charity never condemned. Charity greeted all comers with hope and love, with the best of expectations, no matter how often those expectations might fail. So Poemen had resisted his feelings, until the incident of the mad boy.

He hoped that was an isolated incident, but feared it was not. Some of the newcomers were no more than tax fugitives; others had failed in their previous occupations, and sought only to obtain for free the respect their predecessors had earned by pure living and holy deeds. There was no practical way of keeping such folk out, even if charity would permit it. Scetis was not a monastery with gates to open and shut, an abbot to give orders, a hierarchy to execute them. It relied solely on the caliber of its inhabitants to maintain its standards. But now, imperceptibly, laxness was creeping in. Perhaps the devastation, whatever that might mean, would come as God's punishment for the sins towards which Scetis was insensibly drifting.

But how, exactly? Not devastation from the hand of man, surely. Who would attack it? The likeliest candidates, the nomadic tribes of the desert, the Mazices, the Blemyes, had not troubled Scetis or Nitria for the better part of a century, since their foundation, indeed. They had been deterred, folk believed, partly by superstitious dread of the hermits' supposed magical powers, and partly by genuine respect. The Roman army had no motive and far too many other things to do. And as for the third and only other power in Egypt, Theophilus and his parabolani...Poemen, though no admirer of the Sly Fox, shook his head at the sheer absurdity of the thought. An orthodox Christian Archbishop physically assaulting a religious community? Inconceivable! It could only be by a straightforward act of God. An earthquake, perhaps. Yes, an earthquake was the likeliest.

But, should he then follow Macarius' advice, take up his sheepskin and flee the place? Even in the somber mood that had so suddenly and inexplicably fallen on him, Poemen did not consider this. God had called him to Scetis and in Scetis he would remain, until the end. If it was God's will that he be slain there, then let him be slain, let that will be done.

And with this thought, he knew with a sudden shocked recognition as to what was the matter with him. Accidie! That subtlest and most insidious of temptations, sapping the will and breeding cold despair in the heart, had found a new way to attack him, a way so cunning and ingenious, so well camouflaged that it had temporarily fooled even as old a campaigner as himself. Chastened by this discovery, ashamed of the slowness of his discernment, but not altogether sorry to be reminded once again that no one, ever, in this life dare even dream of immunity from sin, Poemen fell to his knees, thanked God for revealing to him the true state of his affairs, and began to recite one of his favorite psalms:

"...yea, though I walk through the valley of the shadow of death, I will fear no evil: for Thou art with me, thy rod and thy staff they comfort me..."

By the time of the agape, that afternoon, prayer and increased vigilance had fully restored Poemen to his normal self. Warmly, he greeted friends and acquaintances, noticing that the refectory seemed more crowded than usual, several visitors mixing with the regular inhabitants. There was John Cassian, who passed through so frequently one thought he had taken up residence, and over there Photinus, the dapper and knowledgeable deacon from Cappadocia who had attended Moses' ordination. Presumably they had all come to hear the Archbishop's annual message, which Moses was scheduled to read to them after the introductory prayers of the synaxis.

And there was Moses himself, looking, to Poemen's surprise, distinctly ill at ease. After clearing his throat a couple of times, he began to read, almost apologetically, the section of the letter that dealt with the religious calendar. Then he paused, rolled up his eyes as if hoping for some heavenly salvation, and when none was forthcoming began again in a deliberate monotone:

"The Archbishop then addresses us as follows: 'dearly beloved brothers in Christ, I greet you once more in this the last year before the four hundredth anniversary of Our Lord's birth. I will say nothing today about the false prophets who have proclaimed that this anniversary will mark His Second Coming, since, 'the Son of Man will come when you least expect him", Matthew 25.44, and woe upon those who do not keep themselves in perpetual readiness for that hour. I will merely point out the folly, if not the blasphemy, of assuming that the Will of the Almighty is subject to this purely human and purely superstitious obsession with numbers, especially round numbers.

"If only this were the only way in which men believed God's uncreated and immaterial presence to be limited, circumscribed, diminished by the possession of mere human attributes! Alas, it is not.

"All of us are, of course, familiar with Genesis 1.26, 'And God said, let us make man in Our image, after Our likeness,' and most of us, I would hope, will have always understood that verse in a purely spiritual sense, as of God admixing with 'the dust of the ground', Genesis 2.7, some tincture, some reflection, no matter how shadowy or remote, of His Divine essence. But we must recall the circumstances under which even this attenuated representation of the divine was bestowed on Adam, the first man. It was bestowed on Adam before he sinned, before his sin brought death into the world. Can we in all honesty dare to claim that even so faint a likeness of the Divine remained with us once our souls had become fouled with sin, once our bodies had become rotten with corruption?

"Similarly, when Scripture refers to 'the hand of God', 'the face of God' and so forth, we surely should conceive these things as figurative—God's hand, for instance, as merely standing for those agencies, whatever they may be (agencies subtle and far beyond our limited understanding, no doubt) that God uses in order to accomplish His purposes. For if we do the reverse, if we rashly suppose God to be endowed with hands like ours, a face like ours, then quite simply what we are doing is recreating God in our own image. And that is blasphemy—out-and-out sacrilegious blasphemy."

Poemen had observed some of the congregation becoming more and more restive as Moses read on. But at these last words, the unthinkable finally happened: something that had never happened at any synaxis in all Poemen's years in Scetis. A muted but deep murmur of disapproval rolled across the congregation, a dull and rancorous sound that had no single or visible source. Poemen saw Moses' eyes, flashing, search for its source, fail to locate one and then send a baleful glare of warning into every corner of the church. At that glare, and at the silencing of Moses' voice that accompanied it, the murmur subsided slowly and died away, although a restless stir of movement, insuppressible, continued to make itself heard.

Without waiting for the silence to become absolute, Moses began again: "Nor do we need to look far to determine whence this blasphemy comes. Satan may be frustrated but he never surrenders—checked in one place, his cunning wiles are immediately applied in another, which he hopes may be weaker in withstanding him. Once he worked through pagan belief, leading men to worship his demons and himself in the guise of idols that depicted human figures, or even the figures of brute beasts. Now, deprived throughout most of

Egypt of the support he formerly received from pagan worshippers, he has turned to seduce the servants of Christ themselves, those who should be the very first to perceive and to condemn his vile stratagems.

"For this Anthropomorphism, this setting-up of a false and idolatrous image of the True God for worship is no better than paganism, is indeed worse by far than paganism. For whereas some pagans might be pardoned in that they had never been exposed to the True Gospel of Our Lord Jesus Christ, this disgusting heresy afflicts precisely those who..."''

Moses broke off as the harsh and rancorous murmurs swelled again through the church. "I can't read any more of this," he said. "This is unconscionable, needlessly divisive, and seeks to turn into heresy what is surely a matter for the individual conscience. A long time ago, Father Sopatros warned us not to tamper with these things, since they can only lead to futile disputes. But even he said they involved nothing heretical. Enough of this. We shall proceed with the service."

"No, we shall not," someone cried out.

"Who said that?" Moses, his eyes flashing fire, looked from one side of the congregation to the other.

"Read the letter," someone else shouted, and another echoed him, while shouts of, "No, no! Go on with the service!" came from other parts of the church.

"Read it yourselves, then," Moses said, tossing the roll of papyrus into the front row of the congregation. With quick, jerky movements he stripped off his white robe and threw that too to the ground. "And get yourselves another priest while you're about it," he added as he stalked off, his tall lanky frame erect and bristling with righteous indignation, out of the church and into the cool and quiet of the desert evening.

A moment of stunned silence was followed immediately by a redoubled outcry. Hermits ran to seize hold of Theophilus' letter, pulling it this way and that until it tore into several pieces. All over the church, small groups of angry, gesticulating figures argued with one another. Others were following Moses out of the church. It was a scene of total confusion.

Poemen eased his way forward, picked up Moses' discarded robe, shook it, smoothed it and folded it neatly over his arm. Then he signaled to John the Dwarf, who understood his intention immediately and who followed him, catching up with him just outside the church door.

"This is terrible," John said, trying to control the nervous twitching of his hands. "This is exactly what I've been afraid of, all these years. Something that would divide us. Why has Theophilus done this?"

"I don't know," Poemen answered him. "Out of ignorance is my best guess."

"You mean ignorance of Scripture?"

Poemen smiled. "Ignorance of us.

"He always tries to make out," John said, lengthening his stride to keep up with Poemen as they headed for Moses' cave, "that he's one of us."

"I know, but he's not, is he?"

John agreed. "If he'd wanted to divide us, though..."

"He doesn't. Divided, we're a nuisance to him. United, he thinks he can use us as a weapon. Like at the Serapeum. He miscalculated, that's all."

They found Moses in his cave, already on his knees in silent prayer. They waited outside until he became aware of their presence. He turned to them slowly, his eyes, luminous in the soft light, full of sorrow.

"I'm sorry, brothers."

"It wasn't your fault," John was quick to answer him.

"I gave way to anger," Moses said sadly. "Whose fault was that, if not mine?"

Poemen handed him his priest's robe. "Put this on and come back with us, then."

Moses shook his head, refused the robe. "I'm sorry about my anger. I'm not sorry about my decision."

Poemen and John exchanged looks. "You can't possibly..."

"No, believe me," Moses said in a quiet but firm tone. "I cannot and will not be priest of a community that's tearing itself apart. Let them find someone else."

"No one else here's ordained."

"Then let them ordain someone else."

"I don't think he can just resign like that," Poemen said. "Can he?"

"I'm not absolutely sure what canon law has to say on that point." John's forehead wrinkled in concentration "Wait, now I remember...I heard about some bishop, once, in Syria, who changed his clothes and became a builder's laborer. I think they made him go back as soon as they got onto him."

"Well, whether or not," Poemen said, "we all want you to be our priest, and at least some of us will support you, whatever you decide. But what you said deeply shocked me."

Moses stared at him. "Why?"

"Why? Because I never thought you'd give way to pride."

"Pride!" Moses blinked and shook his head slowly, puzzled.

"Yes, pride," Poemen pushed on. "Suppose God's put you where you are so you can heal the community, bring it together. Perhaps because you're the only one who could bring it together. Would you set up your will against His will? If that's not pride, what is?"

Because of his complexion, Moses could hardly turn pale, but when he was deeply shocked a kind of greyish cast came over his features. "I never saw it like that," he said simply.

"Of course not," Poemen soothed him. "How could you? Anyone would have been thrown off balance by what happened back there. And might have said things he never meant in the heat of the moment." He handed the white robe to Moses a second time. "Put it on. We'll go back together. And if they're still arguing, we'll just sit there until they come to their senses."

And indeed they were still arguing, but no longer in several different groups. Many had left, but the remainder had formed an attentive ring around a pair of figures: Photinus, the deacon from Cappadocia, and the old hermit, Serapion. As Moses, with John on one side of him and Poemen on the other, sat down quietly on a bench at the very back of the nave, Photinus was speaking vigorously and eloquently, while Serapion, his face haggard, gazed up at him and every now and then tried to interrupt him, only to have his words drowned in the flood of the deacon's oratory.

"How did an outsider get the floor?" Poemen asked his neighbor in a whisper.

"Oh, somebody asked him what the other churches in the East believed. Once he'd gotten started, you couldn't stop him."

"...for if we assume that God has bodily parts like ours," Photinus was saying, 'then must we not also assume that God experiences the same feelings as we do? We as humans feel rage, envy, greed—we feel these things precisely because we have bodies, because the animal heat of those bodies provides food for these passions. Indeed it is precisely because the physical self feeds these passions that we, as hermits, seek to mortify that physical self—seek to master our feelings by weakening that part of us which feeds them, Whereas..."

"But the wrath of God," Serapion cried out, managing by his cry to stem for a moment the flow of words. "Over and over in Scripture they tell us of the wrath of God..."

"In a purely figurative sense! Do you imagine God having temper tantrums, like some naughty child?" And Photinus, a good mimic, wrinkled and reddened his face, stamped his foot, shook his fist. "No, my friend, the wrath of God means something far more terrible than mere human anger. It means the absolute withdrawal of His love, it means the turning of His back on you, it means His handing you over to the torments of Hell! It means something wholly beyond human understanding, which is why the Scriptures, in their wisdom, compare the inconceivable to things we know well and can understand, like the anger a master feels at his lying or incompetent slave. And if an angry God still seems possible to you, what about a fearful God?"

He approached Serapion moving swiftly and lightly on his toes, then bent and placed his lips close to the old man's ear. "I don't mean a God who inspires fear, I mean one who feels fear," he went on in a voice little above a whisper. "Who is afraid, and doubts, and hesitates, and contradicts himself, just as each of us does! Can you seriously suppose an All-powerful, All-knowing God who is afraid, who doubts, even doubts himself? Who, just like us, sometimes can't quite make up his mind what to do? Do you think God is ever afraid, Father?"

Serapion shook his head.

"Ever in doubt?"

"No, never."

"Or uncertain what he should do next?

"Of course not."

"Tempted, perhaps, by sin?"

Serapion shuddered. "How could you even say that?"

"It's absurd, isn't it?" Photinus stepped back a pace, straightened himself and spoke in a normal voice. "But then if God does not and cannot have a mind like ours, why should we suppose he has a body like ours? Of course the truth is, he has neither. He is eternal, immaterial, uncreated spirit," and he flung his hands on high, "so let us worship him as such! Alleluya!"

And an echoed "Alleluya! Let God be praised!" rolled around the church. Photinus smiled down at Serapion.

"Have I convinced you yet, Father?"

The old man blinked, his eyes moist. "I cannot argue against you, my son...It's just that I feel...I felt...for so long a time...No. You must be right."

Photinus smiled. One or two of the hermits cheered. Then Photinus saw Moses sitting on a bench, behind everyone, waiting. He came towards the priest with light, eager steps. To the astonishment of all, he prostrated himself, reaching forward with his lips to kiss Moses' horny, calloused toes. Moses squirmed in embarrassment, rolling up his eyes, but Poemen made him a quick sign to control himself.

"Father." Photinus said. "Forgive me."

"Why?" Moses asked.

"Because he asked," Poemen hissed under his breath. "Go on, do it!"

"I meant," Moses said, "what am I supposed to forgive you for?"

It was Photinus' turn to look puzzled, "For...for taking over the synaxis, of course. And I, a mere visitor here. May I beg you, on behalf of all of us here, to continue what we so rudely interrupted?"

"There's nothing to forgive," Moses said. "I abandoned the synaxis. Whoever the spirit moved was free to take over." He hesitated, distracted by Poemen's hand urging him to rise; then he said, "But, if you think I'm going to endorse the Archbishop's letter—or even finish reading it..."

"That won't be necessary," Photinus said. "Everyone here is of the same mind now, I believe."

Moses glanced round him. It was true. Most of those likely to hold Anthropomorphite views had already left, and those who remained, like Serapion, were convinced, or half-convinced, or too awed by the Cappadocian's rhetorical skills to take him on.

"Because in my view," Moses went on, as if Photinus had not spoken, "how one sees God is one's own business and nobody else's. God told us to keep the Commandment, not indulge in vain and idle speculation about who or what He is. Discuss it if you must, but I will not tolerate any bullying or any talk of heresy for as long as I am priest of Scetis. Is that understood?"

"Of course, Father," Photinus said meekly.

"Good." Moses strode firmly towards the altar, turned and said, "let us begin by repeating the prayer Christ taught us to say. Our Father who art in heaven..."

"Our Father who art in heaven—" a hundred voices echoed him. "Hallowed be Thy name..."

As the prayer died at last into silence, Poemen heard a muffled sobbing. It came from Serapion. Poemen stepped quickly and nimbly among the benches, put his arm around the old man's shoulders. "What is it? What's the matter?"

"...my God..." was all Poemen could make out at first. Alarmed by the continuing silence, he looked around to find every eye in the church fixed on them.

"They've taken my God away from me," Serapion sobbed.

"Hush," Poemen said, as one might to a child, patting and stroking the old man's shoulder as he bent over him. "Don't upset yourself. We'll talk about it afterwards. Promise."

Serapion broke out abruptly in a loud wail. "They've taken away my God, and now I've got nothing to hold on to! I don't know who or what I'm to pray to anymore!"

Poemen's gaze locked with that of Photinus, and Photinus looked quickly away. The Shepherd spoke in a voice as close to anger as he had ever come in two decades.

"So that's the fruit of all your philosophy? An old man in tears!"

Photinus blushed and did not answer. Poemen wrapped an arm around the weeping old hermit and led him gently out of the church. *How dare they*, he thought. *What can any of them, or I, or any human, know about God?* He is whatever He chooses to be—turn the stone and you will find Me, cut the branch and I am there—He is body, spirit, the air we breathe, the bread that nourishes us, all and yet at the same time none of these, as far beyond our understanding as we are beyond that of an ant or a fly!

"Come," he said to the old man, "take no notice of them. Worship Him in whatever form you want to. So long as you love Him with a true heart, what difference does it make to anyone?"

Derek Bickerton

Chapter 8

Darion subsisted for quite a while on the money he had robbed from the magistrate. By the time it was gone, he had pretty well determined that, short of life-threatening emergencies, he had committed his last crime. He played his flute at fairs, or for the treaders at the grape harvest, he begged, he threw dice with the camel-drivers in their crude wayside taverns, cheating when he had to—a risky business, that. But all the time at the back of his mind, he felt the need to establish himself in some new profession, any profession, it didn't matter what, provided it was not overly onerous and did not involve the shedding of blood.

While pondering this question one day, the memory of the hermit he had rescued from the desert came into his mind. That hermit owed Darion his life. Darion was entitled to some sort of recompense, even if that recompense was no more than a piece of advice. And a hermit was the ideal person to ask for advice. Everyone knew that hermits had powers of discernment beyond those of other men. Besides, they refrained from judgement—it wouldn't bother them that Darion was a robber and a murderer. So he resolved to visit the hermit, ask him, and follow whatever way of life might be suggested, so long as it didn't involve becoming a hermit himself.

So, on a midmorning a few days later, Didymos was busy weeding a field of young barley when he heard someone approaching. He straightened his back slowly and with the awkwardness of one who has spent several hours bent over his own soil. Leaning on his hoe, he spat—not out of rudeness, but because his mouth was full of dust—and gazed at his cousin with suspicion, for he had had both good and bad things from Darion, and never quite know what to expect from him.

"How goes it, cousin?" Darion asked cheerfully.

"Hard," was Didymos' response. "As usual. But you wouldn't know much about that, would you?"

"Hey, steady on!" Darion stared back at him with injured innocence. "Is that any way to greet a long-lost relative?"

Didymos shrugged. "What are you after this time?"

"What am I after!" Darion repeated in a shocked tone, squatting down on the bare earth at the edge of the field. "How can you say such things? I just happened to be in the area, is all, and I thought to myself, while I'm here, why don't I just go visit my cousin Didymos, see how he's getting on? I'm not after anything."

"You always want something."

"Well, last time, as I recall, it was me who did you a favor."

Didymos leaned on his hoe, impassive, chewing a grass blade. "Not much of a favor, that was."

"Well, I paid you, didn't I?"

"Maybe, but the bugger ate like a horse."

"If you're out of pocket," Darion said recklessly, "I'll make up the difference...Are you?"

Didymos was tempted to say yes, but could not, in all honesty. He had in fact made a profit, real if not spectacular, out of Zachary's stay. "I broke about even, I guess," he said grudgingly.

"There you are then...You look thirsty." Darion opened the satchel in which he carried his few possessions and took out his wineskin. "Have some."

Didymos shook his head. "Too early for me."

"Well, at least sit down, you're making me nervous, looming over me like that...Come on, it's only half-and-half."

Didymos, squatting, took the wineskin. "Hm. Not bad...But can't you just get to the point? I've got the rest of this field to clear by sundown."

Darion shrugged. "All right, be that way. Where's the hermit?"

"Alexandria."

"Shit!" For some reason it had never occurred to Darion that the hermit wouldn't still be there, fixed in place, just waiting to give him advice. "You know I never spoke to him. Never even knew his name. What was he like?"

Didymos took another pull at the wineskin. "Decent sort of guy. Good family, I guess, though he didn't want to talk about that. Gave up being a hermit, that's for sure, in the finish he was living with this weird woman who'd been thrown out of a monastery or something, everyone thought she was cracked but he seemed to get along with her all right. Then she drowned somehow, in the last flood, nobody knows exactly what happened, but right afterwards he was offered a good job in Alex and he left, just like that." Didymos snapped his fingers. "Never even said goodbye," he added resentfully. "What's the big interest, anyway? You want money from him?"

Darion was tempted to say, it's none of your business. Then he thought, *What difference does it make?* "I wanted his advice."

"Huh," Didymos said. "That's a new one." Then, when Darion did not expand on his statement, he asked, "Advice about what?"

"What to do with my life."

"That is a new one."

"I'm giving up crime."

Didymos laughed cynically.

"No, I'm serious," Darion insisted. "But if the hermit's gone..." He stood up. "Guess I'll be on my way, cousin."

Didymos seemed to regret his lack of hospitality. "We've got a priest you could ask. The wife swears by him."

"Nah, forget it."

Darion had taken back his wineskin and was turning away when Didymos, pointing at the flute in his belt, said, "Never thought of making a living with that thing?"

"Of course. But it's too chancy. I need a steady job."

"You could work in a temple."

Darion laughed derisively. "They're all closed."

"Not all. Ours was open till this year. And the one in Terenuthis is still open, I know for a fact. They say the hermits of Scetis protect it, though why they would do that I can't imagine. You could try there."

Darion opened his mouth to pour scorn on the idea, then immediately thought better of it. It wasn't the hermit's advice, but if he hadn't come looking for the hermit he wouldn't have received it, so in a sense, indirectly, it had come from him.

"All right," he said. "Maybe I will."

He was a little leery of entering Terenuthis because of what had happened several years before, but he figured that his time spent there had been too short, and his jailers too drunk, for anyone to recognize him now. He approached the temple and was greeted in its gateway by the linen-clad, shaven-headed priest of Isis, who informed him that there was indeed a vacancy.

"I have to be honest with you," the priest told him. "I can't afford a proper salary. No more than pocket-money, really. That's why my last flute-player quit on me. The Christians have just about ruined us. Donations are way down; we get less every year. You can still eat off it—yeah, sure, sacrifice is illegal now, but they turn a blind eye to small stuff, chickens, ducks, even the odd piglet or two, but goats are too dodgy, and as for bulls..." The priest blew through his lips contemptuously. "Forget it! No more beef stew. And you can sleep in the temple, naturally. But you've got to bear in mind that they could come in and close us down any day now."

"Someone told me the hermits protected you," Darion said.

The priest sighed. "Wish it was that simple! I've always got on well with the folks in Scetis, they're not like the rest of 'em, they figure if they leave us alone our people will come over to them in the long run, and seems like they're right, unfortunately. And since the town does a lot of business with them, that attitude has kind of rubbed off on the local authorities. But make no mistake," and the priest shook his head sadly, "if the army moved in, there's nothing they could do about it. All it needs is a stroke of the pen from some city bureaucrat, and you and I are both out of a job...Is there anything else I can tell you?"

"Do I have to believe in anything special?"

"Nah...But if you don't believe in Isis, just have the decency to keep quiet about it. And show a little respect...What do you think?"

Darion did not have to think for long. There seemed little enough to it—morning and evening serenades to the goddess, special performances on her feast-days, a little light work decorating statues... The very precariousness and semi-legality of the job appealed to him, it felt like an appropriate coda to his career. And he wouldn't have to shed blood any more. Not even animal blood. The priest could look after that.

"I'll take it," he said.

Chapter 9

As Theophilus' festal letter made its way south through the monasteries and hermitages of Egypt, it left rage and confusion in its wake. In many churches, the priests didn't even get as far as Moses had done; they flat-out refused to read any of it. But when its contents became known, as they inevitably did, the horror of the more conservative knew no bounds. Of course God had a human shape! How else could you read Scripture? And what was all this highfalutin' Greek nonsense about 'spiritual interpretations'? Rank heresy, which was all it was. And from their own Archbishop! A sense of betrayal ran wide and deep.

No leaders arose; no organization imposed itself. All that happened was that, singly or in small groups, on foot, by donkey or by boat, monks and hermits began to make their way towards the capital. And the rebellious murmurs that came from them spread swiftly, swelled, built up into a roar of execration:

Death! Death to the heretics! Death to the heretic Archbishop!

For the first and perhaps the only time in his life—if you leave out the letter to Maximus with which Eutropius had blackmailed him—the Sly Fox had miscalculated. And for once his network of spies, stunned themselves perhaps by the suddenness and fury of the response, failed to alert him in time.

He had, anyway, much on his mind. On top of his humiliation in the Imperial capital had come the Tall Brothers' defection, amid rumors of financial mismanagement and even outright fraud. According to one of his agents, they had actually claimed that their souls might be in danger if they went on working for him. And then on top of that came the affair of Isidore.

He had never really liked Isidore. He had run him for Archbishop of Constantinople only because he had nobody else who would both make a credible candidate and remain (or so he believed) under his control. Then, when he had tried to build up Isidore's reputation by letting him act as a peacemaker in Palestine, Isidore's bungling had served only to make the dispute increasingly bitter. And when Eutropius forced Theophilus to consecrate John Chrysostom, all the Archbishop's impotent fury had been deflected onto the defeated candidate, almost as if the whole thing had been Isidore's fault. As in a way it was, Theophilus convinced himself. After all, if Isidore had been a halfway-acceptable choice, why would the castrated Chamberlain have picked a rabble-rouser like Chrysostom in his place?

Then another agent brought him the story of the widow Victoria's legacy.

He summoned the old priest and kept him waiting outside his office for an hour before calling him in.

Isidore faced Theophilus across the latter's immense desk. Theophilus was seated, but he did not ask Isidore to sit. Indeed, he did not say anything at all for the space of a full minute, while the old priest, whose arthritis gave him agonizing pain if he had to stand for any length of time, shifted uneasily from foot to foot and tried unsuccessfully to counter the level stare that Theophilus directed at him from his colorless eyes.

When the Archbishop finally spoke, it was without any preamble, and in a harsh, peremptory tone. "You know my instructions about the handling of all legacies to the church." Isidore bowed his head and murmured something that Theophilus affected not to understand.

"I said you know my instructions, do you not? Repeat them!"

"All legacies," Isidore said, "are to be paid first into the Central Fund. Subsequently they will be allocated to their various purposes."

"Have you obeyed those instructions?"

"Well," Isidore stammered, "in one particular case..."

"Have you obeyed them, yes or no?"

Isidore gathered his courage. "No."

"How dare you!"

"In this particular case..."

"How dare you disobey my explicit instructions?"

Theophilus stood up, towering over the priest. "I, and I alone, am responsible for the management of these funds. You are just a clerk, and an incompetent clerk at that, just as you were incompetent at every other job I ever entrusted you with."

He stopped for breath, and Isidore, who had been struggling to speak, broke in, "this was a case in which the testator specifically intended—"

"What do I care what they intended?" Theophilus raged. "What they intended is none of their business, and none of your business, either. It is I who allocate the Central Fund, I and nobody else, understand me? What happened to the money, where is it? Surrender it to me immediately."

"It's already been disbursed." A faint smile of satisfaction flickered briefly over Isidore's face. He might pay, and pay dearly, for his action but it was too late to reverse it, and he was glad about that.

One glance at Theophilus, however, quickly removed the smile from Isidore's face. He thought for a moment the Archbishop was going to have a fit: his face turned red, then a dull purple, he seemed to be choking, spittle flew from his lips. Then, he found his voice. "You... you spent it?"

Isidore, awed, simply nodded.

"You spent my money?"

"It was given to the poor, just as the testator..."

"I don't want to hear any more about the testator!" Theophilus was almost screaming. "The testator didn't give it to the poor! You gave it to the poor! In defiance of my strict orders..."

"It's our duty to give to the poor," Isidore managed to get out.

"Don't tell me what my duty is! I know what my duty is! My duty is to maintain the honor and dignity of this church in a world of heretics, pagans and Manicheans! Not to mention disobedient, incompetent assistants! Get out of my sight!"

"I beg your..."

"I said get out of my sight, are you deaf as well as stupid?" Theophilus' whole body was shaking with rage. With clenched fist he pounded the table in front of him. "Get out before I do you a physical injury! But don't think you've heard the last of this, because you haven't! No, not by a long shot."

Backing nervously, Isidore left the office, torn between consciousness of his own innocence and wild speculation as to how Theophilus would make good his threat. But Theophilus had not thought that far ahead yet—he only knew that his revenge would have to be crushing, something that would not merely terminate Isidore's career but irreparably blight his reputation for the short remainder of his life.

No time to think of that now, though. He had business at the Church of St. Theonas, on the western outskirts of the city. His litter, borne by six hefty Nubian slaves, awaited him in the courtyard below. He stepped in and seated himself, the slaves raised the litter and set off at a dog-trot. If only he could gain the right to use a horse-drawn carriage in the city like the Prefect did! But the civil authorities clung tenaciously to their privileges.

He missed, by a mere five minutes, the solid black-clad wall of monks and hermits, their clothing soiled with the dust of the desert, that came rolling northwards along the Street of the Soma, heading from the ruins of the Serapeum that had served as their gathering-point towards the Caesarium and the Archbishop's headquarters. They chanted as they came: "The hand of God protects us! The arm of God will strike for us! Death to the heretics! Death to the heretic Archbishop!" Along the flanks of the column ran little pagan boys, jumping up and down and shouting, "God has a wienie! God has a butt!", until the monks dispersed them with well-aimed stones.

The black army surged into the Caesarium, through the massive doors of St. Michael's Cathedral, into the guest houses, the ancillary chapels, the administrative building itself. The parabolani came running with their clubs, but the monks and hermits all carried staves, and Theophilus' men were heavily outnumbered. Within minutes, they were running for refuge towards the harbor, leaving a dozen or two of their members sprawled on the pavements with cracked heads and broken limbs. After that, it was just a question of finding some of the Archbishop's officials who knew where he had gone and beating them until their fear of further pain exceeded their fear of Theophilus. Then, the column moved off again.

Theophilus, returning in his litter down Canopic Street, saw them in the distance, a black wall that filled the entire width of the great avenue. Even without knowing what had happened, too far as yet to make sense of the confused rumble of sound, he knew instinctively that they spelled trouble.

"Turn around," he called to the church slaves. "Back to St. Theonas! And move it!"

He was too late. Someone with sharp eyes in the front rank of the column had recognized him. Looking over his shoulder Theophilus saw the leaders break into a run, saw the column lose shape as the faster runners forged ahead of the others. He figured there was a good half-mile between him and the relative safety of the church—they should just be able to make it, though it would be touch and go whether they would have time to barricade the church doors after them. Would it be a smart move to send one of the slaves ahead to alert the vergers? No, he decided, calculating how quickly the front runners were gaining on him. He needed all six bearers just to keep ahead of them. And pedestrians along the street were already turning to stare. The lower classes of Alexandria were totally lacking in principle, they would be quite capable of stopping the litter just for fun, to see what would happen when the black column caught up with it. If that happened, he would need all hands to fight his way through to safety.

The first stone flew through the air.

It landed well short of the litter, but Theophilus knew at once the danger he was now in. The leaders did not have to catch up. If they could disable one or more of his bearers, he was finished.

He felt no fear, only a kind of heady excitement, almost as if the chase were a spectacle in the circus and he himself a thrilled but personally uninvolved spectator. His moral courage might falter occasionally, as it had in that little room high up in the Imperial Palace, but his physical courage had never failed him yet.

Another stone came, and another, but this time they were not falling short—he heard them landing in the street to both sides of them. Then suddenly there came a cry and the litter gave a convulsive lurch, so that for a moment Theophilus had to cling to it in order to avoid being hurled bodily to the pavement. The litter righted itself abruptly as the five remaining bearers redistributed its weight. As it began to move forward again Theophilus, looking over his shoulder, saw the sixth bearer laying in the street, struggling to rise, bleeding from a wound in his scalp. Then the first wave of pursuers swept over him, trampling him, and he vanished from sight. The litter went on, but more slowly. They would never make it to St. Theonas in time.

Behind them the voices were roaring:

Kill him! Kill the heretic Archbishop!"

Theophilus knew now that he was very close to death, perhaps only seconds away. He had no fear for his own fate. He might have cut a few corners, but it was all for the good of the Church, and anyway he was convinced that God would never send an Archbishop to Hell, that would be too damaging to Christian morale, as well as a gross violation of those hierarchical principles which, he felt sure, reigned in Heaven just as they did on earth. But he was not ready for Heaven yet. He still had too much to do: Isidore remained unpunished, Constantinople had to be brought down, the final triumph of the Alexandrian church was still far from accomplished. "God, let me survive just a few years more," he prayed.

And, as if in answer to his prayer, God, or something, put into his head what he had to do.

"Stop!" he shouted. "Stop! Now!"

They took no notice. Seized by panic, they ran blindly on.

"Stop or I'll excommunicate you, you brutes!" he yelled.

That stopped them. Though slaves, they were good Christians—better a quick passage to paradise thirty seconds from now than an eternity of torment after a few more years as slaves. The litter lurched to a halt, and Theophilus, archiepiscopal robes flying, leapt nimbly from it, turned to the mob now no more than twenty paces away from him and strode deliberately towards it.

He knew mob psychology, he had studied it and used it himself. He knew that a show of courage by a single calm and determined individual could cause the biggest and blindest mob to hesitate, if only for a few seconds. Of course, everything turned on what that individual could do in those few seconds.

Just as he had foreseen, this mob, leaderless, momentarily uncertain, the monks if not the hermits in it trained for years to respect authority, slowed and faltered before him, would have come to a complete halt save for the pressure of bodies from behind, which caused the front ranks to take a few more stumbling steps. As their shouts died down in that moment of bewilderment,

Theophilus raised his arms high.

"Bless you, my children!" he intoned. "When I look upon you, I see the face of God!"

A babel of voices, angry, confused, astonished, greeted these words. Theophilus signaled for silence.

"Truly those shining countenances, filled with holy zeal, could leave no doubt in anyone's mind that we are indeed made in God's image!"

"What about the letter?" somebody shouted, and the shout was echoed: "the festal letter!"

"What about the letter?"

"It said God didn't have a body!"

"A forgery," Theophilus lied without the flicker of an eyelash. "A gross forgery, authored by the enemies of the Church, to sow dissension in our ranks. But, praise be to God, I see from this mighty demonstration that it has failed, that it has served only to unite us, to make us stronger still."

"Anathematize Origen!" a monk shouted. "If you want us to believe you, anathematize Origen!"

The shouting, focused now, swelled once again into a roar. "Anathematize Origen! Anathematize Origen!" The shouts synchronized gradually, found themselves a rhythm.

Well, if that's what they want, Theophilus thought. *They need a demon, someone on whom to center and vent the rage they've built up and they won't calm down until they get one.* He was sorry about their choice, for he had obtained much pleasure and profit from Origen's writings. But better a dead theologian than a dead archbishop.

He drew himself up to his full height. "I pronounce Origen and all his works to be anathema, abhorrent to Holy Church, false and heretical doctrine to be shunned and denounced by all true Christians!"

A ragged cheer came from the mob, drowning the minority of skeptical voices. Theophilus thought for a moment that they were about to lift him and carry him in procession through the streets. But no, they were stepping aside, making way for him. Theophilus glanced back to see his litter-bearers standing patiently; even the sixth, injured one—lucky for him the mob was shoeless!—had somehow survived.

"Follow me to the Caesarium," he cried. "Let us join there together and give thanks to God for all His blessings and mercies. Let us renew our vows to defend the orthodox faith and combat false doctrine in whatever form it takes. Bearers, come! The Caesarium!"

It took him the rest of the day to disperse the mob—hours of special prayers, speeches, and interviews. But that day had not been altogether wasted. It had given him an idea for dealing with Isidore. He had pronounced a genuine letter to be a forgery; he would now pronounce a forged letter to be genuine.

It was the third or fourth hour of the night before he could call in his master forger, an aged and decrepit scribe whose hand, however, remained for the moment steady enough for this particular task. Theophilus liked to employ elderly agents because they would die quite soon, even without assistance, and his secrets would be buried with them. "Begin, 'dear Father Theophilus'," he said.

The old man hesitated, stylus poised. "Not Archbishop, your Reverence?"

"No," Theophilus said. "This is an old letter, so don't forget to age it before you give it to me. It continues, 'I am writing to you to make you aware of a circumstance which has caused me much grief and sorrow, and because you will know what appropriate actions can be taken. This matter concerns the priest and former hermit Isidore, presently officiating here at St. Michael's...'"

"That's more than fifteen years ago," the scribe objected.

"Eighteen," Theophilus corrected him. "Before he was appointed to Scetis. I told you it was supposed to be old."

"Continue: '...to whom I went periodically for spiritual counseling. To my everlasting shame he prevailed over my better nature, under the pretense that certain conduct disgraceful among seculars was permissible for a priest and even licensed by the commandment to love one's neighbor. Seduced by these specious arguments as well as by the sums of money he offered me, I reluctantly engaged with him not once, but several times in the abominable act of sodomy...'"

Chapter 10

It was a strange feeling, returning after so long an absence to the city of one's birth. For the first day or two Zachary felt completely disoriented. The noise, the confusion of the streets, after the lethargy of a country village, stunned his senses. The stone buildings weighed on his soul, and the ostentatious display of statues, arches, memorial columns seemed to be saying, only the life of this city matters, the rest is garbage, unworthy of anyone's remembrance.

He did not immediately seek out his family—one shock at a time was quite enough. Instead he took lodgings in a house some distance from what had once been home, and avoided his father's office, only a couple of blocks from where he now found himself working, by making a complicated detour.

In any case, he would have been too busy, at the beginning, for any serious contact with his former life. His employer's business, of which he was now effectively in charge, had been left in chaos by the previous manager, Moreover, although Zachary's previous job had given him some experience of keeping accounts and office management, he had never dealt with sea-captains, insured cargo, prepared bills of landing or paid customs duties. All this and much more had to be painstakingly learned in those first days, along with trade routes, current commodity prices, sailing schedules, shipping rates, and the ever-varying preferences of his customers. He had little time for anything else.

And he was deeply glad of this for it prevented him from thinking about Leila. In the days immediately following her death, and on the voyage downriver to Alexandria, he had remained sunk in a profound depression. It was his fault that she had died. Whether she had willed her own death or fought to the last to avoid, it did not assuage his level of guilt in the matter. If he had never contemplated a move to Alexandria, he told himself, she would be alive still. So guilty had he felt that in the first days after her death he had considered, as a penance, forgoing his new post. Luckily for him the state of the river, too violent at the beginning of flood time to allow regular travel, had unexpectedly given him a few day's grace before his final decision. By then he had realized the truth: life without her in rural Egypt would be impossible. Now she had gone; there was nothing left there for him. He would have had to leave, work or no work.

There were whole hours, days almost, when he became so absorbed in mastering new skills that he forgot her completely. Or rather, there were periods when his thoughts of her were overlaid by the pressure of other concerns. He never really forgot her, for as soon as that pressure relaxed, memory flooded back, and he relived in all horror those moments when, tossed this way and that in the river's irresistible coils, he had seen her head gradually receding from him, and had known that it lay beyond his power to save her. If only he had never told her! If only he had refused the fatal offer, as soon as it was presented to him! For hours after the event, wide-eyed, unable to sleep, he had played and replayed an imaginary past in which these other options had been chosen, so often that he could almost bring himself to believe that this imaginary past was the real one, that she still lived, that any moment she might walk through the door and greet him. But the past remained unchangeable. Gradually, he grew to accept that. During those hours in which his thoughts were distracted from her, he would talk, even laugh at times, like a normal person. But soon the curtain of depression would descend again, leaving his eyes dulled, his speech curt and uninterested. This, plus the contrast between the discipline he imposed and the laxity of his predecessor, made him less than popular among his subordinates.

The days stretched into weeks, the weeks into months, before he finally made up his mind to visit his mother. He thought first he should warn her in some way of his impending visit. His room was littered with fragments of letters that began, 'dear Mother, it has been so long since [I saw you, crossed out] [you saw me, crossed out] we saw each other...', or 'dear Mother, you will hardly have been expecting, after all these years...', or—perhaps his favorite —'dear Mother, I hardly know how to begin this letter...' Unfortunately that last was all too true, so much so that he finally realized there was nothing for it but simply to go there, unannounced.

He had not expected to recognize the servant who opened the door to him, and indeed he did not. To the question, "Who shall I tell her is calling?" he answered, "Her son."

The servant, a middle-aged house-slave with a stoical expression, said, "She doesn't have any sons."

Zachary's heart lurched. He had heard of parents disowning their children, refusing to acknowledge their existence because of some real or imagined transgression, but even after his years of silence and absence he couldn't believe that this could have happened to him.

"Go ask her," he said coldly, "whether she has a son or not. If she says she doesn't, I'll leave."

Puzzled, the slave left him standing in the old entrance hall, with its familiar statuettes in niches and, in the center of the marble floor, the mosaic of an archer about to shoot a baby deer that had distressed him so much when he was a child. He stood there motionless, quite unconsciously placing his foot on the hand that held the taut bowstring, preventing it from shooting just as he had done at the age of three, and let the memories well up and fill his mind. How strange time was, in its inexorable passage! How vivid and alive was his past, yet it had been erased utterly from the world, just as all that he was experiencing now would be erased.

Then, in the distance he heard sounds, a muffled shouting. The measured slap of sandals on tile, again so familiar, and the high-pitched, emphatic voice becoming clear, articulate: "How could you have been so stupid, why didn't you bring him in to me immediately, I said immediately, you can be thankful you're living in a Christian household because otherwise I can't imagine what awful things I might have done to..."

She had emerged into the hall. The voice changed abruptly and in midsentence to an ecstatic squeal of pleasure, the loose sandals slapped faster, and as irresistibly as a force of nature his mother propelled herself across the room and into the arms which, almost too late, he spread out to her, more to bring her to a halt than to express affection. For the next minute or more, she overwhelmed him in her embrace, spluttering barely comprehensible sounds and palpating him with her hands as if to reassure herself that he was physically real. Then, she sprang backwards—still nimble on her feet for her age and weight—and holding him at arm's length, surveyed him critically with her head cocked slightly to one side.

"You're so thin!" she wailed.

"I'm fine, Mother."

"You must be starving yourself; don't you have anyone to look after you?" Without giving him time to reply, she rushed on, "And how cruel of you, all those words without even a year!"

"All those years without even a word, Mother!"

"Don't change the subject! We were mad with worry about you, your father and I, well not so much your father, you know how he always kept everything to himself, but me, just look what it did to me! Look at my grey hairs!"

"Mother, you were..." Zachary had been on the point of saying, you were already going grey when I left, but decided just in time that that would be needlessly cruel. Anyway, truth had always been the first casualty of peace, in their family. "I'm sorry, Mother," he said instead.

"Well, I'm sure you had your reasons, although I can't for the life of me imagine what they were. But anything, anything at all—just a message to let us know you were still alive, I mean can you even imagine how we felt, not knowing whether you were dead or alive? No, of course you can't. Young people have no idea, no idea at all, they hardly know they were born, yet home they come, just as if nothing had happened, expecting everything to be just the same as it always was..."

It was only at this moment that Zachary, foundering in her torrent of words, registered her use of the past tense. "You said "kept"," he began, "you don't mean that..."

"...but of course it can't be, it never is. I mean look at you, you were hardly more than a child when you left, and..."

"Mother!"

"Yes, dear?"

"Is Father all right?"

She stopped and stared at him. "You didn't know?"

"Know what? How should I know? I've been..."

"I thought that was why you came!" she cried out. "I thought you must have heard!"

"Heard what?" he cried in an agony of impatience.

"He's dead! He died last week!"

Zachary reeled as if he had been hit by a club. If his mother and the dutifully-waiting stoic-faced slave had not, between them, somehow managed to catch him, he would have crashed full length to the marble floor. A week ago! And he, Zachary, had been right here in Alexandria, had walked the same streets, had gone to great lengths to avoid his father's office, where a chance encounter might have re-united them. Sunk in his own self-indulgent grief, he had thrown away his last chance to see his father before he died, and say to him...

What?

He had lost consciousness. He regained it, not knowing how much time had passed, lying on a couch, with his mother holding a cloth soaked in vinegar to his nostrils. What had happened to him? Even his guilt-ridden grief for Leila had not affected him in this way. Partly the suddenness of the news might have caused it, when he had assumed so unquestioningly that his father must be alive. But, that couldn't be all. He knew, too late, that he had had an agenda with his father, an agenda he could never now complete. He had loved his father passionately as a child, but his father had seemed to cool towards him as he grew older, and to protect himself Zachary convinced himself that he too had become indifferent, siding with his mother in her deprecatory remarks, even though he had never liked her as much.

Now he knew, too late, that whatever was tough and surviving in him, whatever had brought him through all the trials of the previous years, had come to him from his father. He realized too that his father's seeming indifference had had a purpose, had (whether well-advised or not) been intended not to reveal feelings but to hide them, had been formed as a deliberate policy to make him grow strong and independent. And now, now that he had achieved his father's goal, they could have met as never before, they could have spoken frankly and honestly together, could have expressed their love for one another...But thanks to his blind, selfish, thoughtless stupidity, that chance had gone forever.

"For years," his mother was saying, "we thought you were still in Scetis. The Archbishop told me personally you were there, I suppose you knew that?"

Zachary nodded.

"He explained to us why parents couldn't have contact with their hermits, it seemed awfully severe to me, but you know how a mother..."

"Why hermits couldn't have contact with their parents, Mother," Zachary corrected her.

She blinked. "Whatever you say, dear! It amounts to the same thing, though, doesn't it? So, we didn't worry too much, not at first, until one day the Archbishop, such a thoughtful man, isn't he, I mean for someone in his position, so often bishops and even deacons get so puffed up with pride they won't even give you the time of day...What was I saying?"

"One day the Archbishop," Zachary prompted.

"Huh? Oh, yes! One day the Archbishop asked me whether you were in Alexandria and I was so shocked I forgot to call him Your Reverence, I just said, 'No!', just like that, I said, 'You mean he's not in Scetis anymore?' and he told me no one had seen you there since that pagan temple, what was it called, was overthrown. So you were here," she exclaimed reproachfully, dabbing at the corners of her eyes with a tiny handkerchief. "You were back here in Alexandria all that time and you never even came to see us!"

"Actually," Zachary said, "I thought I had."

She stared at him. "I've no time for your philosophical paradoxes!"

"I'm sorry. It's a long story. I'll explain one day."

She continued to gaze at him searchingly, as if about to interrogate him further, then shrugged her shoulders and went on. "We had no idea where you'd gone; no way of finding you. If you'd even told someone, just one person, then we could have tried to trace you somehow, but you just seemed to have vanished off the face of the earth."

Which is almost what I did, Zachary thought.

"Where were you, anyway?"

"In the interior desert."

Her eyes widened in horror. "Were you mad? With all the lions? And the serpents and everything?"

If only its dangers were so familiar and physical!

"Those things aren't as common as people make out," he told her.

"And how did you live there? How did you get things to eat! No wonder you're so thin! How long were you there for, were you there all that time?"

A recital of his whole story was the last thing Zachary wanted at this particular moment. "Mother, please! All these questions!"

"A mother has every right…"

"I'll tell you, I promise you, I'll tell you everything that happened to me." That was a lie and he knew it but it would give him time to make up some plausible tale. "But not now, please, do you mind? I mean I've just found out my father's dead; I need a little time to…to adjust myself to that."

You don't look exactly shattered by grief, he felt like saying, and all of a sudden he knew something he had never previously admitted, even to himself: that his mother had not really loved his father, that her fits of testy irritation with him had not been, as Zachary used to believe, mere transient moods, but reflected something deeper and more permanent that she had suppressed, most of the time, in order to keep the position that his wealth gave her.

"In fact," he went on, "I'd like to be alone for a little while, if you don't mind. I'll come back," he said quickly, to forestall her, seeing her open her mouth to protest, "I promise I will, tomorrow…well, in a couple of days, say. Then we can talk properly. I can't now. Please understand."

"There's so much to talk about!"

"I know there is. Mother, I know there is. Just be patient a little, please."

She made a pained mouth of disapproval, then said, "Oh well. It's been so long, I suppose another day or two won't make that much difference. You always get your own way, always have, from the time you were just a baby."

"If you say so, Mother."

"Go on with you then. But remember, this is your home, and you have to come back here tomorrow or the next day because we have to discuss what's going to happen to the business."

Zachary had already half-turned to take his leave, because if one didn't make a decisive motion of some kind, his mother would continue to talk indefinitely. Now he stopped. He had totally forgotten about the business. He had totally forgotten that, without a move on his part, he had become rich. The thought, now it had come, left him feeling completely indifferent, as if he were hearing an anecdote about someone he hardly knew.

"What about the business?" he asked.

She seemed astonished that he should ask so obvious a question. "Well... what's going to happen to it, of course? I mean I can't run it, I'm a woman! I'm already negotiating to sell it, but now suddenly you turn up, and as you know perfectly well your father always meant for you to carry it on."

Did he, Zachary wondered? His father had never said a word to him about it. And he himself felt—having been so undutiful a son, having put nothing whatsoever into the enterprise—wholly unworthy either to take it over or to profit from it.

"Go ahead," he said, "sell it."

"You don't mean that!"

"Yes I do."

"Well you may think you mean it but you can't, you're just distraught, you haven't had time to think about it. Go, go now, think about it, think very seriously and come back and tell me what you've decided."

"It'll make no difference."

"Oh yes it will." She ushered him to the outer door, patting his shoulder with a proprietary air and repeating, over and over, her insistence that he should return soon. Out in the street, he felt a rush of relief to have escaped her insistent pressure. Did he love her? Of course, he told himself, one loves one's mother, that's axiomatic. If only she wouldn't go on so! And again he felt a sense of kinship with his father, who must have stoically endured similar pressures over so many years...Why? Because, though she had not loved him, he still loved her? Because he had someone else to love, a secret mistress perhaps, and merely kept his home as a respectable facade? Because he had armored himself with indifference against the blows of fate? Zachary would never know now.

It was evening. He walked, for no reason he could have named, towards the sea and out along the Heptastadion, the long breakwater that linked to the mainland the island on which the Pharos stood. There were a few casual strollers, come to cool off from the late summer heat, or to stare at the constant movement of shipping in the Great Harbor to the east of the breakwater. Their presence did not disturb him. Sunk deep in his own thoughts, he reached the island and clambered over its rocky slopes until, completely alone, he stood gazing out at the darkening Mediterranean, while the afterglow faded from a high fringe of cirrus to his left. To his right, the red glow from the Pharos deepened, hurling its light over the horizon to voyagers invisible from where he stood. Overhead, stars became visible, one by one.

Those stars marked the outermost sphere of the created universe, enclosing earth and its attendant sun, moon and planets, concealing from earthly gaze the domains of Hell and Heaven. Somewhere back there were the souls of his father and of Leila. But where? His father, an unbeliever in a world of believers, automatically doomed to eternal damnation? He could not bear to think that, he knew his father had been basically a decent man, and surely a just God could not condemn him and at the same time save those who lived lives of vileness and then had themselves baptized on their deathbeds. And what about Leila, baptized believer, believing herself damned for breaking the oath she took in the White Monastery? Surely she should have found a resting place in Heaven, not close to the Throne, perhaps, but at least somewhere round the edges?

He did not know. All he could do was pray for their souls, and his own, as he now did, until the last light had faded and only with difficulty was he able to pick his way back to the Heptastadion. He had left the breakwater and was walking down the Street of the Soma when he heard a voice calling out his name.

Turning, he saw a man of about his own age, fair-haired and blue-eyed, with a patrician nose and a wry, humorous smile.

"Do I know you?" Zachary asked.

"You certainly do," the other said, and there was something ingratiating, almost shamefaced about his grin. "I admit it's been a pretty long time, but we had…well, you might say, a lot in common."

Zachary projected backwards, subtracting years from the fellow's appearance, trying to imagine what he might have looked like, when suddenly he knew. His face flushed, a spark of anger danced in his eyes. "I know you. You're—"

"You got it," the other interrupted him. "I'm Cellius."

Chapter 11

"You know," Cellius said amicably, "there's really no call for you to be looking at me like that. I mean, she made fools of the pair of us, so far as I can make out."

Zachary's fists slowly unclenched. He was hardly aware that he had been glaring at Cellius, his look came from a hostility that long brooding had made quite automatic. For years now, the thought of his old rival had scarcely entered his head, and he knew in his heart that time had withered the core of his hatred, leaving only a dry carapace of reflex responses. But the whole episode of Cellius and Celia had remained frozen there, leaving him with no other way to respond. So, he simply stood, baffled, forced to deal with this former intimate as with a total stranger.

"You ruined my life." The words popped out of Zachary's mouth without forethought, leaving him as surprised as his hearer—was it true, was his life really ruined, was that what he actually thought? Cellius blinked in astonishment and took a half-step backwards.

"That's going a bit far, don't you think?"

"Maybe. Maybe not. It was because of what you two did that I became a hermit. And I failed at that, obviously."

Cellius' face took on an expression of lugubrious sympathy.

"You really did, then, it wasn't just a rumor."

"Did what?"

"Became a hermit."

"Of course. Why should that surprise you?"

Cellius gaped at him with an expression of comic dismay; he even scratched his curly blond locks in a pantomime of bewilderment. "Well...I don't rightly know, is the answer to that. I mean we all used to talk about that sort of thing, but... you know, I never thought anyone took it seriously, I mean seriously enough to actually do it. It was just...well... like the kind of fashion in those days."

"The kind of fashion," Zachary repeated, stunned.

"Yeah, you know, the 'in' thing. Like nowadays, it's neo-paganism and this woman, Hypatia, who lectures on pagan philosophy. But listen," Cellius said, seizing Zachary by the sleeve, "we've got so much to talk about, and if I really spoiled your life the least I can do is buy you a drink, even several drinks. I know a great place real close to here; I'm on my way there right now, as it happens, so why don't you come with me?"

Zachary's immediate reaction was to refuse, but before he could open his mouth he realized he had nothing else to do and nowhere else to go but his lonely and cheerless lodgings. Why not take advantage of this fortuitous encounter to forget his own problems for a while, and at the same time to satisfy his curiosity about events that for the very first time in his life he might be able to view objectively? He would stay only for an hour or so, then plead fatigue or urgent business the next day.

Cellius, taking his arm with a familiarity he resented, though not strongly enough to object out loud, led him to a building a few blocks back from the harbor, where he rapped imperiously on a massive iron-studded door. A panel in the door opened, they were scrutinized by someone within, and then the door itself was held ajar for them by a beaming, obsequious Nubian who showered Cellius with thanks for the small coin unobtrusively offered him. They advanced up a carpeted stairway to a room draped ostentatiously with heavy fabrics where a number of men who looked, Zachary thought, rather like his father—prosperous Alexandrian businessmen of middle age—sat around on cushioned sofas with the air of people awaiting some event, a show perhaps, and for whom conversation was a time-killer rather than the purpose of the evening.

"This is Zenobia's place," Cellius said out of the side of his mouth, "and this is Zenobia," pointing to an overweight, overdressed woman with a clown's face who bore down on them, gushing meaningless pleasantries. Zachary, still puzzled to know what kind of place he had entered, since it gave off mixed messages of private residence and place of entertainment, was introduced, and a whispered exchange between her and Cellius, inaudible to him, caused her to clap her hands and summon a young girl, very much underdressed, who took their order. Glancing over his shoulder, Zachary saw a woman crossing the room clad only in a robe of some diaphanous material, so transparent one could see quite clearly her pubic hair. One of the seated men rose from his couch and followed her out.

"Is this place a brothel?" Zachary hissed in Cellius' ear.

"Don't worry about it," Cellius whispered back. "I told Zenobia if we felt like anything later on, we'd let her know. Nobody will bother us till then."

He gestured towards a table of cedar wood, inlaid with ivory, beside which two small couches stood companionably close. "We can talk here; nobody will disturb us." Feeling ill at ease, Zachary perched on one of the couches while Cellius threw himself full-length on the other, signing for the girl to put down the silver flask of wine, the water-jar and the two glasses on the table between them.

"I felt badly about it, at the time," he confessed. "When you took off like that, without a word to anyone. I didn't know you'd seen us, not until Celia told me. I was...well, otherwise engaged, you might say, but of course I guessed immediately what it was all about. If I'd had any idea then that you were going off into the desert..."

"You'd have done exactly the same," Zachary said bitterly.

Cellius burst out laughing, a frank and unaffected laughter that made Zachary warm towards him, despite himself. "You know you're probably right. Gods! Do you remember how it felt when you were seventeen, eighteen, you weren't human, really, just a mass of raging desires. What is it they say? A stiff prick has no conscience? Nowadays, you stop to think, should I, shouldn't I, will it be worth it? But then..." He leaned forward, half-filled their glasses, topped them off with water. "Try this, it's Italian, from a place right by where I was born, it so happens. Think you'll like it."

Zachary lifted his glass, sipped, and at the taste, memories of the last time he had gone drinking in Alexandria came flooding back to him. With a very different companion, that time, but there had been brothels that night too, although nothing approaching the opulence of this one. There flashed through his mind images of riotous drunkenness, and suddenly he knew he wanted to drink tonight, wanted to get drunk, blind stupid drunk, to exorcize from his mind, if only for a few brief hours, the ghosts of Leila and his father. He drained the glass at a single draught.

"Hey! Steady on!" Cellius exclaimed. "This is strong stuff, even when it's watered."

"Can't be too strong for me."

"Well," Cellius said, pleased. "Sounds like we're going to have quite a night of it. While we're still relatively sober, let me fill you in on what happened after you left. Or do you know?"

"I don't know," Zachary admitted. "I came back here just a few weeks ago, I've seen nobody." For some reason he felt unwilling to tell Cellius of his one visit to the city and his meeting with Celia. Cellius nodded, drank deeply himself, and refilled their glasses.

"Well, right after you left, Celia turned against me. At first I thought it was because of you, she blamed me for you leaving, but no, she had bigger fish to fry. You remember who was Prefect back then?"

"Evagrius."

"Evagrius, right. He screwed up somehow, got posted to some shitty province up the Danube, but right then he was riding high. Seems he'd seen her, Celia, I mean, at official parties and stuff like that, anyway he fancied her, and when he offered to set her up as his mistress, she went for it. Must have been insane, I mean can you imagine it?" He gazed at Zachary, round-eyed in wonder. "Of course her family disowned her; nobody would have anything to do with her. She must have known how precarious it all was, even if he didn't get sick of her, officials like that are just over decorated office-boys, send 'em here, send 'em there, whip off their heads if there's any problem.. You know what?" He leaned forwards confidentially. "I think she was a nympho."

"A what?"

"A nympho. You know, crazy for it. Some women are. She was the one who started it with me, you know, I'm not just telling you that to make you feel better about me, it really was, not that I didn't want to, naturally, but I'd have been scared, you know, family like hers." His face looked so open and disingenuous, Zachary had to believe him. "And then there were stories, even while she was with Evagrius, which makes me all the more certain it was compulsive because if ever he'd found out for sure, she'd have been dead! Luckily, it never got beyond slave gossip, but there was even a rumor that one time she did it with a monk."

Cellius broke off suddenly, an impish light sparkled in his eye. "Couldn't have been you, by any chance, could it?"

Zachary tried at one and the same time to say no and take a swig of wine to hide his confusion. The result was a splutter, an incoherent snort and a fine spray of red droplets over the inlaid table. Cellius' face lit up. "Holy Zeus! It was you, wasn't it?"

Zachary nodded sheepishly.

"Well good for you! Serves the bastard right! Here, this calls for a celebration. Girl! Bring out the Falernian!"

The girl went, but in her place returned Zenobia. "You're a naughty boy!" she said, wagging a minatory, multiply-ringed finger at Cellius. "You know very well what I told you! The regular stuff, fine, that can go on the slate, but Falernian? No way! How long d'you think I'd stay in business at that rate? You'll be wanting girls on credit next!"

"Zenobia," Cellius protested. "d'you think it's good business showing me up in front of my friends like that?"

"I certainly do! If he's got no money he's no business here, and if he's got money he can damn well pay for it himself."

"A charming invitation," Cellius said with a wry smirk at Zachary, but Zachary, who was already pulling out his purse—he had spent hardly anything since arriving in the city, and could well afford it—said stiffly, "Of course I'll pay."

"Well you're a gentleman, at any rate," Zenobia screeched. "No need for that now. I'll see you get your bill in due course," and she flounced off.

"Bitch," Cellius said. "I really didn't mean for you to pay, but I only collect every three months and not always then if shipping's held up. The old cow could have had the decency to call me aside, I've always had credit here before, I always pay up, she knows that." The Falernian came, he poured it out lovingly. "Never had this? Oh, you should have! It's the best! Well, here's to the horns of Evagrius!"

"The horns of Evagrius," Zachary repeated.

"May he wear them long and shamefully!" Cellius' expression changed suddenly, from ribald mirth to intimate confidence. "Tell me honestly—what was it like?"

"What was what like?"

"Having her, of course! You know all that time I never once got to fuck her." He reacted immediately to Zachary's incredulous look. "No, I mean it! Everything else you can think of, except that! And then later on, well, that was commercial, so you can never be sure how the real thing would have been."

Zachary gulped. "What do you mean, commercial"

"You didn't know? No, of course you didn't. Well, I'll explain in a moment, I'm getting ahead of the story, I just want to hear all about how you got back to her, how it happened, everything..." He read the expression on Zachary's face. "Oh, I see. Gentlemen don't talk about their conquests, is that it? Oh well. I'll respect that, for now. Not saying I won't try and worm it out of you, when you've had a few more drinks, though." He laughed easily. "You know, I really should warn you about me. If you're still in the holy brigade, that is. I can see you're no hermit anymore, but I daresay the training kind of sticks to you...Well, I'm the type the holy fathers told you never to associate with."

Zachary smiled. "Guess I'll survive it."

"As long as you don't say I didn't warn you! Now where were we? Oh yes, the Evagrius bit. I only got this at second hand, mind you, I'd left Egypt by then. She hung onto him until he got posted and that was it, she didn't want to go to Outer Barbaria and he didn't want to take excess baggage, he figured that even out there they'd still have women. Well, what could she do then? Nobody would marry her, at least no one she'd have, so there was only one thing open to her."

Zachary hadn't wanted to admit it, though somehow he'd known it, all along. "You mean...prostitution?"

"Oh, a very high-class form of it. Not even in a house like this. She got a job in a theater, nothing much, just showing herself off and prancing around a bit, I guess for the advertisement, really, she probably paid them. Had her own place and all, not quite as classy as the one Evagrius got her, but not bad, not bad at all, she was making good money, obviously. So that was the scene when I got back here." He leaned towards Zachary confidentially. "You're probably wondering how I support myself, so I might as well tell you. I got, um, involved with a certain young lady in the Eternal City, incredibly old family, more than one Caesar's come out of it but I'm afraid I'm not at liberty to tell you the name because that was part of the deal. To cut a long story short, I get paid to keep away. A long way away. They figured that would work out cheaper in the long run."

He yawned, stretched himself quite unselfconsciously, and took another drink. "So, here I was, and there was Celia, available to all who had the right price. How could I resist? Sheer curiosity would have drawn me. And it was—" He grinned. "I don't have your scruples—it was, well, quite sensational, in its way." His eyes took on a dreamy look. "She was a lousy performer on stage, naturally I'd seen that, too, but off it...She'd learned stuff that was new even to me. But you know, how can I describe it, it was...mechanical, like you were doing it with some hydraulic machine. I mean you know how it feels when a woman's really into it...Well, maybe you don't; I keep forgetting how different our experiences are. But it's another thing, another thing altogether, I can assure you."

Zachary had by now stretched himself out on the couch, his head only a couple of feet from his companion's. He was listening intently, in a mixture of horrified disgust and utter fascination. "But I went back for more," Cellius went on. "Oh yes, several times. I guess it was the challenge of it. You know, see if I could hit that spark in her. In fact, in the end, I just said to her straight out, I said. 'Celia, listen, this isn't just another customer, this is Cellius. Come on, let yourself go, feel something.' And d'you know what she said to me? She said, 'there's only one man in the world I've ever really let go with.' But she wouldn't say who."

Cellius shook his head reflectively. "Wonder who it was," he mused. "Evagrius, d'you think? Some monstrous black slave she grabbed for a one-nighter? Or do you think..." He laughed out loud. "You! It could have been you!"

Zachary, taken totally by surprise, felt stirred to the depths of his being. Indeed it could have been him! Although the details were now lost to him, he remembered the passion of that night. What's more natural than that she should have shared it? Then he remembered what she had become, but before disgust could seize him, he recalled his own part in shaping her fate. If he had not fled from her the first time, if he had forgiven her for what she and Cellius had done, how different both their lives might have been!

"It could indeed," Cellius was chortling to himself, oblivious to the storm of feelings he had aroused in his companion. "And you a virgin, too, I suppose. At the time."

Zachary nodded.

"Shit! Life's so unfair!" Cellius was only half-laughing now, a tone of bitter envy had tainted his mirth. "What a waste...How could you appreciate it?" he demanded. "You'd got nothing to compare it with! And me, with a couple of hundred I could have compared it with...No, it's really not fair!"

"And then what happened?" Zachary found himself forced to ask.

"Oh," Cellius went on, quickly composing himself, resuming his playboy shell, "I didn't go anymore, after that, it was too painful, and the mechanical stuff I could get anywhere. And then one day I heard she wasn't in town any more, she'd gone off with some rich customer, to Antioch or somewhere, at least that's the story that got around. And there's been no word of her since. I fantasize about her, sometimes," he confided. "I imagine she's come back to Alex, totally broke, all her looks gone, she's begging in the street and I come by and say, 'Celia, if you give me what you gave the mysterious stranger, I'll support you for the rest of your life, old and ugly as you are.' And sometimes she says 'Yes,' and sometimes she says, 'No, I can't,' and then I toss her a coin or two and go on my way."

Cellius drained his glass and replenished it. "Well, that was my story. What about yours?"

Even in a heavily condensed and edited version, Zachary's story took a lot longer than Cellius' to tell, in part because, while Zachary had listened quietly to Cellius, Cellius constantly bombarded Zachary with questions and comments. To him, the life of hermits, even the life of rural villages, was something exotic and bizarre, to be greeted at every turn with exclamations of wonder, even feigned incredulity.

Zachary found himself telling about Leila. He realized too late, with a twinge of self-disgust, that he had only brought her into it to show Cellius that, sexually speaking, he was not as inexperienced as Cellius supposed. But the details of her death had to be drawn from him slowly and painfully, through relentless questioning, and he could not help feeling that he had doubly betrayed her, slain her again, so to speak, by describing to Cellius her last moments.

Not that Cellius was ever tactless enough to pour, on his rural adventures, the sophisticated scorn Zachary had feared. On the contrary, he made an eager and sympathetic listener, and never more so than when Zachary was approaching the end of his tale.

"So your father's dead," he commiserated. "I'm sorry. I hadn't heard. Too wrapped up in my own selfish pleasures, I really should pay more attention to what's going on. I remember when my own father died, I was in Rome then so I saw it all and I remember thinking, you old bastard, you spent every penny and all you're leaving me is debts. Then when he finally went, there I was, bawling my eyes out like a baby. You don't realize till it hits you. How you feel."

Zachary, starting to feel the wine now, had a hard time stopping his own tears. "There's so much you want to say!"

"Don't I know it! Like, 'dad, where did you hide the silver?'...No, I'm just joking. You have to laugh sometimes or you'd burst out crying. You know what the poet said, the tears of things? If I couldn't laugh a bit I couldn't get through the day..." Cellius let pass a moment's respectful silence, then asked abruptly, "He had a business of some sort, didn't he?"

"That's right. Import and export."

"So what happens to that now?"

Zachary shrugged indifferently. "I don't know. My mother's talking about selling it."

"And you're letting her do that?"

"Why not?"

"Why not!" Cellius sat bolt upright in indignation. "Are you crazy, or what? You're, what is it, now, some kind of office manager or something, for some provincial nobody, and now you've got a chance to run your own business, probably several times the size, you're totally insane if you let her sell it."

Zachary hesitated. "You mean...I should run it?"

"Who else? If only I had a chance like that! And I know nothing about it!" Cellius' eyes grew dreamy again. "Know what I'd do, if it was me? I'd buy out this what's-his-name, this boss of yours in the country, I'd amalgamate the two businesses, put in a manager, put in someone to watch the manager so he didn't steal too much, and live like a king off the profits! The baths, the races, villas in the country, a good stable, all the Falernian I could drink, and never do another lick of work as long as I lived!"

Zachary thought about it a while. He had been poor, poorer perhaps than anyone in that room had ever been—first by deliberate choice, then through mere stubbornness. He had heard only of the perils of riches, the evils that walked in the world of pride and greed. But now was it anything more than habit that kept him from sampling that world, finding out if what was said of it was really true?

"Think about it," Cellius said. "If you let go a chance like this, you'll regret it for the rest of your life. And look at it this way. If it doesn't work out, if you're not happy in the business, you can still sell it. But if you give it up now, and change your mind later, there's not a thing in the world you can do about it."

Zachary nodded glumly. What Cellius said made sense.

"And suppose you wanted to feed the poor, build churches, all that stuff Christians do, how could you best do that?" Cellius asked. "On some lousy salary? Or with the profits from one of the biggest firms in the city? It isn't money, it's the love of money that's supposed to be the root of all evil." He gave a self-satisfied laugh. "There, bet you never thought I knew that much scripture, eh? Well, hate the stuff, if you must, but grab onto it whenever you can, that's my advice."

Not the advice they would have given me in Scetis, Zachary thought wistfully. Then he pushed the thought away. That had been a brief episode in his life that was long over now. How could it control him still? The realities of the situation had changed, changed irrevocably.

His face looked so gloomy and preoccupied that Cellius leaned forwards and punched him lightly in the shoulder. "Cheer up, can't you? Nine-tenths of the world would just love to have your problems."

Zachary half-smiled, in spite of himself. "If you look at it that way," he said.

"What other way is there? Think of the millions out there, starving, or working their butts off just to stay alive. Dad dead? Wife dead? So what? That happens to everyone! Not one of them wouldn't give his soul, if he happened to have such a thing, just to be where you are now. Or even just to be in Egypt, if it comes to that." His voice took on a serious tone. "You've no idea what it's like out there. I tell you I'd have been glad to get out of Italy even without the allowance. Hordes of barbarians roaming around, nothing to stop 'em, the place is a shambles. If they had any organization themselves they'd have taken over already. And yet everyone pretends nothing's happening! Fucking patricians hanging around the Senate, you can see smoke from their burning estates from the city walls and they're saying, "Oh, Rome's invincible, we've been here eleven centuries, how could it possibly fall?" Dumb shits! Thank God for the desert, say I, all those Teutonic oafs want to do apart from drink beer and hack one another about is farm, and they can't do that here."

"If Rome fell," Zachary pointed out, "you probably wouldn't get your remittances anymore."

Cellius laughed ruefully. "Think I don't know that? Live for the day, that's my motto, get what you can while you can. In the mood for a woman yet?"

Zachary shook his head.

"Well neither am I right now, to be honest. In that case let's move on somewhere, I get restless if I stay too long in the same place, and I don't see why I should give Zenobia any more of my hard-earned credit."

Now was the time, if ever, for Zachary to take his leave. Part of him wanted to. That part of him knew Cellius to be totally amoral, knew that any contact with him would only lead to bad consequences. But the other part was fascinated by his charm, his brutal candor, and most of all was flattered by the fact that, worldly sophisticate though Cellius was, he still found Zachary, the unworldly ex-hermit, the rural rube, acceptable and perhaps even desirable company.

It was ironic how their relations had shifted, almost reversed. When they were together before, almost ten years ago now, Zachary had been the privileged insider, ensconced in a powerful family, engaged to the daughter of one more powerful still, while Cellius had been the outsider, a foreigner, a young student with no connections clinging to the fringe of society on the strength of his wit, charm and good looks. Now Cellius was the complete man of the world and Zachary, cut off from decent society for nearly a decade, found himself converted into the naive and clumsy newcomer. Yet far from finding Zachary a boor or a bore, Cellius seemed only too anxious to regain his friendship.

As with his last escapade in Alexandria, Zachary's memories became progressively more fragmentary and confused as the night progressed. He seemed to remember being on a boat moored in a canal, but was it there or in some other place that they had witnessed a show of some sort? There had been comedians who told lewd jokes, mimicked sex acts, and hit one another with inflated pigskin bladders. There had been a naked woman who lay on her back while pigeons pecked grains of corn from her groin, her genitals protected from their beaks only by a skimpy triangle of flame-colored silk. But he couldn't remember the face of the woman or any of the jokes. He dimly remembered some hole-in-the-wall tavern where the clientele started muttering about fancy rich folk who came slumming where they weren't wanted, until Cellius showed them his dagger and, with a few swift passes through the air, that he knew how to use it.

He could not remember passing out on a bed, but he must have done that because he remembered, all too vividly, the rasp of stubble on his cheek, a hard male organ pressed against his naked thigh and a hand trying to grope between his legs. He lashed out instinctively, rolled off the bed and leapt to his feet, to see, by the dim light of a single lamp, Cellius ruefully rubbing his jaw and saying, "No need for that, you could have just said no."

"I didn't know you were one of those!" Zachary exclaimed.

"I'm not one of those!" Cellius protested indignantly. "I've just never understood why one should write off half the human race as a source of pleasure. If that's not your thing, fine. I'll respect that. But you never know if you don't try."

"You could have asked first," Zachary said resentfully.

"How could I? You were unconscious. Besides, I've found by experience that no often means yes. You may not believe it, but there is such a thing as male modesty. And some that enjoy it like to say, 'I was forced'."

Zachary arranged his disheveled clothing. He was still dizzy drunk but he had some sense of direction. He could see a door and he headed for it.

"Hey, where d'you think you're going?" Cellius cried.

"Out."

"You can't do that! You're my guest!"

Only then did Zachary realize he must be in Cellius' apartment. And Cellius had somehow managed to get between him and the door, for they were struggling together, shouting, "Let me go!" and, "No you don't!" until suddenly, without quite realizing how he had got there, Zachary found himself sitting in a large armchair with Cellius standing over him waving a flask in front of him and saying, 'drink this.'

"No."

"Yes."

"I'm drunk already."

"This'll sober you up."

"No it won't. You just want to make me…"

"No I don't," Cellius said vehemently. "I swear it. Any oath you like…"

"Because you don't believe in anything!"

"That's not true! I believe in friendship…"

"Fine way you have of showing it!"

Cellius backed off, set down the flask on a table and sat down himself. "Listen to me, Zachary," he said earnestly. "I'm very sorry if what I did upset you. If I'd known it would, I'd never have tried it. If I'd been sober, the thought wouldn't even have entered my mind. What can I say? I'm really sorry. It won't happen again, ever. I'd hoped we were going to be friends, but if I've spoiled that, well, that's entirely my own fault, and I'll have to live with it. Gods!" he cried, banging his forehead with the heel of his hand. "The stupid things we do! The self-destructive...Please don't go. If you go, I'll feel even more awful than I do now."

Now was the time to insist, to leave, but some power stronger than Zachary's will kept him rooted in his chair.

"Will you accept my apology?"

Zachary mumbled something that, since he still did not rise and leave, had to be taken as assent.

"Good! Have another drink with me, to seal it."

"I don't want another drink."

"You may not want it, but you need it. Take it slowly. Believe me, at this stage of the game, if you're careful, you can drink yourself sober again. Well, more or less."

Reluctantly, Zachary sipped at the glass offered him, and after a few moments found, to his surprise, that his head had indeed cleared a little. He saw the reddish swelling on his companion's jaw, and felt obliged to say, "Sorry if I hit you. It was just a reflex. Does it hurt?"

Cellius waved aside his concern. "Nah, nothing! My own fault, as I said. Come, let's go out on the balcony, let's look at the night."

Zachary looked over the balcony. Though he had no memory at all of the many stairs they must somehow have climbed, they were on the top floor of a tall apartment block that commanded a view over the whole eastern half of the city. Rooftops, towers and domes receded into the distance. Here and there, the tops of trees indicated where the rich had salvaged some oasis from the urban sprawl. Over to their left, the sea glimmered in the light of a low moon hidden from them by the building behind them. Beyond that again, high over the harbor mouth, the Pharos raised its unwinking red glow. It must have been late, the tenth or eleventh hour of the night, for this city of half a million people was almost silent, save for the occasional barking of dogs or the shout of a watchman, muted by distance.

Looking upwards, Cellius asked, "Ever wonder what's beyond that?"

It was the same thought Zachary had had, several hours earlier, looking at those same stars from the island where the Pharos stood. "Heaven, I suppose. And hell somewhere down below there."

"You sure?" Cellius' voice was light, teasing, and Zachary suddenly saw again the figure with the shouting mouth he had seen in the ruined temple, and felt the chill breath of cosmic fear he had first felt the day Cosmas the Syrian crashed to his death in Scetis. "Nobody's ever seen it. Nobody's ever come back and told us about it."

"Jesus Christ returned from the dead," Zachary said automatically.

"Perhaps. Who knows? But he didn't have much to say about what it was like there, from what I've heard...Did you ever read Lucretius?"

Zachary shook his head,

"A fellow-countryman of mine who wrote a book called "On the Nature of Things". And in this book he says there is no heaven, no hell, no demons or angels, no supernatural beings at all. And, as follows logically from that—no God."

"Everyone believes in some sort of God," Zachary insisted. "Even Mithraists, they think God is the sun. Even pagans."

"Not Lucretius. He says that everything, everything in the universe, consists of atoms. Either atoms or the void."

"What are atoms?" Zachary asked.

Cellius laughed. "They really don't teach you much, all those monks and clergymen, do they? That's from Democritus—a philosopher, a Greek like yourself. Atoms are like...well, they're a kind of building block, little thingies too small to see that everything's made of. Like, the only reason you're a man, not a plant or a stone, is just the number of atoms in you and how they're put together. But the atoms themselves, they're all exactly alike. And if everything's made of them, then there really is nothing in the universe but them and the gaps between them. The nothingness. The void."

Zachary's mind reeled, trying in its fuddled state to digest this new and shocking information. It was outrageous, of course. It was impossible, unthinkable, something to be rejected out of hand by all decent God-fearing folk. It simply could not be the truth.

A voice whispered somewhere in his head, a small, dry, furtive voice: But supposing it is...?

Memory blurred again. He had no consciousness of the passage of time, but time must have passed, for it was suddenly getting light, the two of them were leaning over the balcony, glasses in hand, laughing. Laughing at what? He had no idea. Everything, anything—a snatch of song, a stupid remark— suddenly seemed hilariously funny. And something very funny was happening to the world. The sun was not up yet, but its glow was visible below the horizon. A brisk breeze blew in their faces from the east, and on that breeze, low cloudlets came skimming towards them. Only to Zachary it didn't seem like that. It seemed to him as if the clouds were stationary, and the building in which he stood was moving, plunging into the east, into the dawn—the balcony was like the prow of a great ship breasting the waves, only it was moving faster than any ship, moving at vertiginous speed into the heart of light, and he aboard it, wild with reckless exhilaration, laughing like a fool, shouting in chorus with Cellius: "Atoms and the void! Atoms and the void!"

Chapter 12

Cellius slipped unobtrusively into one of the rear seats in Hypatia's lecture minutes after it had begun. The hall was, as usual, crowded. One or two of the other students nodded and greeted him surreptitiously. He was popular among them, though many regarded him as a lightweight because he laughed and joked a lot and refused to attend lectures on mathematics. He grinned back at them and then composed his mobile features into a mask of respectful attention.

He didn't give a damn for any kind of philosophy, of course, and he found Hypatia's brand of Neo-Platonist metaphysics, with its talk of the One and the All, completely baffling. He had gone there first out of curiosity, because the lectures were fashionable amongst the younger smart set. And had persisted because they turned out to be an excellent place for picking up women. "I found what she said this morning pretty hard to grasp—do you think you could explain it to me in real simple language?" Coming from a seemingly sincere and certainly handsome male, what woman could resist such a bait? And from the Nature of the Soul, it wasn't hard to shift gears into the Nature of Love, on a suitably high and abstract plane to start with, naturally, but it was amazing how fast things could go downhill from there.

Later on he had acquired a much more material reason for attending. But for that, he would probably have given up the lectures, since there were plenty of other places where you could score. Today, he wasn't even bothering to scan the hall for possible conquests. He ought really to be in the baths, in the hot room, sweating out his hangover. For although he could function effectively on two or three hours' sleep, the night with Zachary had left him with a throbbing headache and the feeling that there were small sand-drifts behind his eyeballs. He felt annoyed, too, that he almost screwed up—the right word, that!—through his inopportune moment of lust. He must have been drunker than he had realized, to run such a risk.

For when he told Zachary he knew nothing of Zachary's father's death, he was lying. One could not live by one's wits in Alexandria without making a point of knowing all that went on there. He had been on the lookout for Zachary for a whole week, certain that, if Zachary was still alive, he would come out of the woodwork when the news reached him. And to find a Zachary so naive, so guileless, now in a position to control a business worth, at the very least, hundreds of thousands of solidi…Well, he couldn't have wished for better luck.

But for now he had a tiresome chore to execute: his weekly report. When the lecture ended, with the usual knot of sycophants forming around their teacher, he joked and chatted for a few moments, arranged to meet someone at the baths in a couple of hours, and then, at a leisurely pace (it was important never to look as if you were in a hurry) he headed from the Mouseion, where Hypatia lectured, towards the Caesarium. He felt it politic to stroll past the Caesarium and on as far as the esplanade that circled the harbor. Here he stood for a while feigning an interest in shipping until he was reasonably sure that no one was following him. Then, he retraced his steps and entered, not the ecclesiastical offices themselves—if a fellow student spotted him, that would be hard to explain—but St. Michael's Cathedral.

That gave him no problems. He might be twitted by pagan or agnostic friends for entering what they regarded as the House of Superstition. However, he had a ready excuse. The wise man, he would say, knowing that no one can be sure of the truth, covers his bets by paying respect to all deities, just in case. He was imagining the laughter that would greet this remark ("typical Cellius!" they would say) while he knelt before the altar just long enough to see if anyone had followed him in. The lamp perpetually burning in the shadows of the sanctuary distracted his gaze for a moment, and he thought, *Ah, Zachary's and Celia's god, much good he seems to have done them!* Then he rose, crossing himself scrupulously for the benefit of any believers present, and headed for a small and unobtrusive door, beyond which, across a cloister and up an echoing stairway, lay the office of Timothy, Archdeacon.

"Come in!" he heard the reedy, irascible voice bark, and with no great pleasure entered the cramped little office walled with pigeonholed papyri.

Timothy regarded him with at least equal distaste. The Archdeacon knew all too well the kind of instrument he was sometimes forced to use to accomplish the Lord's work, but he bore in mind always the old adage that those who sup with Satan need the precaution of a long spoon. His first two recruits for this particular job had been pious youths who could not restrain themselves from jumping up and down and protesting whenever they disagreed with Hypatia, or from asking her what they naively thought were trick questions—questions that immediately exposed them as Christians. And once suspected of spying for the Archbishop, they had been harassed and hounded out of the lectures—not by Hypatia, who was invariably courteous to thinkers of all persuasions, but by their fellow-students. Cellius, who the Archdeacon's near-infallible nose had immediately picked out as a corrupt vessel, could never be suspected of any religious connection, and was accordingly, one might almost say, a Godsend.

For his part, Cellius was only too glad to pick up the gold piece that was his weekly reward. Of all the little earners he had collected, which ran from pimping to studwork with lustful but ageing ladies, this was by far the most regular and respectable. He would have preferred to do without any of them, but the plain fact of it was, he had put so much on the slate that his quarterly allowance had to be spent the moment it arrived, just to keep his credit-lines open.

"Let's go over the lists," Timothy said.

It was important for the Caesarium to know exactly who attended Hypatia's lectures and for how long, who went briefly out of curiosity and who became committed believers. In another decade or two, many of these students would hold influential positions in the city. What they decided could affect, favorably or adversely, the political and financial status of the Church, so it was crucial to know who might have been infected by Neo-paganism. Timothy and Cellius went through the lists together, with Cellius adding a couple of new names, striking one off, and answering Timothy's occasional questions about particular individuals. Cellius then reported on content—any remarks of Hypatia's that might reflect on the Church, anything overly favorable to the Old Gods, any attempt to compare Plotinus' conception of the Godhead, which coincidentally had a triple aspect, with the Holy Trinity.

There had been nothing particularly controversial that week, and Cellius quickly wound down, his right hand ready to receive his coin. But for once, Timothy seemed in no hurry to get rid of him. "There is another little job," he said, "which you might be able to do for us."

Cellius came straight to the point. "How much?"

"Twenty gold pieces."

"What do I have to do for that?"

"Say a priest performed unnatural acts with you."

Cellius made a sour face. "Will this be at a public hearing?""

"At an assembly of the Alexandrian clergy."

"Forget it." It was one thing to be bisexual in private life, quite another to be publicly branded for the less popular half of one's activities. In his experience, nobody gossiped worse than clerics, and if news reached his female clients, he stood to lose more than he gained.

"Would it make it any easier if you were the active? It would look better for us, him being the age he is."

Cellius considered that, but not for long. Less of a disgrace than playing the woman's part, but with a priest! And an old priest, at that... He shook his head.

Timothy sighed resignedly. "If you won't do it yourself..."

"You want me to find you somebody else?"

"Right."

"A finder's fee?"

"It's a straight twenty for the job. If you want to keep five and your contact is happy with fifteen..."

"Done," Cellius said. "I'll need some information, though. Who the priest is, what he looks like, when and where this is supposed to have happened..."

"What does it matter what he looks like?"

"Well, this kid'll look a fool if he can't identify the guy he's supposed to have buggered."

Timothy bit his lip. "I'm not used to this sort of thing," he said grudgingly. "I suppose you're right." And he gave a description of Isidore, which Cellius dutifully memorized, and answered, as best he could, the long string of questions Cellius put to him.

Incompetent idiots, Cellius was thinking, even as he rehearsed in his mind the shape the testimony ought to take. If they have to get up to stuff like this, why can't they at least take the trouble to think it through? And what business do they have doing it, anyway? Aren't they supposed to love one another? Isn't slander, even true slander, let alone made-up stuff like this, supposed to be something they hate and fight against with all their souls? It never occurred to him to ask what this priest Isidore could have done to deserve such treatment. In his experience, Christians were only too ready to stab one another in the back, for any reason or no reason at all.

"You think you know someone who'd do this?" Timothy asked.

"Possibly." Cellius' voice sounded cool, detached, as his mind ran through several candidates. "How soon do you need to know? Next week do?"

Timothy shook his head. "Two days at most. This is urgent."

"If I have to miss one of the lectures..."

"No matter. Do it. You'll still get paid for the other. This has priority."

Cellius hesitated, on the point of asking for more, then decided against it. At the baths that same afternoon he would almost certainly run into the person he now had in mind. A kid of eighteen, perpetually hard-up but with a perpetual hard-on, totally unscrupulous, who hero-worshiped him, or perhaps rogue-worshiped him would be a better term. And so dumb that fifteen solidi would blind him to any undesired consequences. *So long as he's not dumb enough to tell that cow of a mother of his*, Cellius thought. *But even if he does, I'll have got money up front.* He grinned to himself, bouncing the gold coin in his hand, all the way down Timothy's dark and echoing staircase.

Chapter 13

Zachary felt uncomfortable, going to the baths. His discomfort stemmed from a variety of reasons. He had never been there before, and therefore did not know quite what to expect or how to conduct himself. Worse, he had never been naked in any public place, or even naked in front of any other person, if you excluded his mother in infancy and Celia on that night which, more than any other, he had struggled to forget. Even Leila had never shown herself to him naked, nor he to her.

Moreover, he had his religious conditioning to contend with. To the devout Christian, baths were the stalking grounds of Satan: the pleasures of bathing seduced you. The heat of the hot baths weakened your morals as it aroused your lusts, the sight of shamelessly naked bodies inflamed those lusts, while the presence of prostitutes of both sexes immediately outside (and in the case of male prostitutes, also inside) the baths offered ample opportunities for satiating those lusts. His mother had never let him go there. His mother would be very upset if she knew he was going there. But what his mother felt no longer mattered. He was the head of the family now.

Yet a further reason for his discomfort lay in the person who walked by his side, carrying his towels, his bathing garment, his bath sandals and the cylindrical metal box that contained the array of toilet requisites—oils, perfumes, sponges, strigils—that were deemed by prosperous citizens of the Empire to form an indispensable part of the act of bathing. Not since he reached adulthood had he had anyone to carry things for him. He had learned in Scetis that a man should carry his own possessions, and indeed those of others as well, if those others were too old, too weak or too infirm to do so themselves. But, he had been told by his father's employees—his own now, of course, but he could not stop himself from thinking of them as his father's— that a respectable Alexandrian merchant simply could not attend the baths by himself, let alone carry his own paraphernalia, as if he were some impoverished artisan. If they had had their way, they would have sent him out with a separate slave for each accoutrement.

He had finally compromised on a single slave, a eunuch from the Persian border who made a sour face at having to carry everything and generally behaved as if working for someone as lacking in ostentation as Zachary was damaging to his own social status.

So, why was Zachary going to the baths?

Not an easy question to answer. The simple answer was, Cellius had insisted on meeting him there. But then, why was he going to meet Cellius? Recovering from the terrifying hangover that had followed their first meeting, he had resolved to avoid his old acquaintance in the future. The memory of Cellius' attempt on his virtue, too, remained vividly with him. Yet somehow his resolve had withered as time passed. In part this was due to the note, wryly humorous and apologetic, that Cellius had sent round to his lodgings the next day (but how had he found out where Zachary lived?). In part it was due to a growing realization that the advice Cellius had given him had been sound. Why should he hand over to strangers the business his father had built up through years of effort? Strangers who might dissipate all that painfully acquired wealth in idle frivolity and lascivious pleasures?

For the strongest argument Cellius had given him lay in the good and charitable works he would now be able to perform. The life of mad extravagance, of self-indulgent idleness that Cellius dreamed of held no attractions for him at all. But he could justify his existence and atone for his many sins by feeding the poor, helping the helpless, defending those unjustly punished and bringing comfort even to those whose punishment was just.

And what sin would he be committing if, while fulfilling the second of Christ's commandments, he enjoyed himself a little, and experienced at least the more harmless of the many pleasures the world affords?

They entered the baths, and Zachary paid the gatekeeper the ridiculously small fee which that establishment, heavily subsidized by the city government, charged its customers—his slave, who was not going to bathe, got in for nothing. Before him, the exercise yard, where several games of handball were in progress, emptied rapidly at the ringing of the bell which announced that the hot room had opened. He crossed the yard and entered the changing room, a spacious hall flooded with light from windows set in the roof, where there were wooden cabinets for your street clothes and marble benches where you could leave your slave to make sure the clothes didn't get stolen. There he undressed under the supercilious eye of the Persian eunuch, trying his best to hold his discarded clothing in front of him until he could wind the loose, towel-like bathing garment around his waist. But nobody else was paying him the slightest attention. All around him, other men were changing quite unselfconsciously, or simply gossiping with their neighbors in various stages of undress. *Guess I'll get used to it*, he thought, smiling to himself at his own excessive modesty.

Putting on his thick-soled bath sandals and leaving the eunuch to guard his belongings, Zachary walked down a corridor lined with mosaic murals showing condemned prisoners being thrown to wild beasts. Were they

Christians, he wondered? The baths had been there for more than a century, from before the last persecutions. So they could easily have been Christians. He paused to stare at one figure, a man bound to an upright post, being pushed on a kind of wheeled trolley towards an immense lion that had already hurled itself into the air in order to pounce on him. But nothing about the half-naked figure could tell you whether it represented a martyr or a murderer. And certain classes of criminals were still regularly condemned to the beasts for the entertainment of the public. Christians hadn't stopped that old custom.

He entered the warm room. Here the large windows at one end, sited at normal levels, allowed bathers to look out through a pillared cloister into the sunlit exercise yard outside. From semicircular niches in its walls the statues of former emperors gazed down on a broad shallow marble pool of tepid water where bathers waded, sat up to their necks or raced around splashing one another, an activity that brought words of angry reproof from some of the older ones. All were male; the sexes shared these baths, the largest of over a thousand public establishments in the city, but women could use them only in the mornings. Zachary lowered himself into the water, looking around for Cellius, but could not see him anywhere. He felt awkward, being alone here—everyone else seemed to have companions.

After a few minutes he emerged and, following the signs—mosaic sandals set in the floor, toes pointed in the appropriate direction—headed for the hot room. Wandering peddlers accosted him, within a minute he was offered a live turtle, a dish of olives and anchovies and an aphrodisiac. Pushing through what was becoming quite a crowd, worried now lest he miss Cellius in all this bustle, he entered the hot room, a hall similar to the one he had just left, except that the pool was smaller and the space left by it filled with a three-times-larger-than-life statue of Athena, goddess of wisdom. Heat rose from the tiles and he was glad of the thick wooden soles of his bath sandals.

He plunged into the water, heated to a temperature so high that one's first reaction was to pull oneself out of it. But the discomfort quickly passed and Zachary felt himself relaxing, all the stresses and tensions of his new city life oozing from his pores as his body filled with a luxurious warmth. Nobody splashed and screamed in here. In an atmosphere of decorum, men sat with legs stretched out and water up to the jawline in the meter-deep pool, the backs of their heads propped on the marble rim, talking in low voices with their neighbors or lying with eyes closed, seemingly asleep, minds lost in the sensual pleasure of immersion.

A pretty boy on the far side of the pool was sending him knowing looks, and Zachary quickly averted his gaze. None of the other bathers was Cellius, and he was beginning to think his new friend had forgotten him when there was a splash to his left and a body entered the water beside him. "Sorry I'm late. But you'll be glad when you know why."

"I will?"

"Are you free this evening?"

Zachary was. The friends of his youth were scattered or into their own lives now. Of course he could always eat at home, should he decide that two hours of motherly interrogation were better than a solitary meal in a tavern.

"You see," Cellius announced brightly, 'the reason I'm late is I ran into these people and they invited me to have dinner with them. So I said, fine, if I can bring a friend, and they said, yes, certainly."

"Thanks, that was thoughtful of you."

"Think nothing of it. It's a pleasure to be of service to one's friends." Cellius stretched himself like a cat, sighing luxuriously. "Ah, this feels good, doesn't it?...Well. No second thoughts about your decision?"

"Not so far."

Cellius grinned knowingly. "Nor will you have, take my word for it. It was the only thing to do."

When they had both soaked themselves thoroughly, they headed back down the main corridor, pushing their way through a crowd watching a juggler who flipped balls with his nose and forehead as well as with his hands, and then past a man demanding that the passers-by tie him up so they could see how he escaped. Flute music echoed down the corridor from somewhere out of sight. As they passed the mural of the man being thrown to the beasts, Zachary slowed and stared once more, fascinated against his own will.

"Nice piece," Cellius said, mistaking the nature of his interest. "Realistic." He too came to a stop. "Just look at the fellow's eyes! Looks like they're going to pop right out of his skull. You can see he knows he's cat meat in about five seconds."

"Doesn't it bother you they still do that?" Zachary asked.

Cellius looked puzzled, "Bother me? That they make murals?"

"That they do things like that to people."

Cellius' face exchanged puzzlement for surprise. "No. Should it? Why should it?"

"Because it's...it's..." It had seemed so obvious to Zachary that, when challenged, he had a hard time expressing what he felt about it. "How would you like it if they did it to you?"

"They can't do it to me. I'm a Roman citizen of the equestrian order."

It was Zachary's turn to show bewilderment. "Yes, but supposing you weren't. Just supposing. How'd you think you'd like it then?"

"What's it matter? It doesn't last long."

"Long enough, and there's the time before, the time when you know it's going to happen, and then the time you can see it coming—"

"They deserve it," Cellius snapped, turning on his heel and moving on so abruptly that Zachary had to quicken his pace to catch up with him.

"No matter what, they've deserved..."

"It's got to be done. The only way to keep down crime."

"But people have been punished like that for centuries," Zachary objected, "and there's just as much crime as..."

"Maybe, but what you don't understand is," Cellius said with an air of absolute finality, "that if they didn't throw criminals to the beasts, we'd have twice as much crime as we've got already. Get it? Some old women of both sexes may have bleeding hearts over it, but things have always been that way and always will be. Take my word for it."

Zachary gave up and followed Cellius into the cold room. The shock of the icy water on his overheated body numbed his mind and prevented further thought of any type, but the invigorating sense of well-being that filled mind and body as he clambered out of the pool made ample recompense. *The pleasures of the flesh*, he thought to himself. *He could see how seductive such things were, how hard it would be to meditate on God and holy things if one came here every day and spent half the day here as some did. I can see why some hermits make the state of alousia, unwashedness, an ideal. And what harm could an occasional such indulgence do? Surely they went too far*, he told himself.

Going back to the changing room, they summoned their respective attendants. Cellius still couldn't afford a slave, he had hired a freedman by the hour from the local market. They had themselves rubbed dry, then moved to the massage room. Here, side by side on marble benches, naked save for towels thrown across their buttocks, they lay face-down and chatted idly while slave and freedman carefully anointed their bodies with oils carried in alabaster flasks, scraped off any excess with strigils, and massaged them systematically, starting with their shoulder blades and finishing with their calves.

By the time they left the building, dressed, perfumed—Zachary a little embarrassed by the odors he left trailing behind him, but the eunuch with his supercilious politeness had insisted on it—light was fading rapidly from a sky of dusky blue. They walked in the direction of the harbor. "Let me tell you a little about our hostess," Cellius said as they moved along at a decorous, leisurely pace. "Her name's Vibia, she's married, but, well, her husband seems to be off on some business trip most of the time, you know how these things are. They're quite well-off but not super-rich. I figure he probably has...other interests, can't think why, she's a very attractive woman, intelligent too, lots of friends among the intellectuals, you know, painters, theater folk, the odd philosopher. Pagans, a lot of them—does that bother you?"

"Not at all," Zachary said, remembering the tolerance of Scetis.

"Good. They'll be an interesting crowd; you should find them amusing." They entered the hallway of a large apartment block, passed the scrutiny of a formidable doorkeeper, and ascended a broad curving staircase of marble to the third floor. There, they knocked and were admitted to an apartment with a broad terrace open to the elements, which overlooked the Great Harbor. Lamps glowed in the soft dusk of early evening, dimly revealing perhaps a dozen guests: men and women in roughly equal numbers, fashionably dressed, who smiled and murmured politely as Zachary was introduced. Zachary bowed and smiled back, promptly forgetting all their names, until a tall woman in her mid-thirties, wearing a long gown that was cut so low as almost to reveal her breasts, came majestically towards them. "This is Vibia, our hostess." Cellius said. "Meet my friend Zachary who I told you about."

The woman smiled. She had a long oval face, a patrician nose, and lips that sent out conflicting messages—the upper one firm, decisive, the lip of a woman who knew her world and did not brook contradiction mildly, but the lower one full, ripe, sensual, rich with promise. Her thick brown hair, shot with a subtle variety of tints that perhaps did not owe everything to nature, was piled high on her head in a convoluted coiffure that looked as if it had taken her maid a good hour or two to assemble. Zachary, taking the hand that she spontaneously offered, smelt her perfume, felt the warmth of her body and the gentle, intimate pressure of her fingers, and responded with an involuntary tremor. He was glad of the presence of a serving girl who, offering him a silver goblet of wine, allowed him to cool his right palm on a surface still chilled and dewy from the ice (How much had that cost? How far must it have come!) into which the goblet had been plunged.

The conversations his entrance had interrupted quickly picked up again. The group nearest him were discussing a merchant they knew who had recently married and changed, inexplicably, from a wild and inveterate partygoer to a home-hugging recluse—absurd speculations and lewd jokes, their full meaning impenetrable to anyone who did not know the parties concerned, flew back and forth. The man's name rang a distant bell in Zachary's memory, but try as he would he could not remember when or where he might have met this Cleon.

Abandoning that group, he moved to the next, in the midst of which a middle-aged man with a salt-and-pepper beard was orating with an air of absolute certainty that his slightest word would be received with rapt and respectful attention. The house philosopher, obviously; Zachary listened for a while on the fringe of the group, but having missed the beginning of the discourse he couldn't make heads or tails of what the fellow was saying. He looked round for Cellius, but his friend was deep in conversation with their hostess. Feeling awkward again and out of things, he walked to the low wall surrounding the terrace and looked out over the harbor.

He had not been there more than a moment when he felt a presence at his side. Vibia too was leaning on the wall, her elbow touching his, as if by accident. Instinctively he drew back his own arm. Affecting not to notice, she asked, in a low and husky voice, "Well, how do you like my view?"

"It's wonderful" All that divided them from the harbor was a line of single-story warehouses. Beyond the warehouses, the riding lights of ships moored to wharves or at anchor made an intricate pattern, doubled by the reflections in the calm water. Beyond the lights, on its low rocky island, the Pharos reared. Tonight someone had activated the mechanism that rotated its giant reflector, so that it sent out great pulses of red light at intervals of a few seconds, pulses that must appear, to ships below the horizon, like flashes of supernatural lightning.

They stood together gazing, breathing the air, at once mild and exhilarating, of a Mediterranean autumn evening. "Cellius has told me a lot about you," she said, in the same intimate tone. "He told me you'd been a hermit."

"I was once. But that was a long time ago,"

"I'm fascinated by hermits. You hear so many stories about them nowadays. Extraordinary things they can do."

Zachary smiled. "Don't believe everything you hear."

"Well, that's why it's so nice to meet the real thing," she replied brightly. "So seldom you can do that. Or if you do, they just fob you off with a few religious platitudes. I'd love it if you could tell me a little..." She broke off quickly, immediately sensitive to the change in his expression. "No, no, I don't mean here, it's not the right time for that, and in any case I have to go check if dinner's ready, you must excuse me. But some other time soon, I hope. And please don't be shy with my other guests, we're all friends here."

She turned, with a flash of dark and lustrous eyes, a look that to Cellius would have conveyed an unmistakable meaning. It merely left Zachary confused. Did it really mean what he thought it meant? Or was it just a trick of his feverish imagination, ignited by the sensuality of the baths, the fumes of the wine he was drinking? What about her husband, wherever he was? If it really was what he thought it was, how could she act so blatantly in public? And how, if at all, was he himself going to respond?

Crossing the terrace on her way to the kitchen, Vibia passed close to Cellius. "You were right," she whispered.

"Go ahead, enjoy," Cellius whispered back. "But remember who turned you on to him. And handle him with care, he's still a mite ticklish."

"Oh, I'll do that." Her eyes rolled suggestively. "I'll just love doing that."

Chapter 14

"And according to them two-thirds of the highest-quality paper was ruined by salt water before unloading in Ostia."

"There was a storm off Sicily that month, sir," the chief clerk said. "They're right about that part of it."

"But our captain tells me he put into Syracuse and the storm barely touched them."

"I see, sir."

"And they have no explanation for the fact that it wasn't until two weeks after the ship docked that they put in their claim."

"Is that so, sir?"

"According to their contract they're supposed to claim damage immediately. Who was in charge of packing that order?"

"Symmachus, I think, sir."

"Send him to me. And write immediately to our agent in Rome, ask him if he knows anything about this, and if not have him inspect the paper immediately, it should be obvious if there was sea-water damage." Zachary had no idea whether this was true or not, but he had quickly become used to sounding authoritative on topics about which he knew virtually nothing. "If there is damage and it doesn't look like someone just left the stuff out in the rain, have him go down to the harbor and check if the dockers didn't accidentally dunk some of the packages while they were unloading. Oh, and do they have any outstanding orders with us?"

"Yes, sir. Various quantities of myrrh, salt, opium, gum arabic, balsam, rosewater—three dozen bronze lamps, nine statues of Leda and the Swan, five..."

"Cancel them."

"Sir." The clerk hesitated. "They're one of our oldest customers. With all due respect, sir, your father..."

"All right, I mean hold them. Don't ship them. Not until further notice. This whole thing smells of fraud to me. We're taking enough of a chance giving credit to Romans, these days. If the barbarians take over we'll never get paid. Tell you what, just go through the books and work out what percentage of our business went there, over the last year, say. If it isn't too big, I've a good mind to look for other markets, we might lose in the short run but we'll be better off eventually."

"Yes, sir," the chief clerk's face fell. This meant several hours of extra work for him. The old man would never have been so inconsiderate. Or was it just ignorance?

"That's all for now," Zachary said, dismissing him. Sighing, he leaned forward over the correspondence that still remained, seals unbroken, on the desk in front of him. An involuntary yawn escaped him, and he raised his hand to cover it from the view of the clerks, who could see him quite clearly over the low partition that surrounded his desk. His father's idea, not having a separate room for his office, positioning it where he could overlook the whole staff and make sure everyone kept hard at work. That cut both ways, unfortunately. Of course he could change that policy, any policy, but he feared the comparisons that would be drawn. Not like his old man. Not a real workhorse like his old man was. Wants an office to himself now. Thinks himself somebody special, not like his old man...

He had not realized, when he made his decision to take over the firm, how his hands would be tied by his father's invisible but continuing presence. He had not realized, either, the weight and variety of the demands that would be constantly placed on him, the topics on which he would be required to show knowledge or at worst fake it, the continual crises that would harass him—ships delayed, damaged or sunk in storms or by pirates, overland consignments seized by bandits or cut off by sudden outbreaks of warfare, excise charges capriciously raised by foreign despots, rapid and inexplicable fluctuations in exchange rates, payments withheld for reasons that might be genuine or spurious, issues he had to make judgements on with insufficient facts, on the basis of experience he didn't have...

It would be bad enough if he got a good night's sleep. But he seldom did, nowadays. With his new friends he was out every night, to dinners, parties, theaters. And as if that wasn't enough, he had Vibia.

Or, did Vibia have him?

That first night nothing had happened beyond an invitation to lunch the following week, with her and a friend on that same terrace, to tell them what it was like to be a hermit. On such a site, exposed to half Alexandria in broad daylight, and with another female present, he had supposed that, even if she were planning seduction, she would proceed at a decorous pace that at worst would give him time to decide whether he really wanted to become involved or not.

How wrong he had been! He arrived to find the terrace draped in an awning of green silk that made it as private as a walled room. The friend was mysteriously delayed, then sent a message that she would be unable to come. It became quickly apparent that there was no space for anything between panic flight and close engagement.

He took the second course. He wanted her, there was no question of that. Whether he liked her, whether he wanted her in his life, were matters that seemed to shrink in importance as the wine circulated and the heavily-spiced food went down. And he had been continent ever since Leila's death. Within moments of finishing their meal they were on a couch together, and shortly after that, in Vibia's bedroom with the blinds drawn against the low afternoon sun, the door barred, their clothes in tangled heaps on the floor, their bodies moving with tremulous haste to the first climax, then relaxed, then locked in a long, slow, intimate exploration of one another.

Did that experience equal or even come close to his experience with Celia? He asked himself that question often in the days that followed, without ever being able to answer it to his satisfaction. In the first place, he found it hard to remember the earlier experience, and impossible to do so in precise detail, he had spent so many months trying to erase those details from his mind. Then, his feelings towards the two women differed so greatly. He had loved Celia passionately—he was not, or so he told himself, in love with Vibia at all, and such facts were bound to color even the physical side of things.

But the greatest difference lay in the characters of the two women themselves. While Celia had been hardly more than an adolescent, Vibia was a mature woman, with skills acquired over years of pleasing men, and, Zachary suspected, a capacity to use and manipulate them even while reassuring them that they controlled her completely.

She incited and restrained him, alternated feigned modesty with frank lust in such a way that he could never be certain quite how he stood with her. She exchanged intimacies with Cellius in his presence until he flamed with jealousy, then assured him passionately that he alone had access to her body— apart of course from the husband, who made one brief appearance and then was off again on his travels. And with him, of course, it wasn't like with Zachary, just the minimum that would satisfy conjugal demands. And as for Cellius— why, Cellius was nothing more than a friend, an old friend, true, and a trusted confidant whose advice she valued, but those fair-haired Romans with their cold eyes, she'd never gone for that type at all, just the thought of being in bed with one gave her the creeps, and would Zachary please touch her again exactly where and how he had just touched her? Oh, what utter bliss!

So it seemed he could never get enough of her. More than once, temporarily sated by her demands on him, he had sworn to himself that he would not see her again. Each time his resentment had halved with each day apart from her, until it became small enough for his lust to override it. But no matter how much you halve something, as his tutor had explained to him years ago while teaching him Achilles and the Tortoise, you'll always have a little left.

The presence of Symmachus, the packer, standing mutely in front of him, disrupted his thoughts. Yes, the man remembered that consignment. Yes, it had been properly packed, two layers of cloth round each package and reed mats tied around the packages with strong cord. Short of soaking the whole thing in resin, a ridiculous expense, everything had been done that could have been done to make it waterproof. No, nothing short of prolonged immersion should have caused that sort of damage. Of course, if the paper had been stowed in the bottom of the hold, and if they'd shipped even a little water, or had a slight leak that no one had bothered about, over the two or three weeks the voyage had taken, quite a sizeable puddle might have accumulated...

Zachary hadn't thought of that. He realized that he would have to talk to the captain again. And inspect the hold himself to make sure the captain wasn't lying. Of course, if there had been a leak the captain would have had ample time to get it fixed. And all of this was contingent on the ship not having finished loading for its next trip. If he was to have any chance of catching it he would have to go immediately to the harbor, leaving behind the inexorably growing mountain of work he had here.

Sighing, he sent a messenger for a slave to accompany him. That had become a reflex action by now, he realized as soon as the instruction had been given. He didn't have anything to carry on this occasion and he could hardly run any physical risk at midday in the crowded port. It was simply because a person in his position was always expected to have at least one attendant or preferably two (more, except on very formal occasions, began to smack of ostentation), just as a hermit was not expected to have any. In both roles, he realized, his behavior had been shaped by other people's expectations—so why should he find a slave's presence so irksome now when its absence had not bothered him in his other role?

You'll get used to it, he told himself for the hundredth time.

He and his slave pushed their way across the heavy stone slabs of the dock area, dodging hand-trolleys, donkey-carts, camel-trains, avoiding as best they could the patches of camel-dung, rotting fruit and other refuse scattered over the stones. The screeching of ill-oiled wheels and a hubbub of shouts in a dozen different languages assailed their ears; a medley of smells, urine, rotting seaweed, aromatic herbs, unwashed bodies, assaulted their nostrils. Why am I doing this, Zachary asked himself, and answered immediately, because I don't have anyone I can trust to do the job right. His employees were honest and conscientious enough, so far as he could determine, but they lacked imagination: they would not ask the right questions, they would accept plausible lies, they had neither the intelligence nor, what was even more important, the streak of cynical skepticism you had to have in order to come out on top in a deceptive world.

If I could get hold of someone like that, he thought. And then, a moment later: Cellius! Why didn't I think of him before?

Cellius, granted, had made it abundantly clear that he didn't like work. But Cellius had made it equally clear that he was chronically short of money. Besides, Zachary did not need workhorses, he already had plenty of those. He needed a trouble-shooter who would deputize for him at critical moments, be his eyes and ears, give him reports as shrewd and incisive as first-hand experience could provide. Zachary realized he was still hampered by other vestiges of his eremitic days: willingness to believe the best of others, to value the well-being of his neighbor more highly than his own. And Cellius' attitude was the exact reverse of this.

I'll mention it to him this afternoon, he thought.

The good ship Saint Anthony—funny how many of them had Christian names now, where before they had been named after pagan gods and goddesses—was still moored at the quayside. For its next trip, probably the last it would make before the sailing season closed, it had been chartered by the government and was loading wheat for Rome. A string of bare-chested stevedores bowed under their sacks filed up its rickety gangplank, and, regardless of your class or rank, you had to wait till they had all passed or get shoved into the harbor. Zachary was closeted with the captain for a good half-hour, and spent the best part of another hour surveying the hold, as best he could, given that the ship was already more than half loaded and he had to keep dodging the sacks that were hurled down through the hatches with no regard for anyone who might happen to be underneath.

He left the ship little wiser than he had boarded it. He could find no trace of any leak, nor of recent repair, although either could have been concealed by the new cargo. The captain had sworn total ignorance of how his previous cargo could have gotten damaged, and pointed out that all ships on government charter had first to pass inspection by the port authority—no effort was too great to protect the free distribution of wheat that kept Rome going, prevented the large-scale rioting that would inevitably follow any break in the food supply. Indeed, he seemed personally insulted when Zachary insisted on making his own inspection. Well, if it wasn't a leak, what was it? Had they run into any heavy seas before making Syracuse? Yes, naturally, what would you expect? Could one of the hatch covers perhaps have been left off, or have blown off in a sudden gust of wind? No, of course not. And so it went. Either the captain was lying or his customer was. How could you ever know?

"You're late," his mother told him when he arrived at his old home to eat with her.

"I know. I had to go to the port."

"You do too much. You should learn to let other people do things -for you. You're not in the desert now, you know."

"Mother," Zachary said. He did not raise his voice, but he was seething inside, not least because he had just come to the same conclusion. "Did you tell father how to run his business?"

She looked flustered. "Well, that's different."

"It's no different. He was in charge; now I'm in charge."

"Yes, of course you are, dear. But..."

"No but, mother..."

They finished their meal, she in a hurt silence, he in a guilty but resentful one. *It's a good thing she doesn't know I'm going to the circus this afternoon,* he thought. *Then she really would have something to be upset about.*

Chapter 15

The chariot races had already begun when Zachary arrived at the circus. He knew that long before he reached the gate, for he could hear a beast-like roaring a quarter-mile away, and the sound triggered a long-buried memory. He was a child, it was the day his father took him to see the giant figure of the god Serapis, and on the way he had been puzzled by that same roaring. "Is it lions, daddy?" he remembered asking, and his father had simply smiled and said, "No, son, a much more dangerous beast than that."

That figured. The circus lay only a few blocks from what were now the burned and blackened ruins of the Serapeum. His father had never taken him to the circus. The Serapeum you could pass off as educational, it being a library as well as a temple, but nobody could claim that about the chariot races. His father disapproved of them almost as much as his mother. His father disapproved because they were a waste of time; his mother disapproved because there the basest passions were unchained, not just rage (if your team didn't win) or pride and vainglory (if it did) but greed (if you bet on it) and lust (because men and women mixed indiscriminately there, and the women included prostitutes of the basest kind who flaunted their bodies before men whose inhibitions had already been eroded by the carnal atmosphere of the place).

Zachary gazed with frank curiosity at every aspect of the spectacle as it unfolded before him.

The first thing that met his gaze was the facade of the northeastern end of the circus, a pillared colonnade lined with shops, brothels and eating houses. Above the colonnade, a blank expanse of stone, crowned by a cornice with a winged Victory, formed the rear wall of the building that housed the president's box and the starting gates. The entrances were round to one side. Zachary, followed by the slave carrying his cushion, entered a narrow, dark tunnel where the roar of the crowd, rising in pitch and volume as the current race reached its climax, reverberated with deafening force. The sound died to a confused and sporadic shouting as he emerged once more into the light and air.

The stairs gave onto a broad paved walkway, parallel with the track, which divided the tiers of stone benches where ordinary citizens sat from the three or four rows immediately adjoining the arena that were reserved for the upper classes. Guards with heavy truncheons patrolled the walkway to ensure that no spectators sat in seats to which they were not entitled by rank or wealth. The track itself spread out before him, almost a third of a mile long and seventy yards wide, forming an enormous loop whose two sides were separated from one another by a low but broad and solid stone barrier, ornamented every few yards with obelisks and statues. The whole arena had been sunk in a rocky cleft to minimize costs of construction: Zachary had entered at street level but now found himself well above the track, whose sandy surface, laid over layers of finely-crushed rock, was scarred by the wheel-ruts of the chariots and already being worked on by stadium slaves with long rakes in preparation for the next race. The chariots that had taken part in the last one were all leaving the arena through the gates by which they had entered, save for one, parked near the center of the finish line, whose driver was receiving his prize from the sponsor of the race.

Zachary looked around for Cellius and his party. Cellius had told him they would be seated as near as possible to the finish line. But all he could see on the seats below the walkway was a confusion of heads and faces, continually in motion as their owners craned their necks for a better view, stood up, sat down again, exchanged seats, or tried to carry on conversations or arguments with people a dozen seats away. The walkway itself was crammed with guards, people looking for better seats, peddlers hawking sweetmeats and drinks, men with performing donkeys, hirers of cushions almost invisible under their pile of wares, whores swaying their hips as they advertised. One of these bumped into him by feigned accident, almost choking him with a wave of cheap perfume. He averted his eyes and passed on, hearing her burst of contemptuous laughter. Even though nothing in particular was happening, the background surge of countless thousands of voices filled his head like the noise a seashell makes, pressed against an ear.

There must be eighty, a hundred thousand people here, he thought. Nearly a quarter of the city's population. And the city, plus individual sponsors seeking to curry favor with the mob, absorbed the entire cost of it. Nobody had to pay admission—small wonder so many came.

As Zachary pressed on along the walkway, peering into the rows between him and the track, a long, wavering trumpet-blast announced the commencement of proceedings for the next race. Up in the president's box, high in the main building over the starting gates, an official was cranking a handle and a large urn began to rotate. In the sudden hush that fell you could hear, if you were close enough—and Zachary was now within twenty yards of the gates—the thump and rumble of things tumbling about in the urn. After a few moments the official stopped cranking, turned the urn over, caught the single green ball that rolled from its narrow throat, and held the ball aloft in his right hand for the spectators to see. Shrieks of joy came from the upper slopes of the stadium where the poor sat. The official cranked again.

"Here! Over here!" someone was shouting behind him.

In watching the performance with the urn he had walked right past his friends, who were standing and waving to him; Cellius and Vibia, the salt-and-pepper-bearded philosopher he had first seen at Vibia's dinner, a handful of rich young idlers and a rather statuesque woman in her forties with a slight mustache and the air of a bluestocking. Zachary, followed by his slave, made his way towards them, stepping down carefully over the packed rows of seats, apologizing for treading on cushions or the owners thereof, smiling at a man of senatorial rank who frowned back, and finally feeling the warm clasp of Cellius' hand and the embrace of Vibia, who clung to him with such a show of adoration he felt sure she must be trying to make one of her companions jealous.

In a moment, he knew he was right—she had turned to resume an animated conversation with one of the rich idlers. *Playing games again*, he thought. *Well, if that's how she wants it...* Stifling a pang of jealousy, he turned his face resolutely away from her.

"I don't think you've met Hypatia, our teacher," Cellius was saying, motioning towards the woman with the mustache. "She has granted us today the rare honor of her presence. Hypatia, this is Zachary, he's in the import-export business."

"I've heard of you, of course," Zachary said, bowing politely,

Hypatia nodded briefly, looking as if a rather bad smell had just passed under her nose, then turned ostentatiously away and continued to talk to the salt-and-pepper philosopher. Cellius gave Zachary a grin of commiseration, said, "A very deep thinker, Hypatia," and turned his attention to the urn and the balls.

"What's that for?" Zachary asked, hiding his irritation at the snub.

"To decide who gets which starting-gate," Cellius explained, gesturing towards the row of closed double-hinged wooden doors, each in its own semicircular archway, which filled one entire end of the stadium. Between each gate stood a stylized stone figure of the god Hermes, flat-faced, flat-bodied but for one thing. "You can see Christians have been at work there," Cellius said with a sly look.

"I don't understand," Zachary said.

"The Herms. Their cocks have been knocked off."

Now Zachary could see that the stone phallus on each statue had been drastically foreshortened or, in one or two cases, removed altogether. "How do you know it's Christians?"

119

"Who else would do such a dumb thing? They're just good-luck signs, for Jupiter's sake. Nothing to do with sex at all, but you Christers go ape-shit when you think there's the least chance someone might get aroused."

Ignoring the bitterness in Cellius' voice, Zachary said mildly, "don't hold me personally responsible for everything Christians do...You were explaining to me how they decide which gate you get, are the balls numbered, or what?"

"No. Each ball has a different color, and whichever color comes out first, that team gets to-"

"Yeah, but I haven't quite understood about the colors yet."

Cellius gave Zachary a pitying look. "Where have you been all your life? I thought everyone learned that when they were little kids."

"When I was a little kid I was taught that the circus was the devil's playground and to shut my ears any time anyone mentioned it."

Cellius sighed. "All right, there are four teams, each team is known by its color—green, blue, white, red—the Greens and the Blues are the only ones people really care about, don't ask me why, just tradition. This next race is for twelve chariots, three of each color. Whichever team has its color come out first gets first choice of gate, then the team whose color comes out next, and so on."

"The one that wins pick the inside track," Zachary offered knowingly.

Cellius laughed. "It's not that simple. Suppose you get off to a slow start and another rig cuts in ahead of you and another's alongside of you, you're boxed. Then again, if you know one of the other teams has a real fast bunch of horses—"

Another trumpet-blast cut the air, and Cellius abruptly stopped speaking. So did everyone else in the stadium. The suddenness of the silence struck like a physical blow, it startled you into attention and you felt the surge of anticipation that swept the arena. The president moved to the balustrade of his box, a white cloth in his hand. Savoring the hush he had created, he paused for a moment, smiling fatuously, then let the cloth fall to the sand beneath. The official at his side pulled a lever.

In the silence that still held, Zachary heard distinctly the click of a dozen bolts as a machine activated by the lever simultaneously drew them all back. Twelve pairs of twin doors flew open, and from each of them horses burst, yoked in teams of four, each team drawing a light, brightly-painted chariot, the charioteers standing, leather-helmeted, with leather corselets over their green, blue, white or red tunics, leaning backwards slightly with reins wrapped loosely round their waists and held slack in the left hand. Only the charioteers' eyes moved, quickly to left and right, scanning the field, gauging positions, as they tried to predict the order in which the other chariots would hit the break line.

What happened in those first few seconds, Cellius shouted in Zachary's ear—for the silence that preceded the opening of the gates had been followed by a deafening shout the moment the horses appeared—could go a long way towards deciding the result. He did not bother to explain how, for a man in an old-fashioned senatorial toga that Zachary had almost trodden on a few moments earlier was waving a fistful of coins in Cellius' face and demanding stridently that he bet. But Zachary could see for himself what was happening.

In the first hundred yards or so of the race, the chariots had to be funneled from the gates, which filled the entire width of the arena, to the point where a tall stone turning post marked the beginning of the central barrier, and where in consequence the track shrank to half the width of the gates. At that point a white tape, flush with the ground, stretched from one side of the track to the other. The area between tape and gates was divided by similar tapes into twelve lanes, one lane to each gate. Until it reached the break line, each chariot had to stay in its own lane—it could overtake but it couldn't cut in on the rig next to it, under pain of disqualification.

After the break line, the lanes ceased, anything went. It was then, bare seconds after the start, that the orderly, well-spaced array of horses and chariots imploded into a ragged, huddled mass of speeding rigs, running wheel to wheel, fighting to get inside one another, speeding to take advantage of a sudden opening, reining back to block dangerous competitors.

And in the audience itself, total bedlam reigned. Staid citizens bounced up and down, screaming, jerking imaginary reins and waving phantom whips. Others shouted out bets, accepted, refused, doubled up. Men, and here and there women too, hurled abuse at those who supported a different team, shook their fists, stuck out their tongues and gave one another the finger. Here and there, fights broke out, guards rushed up with clubs, the fighters, packed in that confined space, sent innocent bystanders sprawling, and the bystanders themselves joined in, so that each fight spread outwards like the ripples from a stone thrown in a pond. And yet to an observer poised above the arena, those fights would have been hardly noticeable, would have been lost entirely in that vast sea of lurching, shrieking, gesticulating humanity.

Zachary felt overwhelmed by it all. No one could stand in the arena and remain wholly unmoved by the contagious hysteria that swept it. Yet what he felt was more bewilderment than excitement. What could it possibly matter to any sensible person if Green beat Blue, or vice versa? And it was only too apparent to him why Christian philosophers condemned the races—calmness, self-control, peace of mind, all these were shattered and thrown out the window, all the baser passions were stirred up from the moment the chariots burst out of their gates.

The chariots rounded the farther turning post, offside wheels clear of the ground, sand and fine particles of gravel spraying from their nearside wheels. Two chariots all but collided, and a huge collective sigh, almost of disappointment, rose from the slopes. Then they were all into the straight, headed back towards where Zachary and Cellius were standing. By now, virtually no one in the arena was sitting down. The chariots were still closely bunched, the original leader, a Green, cut off by a Blue that had slowed deliberately ahead of him while a second Blue tried to force the Green into the barrier.

"See that?" Cellius shouted in Zachary's ear. "That's Hierax, the Green on the inside. He's the best. That's why the Blues are trying to fix him." He swung his mouth away and screamed, "Go, Green, go! Go for it! Pull out! Smash through 'em! Plough 'em under!"

Hierax did not pull out. On the contrary, the Blue chariot on his right drew closer, forcing him into the sloping wall of the barrier. His inside wheel skimmed the wall and began to mount it, throwing him to one side, "die, you Green bastard," the senatorial man was shouting. "Break your fucking neck!" But Hierax, pulling back hard on the reins, balanced himself and by sheer strength forced his chariot down off the barrier, brought his horses' heads round right under the wheels of the Blue chariot that had now slid ahead of him and, with a flick of his whip over the rumps of his horses, sent them outside the Blue and into the second turn in a wide sweep.

"See?" Cellius said, slapping Zachary on the shoulder. "I told you he was good. But he won't win. Not today." He grinned knowingly. "The Green team manager is my buddy, so I know the strategy. Hierax goes all out in the first few laps, the Blues are scared of him so they'll try to nail him, but see that other Green there, the tall guy running around fifth? He's the sleeper, just watch him go when they get to the last lap. Oh, it's a science, this is! You think it's just a bunch of dumb jocks careering round as fast as they can go, no way, you need a head for this stuff."

"Why do you back the Greens?" Zachary asked.

"Oh, mostly to annoy old farts like him." Cellius jerked his head in the direction of the man he had bet against. "The Greens are the working class favorites, the rich like the Blues. Again, don't ask me why. Tradition. Lost in the mists of history. You should get Hypatia to explain the symbolism of it one day. She fancies herself as a circus theoretician."

The chariots swept past them again. This time a Red was in the lead. Dust particles hung in the windless air like a fog. The noise of the crowd rose and fell like the sea on a rocky coast. In the lulls, if you were close enough, you could hear the thunder of the hooves of forty-eight horses and the rush of a dozen pairs of wheels tearing through the loose sand. To Zachary it was all quite meaningless, a blur of color and movement, yet despite himself he felt his interest aroused—would Red hold the lead, putting down the more popular colors? He found himself hoping so, Scetis had taught him an instinctive sympathy for the underdog. When they came round again and a Blue chariot was leading, he heard to his own amazement his own voice shouting, "Red! Come on, Red!"

Simultaneously, a hand slid around his waist and clasped it. "Why on earth are you shouting for Red?" he heard Vibia's voice asking. "Nobody who's anybody backs Red."

Zachary had sworn to himself that if she approached him he would ignore her, but he found himself saying, "maybe that's why."

"Oh dear. You are weird," she said coyly, pressing against him. Maybe you're nobody I should know."

He shrugged. "Maybe."

"Now you're cross with me," she pouted, "just because I was being nice to poor Andreas there, didn't you know his father just disinherited him, someone had to cheer him up. Such a shame for him, he's quite brainless, so heaven knows how he'll make a living."

Zachary laughed in spite of himself. "I'm sure he'll find a woman to keep him."

"Not this one. This one already has all she can handle."

He felt her hand increase its pressure. Did Andreas just turn her down, he wondered ungallantly, is that what this is all about? But his cynicism could not wholly suppress the surge of gratification that her touch and her words brought him.

"Aren't you betting?" she asked.

"I don't care enough about any of them to bet."

"But that's not the point! It just makes it more fun, that's all. I always bet on Blue, all the nicest people bet on Blue. I bet with Hypatia this time because she said White would win. She did explain why, something to do with some old Greek myth, but I really didn't understand a word of it."

"What's that?" Zachary asked abruptly.

"What? Where?"

"Those things like eggs, over there on the barrier." Zachary had only just noticed them: three hollow metal ovoids, balanced on a crossbar raised above the barrier, just a little way beyond the nearer turning post. As he pointed, the chariots swept by beneath them yet again, and a man on a ladder propped against the crossbar took down the third egg.

"That's to mark the laps," Cellius, his self-appointed circus mentor, cut in. "That means only two left. Watch now, this is when it gets down and dirty."

"You mean it wasn't before?"

Cellius just laughed.

Obediently, Zachary watched. The drivers were taking greater risks now, swinging their chariots directly into the path of a rival so as to overturn him, or bringing their horses right up to the chariot in front of them in the hope that their flying hooves would shatter its flimsy framework, built for speed not strength. Whips were out and swinging, the horses' mouths, lathered with foam, clamped on the bits as their eyes rolled in fear and desperation. The charioteers were crouching now, legs spread to hold their balance, reins wound tight, glancing quickly behind them and then forwards again, as...

"Look at that!"

The screams of the crowd rose to an impossible pitch as a White chariot overturned and its driver flew from it like a projectile, drawing in his head with a skill born of experience and rolling like a ball as the leather helmet hit dirt. And like a ball he bounced, snatched from the ground instantly by the reins that still linked him to his horses and that tightened with a sickening jerk as those horses tried to keep on running their race. A brawny arm swung up, a dagger glittered briefly in the sunlight and the screams turned to a mixture of cheers and catcalls as the man hacked through the reins and rolled clear, to be snatched up by nervous attendants and hustled to the shelter of the arena wall. The driverless horses slowed down as the chariot, skidding along on its side, one wheel spitting broken spokes while the other spun useless in midair, gradually braked them, and the surviving rigs, pulling out to right and left of it, maneuvered frantically to avoid it and at the same time make the turn.

"Shipwreck! Shipwreck!" the crowd at the far end began to chant.

Zachary, craning over his neighbors' heads, saw Hierax's chariot suddenly sandwiched between two Blues. Hierax, his mouth a slit of determination, crouched over his team, lashing frantically with his whip, trying for the only maneuver now open to him—to out speed the rigs either side of him and pull clear. But his horses had expended their energy in the front-running strategy imposed on him by the team manager, and the Blues bore in on him inexorably. The felloe of his offside wheel snapped first, and then, in quick succession, the axle, the spokes of the other wheel, the framework of the chariot itself.

"Shipwreck! Yay, shipwreck!" the crown shrieked in joy.

In a couple of seconds the chariot had disintegrated, dissolved into a flying cloud of splinters. The horses surged on, pulling out the shaft that was now the only intact portion of the chariot, and Hierax pitched forwards head first, dropped face down and was whirled along limp and helpless at their heels. Green liveried attendants swarmed from the shelter of walls and barrier and at the risk of their own lives seized the horses and dragged both them and the limp figure of the charioteer out of the line of the race. The other chariots swept by, heading into the penultimate turn, and now the attendants were bending over Hierax, lifting him, carrying his limp body towards a doorway in the retaining wall.

"He's had it! Had it!" the Blues supporters chanted, echoing the cry of the good old days of gladiator fights when one gladiator was wounded too badly to continue and fell to the ground, eyes liquid with fear, awaiting the crowd's and the president's decision. The Greens wept, tore their clothes, hurled insults and punches at the triumphant Blues. Zachary felt Vibia pressing herself passionately against him, her legs twined about his, and realized to his horror and revulsion that she had been sexually aroused by the sight of another's suffering. He would have moved away from her but by now the crowd, in a delirium of excitement, had poured down from the higher slopes into the upper-class tiers and was packed too tightly to allow the slightest movement.

Yet, though you would never have known it from the spectators' frenzy, the rest was anticlimactic. The Blue chariot that had moved into the lead a couple of laps back held its place. The two Blues who had smashed up Hierax swung into position behind it, wheel to wheel next to the barrier, holding back all the other chariots. The Red who had led earlier made a desperate swing around the outside Blue and tried to cut in ahead but his horses gave out at the crucial moment and he dropped back, screaming and shaking his whip in frustration.

The remaining ten chariots swung into the last straight in a frenzy of flailing whips and rolling sand clouds. One of the surviving Greens tried to squeeze between the two Blues and got close enough to catch the left-hand Blue charioteer in the face with the lead loaded tip of his whip, temporarily blinding him, but the man hung on letting his horses do the work and the lead Blue began to pull away, two lengths, three, a full four lengths ahead as the teams came thundering over the finish line.

"Blue! Blue! Up the Blues! Blues rule! Greens suck! Greens can't get it up! Blues forever!"

The Blue supporters had gone wild, embracing one another and total strangers, slobbering them with kisses, jumping up and down and screaming abuse and contempt at known Greens who stood booing and catcalling at the winner. A disgusted Green, an artisan by the look of him, jumped onto the parapet, ripped off cloak, tunic and loincloth, hurled them into the arena, sent his sandals skidding after them, and stalked off stark naked, to be seized by guards and hustled away down a tunnel. More fights broke out, and an unconscious man was carried past by his friends, bleeding profusely from a scalp wound. Within feet of Zachary and his group, a sweetmeat seller was knocked down, his tray ripped from him and its contents distributed among the crowd by a gang of youths. Nobody tried to stop them. Zachary, unable to get to the peddler's assistance because of the pressure of the mob, shouted futilely at them. They ignored him, and a lot of people just laughed.

Gradually the arena quieted, and a herald with a megaphone appeared at the balustrade of the president's box. The trumpeter blew for silence, and when the noise of the crowd had died down to a dull murmur a distorted voice could be heard booming, "Hierax is alive!" (Cheers). "He is unconscious with broken limbs but the doctors assure us he will recover" (Cheers and boos). "He has been carried to the infirmary" (Whistles). "There will now be a half-hour interval, with entertainment" (Whistles, cheers and catcalls in roughly equal proportions).

"An interval," Cellius complained loudly, furious at having had to pay out to the old fart in the toga. "I don't know what's come over the races nowadays."

"It's the troubles in Cyrene," the pepper-and-salt philosopher said. "They can't get enough horses anymore."

"I don't give a shit what it is, this sucks." A band of singing rope dancers had come out from one of the gates and was proceeding around the arena, twirling their ropes, running, jumping and tumbling as they warbled a currently popular melody. Boos and hisses spattered from the slopes, then shouts for silence. "Just look at them," Cellius sneered. "Is that what they call entertainment?"

"Cellius," Zachary said.

"Yeah."

"There's something I wanted to talk to you about...Something that occurred to me this morning." He hesitated. He was not quite sure how to put this without offending his friend.

"Well, spit it out," Cellius said impatiently.

"How would you like to work for me?"

Cellius blinked, drew back his head, rounded his eyes in comic surprise. "Work for you? As what? Buyer, seller, accountant? Or you want me to beat up irate customers? That's about the only job I'm qualified for."

Zachary smiled. "No, nothing like that. And don't worry, this wouldn't be a regular job. It's just that...Well, there are times when I have to do things that should be done for me, but I don't have anyone I can trust. I'd like to think I could call on you if—"

"I'm flattered," Cellius said. "Flattered you should think so highly of me. Surprised, too. What have I done to deserve this?"

Zachary did not quite know what to say. That Cellius was a man of his own class, his own level of education, who could understand things without having to have them explained in detail, who knew how to act quickly, confidently, decisively—to say all of that seemed either too little or too much, so he merely blushed a little and said, "Oh, just say it's a hunch I have."

"Well, nice of you to think of me," Cellius said. "Naturally, as a friend, I'd only be too happy to help you out any time you needed it..."

"I would pay you, of course. And pay well."

Cellius waved this aside with a dismissive gesture, as a thing of no importance. "Well, we can talk about that when it comes up."

"You mean you'll do it?"

"Why not? Just let me know when you need me." Cellius turned to look down into the arena, where a pair of pancratists had now appeared. Stripped to their loincloths and heavily oiled, they faced off, gestured threateningly and insultingly at one another, then started into their routine of vicious kicks, head-butts, punches to the nape and kidneys and spectacular falls.

"I'm really grateful to you," Zachary said.

"Huh? Oh, think nothing of it." Cellius' attention was focused on the pancratists. "Did you see that?" he asked. "Rank amateurs! The city should be ashamed of itself, putting on stuff like this."

"No, it's not quite like the old gladiator days, is it?" a voice said from behind them. "Give me a bit of good swordplay, any time."

Cellius swung round. "Zachary, meet Dion," he said. "He's the Green team manager I was telling you about just now."

Zachary, who had tactfully refrained from reminding Cellius about the Green sleeper who was all set to win, turned to greet a short, sandy-haired man with a deeply pitted face and merry eyes. "I'm sorry about your man, Hierax," he said. "I hope he does recover."

"Thanks. So do I." Dion grinned ruefully. "Oh well, these things happen. Bit of a blow for us, though. When Green's been going so well."

"Too bad," Cellius agreed. "You're right, though, about the old-time games. They should bring them back."

Dion shook his head. "Not a chance."

"Why not? You know this mob," and Cellius gestured at the spectators. "Nothing it loves better than a spot of blood."

"Who'd sponsor them?" Dion objected. "The Prefect wouldn't, he's in the Christers' pocket. The city wouldn't. And there's no private sponsors left with the kind of cash it takes nowadays."

"You could."

Dion laughed. "Us? The Greens? You think we're rich or something? Besides, you can't have heard what happened in Rome a few months back. The Emperor of the West closed the gladiator schools. That means curtains for the games, even in the heartland."

"So we're stuck with this crap," Cellius said, pointing down at the band of singing rope dancers who were just completing their circuit of the arena. "Oh, well, at least I'm glad you showed up, Dion. I'd have had to go look for you anyway after the races." He turned to Zachary. "Would you excuse us for a moment?"

"Sure."

"Yes, let them go off and discuss their men's things." Vibia said, twining her fingers in his. "Have you noticed how you always ignore me when there are men around?"

"Do I? Do I really?" Zachary, who had never realized this, asked in embarrassment.

"Yes you most certainly do, but I'm prepared to forgive you…this time. Tell me, was that really the first race you ever saw? I can hardly believe it, what did you think of it?"

Well, what did he think of it? Zachary hardly knew, except that the race seemed somehow to symbolize what his whole life was becoming: a strange and heady mixture of fascination and repulsion, a violent collision of forces pulling him this way and that. He was struck by a momentary pang of longing for the peace and silence of the desert. But how could he tell Vibia all this? She would never understand. He muttered some commonplace remarks about the noise, the excitement…

Meanwhile Dion and Cellius were moving slowly along the walkway, talking in low tones. "I have a proposition," Cellius said, "that I think might interest you."

"Go ahead."

"Could you and your Supporters' Club raise a few hundred fighting men? Given a week or two's notice."

Dion's eyes rolled in comic amazement. "What do you take me for? A general?"

"We don't need professionals. I mean street fighters, young hooligans, you know the kind."

"Who's we?"

"I'm not at liberty to tell you that. Not yet."

"Hm." Dion studied him with a guarded look. "What's in it for me?"

"Plenty. Our man is loaded. We can talk figures when you agree in principle."

"I'd have to know more about it than that," Dion said cautiously. "What's it all about, anyway? Somebody want to roust the Jew quarter?"

"Not this time."

"In the city, is it?"

"Uh-uh." Cellius shook his head. "The desert."

"My boys aren't going to fight savages!"

"They won't have to."

"Well, then, it's..." Understanding dawned in Dion's eyes. "Hey, you don't mean it! I'd heard there'd been ructions, but I never thought it had gotten to that pitch."

"Listen," Cellius said, "I didn't say a word, understand? If you want to do business with me, keep your mouth shut."

"All right, all right, keep your hair on! How long for?"

"Two to three days, max."

"All right, buddy. You're on." Dion's eyes twinkled. "Just as long as the price is right, naturally."

"Naturally."

"So tell me more."

The two men moved on, their voices lost in the tumult of the crowd.

Derek Bickerton

Chapter 16

Poemen did not stay long in Nitria. The feared blow from Theophilus did not fall, and Christmas was fast approaching. Poemen did not want to spend Christmas in Nitria. He did not want to hear a Christmas sermon from a disciple of Evagrius Ponticus (dead, alas, this past year) which would lose the little town of Bethlehem in a mist of cerebral abstractions. Nor did he want a crudely literalist sermon from some Anthropomorphite, replete with signs, portents, stars, Magi, gifts, shepherds and other paraphernalia which would equally obscure the mystery of God becoming man. He wanted to hear Moses' blunt, direct common sense, the shrewd simplicity with which the Robber could cut to the heart of any matter. Accordingly, he returned to Scetis so as to celebrate his Savior's birth with those who were closest to him.

He found there the usual fuss about the crèche, of course. For the past several years now, some of the hermits had taken to setting up, in the church, a small model stable, with straw, and a manger, and little cows and horses made of clay, and Joseph and Mary, ditto, and in the manger a Christ-child, a good deal larger than a neonate had any business to be, but then scale obviously wasn't the anonymous modeler's forte. Hermits like Papnoute poured scorn on the crèche: these were idols, whoever set up such a thing was no better than a pagan, it had no place in any Christian's life, let alone in the center of a place of worship. Hermits like Serapion defended it: it made the birth real, and it reminded, as no written scripture could, of the humble circumstances under which God had chosen to manifest Himself in human form.

For two or three years now, Papnoute, backed up by Arsenius, had flat-out asked Moses to remove the crèche. This, however, Moses had refused to do, stating tactfully that while he himself might not have chosen such a manifestation, it would be an act of impiety, worthy only of some pagan or heretic, to remove the crèche once it had been installed. This year, Papnoute had told Moses he was determined to keep vigil in the church. Moses shrugged and said nothing, but when Papnoute and his disciples appeared for their vigil, they found the crèche already installed.

Papnoute knew that Moses had tipped off the makers of the crèche but he knew also that if he accused Moses, Moses would simply assume an air of bland innocence, so that he, Papnoute, would end up looking mean-spirited or ridiculous or both. So he said nothing, though his expression spoke volumes. Poemen, for his part, agreed with Moses—it wouldn't have been his own choice, but what harm could it do, and why not leave untroubled anything that served to confirm even just one person in his faith? If such things offended your faith, so what? As so often before, he found himself mystified by people who praised humility in one breath and in the very next tried to impose their own views on others. At least, as long as Moses was priest in Scetis, such folk would have a hard time of it.

But when Christmas was over, the question arose once more: was Poemen obligated to return to Nitria? He did not want to go. While he had been there, he had seen a hermit—or a monk, many people at Nitria nowadays seemed to be uneasy hybrids of monk and hermit—flogged. Yes, they had made him embrace one of the tall palm trees that grew in the very courtyard of the church. They had lashed his hands together around the other side of the tree, then secured him further with a rope passed around his waist. Then they had torn the tunic from his back and flogged him until he screamed for mercy, until his back erupted in purple weals that oozed blood.

Why? Because in an argument he had struck another monk-hermit. Wrong, obviously. Still wrong, though less so, if the other had provoked him. "He should have waited till he was an Archbishop," Poemen said, quietly but clearly, during an interval in the flogging. "Then, he would have gotten away with it."

The remark was greeted by some with angry looks but by most with stares of total incomprehension. They must all have heard Ammonias' story by now, and many of them had seen the physical evidence that he carried on his face. Yet as far as they were concerned, the two acts, the monk-hermit's and that of Theophilus, had taken place in two totally different and incommensurable worlds. Even Ammonias himself seemed to have a hard time getting the point. But then the Tall Brothers were so withdrawn from the world of earthly things that they seemed hardly to notice the governance of the community where they lived. They merely accepted it as a condition of life—to criticize it would have been as pointless, to them, as criticizing the weather.

After the monk-hermit was cut loose from the tree, Poemen continued to repeat, to everyone with whom he spoke, that punishment of this kind, or probably of any kind, was totally inappropriate, as well as rankly unscriptural, in a community that sought to follow Christ. He found some sympathizers but earned the animosity of many others, including the one who was known as Father-Abbot and who seemed, with his council of seven priests, to represent the reigning authority in Nitria. But for his reputation for holiness—which, he reflected wryly, whether earned or not, occasionally had its advantages—he would probably have been expelled from Nitria. As it was, many must have sighed with relief when he left at Christmas, and would be correspondingly annoyed if and when he returned.

So not to return would satisfy both his own desires and theirs. Yet on the other hand a soft, insidious voice in his brain kept repeating, at the most inappropriate moments: "Stand by the Brothers!" Why should I stand by them, Poemen asked the voice; what good can I do them? He knew, of course, that that was a stupid question. It was not what he could do that counted, it was just his being there, as a solid pledge of brotherly solidarity between the hermits of Nitria and the hermits of Scetis. A purely symbolic presence, naturally. But symbols were powerful things, as the Cross itself bore witness.

He prayed long and often for guidance, but received no revelation. He kept postponing his decision and felt guilty about postponing it. He sought advice from Moses and John Colobos, but received only stuff of the, "on the one hand this, on the other that" variety. Politely, they were telling him that if he couldn't make up his own mind on what he should do, that was his business not theirs. He even went so far as to ask advice of Arsenius, on the principle that if people of like mind to yourself can't help you, perhaps you should consult people of a temperament as far as possible from your own—at least the advice they give will not be a mere mirror image of your own doubts and confusions.

Really, he said to himself afterwards, you should have foreseen what you would get.

"You say you want to give them moral support? Against their own Archbishop?"

Arsenius could hardly have gotten his eyebrows higher, Poemen thought, *if he'd shaved them off and painted on new ones.* As for the italics and exclamation points in his speech, they were truly something to hear.

"I told you what he tried to do to Isidore. And what he actually did do to Ammonias."

"You told me, and I'm sure you believe it sincerely, but I do not, not for one moment."

Poemen gave Arsenius a long and searching look, but he could discern no hypocrisy there–Arsenius too believed sincerely what he was saying. "Have you met Ammonias?" he asked.

"I have," Arsenius replied curtly.

"You know he is a man respected by everyone for his virtues and his way of life."

Arsenius sniffed. "So I have heard," he said grudgingly.

"Do you doubt it?"

"I don't doubt that he could have misunderstood the situation."

Poemen felt a wave of incredulity mounting in his brain. "I saw his face. Somebody hit it."

"I'm not disputing that."

"Are you suggesting he misunderstood who hit him?"

"Neither of us was there. And neither of us know what the context of it was."

"What do you mean, 'context'?"

"Well, what provocation there might have been?"

If I'd said that, Poemen thought, *at least I'd have had the grace to look embarrassed.* Try as he might, he could not detect any sign even of mild uneasiness in the other's manner. "Look, no matter what provocation there–" He was on the point of saying, no Christian, let alone an Archbishop, should go round punching people in the face, when he realized that he ran the risk of judging. "Well, assuming Theophilus did hit him, it doesn't seem unreasonable to fear that he might take some further action against the Tall Brothers, especially after threatening them."

"You have only Ammonias' word for that."

"And I believe him."

"You may be wrong in that. As I said, he could have misunderstood. Or the Patriarch could have been justified in threatening him."

Poemen controlled his anger, not without difficulty. "Justified? How?" he asked, in a tone that suggested he genuinely wanted to know.

"By the Tall Brothers' heresy."

"Now you are saying they're heretics," Poemen said, his tone openly incredulous now.

"No I'm not," Arsenius objected reasonably. "I don't know, and neither do you. But if anyone does, I'd have thought a Patriarch of Alexandria stands at least a reasonable chance of being right about it, wouldn't you? And that in all humility we should at least suspend judgment, rather than jumping to the conclusion that we know better, don't you think?"

Poemen spread his hands. "You are right. Of course you are right. I apologize. I am duly edified, and grateful to you for your lesson in humility, of which obviously I was in need." For after all, what else could he say? To say anything else could only breed anger and dissension. The mistake he had made, he realized as he made his way back to his cell, was not foreseeing how someone like Arsenius would respond.

Arsenius wasn't stupid. On the contrary, he was highly intelligent and highly educated, far better educated, in a purely formal sense, than Poemen himself. Arsenius wasn't evil. On the contrary, he was a man of scrupulous virtue—not quite, perhaps, the kind of virtue Poemen valued most highly, but a kind he could understand and respect, cold though it might seem at times. And yet Arsenius, good and intelligent as he was, turned a blind eye to the evil of Theophilus. Why?

There was only one reason Poemen could think of. It must be altogether too painful for Arsenius to have to admit that the leader of his church, the man ultimately responsible for his own moral welfare, had yielded to the sins of greed, pride, vainglory and anger.

Realizing this depressed Poemen deeply, because it wasn't just a question of Arsenius. The way Arsenius thought was the way that countless thousands of honest, decent, intelligent people, in the church and outside it, thought too. Faced with what seemed like a contradiction in terms—a sin-driven Archbishop—they would deny the evidence of their own senses. Worse, they would deny the evidence of their moral sense. The contradiction between what Theophilus ought to be and what he really was seemed outrageous to them—so outrageous that, rather than accept the evidence, they would make excuses, conjure up extenuating circumstances, twist or ignore plain facts with reckless abandon. Thus by this willful blindness they could convince themselves that they were still living in a normal, virtuous world, with everything in the exact place where it was supposed to be.

In a virtuous world, a world of just people, discreet and discerning, Theophilus would never have gotten to be an Archbishop. People would have recognized and admitted the Sly Fox's nature while he was still a deacon, if not sooner. While scrupulously refraining from judging him, while continuing to behave towards him in a neighborly, even a brotherly manner, they would have made sure that, whatever office fell vacant, somebody else got the promotion. What could he have done about it? Nothing.

Now, there were only two options, both distasteful. You could knuckle under to him, let him ride roughshod over the Tall Brothers and anyone else, however holy, who got in his way. Or, you could form a group, a sect, a party and fight him, as Ammonias had wanted to do. But that course was as futile as the other, for as Moses had said, in no time you would breed a Theophilus of your own. And you would then blind yourself to his vices, for he would be, after all, your son of a bitch.

So the cycle of anger and hatred would go on, until the end of time.

Poemen could only seek for a third way between those options. He would not knuckle under and he would not fight politically. Most of all he would not judge. He would simply try, to the best of his ability, to frustrate evil moves and nourish good ones. And hope that his example would touch others, as a drop of rain touches and moistens the desert sands. A thousand times drops would fall and a thousand times the desert would dry again. It didn't matter. You had to try it again, for the thousand and first time. You had to be God's rain and keep falling. In the faith, mad though it might seem in the eyes of the world, that one day the moral desert would become a green garden.

Benjamin was waiting outside his cell when he reached it.

"Greetings, Father."

"And to you, Benjamin."

"Can I have a word with you?"

Poemen's hearing was not as good as it had been, lately. "Did you say 'with you' or 'from you'?"

Benjamin grinned. "Both, Father. The 'with you' first, if you don't mind."

"Of course not. Come inside."

The year might have turned, but the short winter day had already shrunk to its ending. Poemen lit a lamp, and asked, "Have you eaten?"

"I ate in the market, Father."

So he's been to Terenuthis again, Poemen thought. *Typical Benjamin, forever gadding about; he never learns.* "That must have been this morning," he objected.

"One meal a day is enough for a hermit," Benjamin said stoically.

"Normally, yes, but not if you've been walking all day. Here, I haven't eaten yet." Arsenius hadn't offered him anything, either, but he knew that that wasn't through meanness—the Roman simply got so absorbed in whatever he was doing that he entirely forgot all bodily functions. Now Poemen took a small, hard loaf, broke it in half, and gave half to Benjamin. "Sorry there's no lentils tonight. I ran out of oil."

"That's all right, Father. Aren't you going to give it a blessing?"

Poemen clicked his tongue in self-disapproval. "I'm getting as bad as John Colobos," he said. "Worse, John's improved. All right, in the name of the Father…"

He blessed their frugal meal and the two men ate in silence, squatting on bundles of papyrus stalks. When they finished, Benjamin said, "I picked up some gossip in the market today."

"I knew it," Poemen said. "I don't want to hear it."

"You need to hear this, Father." Benjamin leaned forward, his expression serious. "I overheard you talking to John the other day. About whether to return to Nitria."

"There you go again! Listening to other people's…"

"Well you shouldn't."

"...conversations...Shouldn't what?"

"Go to Nitria."

Poemen gaped at him. "Why on earth not?"

"I'm trying to tell you, Father," Benjamin persisted doggedly. "What I heard in the market. Theophilus, I beg his pardon, our Patriarch, got five of the rottenest monks in Nitria to swear out a formal accusation against the Tall Brothers."

"An accusation of what?"

"They didn't know what. Heresy, I suppose. So then he took this to Archelaus, the Prefect, to ask him for troops. He's going to attack Nitria with the Roman Army."

"Are you sure all this is true?"

"Absolutely certain." Benjamin looked like he was about to make the sign of the cross, but desisted when he felt Poemen's eye on him. "The man who told me, he's a merchant, Cleon of Alexandria, a very pious Christian, John knows him."

Poemen remained unconvinced. "There'd have had to be more than heresy at stake, to call troops out. There'd have had to be some threat to public order."

"I don't know about that."

"Did the Prefect give him the troops?"

"I don't know that either. But they say Theophilus has got both Emperors to sign an order making it a crime to read the works of Origen."

"This is insanity," Poemen exploded. "If it's true," he quickly corrected himself. "I can't believe even Arcadius would be that foolish."

A look of fear crossed Benjamin's face, and he put a finger to his lips. "Father, be careful—"

"Why should I be careful?" Poemen asked. "This is Scetis. God's law is the only law that counts here. If they want badly enough to ferret me out and throw me to the beasts for treason, they can. Besides, I didn't say he was foolish, I said he wasn't foolish...Well, not that foolish."

Benjamin looked at him pleadingly. "All right, but whatever you do, don't go to Nitria."

"Why not?"

"Because it's dangerous."

"But that's exactly why I'm going." He smiled at Benjamin. "I'm sorry I gave you a hard time about the gossip. I've been struggling with this decision for days. Thanks to you I know what I've got to do now. I'm grateful to you, Benjamin."

Benjamin gave his head a puzzled shake. "I don't think I'll ever understand you," he complained.

"It's not hard. I have to stand with the Tall Brothers. If they're in no danger, they don't need me. If they are…"

"You could get killed!"

Poemen's eyes had become very bright and lively, he felt as if he had shed five years in the last five minutes. "So? I've more than used up my Bible span, my life is forfeit to God now. Let Him take it whenever He wants to."

Suddenly, he felt the need to be on the move at once. It surprised him, this sudden surge of almost youthful vigor. Where had it come from, could it be of God? On his last trip to Nitria he had insisted on sleeping before they started. Now he felt wide awake, ready to make the twenty-hour journey without stopping. Before sunset the next day he would have arrived in Nitria.

Watched by a bewildered and still somewhat resentful Benjamin, he picked up his worn leather satchel, pulled down a change of clothes from a peg on the wall, stuffed a couple of small loaves and a goatskin water container on top of the clothes, fastened the satchel, picked up his hermit's staff and threw his sheepskin cloak over his shoulders. That was one of the hidden benefits of the hermit's life. If you did decide to make a move, it was no big deal.

"A word from you, Father," Benjamin reminded him. "Before you go. Give me a word for my salvation."

Poemen paused with his hand on the latch. "teach your mouth to say that which you have in your heart," he said, and went out into the darkness, leaving his cell wide open, so that passers-by or the desert hyenas could take from it anything they might need that they could find there.

Chapter 17

By the first hour of the night, the convoy had already crossed Lake Mareotis and entered the mouth of the River Lycus, a distributary of the Nile that branched off from the Canopic stream and looped round to pass close by Nitria before emptying into the lake. There were five boats in all, rented by the Church from the dock that lay at the southernmost end of the Street of the Soma: flat-bottomed barges with lateen sails puffed out now by a steady north-north-easterly breeze, with ranks of rowers, hefty Nubians, rented along with the boats, pulling oars on either side.

In the bodies of the boats sat the Archbishop's army. They had boarded that morning, at the Soma dock on Mareotis, to the whistles, catcalls and occasional cheers of racetrack fans waiting for boats to carry them back to their homes in the Delta. Theophilus had planned the attack for the previous day, but the previous day was race day at the circus, and the members of the Greens' fan club who formed a substantial part of his army had simply refused to move until the races were over. Now their presence at the dock drew cheers from their own supporters but only derisive noises, gestures and epithets from the waiting passengers, most of who seemed to sympathize with the other colors.

Theophilus was embarrassed by these demonstrations. Heartily he wished Archdeacon Timothy, Dion the leader of the Greens, and the Roman wastrel who had served as their go-between, at the bottom of Lake Mareotis. If only he could have done without them! If only Archelaus, cowardly timeserving fence-sitter that he was, had had the decency to provide him with proper military backing! Then he would not have had the task of trying to weld together this ragtag army of violently contrasting elements.

Standing in the bow of the lead boat, just behind the man whose job it was to alert steersman and oarsmen to obstacles in their path, Theophilus permitted himself a rare luxury, a dream of what might have been. If God's hand (a very palpable object, he was now committed to believing) had not directed him into the Church, what might he not have become. A great general, surely! He saw himself commanding a dozen legions, ordering them into their impregnable tortoise formation, against which waves of Persian charioteers, Numidian cavalry, giant Teutonic foot soldiers with long blond hair and two-handed swords would hurl themselves in vain, then calling in his own cavalry to sweep the surviving stragglers from the field. He saw himself as Theodosius, a mere six years before at the battle of the Cold River, on that momentous morning when God's wind blasting down from alpine heights blew the enemy's spears and arrows back in their own faces while hurling the Christians' weaponry with devastating force into the ranks of the last army to fight as both Roman and pagan.

Well, he had tried. Archelaus had hummed and hawed and finally offered him less than a couple of hundred men, old garrison hands, crafty old sweats with more experience of chicken stealing than sword fighting. Not that Theophilus was expecting much resistance, but there were upwards of five thousand monks and hermits in Nitria, some of them supposedly on his side but still awed by the supposed holiness of the Tall Brothers. So he had had to back up the troops with Dion's circus toughs and his own parabolani, both skilled, in their different ways, at hand-to-hand brawling in the back streets of Alexandria, but both totally unused to desert warfare, along with whatever stray monks he could round up from the monasteries in and about the city.

Well over a thousand in all, that should be enough, given the element of surprise. Surprise was crucial. He didn't want too many casualties. Just the Tall Brothers and Isidore. Maybe even let off Dioscorus, for when all was said and done, a bishop's rank did deserve some consideration. But the earless maniac who had had the impertinence to defy him would not survive the night if the Sly Fox could help it, and the other three might as well go with him. Then on to Hermopolis, boot Dioscorus out of his diocese and send him into exile. Theophilus stared into the darkness ahead, as if by the mere intentness of his staring he could quicken the pace of events, a pace that could never be too fast for him.

There was a moon up and little cloud, or they would not have dared proceed along the Lycus by night. The canal-like stream, dead calm, seeming almost stagnant, was choked with reeds along its flat banks. The lanterns attached to their rigging must have been visible for miles across the fields, and Theophilus thought of having them put out. Then he realized that no one could deduce anything about his force, its nature, purpose or destination from a handful of glowworm eyes moving mysteriously through the lower air. Any persons unfortunate enough to be wandering around this late would merely cross themselves, or utter a prayer to Isis, depending on their faith. They would attribute the lights to those demons of the desert margin in whom most Egyptians, whether pagan or Christian, sincerely believed.

At last the outline of a jetty appeared ahead, and the captain of the lead boat made his way forward to where Theophilus still stood.

"This is it, Your Reverence. This is the landing for Pernoudj."

"We don't want Pernoudj, we want Nitria!"

"I know, Your Excellence. Normally we'd go to the next landing, but the river's silting up, we're liable to run aground and with this mob I wouldn't like to be responsible for the consequences."

"How far from here to the first monastery?" Theophilus asked.

The man scratched his head. "Never walked it. Two hours maybe. Maybe three."

A grumble of disapproval came from those who overheard this. A voice shouted, "Nobody told us we'd have a three-hour hike."

"And back!" another voice shouted. "That's a six-hour hike!"

Theophilus hesitated. He was on the point of ordering the captain to proceed to the next landing. Then he envisaged the chaos that would assuredly follow if they did run aground.

"Disembark!" he shouted. "Legionaries first! Centurion, see the gangplank is manned, make sure your men get off first." He didn't trust the circus fans, they would be all over the map if they didn't have trained men watching them.

The centurion had been lamed in a skirmish with Isaurian brigands, but he seemed to know what he was doing. Quickly, he established a perimeter, within which, as each boat disembarked in turn, the monks, fans and parabolani milled around aimlessly. They also talked, and news of their unexpected hike traveled fast. "They're in a bad mood," Dion said, coming up behind Theophilus on light springy feet, so quietly that Theophilus could not entirely suppress an involuntary start.

He glared at the Green circus boss with distaste. A pagan and libertine, his way of life written visibly in his pitted face and insolent grin. And pagan too were most of the fans—most of the soldiers, if it came to that, even though they fought nowadays under Christian banners. Strange what instruments God sometimes chose for his work!

"They say this wasn't part of the bargain." Dion went on. "They say they want more money."

"They're being paid an exorbitant sum already!" Every drachma, every obol that did not go into his Building Program was like a knife in Theophilus' heart.

"I'll be blunt with you. No money, no fightee."

"This is extortion!"

Dion shrugged, grinned, slipped his thumbs inside the exaggeratedly tight belt of his tunic and, after Theophilus had fumed in silence for a moment, began to whistle insolently.

It was all the Archbishop could do to keep from grabbing that belt in both hands and butting the circuit boss in the face. Caution restrained him. This was no hermit who would respond nonviolently. And even if he could take Dion one-on-one, the fan club would lynch him within seconds, Patriarch or no Patriarch. "Is there," he asked, his voice unsteady, grating, he was so furious at having to ask even this much of such a man, "is there . . . any other way?"

"Like what?"

"Well...suppose they had a few drinks?"

Dion whistled on a rising note. "Got any?"

"Of course." Luckily it had already occurred to Theophilus that his ragamuffin army might need liquid encouragement at some stage of the game. Amphorae of the worst and cheapest wine had been stacked beneath the decking of the lead boat the previous evening.

"Well, we can try it," Dion said. "You want to announce it or shall I?"

"Go ahead." Much as he hated yielding the limelight, an Archbishop should surely not admit responsibility for a drunken orgy. Dion climbed onto a bulwark and shouted for silence.

"Lads! Listen up a minute!" Gradually the milling mob fell silent. "Well, it turns out we either get stuck on a sandbar in the middle of the river for the next few days, or we take a short hike." Groans from the crowd. "What kind of men are you, anyway? I told the Archbishop here what a tough lot you were. Wanna make me look like an idiot?" Mixed groans, whistles, catcalls, but some cheers came from the crowd: Dion was popular with the fans. "All right, here's the deal! We know hiking's thirsty work, so how 'bout a little drink, just to get us going? And then, if we get thirsty along the way, we can have another little drink! And so on and so forth. What do you say, lads?"

He was greeted with a discordant chorus, assent and disagreement in roughly equal parts. One group tried to get going with a chant of, "More money! More money!" but a bunch of Dion's friends, who obviously doubled as a theater claque, broke it up with a rehearsed, rhythmic, syncopated handclap, ONE two-three four-five SIX seven-eight-nine ten, ONE two-three four-five...

"You want more money?" Dion yelled over the racket as the Roman army detachment, their arms grounded, surrounded the bawling fans in silence, grins of contempt on their faces. "Have you had any money yet?"

"No! No!" a dozen voices answered him.

"Right! Well you won't get any if you don't do your stuff. Got it? Now here comes the booze, boys. Those who're ready to march and fight, get lined up for it. Those who aren't, get the fuck out of the way!"

Church slaves from the Caesarium had already started unloading amphorae from the boat, while others ladled the wine into a motley collection of gourds, cracked bowls and other inexpensive containers, of which there were obviously nowhere near enough to go round. Luckily the lame centurion was quick-witted; without having to be told he had already assigned a couple of dozen men to supervise the operation, otherwise the amphorae would have been knocked over and shattered in the first charge of the thirsty fans. With the hafts of their spears the soldiers pushed and pummeled the unruly mob into the semblance of a line, and for a moment Theophilus feared that fighting might break out between them and the fans. But the line settled down as those at its head began to break away with their wine ration, groups of two or three sharing containers, arguing and shouting while they noisily slurped it down.

More amphorae came off the boat and the lame centurion, a natural organizer—*If only I had him as my deacon*, Theophilus thought—broke the line in half and moved the back half up to form a second line. Theophilus saw most of his parabolani in the lines and was on the point of angrily calling in their leader, but thought better of it. If he held them to higher standards than the Greens, they too would riot. As things were, the scene was quieting by the minute, save for scattered bursts of raucous laughter. Theophilus, relieved, told the lame centurion that his men could drink too, there was enough for everyone.

"Thank you, sir. Kind of you, sir. But the lads aren't supposed to drink on duty."

Wish I could instill that kind of discipline in my people, Theophilus thought. He dreamed of the day when Church and State would be as one, when divine law became human law, with all the armament of the state to enforce it—when armies led by bishop-generals and archbishop-field marshals swept the pagan forces off the rim of the world, and everyone worshiped Christ in the same words with the same ceremonies and with identical beliefs, under pain of torture. Tough, but what were a few hours of suffering against an eternity of it? It would be in their own best interests. You had to be cruel to be kind.

It was Dion who spotted the problem. If they were going to offer drinks along the way, as he had promised, they had to find some way of bringing the amphorae, which were far too large and heavy to be carried by hand. So there followed the best part of an hour's delay while a detachment of troops was sent into Pernoudj to commandeer farm carts and oxen to pull them. By that time, everyone was thirsty again, so a second distribution had to take place.

Theophilus glanced anxiously at the stars. It must by now be the fourth or fifth hour of the night, and around midnight the Nitrians would start to rouse themselves for the night office. He could no longer hope to catch them asleep. But at last the parade got going, the soldiers split between the head and the rear of the column, the fans with their green scarves and jerkins singing rowdy circus songs, the monks and parabolani tramping dourly and disapprovingly behind them.

"Hear the news,
Blue must lose,
Up the Greens and screw the Blues!
Greens are keen,
Greens are mean,
Kick that kidney, stomp that spleen!" the Greens chanted. After a while the parabolani, in a spirit of open competition, started to chant the psalms they had chanted on the march to the Sarapeum:

"Let God arise,
Let His enemies be scattered!
Let them also that have Him
Flee before Him!
For He it is
That shall tread down our enemies!"

Theophilus, who already had a headache, had to endure the cacophony that resulted until, after an hour or so, the first drink break stopped their mouths for a while. He noted that one or two of the soldiers had begun to drink and that the centurion was turning a blind eye to it. Dion was in his element, at the center of a group of sycophants, laughing, drinking, cracking jokes right and left; catching Theophilus' eye, he grinned fiendishly and waved him to come on and join them. Scornfully the Archbishop ignored him. He had been looking forward to this march as a time of triumph, but now that time had arrived he could only wish it would be over.

But another hour, another long drink break, and the better part of a third hour of marching passed before the moon glimmered on the roof of a squat tower and the centurion called a halt.

"That's Nitria, sir," he told Theophilus.

"What's that tower?" Theophilus asked, trying to keep the note of anxiety out of his voice. "That wasn't there before. What are they doing, have they built fortifications?"

"Not against us, sir. That's for the barbarians."

"But the barbarians have never..."

Theophilus broke off abruptly. He had been going to say, the barbarians have never attacked ascetics in the desert, when it suddenly struck him, well, maybe they never have, but does that mean they never could? Vague intimations of some vast strategy flashed through his mind—use the monks to control Alexandria, use the barbarians to control the monks—but were lost immediately as he tried to concentrate on what the centurion was saying:

"…got into some argument with the Libyan shepherds, you know, sir, the ones bring their flocks through here every spring for the grass in Scetis marsh, I think they flogged one or two of them and the Libyans took it badly, threatened to come back next year mob-handed. Can't really call 'em fortifications, sir, just a tower they can shut themselves up in, case there's any trouble…"

Theophilus thought for a moment. The noise his forces were making was almost too deafening to let him think—chanted psalms, obscene songs, banging of equipment, whoops and yells, for by now everyone, barring himself and the marching passed before the moon glimmered on the roof of a squat tower and the centurion called a halt.

Chapter 18

Poemen heard their noise from afar. He was awake already, kneeling on a rush mat in his tiny room in the guest quarters of Nitria, for it was now, in these moments of blackness, silence, stillness, that one could approach most closely to God. For if a spiritual darkness forever barred men from seeing God, it seemed that by losing oneself in physical darkness one might occasionally sense, through means beyond everyday senses, God's immanent presence.

When he first heard the clamor explode into that stillness, he thought for a moment that all the demons of the desert must have banded together to attack the home of their staunchest opponents. But within seconds he recognized the voices as human—voices distorted by rage, drink, reckless abandon, but human nonetheless—and knew that the unthinkable had happened: the Church had declared open war on the men of God. He leapt up, fastened his leather girdle around his waist, slipped his feet into his sandals, flung on his sheepskin cloak (for the early spring night still held the dry chill of a desert winter) and hesitated only momentarily before deciding not to pick up his staff, for it was senseless even to look as if you might be opposing violence with violence.

Running with an agility that belied his age, he negotiated a twisting corridor and burst out into the open space behind the church. He was not the only one to have heard the approaching army. Monks and hermits were running in all directions, some to the protection of the church, others away towards the desert, still others, panic-stricken, in no direction you could determine. The noise of the invaders grew louder with every second.

Poemen ran directly to the cells of the Tall Brothers, a plan forming in his head even as he ran.

He found them awake and out of their cells already, but blear-eyed and confused; long nights of anxious vigil had exhausted them. A handful of sympathizers and supporters had gathered around them, all talking simultaneously and giving contradictory advice. Poemen cut through them with an urgent air of command.

"Get them hidden! Now! In the dry well! Move!" He got some cool glances, for he was a stranger there with no authority whatsoever, but Ammonius seemed to wake up suddenly and said, "Yes! He's right, let's go!"

"Where's Isidore?"

"Someone went for him...Look, he's coming!"

"I hope it's big enough for the four of you," Poemen panted as they ran down an alley lined with stone cells. "If not, you'll have to stand on one another's shoulders."

They gathered around the wellhead, gasping for breath. Poemen looked around, but the few people in sight were too busy with their own concerns to pay them any attention. The noise by now was deafening—at any moment the invading hosts might appear. Poemen pulled the wooden cover off the well, whose head, luckily, was built flush with the ground. "Rope!" Poemen shouted, "has anyone got a rope?" He realized immediately the absurdity of his request—who would be going round with a rope in the middle of the night? Why hadn't he thought of that sooner?

"They can climb down, there's enough footholds," someone said.

"No they can't, they'll break their necks in the dark." Poemen thought furiously for a moment. "Take off your tunics."

"What?" Euthymius gasped.

"Take 'em off! We'll tie them together."

"They'll freeze down there," someone objected.

Someone else said, "We can drop 'em in after them."

"Exactly," Poemen said. "Anyway, their body heat should be enough to—there!" He tugged on the string of tunics, making sure the knots held. "Who's first?"

"Me," Ammonius said quickly, and grasping the end of the improvised rope he dropped into the well. "Use your feet!" Poemen shouted. "It may not take your whole weight. Put as much weight on your feet as you can."

Ammonius' reply was muffled by the well. Then he called out louder, "I'm at the end and I haven't hit bottom yet."

Poemen shouted back. "Bend your legs and let go."

They heard a muffled thud, a splash.

"Are you all right?" Poemen shouted anxiously.

"I'm in about half a cubit of water," Ammonius answered. "Otherwise fine."

"There's room for all of you down there?"

"It'll be tight, but yes."

"Good. Catch the others."

Isidore went over, then Euthymius and Eusebius. Poemen threw the knotted tunics down after them, there was no time to untie them; they would have to wrestle with them as best they could in darkness. "Get moving," he said to the others. "Scatter, get as far away as you can." He threw the wooden lid over the hole and had started to kick stones and dirt over it when the first invader burst into the small open space that surrounded the wellhead.

He was too drunk to understand what Poemen was doing—almost too drunk to stand. He reeled around, rocking on his heels, then the sight of some fleeing hermit caught his attention and with a whoop he was off in pursuit. Poemen breathed a sigh of relief, spread his sheepskin over the uncovered portion of the lid and knelt down upon it. Almighty God, he prayed, if it be Your will that the Tall Brothers and Isidore be saved, blind the eyes of these impious men to what has been done here. But if it be not Your will, let that will be done and I will try to understand it, and if Your grace will not allow me to understand it, so be it, for You are the Almighty and Everlasting God and I am nothing, a mote in the whirlwind of time, were it not for Your love.

A stream of figures poured suddenly into the open space: monks and hermits trying to flee, a few of them resisting, and behind them a mixed rabble of soldiers and civilians, screeching abuse, lashing out with staves, clubs and the butt-ends of spears. Men fell with bloodied heads and sprawled senseless or picked themselves up and tried to keep running. The whole melee swirled for a moment around Poemen's motionless figure and swept on, miraculously leaving him untouched. But immediately after them he heard a measured tramp, and a detachment of relatively sober soldiers loomed over him. He felt his arms caught, let himself go limp as they pulled him to his feet. But immediately an authoritative voice said, "Let him go." Released, he fell to his knees and remained there, gazing up inquiringly at the man who confronted him.

"Who are you?" the lame centurion asked.

"Poemen the Shepherd of Scetis."

"If you're from Scetis, what are you doing here?"

"Merely visiting," Poemen answered mildly. "It's the custom among hermits to visit other communities, to be edified by the wisdom of holy men that they don't normally meet."

"What are you doing out here?"

"Praying."

"Praying that God strike dead your Archbishop?"

"Certainly not," Poemen said, genuinely indignant. "I wouldn't pray that about my worst enemy. If I had one."

"Why out here?"

"Because it's more uncomfortable. The more uncomfortable it is; the more merit we gain."

The centurion gave a grunt of mingled contempt and bafflement. "Do you know the Tall Brothers?"

"Of course. Everyone knows them."

"Where are they?"

Here's one lie I'll certainly be forgiven for, Poemen thought. "I don't have the faintest idea. In their cells, I should imagine."

"No they're not. They've hidden themselves somewhere."

"Have you tried the tower?" Poemen asked innocently.

"We're storming that right now," the centurion said. "The fools tried to defend it. We'll soon find out if that's where they are. But wherever they are, we'll get them."

"Well, sorry I can't help you."

The centurion had already turned away. Poemen breathed a prayer of thanks to God. He remained kneeling, utterly motionless, even while a drunken Green pulled his nose and slapped his face.

"This one alive, you think?" the Green said to his buddy. He had his dagger out. Through half-closed lids, Poemen saw the glimmer of moonlight on steel, and braced himself, mentally and physically, for the killing blow.

"Nah," his buddy said. "Lay off. You know what we were told."

"I was only going to prick him," the first protested. "See if he's alive or not."

"Well, lay off, anyway. Hey, that one's alive." A hermit had just run blindly past them, and as automatically as if they were greyhounds after a hare they took up the chase, whooping and yelling.

Poemen continued to kneel, while all around him a scene of utter confusion unfolded. Some of the invaders carried torches, and before his eyes one ran inside a cell and deliberately set fire to the dried palm-leaves and baskets stacked therein. The material caught with a whoosh of flame that spouted briefly through the cell window before settling down to a steady roar.

The incendiarist ran out, shouting and laughing, and he and his friends began to set light to the material in other cells. Monks ran by with their heads and faces bleeding, a stout one who still swung his staff gamely was knocked down and stomped into unconsciousness. Poemen heard distant screams from the direction of the tower, and assumed it had been captured. Smoke began to rise from the direction of the church. A monk ran by screaming, "the Holy Sacraments! They're burning the Holy Sacraments!" Anyone above average height whom the invaders could catch was being bound and dragged off for interrogation on suspicion of being a Tall Brother.

Suddenly Poemen's mind, which had been passively absorbing all this, snapped to attention. A figure was approaching him directly, a figure that advanced through all this chaos with a stately dignity, clad in full archiepiscopal regalia—silk cassock and surplice billowing in the same night wind that was fanning the flames, solid gold chain and crucifix around the neck, the tall, gold-embroidered headgear making its wearer seem of more than human stature. His staff of office, silver handled, swung from his left hand. *A crook*, Poemen thought, *a shepherd's crook. He's supposed to be a shepherd, too! If only I'd had one like that in the old days!* It was all he could do to repress an ironic smile.

Theophilus stopped directly in front of him, not repressing the frosty smile that split the smooth oval of his face without reaching his eyes. "Poemen the Shepherd," he said. "We meet at last."

"Indeed we do, Patriarch."

"You managed to avoid me, you remember, ten years ago in Scetis."

"I was not avoiding you," Poemen said quietly. "We both of us had our own pressing concerns. We just never happened to meet."

Theophilus shrugged, dismissing the issue. "Well, here you are now, anyway. If we had met then, I would have humbly asked you for a word to aid my salvation. Now I must ask you why you have offered help and comfort to the enemies of the true faith."

Poemen remained on his knees—not for Theophilus' sake, but for the God to Whom his prayers had been so rudely interrupted. It would seem more like obeisance to the Archbishop, he figured, if he were to scramble guiltily to his feet. "I don't know what you mean," he said.

Theophilus' eyes flashed. "Yes you do! You know perfectly well what I mean! Do you think I don't know that you've been keeping company with the Tall Brothers? I know everything that happens here, everything, I tell you!"

If you did, you'd have moved me off this wellhead, Poemen thought impishly. He cocked an ear to hear if he could detect any tell-tale sound from beneath, but even if there had been one it would have been drowned in this all-encompassing babel.

"I've been keeping company with any number of people," he said. "I'm not solitary enough. It's a weakness in me that I pray God will remove from me."

"They have been excommunicated," Theophilus thundered. "No true Christian should associate with them in any way." Poemen bowed his head humbly and made no answer. "Where are they now?"

"I don't know."

"You're lying!"

"No."

"I can force you to tell me!"

"You can certainly try," Poemen agreed readily, "but if I don't know, that won't help a lot, will it?"

A spasm of rage twisted Theophilus' face, he reached out with both hands and seized Poemen by the throat.

Poemen's head tipped back, and Poemen's eyes looked fearlessly into his. And then an extraordinary thing happened. Poemen smiled—not a smile of defiance or contempt, but a perfectly candid, trusting smile, a childlike smile, which said as clearly as words, "I know someone as responsible as you isn't going to do anything you might regret afterwards."

Theophilus made a choking sound and his hands, as if of their own volition, relaxed their grip on Poemen's neck. He took a step backwards.

"Don't try to pretend you don't share their heresies."

"What heresies?"

"Don't bandy words with me!" Theophilus, surprised himself by his sudden loss of momentum, was working himself up again. "Answer me these questions and answer them directly…Is the Son equal to the Father, or beneath Him?"

"I don't know."

"What do you mean, you don't know? Of course you know! Equal or beneath, one or the other—answer!"

"I don't know."

"Then, you don't believe that the Son and the Father are equal?" Theophilus cried triumphantly.

"I know that is what the Church teaches," Poemen said humbly, "and therefore I have no trouble in accepting it. But you asked me a personal question, and I had to answer that I don't know, because of my own direct knowledge. I don't know such high things, cannot know them, do not presume to know them, being the least among God's children."

Theophilus bit his lip. "Shall we have material bodies after the Resurrection?"

"I don't know."

"Are the stars living beings?"

"I don't know."

"Where do our souls come from?"

"I don't know."

"Can the Devil be pardoned?

"I don't know"

"Did the Son of God become Man or merely take the form of Man?"

"I don't understand the difference."

A crafty look bridled the rage in the Patriarch's eyes.

"Then, how do you interpret Philippians chapter two verse seven?"

"I don't."

"What do you mean, you don't? If I was your disciple and I came to you asking the meaning of that verse, is that all you'd tell me?"

"I don't have any disciples."

Theophilus, on the point of explosion, knotted his hands together to stop them from striking out blindly. "But IF you had a disciple—"

"One reason I don't have disciples," Poemen said, "is because I simply don't feel myself competent to answer questions like that. I can talk about the passions, and how to fight them, and the ascetic way of life. But those other things…" He shook his head sadly. "I just don't have the depth for that. Sorry."

"On the contrary," Theophilus ground out. "I think you're an extremely clever man pretending to be a fool. But look out! You and all your friends in Scetis who think you're a law unto yourselves. I know you, all of you, I know who you all are. I shall make you bow down! Every last one of you. I shall make you accept the Church's yoke!"

And with a swirl of his vestments he was off, stalking away into the smoke and confusion he himself had created.

Poemen stayed on his knees, still recovering from the strange catechism to which the Archbishop had subjected him. Aimed at trapping him in some heresy, of course, and involving him in the same fate as the Tall Brothers. And, he had not seen his replies as clever subterfuges; he genuinely did not know the answers to the questions Theophilus had asked. If he had dared to be completely honest, he would have said that perhaps no one knew the answers. Not because he lacked humility, no, he knew all too well that there were countless minds, in the Church and doubtless out of it, far subtler and more perceptive than his own. He simply believed there were things beyond any human understanding. And he did not see why it was necessary to understand them. Could you not love and worship God and His mysteries without slicing Him up and spreading Him out as if He were a chunk of meat on a butcher's block?

Gazing around him he suddenly noticed, borne aloft amidst the smoke, burning scraps of paper. One blackened but still partly unburned fragment landed only a foot or two away from him, and he saw to his horror that it was a page of the Bible. *They're burning the Holy Scriptures*, he thought, hardly able to believe what he was seeing, but knew immediately that the act was not necessarily a deliberate one. If they fired the church and the cells of individual monks, they could hardly avoid burning any books placed there.

Though the blasphemy of it still made his soul curl up in distress, he could not resist reaching out to pick up and read the half-burned fragment.

How ironic if it were Philippians 2.7! No, it was Ezekiel 19.13-14. A finger of ice curdled his neck with gooseflesh as he read:

"Now it is planted in the desert
in a dry and waterless land.
The stem of the vine caught fire,
fire burned up its branches and its fruit.
The branches will never again be..."

Be what? Strong? Whole? The writing dissolved in ashes that crumbled at Poemen's touch. The hairs at the back of his neck were still erect with awe. *God, truly You know everything*, he thought, *down to the smallest and guiltiest secret of our hearts.*

Now the victorious mob was streaming past him in the opposite direction, some of the racetrack ruffians carrying the pathetic loot they had taken from the cells—iron cooking pots, water jars, sheepskin cloaks, the occasional leather-bound volume. Most of them ignored him, but a few jeered, and one of them whacked him across the shoulders with a stick, not with any particular malice, but as a boy might lash out playfully at a fence post or tree trunk that happened to stand in his path. Though the blow was not particularly hard, Poemen fell forwards and felt it wisest to remain in a prone position until the last of the mob had gone by.

The night wind that had fanned the flames died down, and day began to dawn, though its onset was retarded by the blanket of smoke that now hung over the settlement. By this time the noise had abated considerably, and over its background Poemen was able to distinguish a loud booming voice coming from the direction of the church. The voice was reading a long list of names. Puzzled at first, Poemen suddenly realized that it could only be a list of the monks and hermits who were being expelled from Nitria—probably from Egypt. Theophilus had said he knew everything that went on there, and Poemen didn't doubt that for a moment. It stood to reason that his spies would have compiled a list of everyone with Origenist sympathies.

Poemen listened for his own name, but did not hear it. Of course he might have missed it at the beginning, but he doubted whether the Sly Fox, at this stage, would try to expel hermits from Scetis. No matter what he did in Nitria, ascetics who wanted to turn a blind eye could always say to themselves, well, they were getting awfully slack over there, they probably had it coming to them. But if he started attacking other communities, he ran the risk of them all uniting against him.

The voice stopped at last, and the background noises too gradually died away. By now day had dawned, and soon the slant rays of the sun cut through the smoke-clouds which, obedient to the breeze, began to drift off southwards. Rising and looking around him, Poemen saw blackened walls but no flames— all the fires seemed to have burned themselves out. A young hermit he did not recognize was picking his way towards him.

"They've gone," the hermit said. "We can get them out now.

"Get who out?" Poemen asked innocently.

The other stared back at him, dumbfounded. "You know perfectly well who."

"I haven't the faintest idea what you're talking about."

"Are you mad or something? The Tall Brothers!"

"Well, I've no idea what happened to them," Poemen said, perfectly straight-faced.

"They're right under your feet, man," the stranger snapped. "I know, because I was here when you put them there. You really don't know who I am?"

"Frankly, no."

"I'm Mark. Ammonias' disciple."

"Forgive me," Poemen said sincerely. "My memory's not what it was. I thought you might be one of Theophilus' spies."

"You see what he's done," Mark said resentfully. "Made us all suspicious of one another." He bent down, groped in the dust for the lid of the well, and started to pull it aside.

"Wait!" Poemen exclaimed. "It could be a trap."

"How?"

"He could sneak back."

Mark shook his head. "No way. I talked to some of them. He's paying them by the day, and you know what he's like about money. They're off to Hermopolis, and if they're not back in the city by midnight it's another day he owes them for. Anyway, he probably thinks someone tipped us off and we're halfway to Palestine by now."

"Was your name on the list?" Poemen asked.

"Sure."

"So why didn't he stay to make sure you all left?"

"I've told you why," Mark said, in the tone of restrained impatience young men use when their elders seem slow on the uptake. "In any case, we have a week to get out of Egypt. If we're caught after that, we can be arrested and thrown into jail. Orders of the Prefect. He didn't have to stay."

Poemen, though still uneasy, had to be satisfied with that. He watched while Mark removed the lid, uncoiled the rope he had hidden under his tunic and threw it down. One by one Isidore and the Tall Brothers scrambled out.

"What happened?" Ammonias asked.

Poemen started to speak, but Mark with his brisk businesslike air cut across him, gesturing at the burned and blackened walls around him as he spoke.

"Was anyone killed?" Isidore asked.

"Only one that I know of. Young guy, just joined us. They fired the tower when nobody would come out—thought all of you were in there. The others jumped for it. He was too scared."

"You mean he was burned alive?" Ammonias asked in horror.

"Afraid so."

"May God protect his soul!"

There was a moment's silence while they all prayed with lowered heads. After a moment, Ammonias said, "We had better leave right away."

A murmur of agreement came from the others. "Where will you go?" Poemen asked.

"Sinai first, I guess."

"I wonder if that's far enough," Poemen murmured.

"We'll go to Ultima Thule if we have to," Ammonias said stoutly. "There must be somewhere in the world where the Sly Fox's writ doesn't run."

They said their farewells there and then, next to the wellhead, for the Tall Brothers would travel due east across the delta while Poemen returned to Scetis. It was a touching moment for the Shepherd. He had grown fond of the Tall Brothers—their theology was too rarified for his taste, but he respected them for their steadfastness and their singleness of heart. He knew, and they surely did also, that they would never see one another again in this world.

He felt relieved, rather than hurt, that in the confusion of the moment they had forgotten to thank him for saving them from the wrath of Theophilus; this would only have made him feel uncomfortable. Thanks feeds the vainglory latent in every soul, makes it all too easy for one to think what a fine fellow one was, how courageous, how resourceful. And from such seemingly innocent feelings there could grow a great bush of self-satisfaction, and the bush would bear fruit of lordliness, impatience, intolerance of those deemed less able.

It was really nothing, he told himself. I mean, wasn't it just what anyone would do?

Chapter 19

Zachary's affair with Vibia continued to sputter on. He was bored with her now, but she clung to him. Not, he suspected, because of any feeling for him. She had developed an insatiable appetite for gifts, and a way, when he refused, of making sly remarks about his meanness that drove him, in a fury, to buy her what she wanted, if only to shut her up.

"Just drop her," Cellius urged him. "Tell her you're through, it doesn't work anymore, the old magic is gone. I can set you up with a beauty, half her age, and breasts like ripe melons..."

"You mean squishy?"

"Very funny. Unripe melons, then. Eyes like amethysts. Hair like...well, great hair. Dancer. Come to the theater tonight, get a look at her, judge for yourself."

Zachary went; he had nothing better to do. In the clear summer night the open-air amphitheater was packed. Cellius pointed her out in the fifth number. She couldn't dance, she just gyrated her half-clothed body more or less in time with the music, but the audience whistled and stood on their seats, and when she left the stage, a solid block of Green supporters in the higher seats set up one of their rhythmic handclapping routines and kept it going until the troupe came back for an encore.

Then there was a comic sketch, two men and a third in drag with a colossally tall blonde wig. One of the two men acted like he was half-asleep all the time, shuffling around the stage with his mouth half-open. He was obviously the husband of the drag queen, who alternated between berating him for his incompetence (including his impotence) and passionately kissing a handful of chicken bones, wrapped in a cloth, which she assured the audience were the bones of the holy martyr St. Pudenda of Stupromundum. Then the third actor stole onstage with a gross excess of caution, rolling his eyes at the drag queen, leering at the audience, and jeering contemptuously at the open-mouthed one, who appeared totally oblivious of him. The audience was going wild, even Cellius was bouncing up and down on his seat, screaming with hysterical laughter.

Zachary didn't see it as all that funny.

"You don't get it?" Cellius asked incredulously. "The one that drools all the time, that's the Emperor, everyone knows he's two bricks short of a load. The tranny is the Empress Eudoxia. And the third guy, that's Count John, they say he's the real father of the heir to the throne."

"And they allow this?"

"How can they stop it? No one's said who they're supposed to be. So shut up and listen, this is great stuff."

Count John had approached Eudoxia and was pinching her padded boobs and groping her in full view of Arcadius. Eudoxia squealed coyly—"Not now, darling, wait till it's his beddy-bye time!"—and tried unsuccessfully to dodge him, clutching her clothful of chicken-bones to her bosom. Count John whipped up her skirt and there popped out an enormous artificial phallus, bobbing and quivering like a live thing. The audience shrieked uncontrollably.

Suddenly a trumpet sounded. A herald had come out by the edge of the stage, accompanied by a uniformed official. The characters onstage froze in awkward postures and fell silent. Behind the official, almost hidden by a low wall, Zachary could make out the helmets of Roman troops. The trumpet blew a second time. The tumult in the vast half-circle of seats gradually died down.

The official began to make his announcement. The theater was closed until further notice. The audience should leave quietly, without making any...

That was as far as he got. The higher seats erupted as the Greens claque and most of the rest of the audience came pouring down the steep steps of the aisles. The herald had already run for it. The official, quickly rolling the papyrus of his announcement, made to follow him at a more decorous pace. A cohort of troops came trotting out from behind the low wall, their short swords drawn. Cellius grabbed Zachary by the arm and pulled him to his feet. "Let's get the hell out of here!"

Luckily their seats were in the front row on the side furthest from where the troops had entered. They ran across a corner of the stage and alongside the low building that housed the performers' dressing-rooms. Behind them they heard confused shouts and screams, the clash of wood on metal, metal on metal as the theater mob tried to overwhelm the troops by sheer numbers. Cellius, who obviously knew his way around here, opened a door and led Zachary through several small rooms and corridors filled with hysterical artists of a wide variety of races and sexes. They literally ran into the girl, Cellius grabbed her and they left via another doorway and an alley down which other members of the audience were fleeing. Two blocks away was a tavern where theater folk habitually hung out. They sank, relieved, onto an angled bench round a corner table.

The girl, whose name at least for professional purposes was Ariadne, expressed her gratitude for their rescue. She couldn't be much more than fifteen, Zachary decided, though she handled herself as if she had been around for more years than that. She was as lovely as Cellius had claimed, but there was an emptiness about her—she could make herself whatever you wanted her to be, precisely because she had no center of her own Suddenly, after weeks without even thinking of her, the memory of Leila flashed into Zachary's mind. The contrast was absolute: Leila's undistinguished looks and the hard, quirky core of her being. He felt a sudden pang of loss—a loss that the expensive wine Cellius had ordered might temporarily alleviate, but could not entirely dispel. He tried to look as if he were enjoying himself.

They gossiped aimlessly about personalities and current scandals, cooling down gradually from the excitement of the riot. Or, at least the two men gossiped. Ariadne composed her face, arms and upper body into a stylized listening posture and threw in an occasional, marginally relevant remark. They speculated about what would happen to the principals in the Arcadius sketch— a whipping, for sure, perhaps a few years in the mines, though an excessive punishment would rouse too much sympathy and rebound on the heads of the administration. They talked of the insulting sermon John Chrysostom, the new Archbishop of Constantinople, was supposed to have preached about the Empress Eudoxia, the real one, that was, comparing her to Jezebel, and wondered whether even someone as popular as John seemed to be could get away with it. Then, the Prefect of Egypt, Archelaus, was supposed to be having an affair with a married woman, nobody seemed to know who—that, however, did not deter them from guessing. Nor was that the Prefect's only problem. It turned out that the parents of the young hermit burned to death in Nitria were influential people and had lodged a strong complaint to the Prefect's office. Theophilus of course had insisted the man had died as a result of the monks' own violence, and the Prefect, between a rock and a hard place, was desperately seeking to pacify both parties.

As they talked they were joined by other friends or acquaintances who had escaped from the theater, and soon seven or eight of them were crowded around the table, talking in animated groups. A serious man with a neatly trimmed beard buttonholed Zachary and said, speaking of this Nitria business, what did he as a former hermit think about it? Zachary could not recall seeing the man before and wondered where he had gotten the hermit story, since he himself never publicized it. Smelling a Caesarium spy, he said merely that it was a bad business all round. Yes, said the serious man, they're hunting the Origenists throughout Asia, the Archbishop has threatened to excommunicate anyone who has anything to do with them. They're old and sick, some of them, he's hounding them to their deaths. Zachary said how sad it was, refusing to be drawn further. And what do you think about Origen, anyway, the man asked.

At this point Zachary felt Ariadne tugging at his sleeve, glanced sideways, noted her pouting expression and was relieved to find any reason to excuse himself. "What's the matter?" he asked her.

"Do you really have to talk about all this boring stuff?" she murmured into his ear.

"No," he said. "I guess not."

"Is it true that you're very rich?"

"Rich beyond the dreams of avarice," Zachary said lightly, fascinated by the frankness of her greed.

"I like rich people. Rich people are so much nicer than poor people, don't you think?"

"I really hadn't thought about it."

"Have you ever been to Constantinople?"

"No, never," he said, thinking, she's got a mind like a grasshopper. More wine kept appearing on the table, he had no idea who was ordering it.

"Don't you want to go?"

"Not particularly."

She made a spoilt-little-girl face with such practiced skill Zachary could only assume that someone somewhere must have told her how cute it looked. "I'm longing to go."

"What on earth for?"

"Oh—to see the court, and all those fabulous ceremonies, and all the clothes they wear, it's so provincial here. Don't you think it's awfully provincial here?"

"What'd you expect?" Zachary said. "It's a province."

She clapped her hands gleefully. "You're right! You know, I'd never thought of that."

He stared at her intently to see if she was making fun of him, but she was not. She was perfectly serious.

"Take me there," she said, squeezing his arm and pressing one of her unripe melons against his side.

"To Constantinople? Sorry. I'm much too busy."

"You said you were rich!" Her voice was hurt, reproachful.

"I wouldn't be rich if I didn't work at it."

Hand and melon were withdrawn. "I thought you meant really rich. Really rich is where you do absolutely nothing but sit around all day and give orders and people just bring you things."

"So I'm not rich," Zachary said. "At all."

More wine appeared. Even if he did not finally go home with her, Zachary foresaw yet another late night and another bleary-eyed morning with fogged brain and carpet tongue. Why do I do this, he asked himself, is this really what I want out of life? This light, effortless but ultimately pointless talk? These drinks that give you the illusion that your spirit is soaring, freed from the limitations of normal flesh, but of course it is an illusion, as you relearn each next morning? This sex-on-demand from someone who you wouldn't really care very much if you never saw again? Pleasures that turn to ashes the moment they are tasted. Leaving only the desire to repeat them in the insane hope that, next time, maybe, they would become real and would last...

But if not this, what is it that I want?

Zachary could not answer that question, had not been able to answer it since the collapse of the temple in the desert oasis. He had thought, after the years in Tebtynnis, that he had recovered from that cataclysmic, soul-shaking event. He knew know that his recovery, like so much else in his life, had been illusory. He was still drifting rudderless, ignorant of his true destiny, while his allotted span of life whirled past him irrecoverably.

He was about to complain of a headache and leave when a word spoken on the other side of him caught in his mind and made him say to the serious bearded person, "Excuse me, what was that you just said?"

The man, who had been deep in conversation with Cellius, looked up abruptly, startled.

"I'm sorry?"

"You said a name just then. You mentioned a name."

"Celia," the man said. "You know someone of that name?"

"Who's Celia?" Ariadne asked. "Is she famous?"

"Zachary knows her all right," Cellius said dryly. "Knew her, I should say. In more senses than one."

Why does the mere mention of her name have such power over me? Zachary thought. *Why has my heart suddenly begun to pound as if it would force its way out of my chest? Why do I feel as if I can't breathe, as if I were suffocating, when it was all so long ago?*

"I was just telling Cellius," the serious man said, "something someone told me about her the other day. But it sounded so ridiculous I really couldn't believe it, I mean nobody who knew her could believe it. I think someone made it up, for a joke."

"What was it?"

The man made a dismissive gesture. "It's so dumb I'd really rather not repeat it."

"Do tell!" Ariadne cried, clapping her hands together. "I love dumb stories. The dumber the better."

"One day you may even understand one," Cellius said nastily. But, he did not take his eyes from Zachary's face. He was staring at Zachary quizzically, with frank interest, waiting to see how he would react. Zachary's knuckles went white. "Just go ahead and tell it anyway," he said in a hoarse, unsteady voice.

The man looked at him as much as to say, hey, where are you coming from? "Just somebody told me that she'd become a nun."

Chapter 20

Celia was living, according to what the man had heard, in a town called Panephysis. All he knew about this town was that it lay in the Delta somewhere. Even Cellius, who in Zachary's experience had never once confessed ignorance, did not seem to have any precise knowledge of its whereabouts. Zachary was not able to learn any details of the institution within which she was lodged, save that it was reputed to be "very strict".

Zachary never doubted for a moment that the story was true. Why would anyone invent it? And there was a dramatic irony in the mirror-image trajectories of their lives—hers from the pursuit of worldly pleasures into asceticism, his from asceticism into the pursuit of worldly pleasures—that, for him, placed the stamp of conviction on the story. If it wasn't true, at least it ought to be true. And he knew that something inside him would never rest until he found out whether it was true or not.

The wonder of it, and a persistent feeling that the course of her life ran in a purer and truer direction than his, stayed with him during the days that followed. He eventually found someone who knew the town and told him it was a strange place, way out on the north-easternmost lip of the delta. It was surrounded by an area that the sea had once overrun and then, retreating, had left sterile, a waste of barren salt flats that even in bright sunlight gave off a melancholy air.

What would have possessed her to choose such a place, Zachary wondered—was it pure chance or had she chosen it deliberately, in atonement for her former life?

He asked his informant if there was a nunnery there. Well, that he couldn't say for certain. Certainly there were hermits there. Hermits, in a town? Well, you should see the town. So there could be a nunnery there too, those things were springing up all over the place and if they went on at this rate, there'd soon be no women left to have babies, the informant complained. But since the end of the world was scheduled for the year 500, maybe it wouldn't matter all that much.

"You want to go look for her, don't you?" Cellius said accusingly one day, after Zachary had maintained an unusually long silence.

Zachary came out of his reverie with a start. Yes, he admitted to himself for the first time, I do want it. Always this uncertainty in his heart, this lack of trust in his own feelings, so that other people had to tell him what he felt! To hide his confusion, he said, "And what about you? You still fantasize about her?"

"I do what?"

"Fantasize about her. You told me you did. That first night after we met again."

Cellius stared at him, and Zachary had the uncanny feeling, not for the first time, that there was no continuous Cellius, that he recreated himself from moment to moment, said whatever seemed appropriate to say.

"I did? What did I tell you?"

Zachary remembered it vividly.

"That if you found her penniless in the street you'd ask her to give you what she gave to some stranger, and if she wouldn't you'd throw her a coin and walk away."

"I said that? Then I expect I did," Cellius grumbled. "Certainly the part about the coin, that rings true. Low denomination, naturally. If there's any such left by then. But frankly I wouldn't cross the street to go looking for her, let alone to a hole like Panephysis. You're the sentimental type. I'm not."

Zachary did not dispute this judgement.

"Why don't you just go, then?" Cellius asked. "Get it out of your system. Go on, the break will do you good. And you might be fit to live with again once you've done it."

"Adjari is coming from Taprobane any time now." Adjari was the Indian merchant from whom they bought spices.

"So?"

"We owe him, oh, several thousand solidi, must be, by this time. Ask Ptolemy."

"No problem. I can settle with him."

"Not if I'm not here."

Cellius smiled engagingly. "I said no problem. Just leave the strong room key, I can take care of it."

An alarm bell went off in Zachary's brain. He realized later it wasn't the words that had triggered it. It was the smile. Cellius hadn't really needed to smile, not right on top of that jarring moment when his guard had gone down and Zachary had glimpsed for a moment the shifting sands of his soul.

"I'd better stay," he said.

"What's the matter?" Cellius asked, just a touch of reproach in his tone, but handled lightly, humorously, as if he couldn't quite believe what he was hearing. "You don't trust me?"

"It's not that." Zachary improvised quickly—he could be wrong, and in any case he didn't want to offend Cellius. "Just anything could happen, you could be robbed, killed, you could drop dead in the street and someone just take the key off you."

"Charming imagination you've got," Cellius said dryly. "In any case, any of those things could just as easily happen to you."

"I know that," Zachary admitted. "But then it's my responsibility."

Cellius shrugged. He seemed unwilling to press the issue. "But if you don't go pretty soon, you know, you won't make it."

"Why not?"

"When the Nile floods, Panephysis is an island. Big boats can't make it through the shallows, and little ones, well, the owners just won't take you that far."

The vague suspicions that Cellius had awoken began to harden and take shape in Zachary's mind. How come Cellius suddenly knew so much about a place whose very whereabouts had been unknown to him a few days before? He must have researched it.

"Why are you so suddenly anxious for me to go?" Zachary asked, trying to keep his tone casual.

Cellius gave a shamefaced smile. "I can be curious, too."

"But you just said you wouldn't cross the street to see her."

Cellius sighed. "All right. You've made your point. I try to be hard-headed, cynical, man-of-the-world about her, but…Well, Celia—you have to admit she'd be an event in anyone's life."

"That's true."

"Someone you can't shake off just like that."

"And you'd like a first-hand report of this miraculous transformation? Is that why you've been bugging me to go?"

Cellius nodded, shamefaced.

You're lying, Zachary thought. *And you're nowhere near as smart as you think you are. You've underestimated me, all along, you think that because I followed the eremitic path I'm a holy innocent, I can be duped like any fool. Well, I still don't know quite what you've got in mind, but forewarned is forearmed.*

One problem solved itself. Adjari appeared the following day and was paid. It seemed unlikely that in the next few days they would need cash. And without access to the strong room, what could Cellius do? There was only the one key, and that had been in Zachary's possession ever since he took over the business. Besides, if Cellius had somehow managed to filch it from him long enough to have a copy made, why would he have suggested looking after it in Zachary's absence, and risked raising his suspicions?

Even so, he called aside Ptolemy, his head clerk, and warned him to be more than normally vigilant during his employer's absence. If he found anyone, anyone at all without exception, behaving suspiciously in any way, Ptolemy should have the guards seize that person, eject him immediately from the premises and make sure he did not re-enter them. He was careful not to mention Cellius by name, but something about Ptolemy's reaction—his lack of surprise, a knowing look that flickered across his stolid face—made Zachary think that his suspicions were probably shared. Ptolemy was nobody's fool, he had had ample opportunity to get Cellius' measure, and Zachary had sensed for some time that he had reservations about the Roman.

So why not go now, rather than any other time? For Zachary was convinced he would never have peace of mind until he knew for certain what had become of her.

Chapter 21

The light, two-wheeled carriage rolled eastwards along the abominable road. It had been going for many hours now, and Zachary's buttocks were sore from bouncing on spring less boards as the iron tires of the wheels slipped into deep ruts or jarred on boulders. It was still broad afternoon, but the sunlight, sieved through a layer of high cloud, gave a lugubrious look to the flat marshes with their sparse reeds and barren mud banks rimmed with white encrustations of salt. Off to the north, towards the invisible sea, the cloud-cover grew gradually denser until the sky above the horizon looked like one enormous, three-day-old bruise. In all this wilderness, there was no sign of habitation.

"How far now?" Zachary asked.

"Be there by dark," the taciturn driver assured him.

Another three hours, at least, Zachary thought. Was he mad, to be doing this? What did he hope to gain from it?

He truly did not know, but something. Something surely, he felt, of inestimable value to him. Her fate and his were entangled in some way that he had not yet understood. If he could understand it, he felt that the full meaning of his life would finally become clear to him.

But there was more to it than that. He just wanted to see her, one more time. He knew he could expect no more than that. He knew he might not get even that, she might refuse to see him, as so many ascetics refused to see significant persons from their former lives. In her case, you could understand that. There were too many things she would not want to be reminded of.

Two nights before, on the eve of departure, he had dreamed he was back walking on the riverbank where Leila had died, and a flock of birds suddenly rose from the grass at his feet and went whirring away over the water. Quail. Quail were a bad omen for a journey. If you believed in that kind of rubbish.

The pale shadow of the carriage, the only shadow in that flat treeless landscape, was lengthening in front of them by the time Zachary began to make out, silhouetted against the bruised horizon sky, something that looked like an uneven lump of rock. This unique pimple on the scenery expanded slowly as they drew nearer, gradually resolving itself into a tiny walled town, raised like an island above barren salt-flats and shallow, stagnant pools.

As they approached more closely, he began to notice signs of wear–a roof almost stripped of its tiles, a tower decapitated in some storm and its irregular brick stump never repaired. Even the town gate hung at an angle from a single rusty hinge, but two old men, straining with it, having to lift it because of the broken hinge, were struggling to shut it. Against what? Who would want to come out here, and what would they have worth stealing, anyway?

The driver wheeled the carriage around and stopped abruptly, facing back in the direction they had come.

"You're not driving in?" Zachary asked, startled, and without waiting for a reply called out to the two old men, "Hey there, just hold it a minute."

"No," the driver said. "I'm going home."

"At night?"

Wordlessly, with his whip, the driver tapped the two carriage lanterns, ugly iron boxes with wafer-thin strips of mica in front that hung either side of his vehicle.

"But I thought you..." Zachary's voice tailed off. He realized he had forgotten to make any arrangement with the driver about returning, he had been in such a turmoil of mind that he had simply assumed the fellow, after carrying him all day, would surely wait for him. "Look," he said, "I won't be here more than a day, just wait for me, take me back. I'll make it worth your while."

The driver shook his head. "Sorry. Flood's coming."

"And?"

"I don't want to risk getting trapped here, is all," the driver said in the longest speech he had uttered all day. "You can't blame me. I got regular customers back there."

"So how do I get home?" Zachary asked.

"Rent something here."

"Is that possible?"

"Sure," the man said vaguely and unconvincingly.

Zachary shrugged, seeing it was useless to argue. He descended from the carriage, lifting the bag with his belongings—he hadn't wanted any servant to accompany him on this trip—off the seat and paying the driver, who curtly touched his forelock with his whip in acknowledgment and immediately set his two horses in motion.

Zachary walked towards the two old men, who had set the gate down and were leaning on it, staring at him with frank curiosity—he had the impression that not many travelers came this way. They exchanged greetings, friendly on his part, cool and cautious on theirs. "Is there an inn here?" he asked.

The two men looked at each other. One of them laughed. The other said. "Well, sort of."

"What do you mean, sort of?

"Well, if there was any place else to go, I wouldn't recommend it."

Zachary asked its whereabouts and was given vague directions. He had already squeezed through the gap between the partly-closed gate and the wall before he turned abruptly and asked, "Why do you bother?"

They gaped at him.

"With the gate? Who'd want to do you harm here?

"Saracens," one of them muttered.

"Out here?"

"We're not that far from Sinai," the other said, and Zachary noticed a slight trickle of drool from his almost toothless mouth. "They came once, didn't they?" he said to his companion.

"Ah, they did that, all right."

"Forty year ago, weren't it?"

"More like fifty. Oh, they didn't half make a mess of things, they did."

"So you see," the first old man said. "We got to be careful."

"Of course," Zachary said. Then, "there's a nunnery here?"

The two men exchanged startled looks.

"A nunnery. You know what a nunnery is?"

They blinked, puzzled; shook their heads.

Morons, Zachary thought, *and senile too. No point explaining to them. The innkeeper will be sure to know.* He walked on into the town, which seemed unnaturally quiet for the time of day. Its streets had been paved once but the stones were cracked and broken, treacherous to the foot—he was glad it wasn't dark yet. There seemed to be hardly anyone about. He glimpsed figures across squares or up alleyways that vanished immediately as he approached, almost as if they were deliberately avoiding him. The houses, half of them obviously vacant, were falling into ruin: window-frames empty, door-jambs crumbling. The place was a ghost town. Either the Saracen raid or the sea's invasion, or a combination of the two, had ruined it. Small wonder hermits had begun to colonize it.

He found the inn at last, thanks to a faded sign on which the image of a large rooster could still be made out. The door was ajar so he entered, wincing a little at the faint smell of mingled mold and urine that assailed his nostrils. He called out, but at first no one answered him, the place seemed deserted. Then he heard shuffling feet and a man in a grease-stained tunic and apron confronted him.

"This is an inn, isn't it?" he asked.

The man nodded.

"You have a room?" The question seemed superfluous, the place looked as if it hadn't seen another guest in months.

The man nodded again and took Zachary's bag.

"Can I get something to eat here?"

The man shook his head.

"Where, then?"

The man pointed down the street, then carried Zachary's bag up a narrow staircase. Following him, Zachary came out into a narrow corridor, open on one side to reveal a cramped, cobbled courtyard beneath. On the other was a row of doors, giving onto a series of narrow cubicles with tiny windows to the street. Most of their doors stood ajar and a single glance sufficed to show they were completely empty. His host stepped to one side and signed for Zachary to enter one of them. Inside this was a narrow bed with a filthy, torn mattress, a chamber pot and a candle stand, nothing else. The man lit the candle, it was already hard to see in the room.

"Is this the best you have?" Zachary asked. The man shrugged.

"Can you tell me if there's a nunnery in town?"

For answer, the man opened his mouth wide and held his jaws apart with both hands. Zachary felt a wave of nausea rising in his stomach, and turned away. The man's tongue had been cut out. In the hollow, stinking cavern of his mouth, there was nothing but a raw, scarred, swollen stump.

Fighting the nausea, Zachary sat down on the bed as the man closed his mouth, turned, and went back downstairs. He had not sat there for more than a moment when he sprang to his feet. He had felt something moving in the mattress. He examined it, and indeed it was alive with bedbugs. How do they live, he wondered, if nobody stays here? Do they suck one another's blood? He took the candle and ran it over the mattress, not caring about the blobs of hot wax that fell on it, not caring even if he set it alight, it would be no great loss. Indeed, the material singed here and there as bugs popped in the candle-flame's heat and others raced desperately for cover. He continued until he could see no more—though he did not doubt there were more, concealed within the entrails of the mattress and then repeated the procedure with the ratty blanket.

When that was done, and it took some time, he made his way downstairs and groped along the unlit street outside. A block away he found a hole-in-the-wall tavern with two men who looked and smelled like camel-drivers eating bowls of rancid stew. They glanced at him suspiciously and then returned to their muttered conversation in a tongue unknown to him. Zachary ordered wine, which was undrinkable, and the stew, which turned out to be the only thing on the menu. The waiter, or cook, or owner—probably all three, no one else was in sight—picked his teeth with the blade of a small pocket-knife and said well, what exactly did you mean by a nunnery? Women monks? One or two of the hermits had women, or were women, he believed.

But you mean like a proper place, with abbots and stuff? Not as he knew of. Mind you, he didn't know everyone in town. Didn't care to, there was some you'd prefer not to. Best thing he could tell Zachary was to wait until the morning and then ask one of the hermits, too late to do anything that night. Ask for Joseph, he was easier to get on with than some of the others.

That was all. The camel-drivers paid and left and Zachary finished his meal alone by the light of a single guttering oil-lamp. From the kitchen came sounds of a man's and a woman's voice alternating, rancorous but taking their time about it, as if in the middle of some argument that had begun long before Zachary's arrival and would continue long after his departure. He too paid and left. There was no point in stumbling around in the dark so he returned to the inn. The door had been locked during his absence and he had to bang for many minutes before his mute host unfastened it. The candle in his room had gone out and he had no means of relighting it. He stretched out on the bed, frustrated and depressed, to find that indeed he had not succeeded in killing all the bedbugs.

He was tired from his long journey and despite the bugs he soon began to feel drowsy. He remembered nothing more until the first grey light leaked through his cracked, cobwebbed window and it was day again. He lost no time in inquiring for Joseph. There were still only a few people around, but so great was their talent for misdirection that mid-¬morning had almost arrived by the time he found himself knocking on a newly-repaired door in a narrow building that backed onto the town wall, and heard a quavery old-man's voice answering him.

"Joseph?"

"What do you want?"

"A word for my salvation," Zachary said, thinking that if Joseph was one of those hermits who hated strangers, this approach had the best chance of working.

The door was unbarred, and Zachary saw a stooped, limping man of frail physique with a bald crown covered in age-spots and surrounded by silvery wisps of hair. Without looking at Zachary, the hermit hobbled back to the center of his barren cell, said "Let us pray" and without more ado fell to his knees. Zachary, used to the more casual manners of Scetis, hesitated for a moment and then followed suit as he was clearly expected to do. He realized with a twinge of guilt that this was the first time he had even gone through the motions of prayer since he was carried unconscious from the desert. And to what God could he now pray? The God whom he had rejected, from whom he had been in flight, all these years? What would those prayers be worth, to that

God? He did not know.

He repeated the Lord's Prayer, mechanically, because he still remembered it and because he found no words of his own to offer. The thought of praying that he might find Celia flitted briefly through his mind, but to ask favors from a God he had rejected seemed insulting and he dismissed the thought.

After a while Joseph rose, his joints creaking, and said, "Well, what can I do for you, my child?"

"I was told there was a nunnery here, Father."

The hermit was slow in answering. Zachary had the impression that all his bodily processes had slowed down, that it took a long time to get messages from his ears to his brain and from his brain back to his mouth.

"A nunnery, my son? What would you want with a nunnery?"

I can hardly say, because an old lover of mine is there, Zachary thought. "I have a sister," he said. "Somebody told me my sister was in a nunnery here."

The old man wet his lips and shook his head slightly. Zachary wasn't sure if it meant a negative or merely the palsy of age until Joseph said, "there's no nunnery here."

"Has there ever been?"

"Never to my knowledge, child, and I've been here..." The cataracted eyes rolled up as he calculated, "Oh, more years than you've been alive."

"But there are some women here."

The old man cupped his ear with a blue-veined hand so thin it was almost transparent.

"Some women, Father. Here in Panephysis. Someone told me there were."

"I have nothing to do with women, my son."

Zachary curbed his mounting irritation, it wasn't the old man's fault if his brain and his senses were failing. "Father," he said softly but urgently, "I'm trying to find my sister. It's very important, it's," his mind improvised quickly, "an inheritance, to do with an inheritance, she has to decide what to do about it."

The bleary eyes watered but the mind seemed to be back on track. "How old is your sister?"

"Same age as me..." *No*, he thought. *Impossible unless we're twins*. "...I mean, just a year younger than me."

Again the old man shook his head. "No, my child. We do indeed have two females among us but they are old, one almost as old as I am. I'm sorry I can't help you."

"Think nothing of it, Father, I'm sorry I wasted your time." Zachary had turned to leave and was halfway through the door when he heard the quavery voice saying. "My son, what of your soul?"

"What about my soul?"

"Those who come here always ask advice of me, for their soul's sake," the old man said in a tone of hurt and disappointment, and Zachary realized that for the old man's sake, not for his own, he had to stay. *If this one's the easiest to deal with*, he thought, *I wonder what the others are like.*

"Consider the lusts of the flesh, my child," Joseph said when his visitor was safely seated. "Is not your soul tormented by the lusts of the flesh?"

"Indeed it is, Father. Most dreadfully."

"Ah, what a suffering that is! Not that I remember it, of course. But you must fight them, son, you must gird yourself with the armor of the spirit and fight them…"

It went on for a good half-hour like that: basic-training stuff Zachary had heard a hundred times. He nodded at the right moments, gave all the right responses while his mind was miles away, wondering how and why he had come on this wild-goose chase, what was going wrong in his business back home, where in the world Celia might really be. As the old man wound down he felt in his purse, detached a gold solidus and placed it unobtrusively on the window-ledge. He left bowing, smiling, saying how edified he had been by the good advice. As he closed the door behind him he saw his action had not after all gone unnoticed—the hermit was staring incredulously at the gold piece, his eyes filling with tears.

Now to get out of here as fast as he could.

He went looking for somewhere he could rent a carriage. Again, he was referred from one place to another, fruitlessly. Finally, he decided to try the owner of the eating-house, the only person in the whole place who had halfway made sense.

The man greeted him without seeming to recognize him. *He has so many customers*, Zachary thought. When he stated his business, the man just laughed.

"What's so funny about that?"

"Got a moment?" Zachary nodded, puzzled. "Then follow me. It's well worth seeing, anyway."

Zachary followed up two flights of stairs and came out in what looked like the ruined stump of the brick tower he had seen from the road. At this height, you could see over the rooftops and the city walls to the desolate wastes beyond. But somehow, today, the scene looked different. It took Zachary a second or two to figure out, everything was so featureless, all the colors so neutral, muted. Then he realized that the southern horizon, which should have been land, was a continuous stretch of water, in which the low clouds, reflected, merely gave the illusion of land.

"What the..."

Then his eyes fell from the horizon to the land just beyond the walls. Over it, only a foot or so high, if one could judge from that distance, but with bigger ripples backing it, there came a solid wave of water that moved towards them faster than the speed of a circus chariot. Even as they watched, it broke against a far corner of the walls and spread, obliterating the stagnant pools and salt-encrusted banks, sweeping around the town on either side, surrounding it.

"Mother Nile," his companion sighed with a sound almost of satisfaction. "Quite a sight, eh? Be like that for the next, oh, two to three months."

Chapter 22

By mid-afternoon, Zachary had found that it was still possible, at least in principle, to leave Panephysis. No boatman would take his boat to the nearest dry land—it was too far to row, and while the north wind might blow a sailboat there, it would take prohibitively long to tack one's way back, even if the maritime skills of the inhabitants of Panephysis were up to that. What you did, you rented a boat to row you out to the deep-water channel, a couple of miles away, and then waited for a big boat to come by. How often did they come by? Ah, that you couldn't tell. Might be several in one day, mightn't be any for a week. You took your chances.

Zachary, his skin red and swollen now from the bites of the bugs, rented a boat and an oarsman and tried his luck. The boat sat in the channel, rocking gently in the slight swell that found its way inland from the still-invisible sea. Though the afternoon was cloudy, the still air and high humidity, added to the normal summer heat, made him feel as if he were choking. The boatman, resting on his oars, occasionally pulling on one or the other to keep their bow to the current or stop the boat drifting, tried to ask personal questions and sulked when told to shut up. The light began to fade with no sign of a boat, and Zachary resigned himself to another lonely, barely-edible dinner and another verminous night in that travesty of an inn.

The man in the bar by the theater had said he didn't believe the story about Celia. *I should have listened to him,* Zachary thought. *But I didn't. I didn't like him because I suspected he was one of the Archbishop's spies, and because I didn't like him I ignored his disclaimer. He was only trying to be honest. I ignored his disclaimer but I believed his story because I wanted to, because I found it dramatically appropriate to believe that Celia had forsworn the world, and because I wanted to believe I understood her nature better than he did, saw through the lewd surface of her life to the unrefined gold beneath.*

The next morning, he was up at dawn, and out in the channel shortly thereafter with a more congenial hand at the oars. Now a wind blew, the waters were choppy, even a whitecap or two appeared here and there. Zachary's stomach began to roll in time with the boat. "Better for you, though," his new oarsman said, spotting his discomfort. "If it's like this back here, what'd you think it's like out there? Weather like this, boats that take the coast route will come inside, long as they know the channels. We'll get you something, never you fear."

Within an hour he was proven correct. A sail loomed on the northeastern horizon, bearing down fast. They pulled into the center of the channel and hailed it. Someone threw down a rope. Zachary, with a relief almost as great as he had felt when he first saw the temple in the desert—though then he had been in danger of death and now of mere discomfort—hurled his bag on board and scrambled up after it, helped by several pairs of anonymous hands. Already, when he stood erect, the boatman was twenty or thirty yards astern of them, waving cheerily. Zachary waved back, then stared at the receding outline of the town, thinking automatically, thank God that's over, that I'll never have to see that place again.

A man was leaning on the bulwark beside him, a tall man, in his fifties, good-looking in a rough-hewn way, who's clothes as well as his manner showed he was no sailor. "Where are you headed?" the stranger asked.

"Alexandria," Zachary answered. "Is this your boat?"

"It is, as a matter of fact, and that's where we're going."

"Tell me how much I owe you for the passage."

The stranger waved a dismissive hand. "I don't normally take passengers, but I felt sorry for you out there. Panephysis is a ghastly hole. I went once; once is enough."

"Most kind of you," Zachary murmured.

"Besides, your face looked familiar—sure I've seen you around somewhere."

Zachary felt the same way about the stranger. They probed one another's memories for a few moments, then the stranger said, "Sorry, stupid of me, I should have introduced myself, Cleon of Alexandria, merchant, wholesale and retail."

"I've heard about you," Zachary said. "I'm surprised we haven't met before. You know a friend of mine, I believe—a Roman, name of Cellius?"

"Of course! Of course!" Cleon seemed delighted by the discovery. "Charming fellow. Very amusing. But then you must be…"

"Zachary. You probably knew my father."

"Indeed I did, God rest his soul. I attended his funeral, could that have been where…"

"No," Zachary said. "I was out of town at the time." He didn't want to get into that any more than he had to.

"Well, anyway, this is really extraordinary!" Cleon said, embracing him vigorously. "I mean to meet out here for the very first time, of all places… Except I can't get it out of my head that it's not the first time. Oh well. It'll come back to me, I'm sure. You know how it is, you rack your brains about something for hours at a stretch, can't think of it to save your life, then you put it to one side and lo and behold out it pops when you least expect it!"

Zachary agreed, smiling a little wanly. He really would have preferred not to have to make conversation, to retire somewhere where he could try to figure out why the failure of his mission had caused him to feel so depressed. What would he have gained if he had met Celia again? He didn't know. Probably nothing. It didn't make sense.

They chatted aimlessly for a while about mutual acquaintances, then Cleon said, "Wait...It's coming back to me...Only you looked different then. Leaner. More sickly, if you'll excuse me saying so. Plus, you were dressed differently—look, I hope you're not offended by the suggestion, but were you ever by any chance a hermit?"

Zachary admitted it.

Cleon's face, animated at the worst of times, lit up. "Now it's really coming back. There were two of you, weren't there, you and another hermit, an older guy..."

"Benjamin."

"...and you'd just pulled down the image of Serapis! Well, I don't mean you two personally, but you were part of that, weren't you? A whole army of you, and I got so drunk that night, that was in the days before I straightened myself out of course...Oh, no wonder I didn't remember you."

"You tried to take us to a brothel," Zachary remembered.

"I did? Oh no!" Cleon laughed shamefacedly. "No, that part I'd completely forgotten, you can see why, trying to get hermits to sin mortally, and me a Christian, too, supposedly. I mean I was one even back then but I just didn't take it seriously enough. It's different now. Plus, if I did happen to do anything like that my wife'd never let me forget it!" He gazed at Zachary anxiously. "Tell me...I didn't—succeed, did I? I mean in getting you to. It's a mortal sin on my soul if I did, I'd have to atone for it..."

Zachary smiled. "We resisted temptation," he said. "That night, anyway."

"Oh, I'm so relieved! That would have been a terrible thing to have on one's conscience, I mean wouldn't it? But since I met my wife, I'm sure you've heard, Cellius is always ribbing me about it, I mean that's why you and I haven't met before. I used to party all the time, when I was in town, I expect Cellius told you, but then somehow ever since I married it's been different, my wife was much more religious than I was, she'd actually been a member of a monastic institution before we met, not here, up the river someplace..."

Zachary felt a sudden flash of intuition. Absurd, impossible.

"What's her name?" he asked.

His voice was so low and choked that Cleon didn't hear him.

"…and naturally one hears jokes, you know, about being henpecked and that sort of thing, but I can assure you it's nothing like that, its…Well it's hard to explain really. If you knew her you'd understand, you really should meet her, I'll invite you for dinner one evening, just you, if that's all right with you, she and Cellius don't exactly…well…. You know how it is, a man's friends, especially ones he knew before he was married, it's always a little…you know, touchy. But it's a funny thing, I've never felt better, physically I mean…"

"What's your wife's name?" Zachary repeated, louder this time.

"…and mentally too, it's surprising how you don't actually miss…Oh. Leila.

"Her name's Leila. Unusual name. Rather a nice one, though, don't you think? Oh yes," he laughed indulgently, "she keeps me in order all right. You bet."

Zachary felt his legs give way under him. He clutched at the bulkhead, while the vast expanse of sunlit floodwater that surrounded them seemed to wheel in a vast circle about his swimming head. But the other seemed not to notice anything wrong.

"Amazing the way we met," he went on. "Just around this time of year as a matter of fact…No, must have been earlier, because I was way up river, in this very same boat as it happens, and the flood had only just started. I remember because we'd put into the side early even though I was in a hurry to get back because it simply wasn't safe, under those conditions. But when this happened it was quite dark, if we hadn't had warning lights hung over the side I'd never have seen anything, but by pure chance I happened to be standing there and watching the water race past me and I remember wondering, yes I actually did wonder this, how long you'd last if you fell in. And then all of a sudden there's this…bundle floating downstream towards me, it never occurred to me it was a person, it looked just like a bundle of brown rags, and so for the hell of it, I beg your pardon, I mean just on a whim I grabbed a boathook and snagged it as it went by."

The lights, Zachary remembered. He had seen lights downstream of him that night without ever really thinking what they might mean. He tried to pull himself upright, he desperately did not want Cleon to notice anything wrong.

"Of course," Cleon went on, "the moment I snagged it I knew it wasn't just rags, I mean I felt the weight under there, right off the reel. It's a wonder the current didn't pull her out of my hands, as it was I almost fell and if my captain hadn't come by at that instant I don't know what might have happened. Anyway, I yelled out to him and between the two of us we managed to get her on board. Unconscious, of course. I thought she was a goner. But my captain said, sometimes an air-bubble can get trapped in their clothes, and to be honest with you, but for Heaven's sake don't ever tell her I told you this, she'd kill me if she ever found out I'd told you, her skirts were way over her head, wrapped around her head, as a matter of fact, so she was stark naked from the waist down. So my captain says, it's always worth a try, and he turns her face down on the deck and gets his knees under her shoulders and just squ-u-u-e-e-ezes her...Well, to cut a long story short, water starts pouring out of her mouth, he squeezes some more, she starts sort of coughing...We took her down below, gave her some wine..."

He turned to face Zachary directly for the first time. "Seems she'd just been walking on the bank and it collapsed on her...Is anything the matter?"

"No. No, I'm fine."

"You look white."

"Well, actually, it's my stomach...I must have eaten something bad in Panephysis."

Cleon sighed reminiscently. "Same thing happened to me. They can't grow anything, everything's shipped in, but boats only stop once in a blue moon so it goes rotten—which reminds me. Time to eat. If I gave you some decent food, think you could hold it down?"

Chapter 23

The wave of euphoria that overwhelmed Zachary, once he fully realized that Leila was still alive, sustained him through the rest of the voyage and indeed until he arrived home.

Somehow, he managed to keep his reaction hidden from Cleon. Much as he would have liked to see Leila again, he knew that for her sake he never could. By what you could only describe as a miracle of God's grace she had been saved from certain death, and by a miracle equally great she had fallen into the hands of a man who, whatever his shortcomings, would at least treat her decently and care for her. Zachary's reappearance in her life could only destroy whatever happiness she had achieved. So when, on their arrival, Cleon pressed him to fix a date when he could have dinner with them, he had begged off, pleaded prior commitments, promised—quite dishonestly—that he would get back to Cleon at the earliest opportunity. He was relieved when he could make his escape.

Still, the mere thought that she still lived, that his failure to save her had not doomed her, filled his heart with a warmth and a sense of well-being that sent him, late the following afternoon, walking briskly through the eastern suburbs of Alexandria, not even thinking to hire a litter, so intent was he on experiencing his own joy and on thanking God for His mercies. How long since he had uttered a prayer of gratitude! Whether God derived satisfaction from his prayer, he could not tell, but he knew that it fell like spring rain on a heart he had thought would remain dry and barren forever.

When he arrived home a servant told him that his mother was out, had gone to a banquet organized by the Archbishop for his most reliable donors. Since Zachary was not expected, no food had been prepared for him. He ordered a meal to be cooked immediately, called for wine and sat down to wait. Now that he could no longer express his feelings through activity, the mood that had sustained him ebbed gradually and gave place to uncertainty. He realized that anyone as garrulous as Cleon would surely tell his wife the experiences of his journey. Oh yes, dear, I gave a ride in the boat to someone called Zachary. Well, did you now! It was not that common a name, and when he mentioned hermits she would know for certain.

It hadn't sounded, from what Cleon had said, as if she had told him that she had lived with another man. She probably had had the good sense to keep quiet about that, even feign amnesia from her terrible experience…But what if she thought he would show up in a few days' time? Might she not, fearful that he would give her away, pre-empt that possibility by a confession? He prayed that she would trust him, say nothing. He dreaded being once more the cause, however inadvertent, of her unhappiness.

Try as he would, this thought cast a spreading shadow over his mood. And within that shadow, other worries began to multiply. What had happened with the business during his days of absence? How many of the countless things that could go wrong had gone wrong?

By the time he had finished his meal it was too late to go to the baths, and he had no desire to visit bars or theaters. Yet it was still too early to go to bed. He decided to visit the office, even though there would be no one there but the watchman. Ptolemy would have put any correspondence for him on his desk, he could at least fill his time by reading that and perhaps answering any of it that seemed urgent. It was still light outside and though the air had begun to cool a little it felt thick, buoyant and balmy. People were walking at a leisurely pace, and even though the streets were crowded there was a relaxed, holiday atmosphere about the evening, a good mood, not the tense edginess that Alexandrian crowds so often generated.

Despite this, and for reasons that he did not understand, Zachary felt tense. When he accidentally bumped into another pedestrian he snapped at him, leaving that person too surprised to feel resentful. The watchman was not at his post and Zachary, who did not carry a key for the outer door of the building, had to clap and whistle until the fellow came shuffling back from a food-stall around the corner, still licking his lips.

Zachary reproved him, feeling mean even as he did so, for the fellow had to eat sometime. The man admitted him in a sulky silence.

Sure enough, the faithful Ptolemy had piled his mail on his desk. Since the light indoors was already too poor to read by, he called in the watchman and had him light a couple of lamps from the lantern he carried. In less than an hour, he had read all his letters, but felt too restless to answer any. Although nothing in the office seemed out of place, he could not manage to rid himself of a vague floating feeling of disquiet, of something badly wrong somewhere. This is absurd, he told himself, if you were superstitious you'd swear someone had put a spell on you.

He walked to the second-floor window and opened it, letting the cool air flow into the stifled, stagnant office. By now it was quite dark in the street outside, although the eggshell sky above still held as it were an echo of the sun's last light. Low down in that sky, barely clearing the flat rooftops, a single star throbbed, white-hot. Lamps burned on the walls of his and the other business houses. The watchman dozed, cross-legged, directly below him, his lantern between his knees. No one else was in sight. What could there be in that peaceful scene to cause anyone disquiet?

I'll just check the strong room, he said to himself, and then I'll go home.

He felt a sense of absurdity, for the key had been in his possession throughout his trip, and no duplicate existed. He unlocked, first, the wooden outer door of the strong room. Pulled ajar, this revealed a massive iron gate, its bars set too close for even the thinnest thief to squeeze through that constituted the strong-room's real protection. This too had a lock which opened to the same key, but only if a secret spring had first been pressed, otherwise the key would not enter the lock and anyone who had stolen his key would assume that a different one was required for it. Groping in darkness round the stone jamb of the gate, he released the spring, unlocked the gate and then went back and brought a lamp. How still everything was, at this time! He had never been there at so late an hour—even the sounds from the distant streets, where crowds still circulated, could hardly be heard.

The lamp lit the interior of the strong room, its dusty, unswept floor, its shelves stacked with bags of coins and bullion bars. To the left was the Egyptian currency, to the right the Imperial gold...

Even then it took some moments before he saw it, for bags had been rearranged to diminish, though not to hide—nothing could hide—the reduction in their number. Surely he was dreaming! It wasn't possible! The vault was impregnable, and yet he knew, with a sick certainty that forced itself on him despite his resistance, that there were less than half the bags that had been there before. He flung himself on one of them, panic-stricken, certain that its contents had been replaced by worthless tokens of iron. But no, the bag still contained gold. He sank back, relieved that at least that fear had not been justified.

I'm going mad, he thought. *In a moment I'll come to my senses and see that everything's here. I should go home, get a good night's sleep, come back in the morning, everything will be just fine.*

He knew as he told himself this that it was a lie. More than half the bags had indeed vanished.

He glanced down. On the floor, in the dust, there were footprints. He placed his sandal in the prints and they were an inch or so longer than his sandal. The only people who had ever set foot in the strong room were himself and Ptolemy, and Ptolemy's feet were smaller than his.

He felt goosebumps crawling down his neck and back, for only some supernatural agency could have penetrated so well-guarded a place. His fevered mind created an illusion of movement in the shadows, he cried out aloud and raised the lamp as high as he could to cast its beams into corners that might be concealing—he dared not even think what they might be concealing...

Nothing, of course. Only, on the floor in a corner, a small piece of broken pottery of the kind that people who ran out of paper or couldn't afford it used to scrawl messages on. Curious, for no such object had any business to be here, he stooped to pick it up and saw that it did indeed contain a message;

"Sorry! Forgive me."

"You...BASTARD!" he screamed with all his force, indifferent to whether he was heard by neighbors or by the watchman dozing outside. Luckily, as he realized immediately, the thick walls muffled the sound. The last thing he wanted was for news of this to get around, everyone he owed money to would descend on him simultaneously and there might not be enough to pay them all off. There was no way now in which he could calculate the loss. Ptolemy would know to a drachma how much the vault had contained, but if he had to guess he would say at a minimum several hundred thousand solidi. A fortune! Cellius would have had to hire slaves to carry it all.

The light had revealed to him something else, something whose significance he did not appreciate until he brought the lamp up close to it: a small shapeless heap, half-hidden by the end of the lowest shelf, which on examination resolved itself into a small pile of rubble. He glanced at the wall above and behind the pile and saw immediately what had happened. Someone had mined through the wall from the outside and then packed the hole with rubble.

Frantically he tore at the rubble with his bare hands as if he expected to find the thief and his loot hidden behind it. Soon his fingernails were broken, his fingers torn and bleeding but he kept on. The wall was feet thick. But whoever had made the hole had not bothered to fill it entirely, and in a few minutes he squeezed through a narrow passageway that led to a completely empty room beyond.

It was clear to him now. Though Cellius had never entered the strong room he had seen Zachary use it and therefore knew exactly where it was. He could easily have taken measurements and worked out what lay beyond the back wall of the strong room. A vacant office, presumably. Cellius had worked out where this office was, found out who owned it and then rented it. And during the five days Zachary had been absent, he and his accomplices had simply tunneled through the intervening wall.

Zachary staggered out of the strong room, forgetting to lock gate or door, remembered, went back and locked both of them, wondering even as he did so what use it was, since anyone could now enter through the tunnel. Then he sat down at his desk and put his head in his hands

It was not the magnitude of his loss that distressed him. Deeply damaging as it was, the firm could survive it. The bullion remained—too heavy to carry, probably—and the Egyptian drachmas—too low a value in ratio to their bulk. Even some of the gold coins remained. No, it was the treachery of it that distressed him so deeply, the treachery of the man he had sincerely thought was his friend, whom he had trusted so much he had almost given him the key. Betrayal of any kind leaves one feeling violated, but betrayal by a trusted friend strikes a sword into the soul.

Suddenly, out of nowhere, the words of Matthew Chapter 6 burned across his mind: Lay not up for yourselves treasures on earth, where moth and rust corrupt, and thieves break in and steal, but lay yourselves up treasure in heaven, where neither moth nor rust doth corrupt, and where thieves do not break through and steal. For where your treasure is, there shall your heart be also.

How often he had heard those words, so often that they had become a mere formula, devoid of meaning. Now they struck home with terrifying force. Indeed his heart had been here on earth, in the pleasures of earth and in the wealth that had seemed so solid, even like the name of the coins of which it consisted. Solidi! Yet how vain and phantom-like that wealth now appeared to him! The things of the world could indeed be taken from one in a matter of moments, whereas the things of the spirit...

What things? He had thrown them aside, trampled on them, rejected them. Were they really more real, could they ever be real to him again? Or, had his pursuit of the things of the world burned out his heart, left it useless, ruined, unfit to contain God's grace? He felt, in those first moments of despondency, as if he had lost both earth and heaven, and had been left to wander condemned in a dreary no-man's-land that was neither one of them.

He forced himself to move. Calling to the watchman to let him out, he circled round to the next street and located the watchman for the building that backed onto his. Slipping a coin into the man's hand, he said, "You know the Roman, the tall fair-haired one, who rents the office here?"

The man knew immediately, as he had expected. "Oh yes, sir. But he's gone, I'm afraid."

"Gone? Gone where?"

"Oh, he never told me that, sir."

"What makes you so sure he's gone?"

"Oh, the furniture. Took it all, cupboards, desks..."

And the money inside of it, too, Zachary thought bitterly. *Smart move!*

"And, when was this?"

"Day before yesterday, sir."

Zachary gave him another coin, made the man memorize his address and promise to report to him immediately if, at any time that night, the blond Roman or anyone else for that matter visited the office, there was still an outside chance that they had left the remainder of the loot to be picked up later. "You needn't worry about deserting your post, I'll give you a gold piece and a job, too, in case you get fired from this one." It would only be for a night, next morning he would have masons in and repair the wall, probably have metal plates set in it for good measure.

Then he went home.

His mother had just returned, in all her finery: layers of silk, neck festooned with gold, greying locks tortured into some fancy style and kept there with jeweled combs. Why would one doll oneself up like that for a quasi-religious occasion? His mother started to say something but he cut across her.

"I've been robbed!"

Her shadowed, baggy eyes flew open in shock. "No!"

"Yes. By the man I thought was my friend. By…"

"Cellius? I always knew he was rotten!"

"Well it's a fine time to bring that up now, Mother," Zachary said in an exasperated tone.

"Well, it serves you right for never paying any…"

He fought down a mad impulse to say, "don't you realize, stupid woman? We're ruined!" Instead he said, "You should know he took the best part of a million solidi, it won't put us out of business, but it will take a while to recover." On the way home he had realized that this was no sudden lapse on Cellius' part but something he must have been planning for months, perhaps from their first meeting. Doubtless it was him who had produced the false rumor about Celia and planted it with the serious bearded man in the theater tavern, probably a co-conspirator. How cunningly he had done it, with all the disclaimers to make it sound more plausible! So that Zachary himself would seek out the hook, would insist on going to Panephysis, insist all the harder when Cellius treated the proposal with indifference.

And then, at the crucial moment, the casual request that he leave the key. Zachary's refusal had left him only one alternative: outright burglary. He must have had it in mind as a fallback strategy all along, must have rented the next-door office, rented or bought the necessary tools…

"You realize how he got me out of the way, do you?" he asked his mother.

His mother blinked. "Of course not. You never told me where you were going. You never tell me anything."

"I'm telling you now. He told me, I mean he had one of his friends tell me that Celia—you remember Celia, don't you?"

"I remember her all right, and what a lucky escape—"

"Yes, well, never mind that—he had his friend tell me that Celia was in a nunnery at Panephysis! I mean what nonsense! And like a total idiot I believed him."

Her hand was over her mouth, she was staring at him with rounded eyes. "He told you that?"

"Yes!"

"But it's true!"

"It's WHAT?" Zachary felt the solid ground under him lurch as if in earthquake. He had a sudden vision of Panephysis, of himself stumbling around its Stygian alleys while from the roofs above a coifed Celia signaled frantically and cried out, "What's the matter with you? Can't you see me? I'm right here!" Was it possible she had been there all the time? Would he have to, God forbid, go back there?

"She can't be, mother, I searched the whole town, I..."

"No, no," his mother insisted. "You misunderstood me. I never said she was in Panephysis, why on earth would she go to a place like that? But she is in a nunnery. Right here in Alexandria."

For a moment, Zachary was struck speechless. Finally he found his tongue.

"Mother!"

"Yes, dear."

"How long have you known this?"

"Oh." Her lined eyes swam vaguely. "Well...months."

"But it never occurred to you to tell me?" Zachary ground out in a bitter monotone.

"Well frankly, no, dear. She never was any good."

"That's beside the point. You realize, do you, that if you'd only had the sense to tell me, months ago, even just a week ago, we wouldn't have been robbed?"

She blinked at him—he knew if he pushed her any further, there would be tears. "How was I to have known?" she wailed. "It was all so long ago. And honestly it just never occurred to me that you'd care."

Derek Bickerton

Chapter 24

The beach was steep, pebbly, strewn with seaweed. Zachary's booted feet skidded on wet pebbles, squelched the damp bladders of the seaweed. The late sun, hanging low over the low bluff immediately ahead of him, shone directly into his eyes, almost blinding him. The bluff itself and the series of caves dug in its sides never seemed to get any closer.

His destination was not, contrary to what his mother had implied, in the city itself, but on the coast some miles to the west of it. To reach it you had to leave the main coast road—the road along which he had walked on his way to the interior desert after the fall of the Serapeum, and on which his rented carriage now awaited his return. Doubtless this site had been chosen deliberately by the founders of the institution to discourage casual visitors. Now the small tide of the almost tide less sea, backed by a northerly breeze, pushed shallow waves over a shelf of rock, sluicing the pebbles and forcing Zachary to detour. The only sound was the hiss and suck of water over the pebbles, and the rhythmic crunching of his boots.

When he reached the bluff, the breeze had fallen, the sea was glassy calm, the sun on the point of setting in a cloudless west. Seabirds, calling plaintively, emerged from nowhere and circled the bluff, preparing to settle for the night. The rocks were splashed and stained with their droppings, as was the worm-eaten wooden door, let into the side of the cliff, which seemed the only way to enter the place, since the caves he had glimpsed from a distance now appeared to be sealed with iron grids. He knocked, and after a while a female voice asked him to state his business.

"To speak with Sister Celia."

"There is no Sister Celia," the voice replied, "and if there were she could not speak with you."

Stifling his irritation at the speaker's smug, self-righteous tone, Zachary said, "then let me speak to the Abbess or Mother Superior or whoever is in charge of this place."

"The Lady Mother cannot speak to you either," the voice said in the same tone.

"Then can you give her a message for me?" Zachary forced his voice into an unctuous politeness.

"No."

"Why, won't she speak to you, either?"

"None of your business," the voice snapped in a more human tone.

"Well, if you ever do get to speak to her, you might mention how disappointed I am that her establishment will not receive the donation of a hundred solidi I intended making."

There was a moment's silence. The voice said, "Wait here."

Zachary waited. Where he now stood, the sun had cleared the bluff and was about to sink into the blue-green, waveless sea. It shone at an angle over his right shoulder, and he suddenly realized that only now, in the last few moments of a summer evening, could sunlight ever reach that door. At any other time, the steep bluff in which the caves were built would have blocked its light. Realizing this filled him with an immense sadness. He did not quite know why. In Scetis, the sun had been his enemy; in the interior desert, its searing light and heat had all but destroyed him. He would have given anything then for such deep shade. But now it somehow seemed better to have the sun as one's enemy than not to have it at all.

Even as these thoughts were passing through his mind, he heard a grating sound, and a panel in the door was pulled aside. Behind the panel was a metal grille, and behind the grille, touched by a faint beam of sunlight, was something that might have been a woman's face.

"Thank you for your generosity, sir," a new and softer voice said. "But we have everything we…"

The voice hesitated for a fraction of a second, then picked up again and went on smoothly, "…need here. I would prefer it if you found someone who was truly in need, of which there are many in the city."

Zachary tried to answer, but could not. He had instantly recognized the voice, even though it was a decade since he had heard it. And that she had recognized him too he knew from that fractional break in her voice when for the first time she had looked at his face directly through that iron grille. The other, the sister who first answered the door, could not have told her what name he had asked for, or she would have known, immediately.

"Celia," he finally managed to say. "You are Celia."

"Celia is dead." Did he imagine or really hear a faint tremor in the voice, as of one struggling, almost successfully, to pretend that nothing out of the ordinary was happening here?

"You are Celia," he repeated.

The shape, the vision, barely visible behind the close-set bars of the grille, but touched with gold by the last soft rays of the sun, said, "I am Mother Perpetua, and I swear to you that Celia is dead."

"You were Celia," he said, "and I am still Zachary, the only man you ever loved truly with all your heart. Just as you were the only one I truly loved."

The light left the grille as, behind him, the sun vanished into the mirror-still sea. Since, for several seconds afterwards, no sound came, he thought she must have left, although the panel in the door remained open. In the silence, he could hear the soft suck of the tide at the weed-covered rocks behind him. Then, the shadowy shape moved, only its movement separated it from the shadows. "Celia," he said. "I'm sorry. Mother Perpetua…"

"The past is dead," the voice said, and now he knew she was barely in control of herself.

"Maybe for you," Zachary said, "though I doubt that. But, for me…No, for me it's not dead."

He was not mistaken. Though it was too dark already for him to make out any detail of the face beyond the grill, he could hear her weeping.

"Please," she said in a soft breaking voice. "Respect my vows."

The identical words, he remembered, that he had used to her when she seduced him. But, he could not be so cruel as to remind her of that now. "It would never cross my mind not too," he said urgently. "No matter what I may feel towards you, I will always do that. But I can't make myself ashamed of what I feel…felt. I won't talk about the past. I only wanted…" His voice trailed off. "I don't know what I wanted. I suppose…I just wanted to see you again. One more time. Why? I honestly don't know. But I wanted it, more than anything."

She said nothing. But, the weeping had ceased.

"Can't you open the door?" he asked. "I would like just to see you."

"That's not possible."

"It is. If you're in charge here? Are you really in charge here?"

"Why would you doubt that?" For the first time he heard something of the light, confident tone of the old Celia. "You think I'm not capable?"

"No." He smiled, "I would never think that."

"Or unworthy. Though that would be true enough. There are some here whose laces I'm not fit to tie…It's to protect them that I stand between them and the world."

Zachary remembered Scetis. The worthiest were those who most sincerely denied their own worth.

"It would never occur to me to think you unworthy, either," he said. "I know what it takes to renounce the world. I couldn't do it. I tried. I failed. It drew me back into it." He laughed ruefully. "I just told you the story of my life. Don't worry, I shan't ask you for yours. Just want you to know how much I admire…Admire. No. Wrong word. Maybe 'envy' would hit it better."

"Our life here is hard," She had ceased to be Celia, she was Mother

Perpetua again, safe in the armor of her position. "There is nothing here to envy."

"I could envy your peace."

For a moment she did not answer him. In the silence he heard the screech of a low-flying bat that came zigzagging round the buff and across the eggshell green of the horizon sky, still bright from the invisible sun. Its demonic presence passed; the elegiac light remained.

"Peace?" she asked. "What do you mean, peace? When I think of the foulness I did, and made others do. No repentance can undo that. No penance, even. If it lasted a lifetime." Again over the hushed suck of the tide, he could hear her weeping, though it was now so dark he could no longer make out even the shadow of her face. "Zachary!" she cried out suddenly. "I made you break your vow of celibacy! I asked you just now to respect my vows, but what right had I, when I couldn't respect yours? The moment I saw you I should have fallen on my knees and begged your forgiveness."

And her voice dissolved in a passion of tears. *This is ridiculous*, Zachary thought. *Here we are, not three feet away from one another—close enough to touch if this stupid piece of wood wasn't between us. If she would open the door and let me touch her, not in desire, in a pure and brotherly love to comfort her, I would comfort her.*

"There's nothing to forgive," he said.

"There is. Don't try to be kind. You know there is."

"No. Whatever sin there was…was mine too. I didn't have to do what I did. Why won't you open the door?"

"Do you really want to risk starting all that again?"

Zachary knew, the moment she said this, knew with absolute certainty that, no matter how she would deny it, what she had felt for him was not totally dead, and she dared not open the door for fear it would revive. If she would give to me, Cellius had said, what she gave that mysterious stranger, I would support her for the rest of my life. Zachary had indeed been that stranger, he knew it now. Perhaps it was better for both of them that the door remained shut.

"Celia," he said, and this time she did not reject the name, "I want you to know that I loved you. Yes, I know, I loved you in the flesh. But it was more than that, it was never only that. And now…now I can no longer love you that way…I want you to know I still love you. I want only what's best for you, so if you want me to go now, if that's what's best for you, I'll go. Only give me your blessing before I go."

She did not speak. They had entered a place where there were no landmarks, no compasses. Though neither of them knew quite how to proceed in that place, neither wished immediately to leave it, without savoring the wonder and strangeness of it.

"I'd rather you gave me your forgiveness," she said at last.

"For what? There's nothing to forgive. If there were, I would have forgiven you already. What happened, happened through my own weakness. Everything that has happened," he added, thinking now of his betrayal by Cellius, his own descent into a slough of lust and greed and self-love.

It came to him in a sudden blaze of certainty what he must do now.

"I'm going back to the desert."

When he uttered those words, the last words he had expected to utter in that context, it was as if an enormous weight was suddenly lifted from his heart. As if his spirit, weighed down in that dark and shadowy space under the bluff, had been set loose to soar upwards like a bird, into the fading aquamarine of the heaves, in pursuit of the light. He felt a lightness in his limbs, his body, his whole being. He wanted to leap. To dance, to run fast and far over the sand and scrub and sun-crumbled rocks, to that land of dust and salt marsh under an implacable sun...to Scetis.

"Do you truly mean that?" she asked him.

"If you make me a promise, I do."

"I cannot promise you anything..." she said urgently.

"Wait, wait. Listen to what I ask first. This is nothing sinful..."

"I don't know what..."

"Just listen! How many times does the gospel say we should forgive those that injure us?"

"Seventy times seven," she said meekly.

"Do you think, knowing our frailty, He would forgive less often than He told us to forgive?"

"I suppose not," she said, doubtfully, reluctantly, not sure where this was leading.

"Then, don't you think, if you repented sincerely, as I know you did, that He has already forgiven you? And that the intention born just now in my soul was His sign to you that you were indeed forgiven? That you could find peace at last?"

He wished he could have seen her face, how she responded to that. He could only guess at the conflict of hope and fear that might be revealed there. "Tell someone to bring a lamp," he said.

"No," she said quickly. Then, "What did you want me to promise?"

"To believe what I just told you."

He heard her sigh. "If I could only..." Then with a quickness of wit that reminded him of the old Celia, she said, "You're just telling me that because you don't want me to suffer, my suffering makes you uneasy too."

Zachary shook his head. "Wrong, Mother Perpetua. I really am going to the desert."

"Because your soul wills it or because you're doing penance for me—because you think if you share the weight of my sins God will lighten the burden on my soul?"

Zachary did not answer this for a long time. The question was just and required his deepest discernment. He knew that he, Zachary the romantic, the sentimental, would be quite capable of such an act of self-sacrifice. But if he admitted that..."

"If it's the second," she said, with a scary prescience, "you must know it's unacceptable."

"Unacceptable?" he asked, his own mind working fast now, as if energized by his unexpected decision. "To you or to God?"

She hesitated only a half-beat. "To me."

"Of course. But not to God." He knew—and she could hardly fail to know, for the tales of it were legion—that many righteous persons had taken on themselves the burden of a friend's sin, and that God had rewarded their selflessness by pardoning the sinner and granting signs to show that He had indeed done so. "So would you set yourself up as more demanding than God?"

Even in the dark, with the door between them, he could sense her shudder of rejection. "No, no, of course not. But what you're doing isn't just penance, it's a whole way of life. And that way is worthless to yourself and God if you haven't chosen it sincerely. Have you?"

Again, Zachary was slow to respond. In this strange place where they now found themselves, nothing less than total honesty would suffice.

"It's true...That was an element in it, at first. After all, if I'd shared the sin, the least I could do would be to share the atonement. And you're right, of course. If I loved you, and I do, I'd try to save you pain. I might have done it for that reason only. I'm quite capable of it. But then, the moment the thought formed in my mind, I knew my soul truly willed it. For its own sake. And that if at this moment an angel descended and told me your slate was clean, it would make no difference. I'd still go back to the desert. And give thanks that you'd put it in my heart to go there."

"That God put it in your heart to go there," she corrected him.

"True...A week ago, I'd never have dreamed that."

"And now?"

"I don't know. But I'm going to find out."

"You no longer believed in God?" she asked incredulously.

"Tell you the truth, I don't know whether I did or not."

"I never ceased to believe," she said passionately. "You would never have guessed that, from the way I lived, but I never stopped believing, and that made things worse, of course, I always knew that what I was doing was wrong. And because I sinned so consciously, deliberately…"

"You felt you could never be forgiven," he finished for her.

He took her silence for assent.

"Promise me you'll believe you're forgiven now."

"How can I promise that? How can I believe it?"

"Then believe at least it's possible you've been forgiven. And pray for a sign."

She sighed, "I'll try, Zachary. I can promise that. No more than that."

Zachary inclined his head. "So be it. Now give me your blessing."

She made a sound that might almost have been a laugh. "Maybe I should ask for yours. When I saw it was you I prayed, Oh GOD, I can't stand this, take this away from me. But He didn't, and now I'm glad you came. You have my blessing, for what it's worth, and gladly. But," she went on in a tone of sudden concern, "how will you find your way back in the dark?"

"Don't worry," Zachary said. "If God wills that I fall in the sea and drown, that's His business,"

"Faith is one thing," she said. "Foolhardiness is another, Stay there. I'll bring you a lamp."

"As you wish…thanks, anyway."

He waited for several minutes. Although by now the sky had almost totally darkened, there remained enough light to be caught and reflected in phosphorescent streaks from the barely-perceptible ripples that continued to break, with a gentle suck and a faint withdrawing hiss, on the rocks a few feet from his heels. A star or two appeared. On the horizon, a moving light betrayed the presence of a ship, sailing eastwards towards the beacon of the Pharos. That beacon itself was hidden from Zachary by a bend in the coast, but to the sailors nearing shore it must blaze in the sky like a captured meteor, promising home, safety, rest. What beacon in the night, equally unseen by his eyes but visible to his soul, had turned his life's voyage to the south, to the desert?

The door opened a fraction, and a lamp was thrust through the gap. A soft, long-fingered hand and a slender wrist glowed with a living warmth in the circle of light that the lamp cast. He reached out, and for a fraction of a second their hands touched. It was as if a bolt of lightning had passed along his arm—

that fleeting contact was somehow more intimate than the most passionate kiss, the most sensual embrace. She snatched her hand away, and with a strange mixture of joy and sadness he sensed that she had experienced an identical feeling.

"God bless you and keep you, Mother Perpetua."

"And you too, Zachary, my brother in Christ."

Clutching the lamp, he hurried off down the beach, for his masculine pride still flourished too strongly for him to let her see, in the lamplight, the tears that were welling up to fill his eyes.

Chapter 25

One morning after synaxis, Mother Theodora told Poemen something that amazed him.

"Arsenius was in Alexandria last week," she began.

"Oh yes?" Poemen said politely, wondering, why is she telling me this? She hates gossip as much as anyone.

"He had to go; he needed medicine for his stomach, and he doesn't trust anyone else to get the right kind."

"Indeed," Poemen said noncommittally, thinking, she has to say this to show that his trip wasn't frivolous. All right, get to the meat of it.

"But this time, he didn't stay in the Caesarium."

"Ah."

"So the blessed Archbishop Theophilus..." surely Poemen was mistaken, could there really have been a note of irony in her tone?..."heard he was in town and sent people to find where he was staying. And as soon as he found out, he went there in person and asked Arsenius why he hadn't come to the episcopal guest house as he always had before. But all Arsenius would say was he was quite comfortable where he was, thank you. So Theophilus asked him for a word. And Arsenius didn't answer right away, then he said, "Will you promise to do whatever I tell you to?" Theophilus promised. Then Arsenius said—you'll never believe what he said!"

"Try me," Poemen said.

"He said, 'If you hear Arsenius is anywhere—don't go there!'!"

Poemen gaped at her. "He said that?"

"I had it from someone who was there."

"Not Arsenius."

Theodora snorted. "He's not going to tell anyone stuff like that. Or anything about himself, if it comes to that. He's too good a hermit to do that... But you're not pleased?"

"I'm not sure that I ought to be."

"Well, you were one of the first to see what Theophilus was really like," Theodora said in her blunt, forthright fashion. "You and Moses. Shouldn't you be pleased when other people finally see the light?"

"I don't know," Poemen sad. He wasn't just being modest or evasive—he really didn't know. "I just don't feel comfortable about it. I don't want to feel glad because someone else is put down—not even someone like Theophilus."

"Oh, you!" Theodora exclaimed. "You're just a born contrarian. I really believe you'd feel sorry for the Devil himself."

"That would be Origenism." Poemen said, straight-faced.

Theodora shook her head at such levity and hurried off to her cell. Poemen was left to wonder over her news, surprising as it was, the wording of it rang true. Arsenius wouldn't judge, wouldn't condemn—in his icy rectitude he would simply cut Theophilus out of his world.

A couple of days later, around the tenth hour, Poemen was setting out bean plants in the sandy soil. He had decided to become more self-sufficient. Although he insisted to himself he was still as strong and vigorous as he had been at thirty, his body didn't seem to be listening. Objective evidence came from the lengthening time it took him to finish a basket, and the smaller number of baskets he produced each week. That meant less income, less money he could use for charity. He did not want to reduce his giving, so he could only reduce his living expenses. Moreover, a shift from a mainly bread to a mainly vegetable diet was one of the rites of passage that, in Scetis, marked the transition to old age.

Stooped over, twisting his digging stick to make holes for the plants Moses had given him, he did not see Arsenius until the ex-tutor was almost upon him.

"I owe you an apology," Arsenius said.

"I think not," Poemen said, stretching painfully as he straightened his back. "You've never done anything to offend me."

"I didn't listen to you."

"That's no offence. I talk too much, anyway."

"Yes it is," Arsenius persisted. "If someone shows you the right path and you ignore them. I must apologize."

Poemen stared at him quizzically. "You're referring to our last conversation, I take it."

Arsenius nodded. "After Nitria—well, that started me thinking."

So it wasn't my drop of rain on the desert, Poemen thought. I was the brute force of unavoidable fact that had changed his mind about Theophilus. Still, if he hadn't first spoken…

Shut up, he told himself. *Don't go seeking praise, least of all from yourself.*

"It was hard for me," Arsenius went on, "having been part of the establishment myself, even if a much humbler part than some people here seem to think. It makes you see things in terms of power. Of hierarchy. Someone in high office, it seems perfectly natural if they seem a bit arrogant and high-handed sometimes. You expect it. Even among God's anointed, you tend to tolerate it." Arsenius sighed deeply. "It took Moses to show me my error. He said, 'two men on horseback were carrying a piece of wood, crosswise between them. They came to a church and tried to enter it. But the wood was too wide to go in crosswise, one would have to lead and the other follow. So they just stood there arguing. Neither would yield'"

"And did Moses explain his parable?"

"The men on horseback were leaders of the Church. The piece of wood is the yoke of righteousness, which they should bear humbly, as equals before God. But their pride will not suffer them to do this, so they cannot enter the church, which represents the Kingdom of Heaven."

"That's good," Poemen said. "I must remember that."

Arsenius turned his lined face to Poemen with an expression of wonder. "Doesn't it amaze you, though, how these simple Egyptian peasants can sometimes see into things much more deeply than we educated folk? Sometimes it's like they speak a language I don't even know the alphabet of."

"I'm not sure who you mean by, 'we educated folk'."

Poemen's tone was frostier than Arsenius had expected. "Why, people like you and I, I mean…"

"I'm one of those simple Egyptian peasants."

Arsenius was flabbergasted. "But I'd always assumed…I mean, you speak excellent Greek…"

"Thanks."

"…you've read widely, you understand the world, you-"

"Who am I?" Poemen asked abruptly.

"Why, Poemen, of course."

"And what does that mean, in Egyptian?"

"I don't know."

"It means 'shepherd'. The Shepherd, that's what they call me, in any language."

"Of course," Arsenius admitted, "but I'd always assumed that to mean… well, it was a sort of courtesy title, on account of your…your pastoral care…"

"I'm not a priest."

"I know, I know, but you're always giving help and guidance…"

"You shouldn't say that." Poemen's habitual good humor was quite restored now. "Bad for my humility. Anyway, things don't work like that round here. People may talk in riddles and parables but when it comes to everyday stuff, they're very literal-minded. Names mean what they seem to mean. Moses the Robber was a robber. Paul the Barber was a barber—still is, it's a trade we need here. And Poemen the Shepherd was a shepherd. Of real sheep. Goats, too, naturally."

Arsenius shook his head. "I would never have believed it. How on earth did you learn so much?"

"I know all too little, I'm afraid." Poemen paused a moment, as if considering. "Well, I suppose my experience was a little different from the average shepherd's. I don't normally ever discuss the past, but since you've opened your heart to me...You really want to know?"

Arsenius said he did.

"All right. This goes right back to the last persecution. There was a Christian, an Alexandrian philosopher, who was martyred. But before they arrested him he sent his wife and children into hiding, up in the Thebaid. And they took with them all his books and papers, because there was always the chance he'd be condemned to the mines and get out one day. Instead, they threw him to the beasts in the amphitheater at Nicopolis. His two sons grew up in the village there, neither had any taste for learning, they became day-laborers and had children of their own. The books were thrown in a cellar and forgotten. Well, one of those children became a shepherd when he was eight or so, just as I did. He was my best friend."

Poemen's eyes misted slightly. They had been as close as David and Jonathan. Yet he had not thought of the other for many years, had no idea whether he was alive or dead.

"Well, we were curious, as boys are. We found all these books rotting in the cellar. And we wanted to know what it all meant. So I went to the local priest, the pagan priest, that is, there were very few Christians in the villages back then, and persuaded him to teach us to read. I think he just wanted to convert the other kid. His family was Christian. Mine was pagan. My friend was kind of slow and soon lost interest, but for some reason I took to it like a duck to water. Used to always take a book with me, when I was out with the sheep. It's not that exacting a job, not if you have a good dog, as I had. I just read and read, anything I could lay my hands on, pagan, Christian, gnostic, Manichaean...The other kids teased me no end about it. The black eyes I got—and gave...Not a very edifying childhood, I'm afraid."

"Not like our blessed Archbishop," Arsenius said, deadpan. "Pagan statues would come crashing to the ground the moment the patter of his infant feet was heard in the distance."

"So, you've heard that rubbish too. Does he make it up himself? No, just flatterers, I guess...Anyway, it all turned out for the best, I got converted. Just reading Clement—and Origen, of course—but the Gospels more than anything else. The miracles and fulfilment of prophecies never did much for me, you could find stuff like that in the pagan books, but when He talked about how you should live...I just knew that had to be the truth, you didn't find stuff like that anywhere else. At least I knew what I wanted to be when I grew up."

Arsenius nodded sympathetically. "I envy you. I was raised Christian, but I'd lived longer than Our Savior did before I started taking it seriously." He broke off, his eyes fixed on something beyond Poemen's right shoulder. "I shouldn't be wasting your time like this," he said. "Here comes someone else in need of your counsel."

Poemen turned and squinted into the rays of the declining sun. Approaching him, coming slowly and covered with dust, he saw a dark-haired man of about thirty who he did not immediately recognize, although there was something vaguely familiar about him.

"I'll be off," Arsenius said. "Thanks for the talk."

"It's nothing...Hope we can talk again soon."

Poemen shaded his eyes and stared fixedly at the approaching figure. Not currently resident in Scetis, but could be someone who at one time—

Got it!

"You're Zachary." he said. "Former disciple, first of John the Dwarf, then Papnoute. Left to pull down the Serapeum, never came back. Greetings."

Zachary stared at him. "You remember all that?"

"That's nothing. I only just this minute recognized you. A real hermit would have known three days ago you were coming." He smiled warmly. "Anyway, I'm glad you're back. You had potential. I remember that, too."

"There's a condition attached," Zachary said stubbornly.

Poemen's smile faded. "Go on."

"I have to be your disciple."

"But I don't take disciples. Everyone knows that."

"I don't care. I've made up my mind."

"YOU have made up YOUR mind?"

Zachary did not even notice the change in tone. He continued to stare fixedly at the old hermit, as a prisoner might stare at the judge who is about to pronounce sentence upon him.

"And what will you do," Poemen asked, "if I don't take you? Go back into the World?"

"If you won't take me," Zachary said, "my soul will die."

Derek Bickerton

Chapter 26

"Oh," Poemen said. "Oh dear." He laid his digging stick, which he had retained in his hand all through his conversation with Arsenius, against the wall of his cell and sat down heavily on a slab of stone. "Why?" he asked plaintively.

Zachary hardly knew what to answer. He could not even remember at what stage of his journey the thought had become fixed in his mind. Not when he first decided to return to Scetis, or for some time afterwards. He had been too deeply involved in practicalities—finding a buyer for the business, arranging for a fund to support his mother, convincing his mother that he had left her enough to live in the style to which she was accustomed. Then, there was the surplus to dispose of, for charitable ends but without involving Theophilus' church. Finally, he had arranged a trust with Ptolemy and Ptolemy's friends, insisting that it be used only to help the needy, whether they looked deserving or not—only God could tell who was truly deserving.

Finally, there were his slaves to be freed. Though the Gospel said nothing explicit on this point, and although most authorities from Paul on had implicitly condoned the practice, Zachary could not for the life of him see how a true Christian could enslave anyone, least of all a fellow-Christian. His mother complained bitterly—a firm with slaves obviously commanded a higher price than one without—but for Zachary the act was doubly recompensed by the looks on his slaves' faces as they lined up to receive their signed and sealed certificates of manumission and the handful of coins that traditionally accompanied it.

That was his last act as a secular. When it was completed, he had literally no possessions beyond the clothes he was wearing. The thought of this filled him with a boundless elation. He was free, free at last from the encumbrance of possessions. All his former friends, the idle, drunken crowd he and Cellius hung out with, would have seen his act as a sacrifice of freedom, the irrational acceptance of a state of needless deprivation. But to him it was a release from pleasures that no longer pleased, from luxury that stifled the soul, from the unceasing demands of the world and the flesh. Demands each of which seemed to follow naturally, inevitably from the one before it, but which taken all together amounted to an insanity, a vast charade that, in the light of eternity, made no sense at all. He had begun even to feel grateful to Cellius for taking his money.

This sense of elation carried him clear of the city. But with every mile closer to Scetis, doubts and uncertainties began to gather like clouds on the sunny morning of a day destined for rain. How would he live when he got there? Whose disciple would he become? He could not go back to John, he would not go back to Papnoute. But what assurance did he have that any other mentor would improve on these? It was there, in the middle of his journey, that his present goal had jelled out of all these uncertainties.

"But why me?" Poemen asked again.

"Do you remember my very first synaxis, when I was here before? And I fell asleep, and you put my head on your lap?"

"Did I? Did I really? I don't remember that."

"Well I do. I never forgot it. Even though you did things I didn't understand. Like when John got robbed. Or when you sent me to Papnoute. No matter what my mind said, I knew in my heart that you...I don't quite know how to put this...it was like, to me you WERE Scetis, you stood for everything it meant. And I just suddenly knew I had to become your disciple or die."

Poemen shook his head gently. "It just doesn't work that way."

"Why doesn't it? My soul longed for it so!"

"I can give you several reasons," Poemen said, the impish spirit that lurked in a corner of his brain completely stilled now. "Let's leave out of account my personal predilections, they're the least important part of it. Just start by considering what you said just now. Remember what it was?"

"I've made up MY mind," Zachary repeated obediently.

"I think you realize now what you said. Or didn't say."

Zachary thought a moment before replying. "I should have said, I felt..."

"You should have SAID?"

"I should have meant."

"That's better. Go on."

"That I felt God willed that I should..." Zachary broke off, aware of yet another problem with his words.

"Exactly. Not my will but Thy will. The first lesson a hermit must learn. Without it, you might as well stay a secular for all the good you'll do."

Zachary bowed his head and remained silent.

"Didn't you realize that was what they meant, the old men. When they talked about a hermit being like a dead man? They didn't mean an apathetic lump. They meant someone wholly purged of selfish impulses, who wants nothing, hopes for nothing, fears nothing. So what does that tell us about the content of your wish?"

"It was wrong, Father."

"Why was it wrong?"

"Because it was not for me to choose who should be my teacher."

"Good," Poemen said. "You may be saved yet." He leaned forward and patted a slab of stone at his side. "Sit down, Zachary. This may take time, and you're tired. If you hadn't started out the way you did, I would already have invited you into my cell and offered you food and rest. But there are times when even the duty of hospitality must take second place. There are serious things that have to be sorted out here. Sit," he repeated, for Zachary, tired as he was, still seemed reluctant to obey him.

"You see," Poemen went on when he was seated, "the first duty of a hermit is to his elder. Not because there is any system of rank or hierarchy here—there isn't. In fact, if there were, it would violate the whole spirit of the place. But simply because following Christ, learning how to truly obey the Commandment, is a matter of experience. It's not something you can learn from books, even the holiest of books. Nor from revelation, either. God's grace can set your feet on the path—it can't walk that path for you. So we, the old men, must make you go through what we have all gone through ourselves. Not because we had to do it and want to get revenge on the next generation. But because it's only through such an apprenticeship that we, that anyone could have advanced even the little we've advanced. There is no other way."

Zachary remained with his head bowed. He did not interrupt. Poemen took a deep breath and continued.

"Then, consider the implication of what you said to the person you said it to. I don't mean me personally. Whoever you said it to. 'Or my soul will die,' you said. What would those words put on them?"

"Responsibility," Zachary murmured, almost inaudibly.

"Good. What else?"

"Guilt."

"Exactly. First, you tried to make someone else responsible for the well-being of your soul. You can't do that, Zachary. The only person responsible for the well-being of your soul is you. You can't abrogate it. You can't delegate it. It's yours, for ever and ever…Now tell me about the guilt."

"Father, I…"

"Go on. Just tell me."

Zachary composed himself. "The person to whom I said those words will feel guilty if he does not do what I ask of him. He will bear the guilt for—"

Poemen raised a warning finger. "Think carefully, Zachary. He will bear the guilt?"

"No. May feel he bears the guilt. He cannot truly bear it because the guilt is mine."

"Good," Poemen said, smiling. "You're not yet beyond all hope. He won't bear the guilt but he may still feel it. Will that be pleasant for him?"

"No, Father."

"Why not?"

"Because it's not pleasant to bear guilt when one is guiltless."

"Tell me how that relates to the Commandment."

"It is a breach of the Commandment."

"Because…"

"Because if you truly love your neighbor as yourself, you don't cause him to suffer. Not in any way it's in your power to avoid."

Poemen shifted his position, for the stone was hard and his bones less well covered than they had once been. "I see you remember something from your time here," he said. "Let's see if you remember the most important thing a hermit can have."

"Obedience?"

"No."

"Charity?"

"No."

"Asceticism?"

"No."

"Repentance?"

"No."

"Freedom from sin?"

"No. No one ever gets that. Not in this life."

Zachary threw up his hands. "I don't know."

"Discernment. You can have all those other things—except sinlessness, of course—but without discernment you'll never make real progress. You can be obedient, love your neighbor, mortify the flesh, weep for your sins until your eyelashes fall out. You're still at the Calumniator's mercy if you can't exercise interior vigilance, monitor your thoughts, tell what's of God from what isn't…Look at you today, full of fervor. You rehearsed that little speech you made to me, didn't you?"

Zachary hung his head and muttered shamefaced assent.

"Sounded good, didn't it? 'Make me your disciple or my soul will die.' Dramatic. Guaranteed to get results. To make any poor old hermit proud you had chosen him and ashamed if he didn't come through for you."

"Forgive me, Father!"

"Nothing for me to forgive, since I wasn't taken in by it. Forgive yourself for being such an ass, if you can see your way to it."

Silence fell. Poemen looked at Zachary. Zachary looked at the ground. *Poor kid*, Poemen thought. *He looks deflated. Oh well. Somebody had to do it.*

"Where does that leave us?"

"I don't know, Father."

"I'll tell you. You'll do as you're told. Right?"

"I suppose so, Father."

"You suppose so."

"I mean, yes, Father."

"You'll go where you're directed."

"Yes, Father."

"You'll take instruction from Father Papnoute, if advised to do so."

Zachary gritted his teeth. "I will, Father."

"And no more romantic nonsense about your soul dying."

"No, Father."

"Good." Poemen glanced at the sky. "It'll be dark in a few minutes, and if I don't get these poor bean plants into the ground, they won't last the night. Come on, help me."

He rose to his feet, impatiently waving away Zachary's offer of assistance, thinking, do I really look so decrepit? "Just stick the roots in the holes I make. Push the soil in around them, water them in with the water from that bucket, then tread the soil down firmly." He went ahead, making holes with his digging stick, not even looking back to see if Zachary was doing it right. When he had completed the row, he turned and leaned on his stick while Zachary, clumsy with haste and his anxiety to please, finished his share of the task. From the darkening slope of the escarpment above, the cry of a hyena echoed. Smoke from a cell where some hermit was cooking late rose, almost vertically, into a luminous green sky. The thin dry air lost heat quickly. Zachary shivered through his sweat.

"You see all those stones," Poemen said when he was done. "Know what they're for?"

Zachary shook his head, catching his breath. He had not worked with his hands since the harvesting at Tebtynnis, how many years ago?

"I'm extending my cell," Poemen said. "Adding another room. Maybe even an outer wall, protect the garden, now that I've got one."

"Is that so, Father?" Zachary's tone was dutiful, polite, trying to conceal his lack of interest. *He still doesn't get it*, Poemen thought with an inward chuckle.

"You see, as a hermit ages, the solitary life gets more and more difficult for him. Things he can't quite manage on his own any more. Or that take too long now, take his mind off his real business. Which, however, gets ever more pressing as his life draws to its close. You see what I'm getting at."

"Yes, Father," Zachary said in a tone that meant he did not.

"That's when, whether he likes it or not, he has to have someone live with him."

The light was fading fast, but not too fast to hide Zachary's expression. It changed in seconds from indifference to bewilderment, then to uncertainty, then to a kind of wild hope. "Father—you mean…"

"I mean I must soon take a disciple."

Zachary flung himself at the Shepherd's feet, clutching at his ankles. "Father Poemen!" he cried out, "Could I…Would you…"

"If we're going to live together," Poemen interrupted him firmly, "there's a few things you have to understand. And one is that I can't bear displays of excessive emotion."

Zachary released the hermit's ankles. Kneeling, gazing up with a desperate appeal in his eyes, he said, "do you mean that? Truly? You would let me live with you?"

"Isn't that what I just said?"

"But after…after all those stupid things I…Why me?"

"Because you were the first to ask," Poemen said, beginning to walk towards his cell. "Isn't that what the Scripture says? Ask and you shall receive? Now get off your knees and let's go find something to eat."

Chapter 27

When Zachary awoke the following morning, he felt a sense of complete disorientation. He had been dreaming of Alexandria, and on opening his eyes expected to see his familiar room. Instead, a low roof of palm-thatch confronted him, balanced on a wall of undressed stone cemented with dried mud. He lay on his back, on the floor, separated from it only by a layer of reeds, puzzling for a few seconds over what bizarre transformation could have affected his home. Then memory brought a rush of images—the long trail across the desert, his awkward interview with Poemen, his final acceptance as the Shepherd's disciple. He had achieved the goal he had set himself, if not quite in the way he had anticipated. So why should he feel so lost, lonely and afraid?

He was alone, for sure. A vacant pile of rushes at the other side of the cell showed where Poemen had spent the night, but he had risen (doubtless hours ago, for it was full day) and gone about his business. The fear, the loneliness certainly did not stem from that, any more than from the fact that he no longer found himself surrounded by servants poised to provide for his every need. He had, after all, gone without that for most of his adult life. No, he knew at once what it was he feared.

Failure.

He had failed at the ascetic life before, when he had had all the vigor and optimism of youth to sustain him. What made him think he could succeed a second time? The impulse to return to the desert had come suddenly and unexpectedly, and he had acted on it without giving himself time to reflect. Why had he not taken a few days, weeks even, to see if the desire persisted? Whether it represented the real will of his soul, or just its rebound to a rapid series of events—the news of Leila's survival, Cellius' betrayal, his talk on the beach with the transformed Celia. Small wonder that such happenings should force on him the re-evaluation of a life already becoming burdensome to him! But any such re-evaluation should have been carried out at leisure, with the full awareness that feelings, no matter how strong, can change fast, and form but a fragile basis for a drastic change in one's life.

Impulsiveness, impatience, lack of foresight—these had been his weaknesses throughout his life.

Was he doomed to remain forever torn between two lives, neither of which could wholly satisfy him—the life of the flesh and the life of the spirit?

No, he told himself. He would not tolerate it. He might no longer possess the full vigor and optimism of youth, but he must surely have gained at least some of the strength that maturity is supposed to bring. Hopefully, the capacity to persevere.

This time he would persevere. No matter what obstacles were placed in his path, he would overcome them. No matter what hardships presented themselves, he would endure them. No matter what temptations arose to draw him from his chosen path, he would trample them down and thrust them into oblivion. So resolving, he rose and went to the door of his cell.

Outside, the sun still hung low over the escarpment. Long shadows broke the monotony of the valley floor. In the distance, a single camel and its driver, in search of nitre or hermit baskets, crawled over the barren landscape. There was no other moving object in sight.

Contrasting the immense emptiness of that landscape with the fevered activity that would have greeted him anywhere in the city, Zachary felt himself overcome by a sense of his own unimportance in the scheme of things. A moment ago he had been worrying about the future and his ability to cope with it. His future. His ability. As if the tiny vulnerable creature he was had only its own resources to battle with an alien and hostile universe.

He had feared, quite rightly, that those resources would prove too small. So what if they did? He had the far greater resources of Poemen to call on. That was the whole point of the teacher-disciple relationship. And behind Poemen stood God, Whose resources were infinite. How could he have supposed he would succeed at anything without God's help? Inexhaustible strength would not be required of him. All he had to bring was purity of intent and an undivided heart. And, of course, discernment. But discernment could be learned. The other two had to be born of his own spirit.

As he stood there, letting this realization sink in, Poemen appeared, a wooden yoke around his neck, two woven palm-frond panniers hanging from either end of it, each laden with stones so that the two loads balanced. Even so, Zachary was amazed at the weight the old man could still carry. And he was bringing them to build a home, not for himself, but for his disciple. He had not woken that disciple, knowing him to be tired after the long walk across the desert. He had quietly, humbly got on with the job by himself. Zachary, overcome with a mixture of gratitude and shame, ran to him, removed the yoke from his shoulders, and carried it to where a wall was already beginning to rise.

"Father, you shouldn't! You should have woken me! You'll kill yourself, carrying loads like that."

Poemen smiled and shook his head. "When I can no longer endure hardship or make myself useful, it'll be high time for me to go."

"I thought you had a donkey for stuff like this."

"I did. But he paid the debt of nature. A camel-driver offered to buy his corpse from me. They could have fed his meat to the dogs, made leather from his skin and ground up his bones for fertilizer. Quite a bargain. Somehow I couldn't, though. See that stone? I buried him there. Papnoute thought it was ridiculous. I daresay he was right, they don't have souls. Just that he seemed to look at me so reproachfully, even when he was dead. Irrational creatures are blameless, never forget that."

For the next few days they worked on enlarging the cell, and though they maintained Poemen's regime of prayer and meditation, little was said about Zachary's way of life. When the work as done, there were three rooms, an inner one for Poemen, and two outer ones, one for Zachary, one to cook and eat in. Outside the cell a low wall enclosed the herbs and vegetables. "A palm tree would look nice," Poemen said, regarding the finished effect, and remembering the trees in the courtyard of the church in Nitria, now burned or uprooted by the invaders. "Some might think it's frivolous. I ask them why God bothered to make trees, in that case. Next time we go to the marshes for reeds, let's dig up a little one and bring it back."

Fleetingly, there crossed his mind the prophecy of Macarius—when you see trees in Scetis, it is at the door. Nonsense, he told himself. If Scetis is truly to be destroyed, whoever destroys it will hardly be influenced by trees.

"Now," he said, turning to Zachary, "we have to decide how you're going to live."

"However you tell me to, Father."

Poemen shook his head. "In that case, I suggest you get yourself enrolled in a monastery. They'll tell you when to get up, when to go to bed, when to pray, when to work, what to eat and how much. You won't have to make a single decision. Is that what you want?"

"No, Father."

"I didn't think you did. This is not a cenobium and I am not an abbot. I don't give orders. If you choose to imitate me, fine. If you want to make your own Rule, fine too. Except if I think it's bad for your soul I'll tell you so. But even then, you're free to ignore me, if you choose." And Poemen turned, as if everything had been settled, and started setting a new batch of reeds to soak.

"Father?" Zachary's voice was hesitant, apologetic.

"Yes, my child?"

"I need more help than that. I don't know how to begin."

Poemen relaxed, squatted down on a papyrus stool and motioned to Zachary to do likewise. "Now you're getting it. Asking for orders is one thing, asking for help quite another. I shall ask you for help, quite often, I'm sure. In fact, I'm going to start by doing just that. Please help me by not calling me Father anymore."

"But, Father..."

"There you go again."

Zachary felt acutely uncomfortable. "But it's a mark of respect! How can I show my respect for you unless..."

"You can show your respect," Poemen cut in sharply, "by respecting my wishes. Calling me Father is like inviting me to consider myself your superior, and I want to avoid that, at all costs."

"But everyone else calls you Father!"

"I can't stop everyone. But at least I can try and stop you constantly bombarding me with it."

"As you wish, Fa—You see?" Zachary grimaced ruefully. "I can't help it. It's just natural."

"We didn't come here to be natural," Poemen said sternly. "We came here to do violence to our nature, at least any part of that nature that stops us from seeking God. Well, try your best, anyway...You wanted to know how to begin."

Zachary nodded, not trusting himself not to say "Father" again.

"One normally begins with repentance."

Zachary thought of his life in Alexandria—the descent of his soul into the slough of material things, the nights of sottish drunkenness, the indulgence of lust with the Vibias and Ariadnes, the times he had listened approvingly while Cellius scoffed and sneered at spiritual things. "I will fast," he said. "I will go without sleep. I will keep silence. I will wear a hair shirt." He had heard about hair shirts in Alexandria, they were the latest thing in asceticism. You had a shirt made of an animal's skin, but you wore it inside out, so that the hairs constantly irritated the skin. Wearing them made you feel so uncomfortable that you acquired a great deal of merit, so they said. There were also some who attached heavy chains to themselves, as if they were prisoners, but he felt that might be going a bit too far.

"Yes, I'm sure," Poemen said. "But are you going to repent?"

The question took Zachary by surprise, leaving him baffled. Surely the things he had described were repentance?

"You see, you can do any or all of these things without actually repenting at all. You can even use them as a substitute for repentance. Likewise, you can truly repent without doing any of these things, though it may help if you do one or two of them. Impresses it more on the mind, so long as you do them right."

He stared intently at Zachary to see how he was taking this, and was pleased to note that his look of puzzlement had been replaced by one of earnest attention.

"But no hair shirts. Not in my cell. If you wear them with nothing over them, that's like advertising to the world, 'Look what a great ascetic I am!' And that is pride, and displeasing to God, as well as being vulgar and disgusting in itself. If you hide them under other clothing, that's still wrong. In my view at least. The itch distracts your mind. When you should be thinking of your sin, you're thinking of your skin."

"But isn't the same thing true of hunger, when you fast?"

Poemen smiled approval. "A good question. Always ask questions. Some old men discourage it. Very short-sighted, in my opinion." Shut up, Poemen, he told himself, you're running off at the mouth again. Isn't this just what you always dreaded, if you took a disciple? Sententiousness, self-righteousness... Just answer the man's question, can't you? "Yes, it's true of hunger, to a much lesser extent. You can go without food for many hours and not suffer too much, especially if your mind is engaged in something that matters to you. Besides, hunger is a natural distraction, so the body has its own ways of adjusting to it. But with a hair shirt, the discomfort starts from the moment you put it on. In fact if it wasn't so uncomfortable..."

His voice tailed off. Something had occurred to him that he hadn't thought of before, or at least, not so clearly. If pomposity was the downside of the teacher's role, then this was the upside—the need to explain to another bringing one's own thoughts into focus.

"I think what it is," he went on, "is that people confuse two things, doing penance and punishing themselves. It's understandable. If you've done something you repent of, you feel you deserve to be punished. And you feel too that if there's some kind of balance between the pleasures the sin brought you and the pain of the punishment, then one has somehow wiped out the other. There'd be no point in wearing a hair shirt if it didn't itch—it doesn't purify body and mind as fasting can, it just itches. And none of this has anything to do with repentance. Repentance is exposing yourself to God AND TO YOURSELF. I mean, you knew all the time that God knew what you were doing, the only way you could shrink the shame of it was by blinding your own eyes and pretending you weren't sinning at all, really. Or at least, not badly. That's why the most important thing is simply to open your heart, confess to yourself and to God, to a third party too, if you like...but confess everything, every dirty little thought, every dirty little secret. And, need I add, learn to truly hate those things and truly mean to amend your life."

"I hadn't thought of it quite like that before," Zachary admitted.

Well, neither had I, Poemen thought. *So why not be up front about it, instead of passing yourself off as the fount of all wisdom?* "As a matter of fact, neither had I. There's a lot to be said for this disciple business, after all—I should have gotten into it years ago...No, I've always felt repelled by hair shirts, scourging oneself." He made a choked sound of disgust. "But I never fully understood why. I do now. It's God's job to punish sin, not ours. To do it to ourselves is arrogance, rank impiety. Our job is to repent, not punish. Well, enough of that. What about the timing?"

Zachary, still trying to absorb what he had learned, was thrown off balance by this change of topic. "Timing?"

"We have to decide how long this repentance should take."

Zachary thought for a moment. The weight of his offences lay heavy on him, the years of selfish, thoughtless indifference. For as long as he could remember, he had heard the words 'to hunger and thirst after righteousness'. But never before had he actually experienced the sensation itself—a longing for purity of heart so intense that it ached within him like a physical hunger.

"Perhaps...three years?"

"Three years!" Poemen looked shocked. "Don't you think that's rather a lot?"

"A year, then."

"Still a lot. It seems to me."

Zachary racked his brains for some appropriate figure. He remembered Jesus in the wilderness. "Forty days?"

"No," Poemen said. "Important though it is, repentance is not the main event. It's just a prelude, something you have to get out of the way before you can start the serious business. Know what I think? I think if you repent with your whole heart and truly don't intend to sin again, three days is plenty. God should accept that. If you open your heart to Him, He'll usually let you know whether He has or not. If you're not sincere, you could go through all the motions for thirty years and it wouldn't do you any good."

"It seems like very little."

"That's all right."

"What do you mean, that's all right?"

"What I said. If it's little, fine. So are you. So am I. Less than the most irrational of God's creatures, who as I said just now are blameless. Something neither of us can ever say honestly. Not in this life at least."

Zachary shook his head, still puzzled. "You'll have to bear with me, Fa— I'm sorry! Force of habit."

"Forgiven."

"What I don't see is...I mean, if my sins were many and serious, surely that requires something equally...See what I mean?"

"I see what you mean all right," Poemen said. "It seems obvious. So obvious it seduces many sincere hermits. Because they are humble, which is fine, and feel compunction, which is fine, they condemn themselves, which is fine, as the worst among sinners, which is not so fine, because it brings in the spirit of competition. If I've sinned worse than you have, then I have to repent longer and harder and more painfully than you. And thus the seeds of pride are sown in my heart, for I must indeed be a great and important and holy fellow to have repented for so long, so bitterly, and so forth. How familiar are you with the Nile delta?"

Zachary just sat there blinking. "I beg your pardon?"

"I said, how familiar are you with the Nile delta?"

"I'm sorry, but what's that got to do with pride?"

Poemen shook his head sadly. "When I said it was good to ask questions, I meant intelligent questions. When I ask you a question, answer it. You'll see soon enough where we're going. He who has ears, if I may borrow from Scripture...Well, for most of its course the Nile is a single stream, right?"

Zachary agreed.

"But as it approaches the sea, it finds its way blocked by sandbars, by the silt from upriver that it's dropped in its own bed. What happens?"

"It spreads into many channels."

"What happens if one of those branches gets blocked?"

"It finds another way round."

"Apply the parable."

Zachary threw up his hands. "I can't! Please explain it to me."

"All right. Most of us see pride as a single stream. We think of kings, emperors, archbishops even—leaders strutting before their people, behaving with the arrogance of the powerful the world over. Not a vice for humble folk like you and me. Wrong. Pride will find a way in. Just like the Nile, it seeks its sea, but its sea is the human heart. To reach that sea, it will break into a hundred subtle channels. And if you think you've blocked it just by adopting a life of humility, think again! Pride is infinitely patient, infinitely ingenious. It will find its way into your life where you least expect it."

"How can I overcome it?" Zachary asked.

"I like that," Poemen said, smiling. "Not, can I overcome it, but how can I? In the last analysis, only by interior vigilance, by constantly monitoring every thought and feeling. But a good start is to accept your own littleness, not reluctantly, but gladly and gratefully. Repent modestly, not excessively. Then, you can start to seek God, but modestly too of course, not expecting anything at all in the way of spiritual experience…"

Zachary starred at him. "Nothing at all? Then why…"

"Enough of this talking," Poemen said abruptly. "Plenty of time for that when you're through repenting. If we don't work, we don't eat."

Zachary gazed down at his hands, swollen and blistered from several days of hauling stones and fitting them together. "That wasn't work?"

"Did you get paid for it?"

"No."

"Then it wasn't work. Come on, don't tell me you've forgotten how to make baskets?"

Chapter 28

Adultery and fornication, with Vibia. Fornication with Ariadne and an unknown number of whores and pickups, names lost in an alcoholic blur, that he had had mostly to annoy Vibia. Drunkenness, unnumbered times. Blasphemy and impiety, mostly passive, listening to Cellius as he raved about the barbarous superstitions of Christers, or atoms-and-the-void. Anger, at his mother, his employees, his clients. Greed that had driven him to the edge of naked fraud. Avarice that had led him to accumulate wealth beyond any reasonable need while making specious excuses for his lack of charity. Pride in a way of life that rejected all restraints.

Poemen interrupted his self-scrutiny on the afternoon of the second day. "Get yourself ready. We're leaving for synaxis."

Zachary did not want to disturb the current of his thoughts. "But I'm not through repenting yet," he complained. "I'm not even sure I've finished counting my sins, let alone repenting them. Is it right for me to stop in the middle, just like that?"

"It's not just right, it's essential. If it throws you out at all, just start over as soon as you get back."

"Is it really so important? The synaxis, I mean. We pray all the time, anyway."

"Remember Cosmas the Syrian?" Poemen asked.

Zachary nodded. "I was there."

"I know you were. Things like that you never forget. Madness, believing you can fly like an angel, surrendering to all manner of diabolic temptations— you don't get there by missing just one synaxis, or two, or even three. But make a habit of it, and you're gone. Know why?"

"Tell me."

"Because we're not isolated grains of sand. Each with his own little soul, his own little salvation. We're more like leaves on a tree. The tree is community. It bears us, and we feed it. Mutual dependence. Without us, the tree is nothing. Without the tree, we are nothing. It's not the prayer itself, it's the praying together, eating together, sharing of word and thought, a thousand things…"

Zachary stood up.

"I'm sorry, I didn't mean to argue with you, I just wanted to understand. I'm ready to go, if you are."

"No you're not. You think you are, but you're not."

Zachary looked round him, puzzled. In the city, Poemen's remark would have made sense. People in the city would not regard themselves as ready until they had put on their finest clothes to go to church in, and, if they were of Zachary's station, called slaves or servants to accompany them. But here Zachary didn't have any finest clothes, any clothes finer than those he already had on.

"Your mind's full of your old sins," Poemen reminded him. "Do you want to take all that baggage to the agape?"

Zachary shook his head.

"Empty it all out."

"How do I do that?"

"Repeat the Jesus prayer, the prayer of the Publican, anything. Repeat it until there's nothing else left in your mind."

A half hour later, Poemen asked, "Have you emptied your mind?"

"Yes."

"Stop praying. See what comes into it."

After a few moments, Zachary said, "Nothing's come into it."

"Be patient. It soon will. Just let the thoughts come, whatever they are. But watch them very carefully and closely. If any are impure, throw them out."

After a while Zachary said, "Can I have some help?"

"Of course."

"Can I tell you my thoughts? I don't trust myself yet to be sure what's impure and what isn't. Not in every case."

"Go ahead."

"I didn't want to go to synaxis because I was afraid of meeting John."

Poemen looked startled, then incredulous. "Colobos? That's ridiculous. Anyway you're certain to meet him sooner or later. Might as well get it over with."

"That don't make it any easier."

"So what's hard?"

"You don't remember? Why I stopped being his disciple?"

Poemen dismissed the matter with a wave of his hand. "Because he had impure thoughts about you? That was years ago. He's long since overcome all that."

Zachary avoided Poemen's gaze. "Maybe, but as soon as he sees me, he'll remember. And that makes it very embarrassing."

"For you?"

"Yes. I won't know what to say to him. I'm worried I might say the wrong thing."

"You've forgotten the Commandment," Poemen said severely.

Zachary shook his head, equally firmly.

"Yes you have. Can't you see how to apply it here?"

"I'm afraid I..." Zachary began. Then his voice tailed off. He did see, or at least thought he might have a glimmering. "You mean...do you mean I should be more concerned about his feelings than my own?"

Poemen's eyes twinkled. "We'll make a hermit of you yet. Yes, Zachary, that's exactly what I meant. He might feel just as embarrassed as you, or more so. So your task as a brother is not to agonize over your own feelings but to do all you can to make things easier for him. Shouldn't be too difficult. Weren't you fond of him?"

Zachary remembered the tiny bustling hermit, bobbing in and out of his burrow, the absurd parables he told, the kindness and innocence that shone through all he did. "Yes I was," he said. "Very much."

"Let him know that. Without going overboard, mind, too much praise is poison to the soul. Concentrate on making him feel at ease with you, and I guarantee you'll be too busy to worry about your own feelings...Well, any more thoughts you'd like to share?"

For as Poemen explained to Zachary, he himself never attended synaxis without examining his thoughts for at least an hour, to ensure that no evil went with him to the communal feast. Since today he had undertaken the same task on behalf of Zachary ("Not that I'll make a habit of it," he warned, "you must learn to do it for yourself"), they were late in setting out, and walked quickly through the late summer heat that settled in the hollow under the escarpment.

"Did anyone ever tell you what the name of this place means?" Poemen asked.

"I don't think so."

"Scetis is the Greek name. From the Egyptian 'shi-iet'. Two words that mean 'heart', and 'to weigh or 'to measure'. Scetis means 'to weigh or measure the heart'. It's the place where the heart is weighed, measured, tested...You know what the old men mean when they talk of having a single heart?"

Zachary hesitated. It was one thing to have a concept in one's mind and quite another to truly understand it and live it. To do that, you had to have experienced it. Could he honestly say that for one moment of his life he had truly known singleness of heart?

"I know what the words themselves mean," he said, "but..."

"Almost everyone has a divided heart," Poemen said. "A heart divided between love of God and one's neighbor, on the one hand, and on the other love of the self, of the world, of the passions and pleasures of existence. A single heart is the prize of purity all of us are striving for here, here where the heart is weighed and, all too often, found wanting. A single heart, dedicated solely to the love of God and of others, all others, enemies as well as friends, perhaps especially enemies, since loving one's friends is easy and loving one's enemies infinitely hard...When they weigh your heart, will they find it single or divided?"

Zachary hesitated. "You mean as it is now, this moment?"

"Yes."

Zachary sighed. "Divided, I'm afraid."

"You're honest. That's good."

"I would give anything to have singleness of heart."

"Wouldn't we all?" There was such wistfulness in Poemen's tone, Zachary turned to gaze at him, bewildered. "But surely, you of all people..."

"I often ask myself," Poemen said sadly, "if such a heart is possible, this side of the grave. If I may compare the holy to the unholy, it's like those illusions that demons sometimes present you with in the desert. You think you see pools, streams, palm-trees. You approach them, and just as you seem to be getting near, they vanish."

"But this is not an illusion," Zachary said.

"No, of course not. If we could truly purge ourselves of the passions, we would have achieved singleness of heart. It's only our own weakness that prevents us from reaching it." And Poemen, shaking his head, fell silent and remained so until they reached the refectory.

By then the big room had almost filled. Moses was already saying grace and everyone present sat poised to start eating. Glancing around, Poemen saw that two of the few spaces left were either side of the hermit who, according to Anoub, had sodomized the mad boy. He hesitated only for an instant before taking one of these seats and motioning to Zachary to take the other. As he stepped over the low bench and sat down, the man turned to glare at him from small leaden eyes under a sloping forehead.

Poemen smiled back. "I think we haven't met. I'm Poemen and that's my disciple Zachary."

The man turned to glare briefly at Zachary, but made no attempt to introduce himself.

"Been here long?"

"Long enough," the man grunted, bending low over his vegetable stew.

"You don't find this place to your liking?"

"Place is all right. The people."

"What's wrong with them?"

The man spooned his plate bare before answering, "They all hate me." The other side of him, Poemen saw Zachary trying to look as if this was a normal conversation.

"Not very Christian of them, if that's true," Poemen said mildly.

"Course it's true," the man said belligerently. "Why do you suppose no one will sit by me?"

"We sat by you," Poemen pointed out.

"You don't know what I did."

"Yes I do, as a matter of fact, but I wouldn't have brought it up if you hadn't."

"You're a hypocrite," the man said, standing up. His body shook so violently with repressed rage that the spoon rattled in his empty bowl as he picked it up. "A mealy-mouthed hypocrite. Worse than the rest of 'em. At least they're honest about it." He climbed over the bench and stalked off.

Zachary gazed questioningly at Poemen. "He sodomized a mad boy," Poemen explained. "I imagine the brothers are trying to freeze him out. Useless, of course."

"You mean they haven't expelled him?" Zachary asked, amazed.

Poemen shook his head. "First of all, there's no 'they'. There's an informal council of elders, who won't even try to throw anyone out any more, since every time they tried, Moses or Bessarion or someone would demonstrate against it. Rightly so, in my opinion. Judgement is God's business, not ours. And now that Moses is priest here, he'd never stand for it. However, that apparently doesn't stop people from applying informal sanctions."

"I wouldn't call that useless," Zachary said. "From what he said I doubt he'll be here much longer."

"You misunderstand me. I didn't mean they couldn't get rid of him. I meant that getting rid of him was useless."

Zachary felt again the sense of moral vertigo, of normal civilized standards turned upside down, that he had first felt when Poemen told John to get his assailants out of jail. "I don't follow you."

"Why not? It's quite straightforward."

"For you, maybe. But—"

"But what?"

"Surely, anyone like that will corrupt others—"

Poemen grinned. "The bad-apple-in-the-barrel theory. Appealing, I grant you. I've been tempted myself. But it's baseless, of course. Why? Because you can't be corrupted by bad example if you yourself haven't started to go rotten already. All the bad-apple stuff is just an excuse."

Zachary, remembering his own experience with Cellius, felt the justice of this in his own heart.

"Now, suppose he goes away," Poemen went on, "voluntarily or otherwise. Has he changed? Not at all. He's as committed to evil as he ever was. Probably more so now he's embittered by having been ostracized. But the people he goes amongst won't know that, so he has more opportunity to do evil there than he had here. And again, someone will be hurt by it. Is that what you want?"

Zachary had to admit it was not. "But the community has to be protected," he insisted.

"And we're too weak to protect ourselves? More able here than anywhere else he might go, I would have thought. Not even taking into account that nowhere else is he as likely to repent."

"You think someone like that can repent and be saved?" Zachary asked doubtfully.

"I don't think it. I know it. And can give examples."

"In every case?"

Poemen thought about that for a long time. "I don't know the answer to that," he said finally.

"You didn't seem to be doing too well with this one," Zachary couldn't resist saying.

Poemen laughed out loud, his laughter, as usual, drawing reproving looks from some of his neighbors. "No, I didn't, did I? What was it he called me? A mealy-mouthed hypocrite? Oh well, an insult or two is good for the soul. You don't win all the time, except in those cheer-up stories hermits keep telling one another. Doesn't mean you can stop trying."

"Even if you think you can't win?"

"Especially if you think you can't win! People have been doing it the other way, the practical way, the common-sense way, for thousands of years now. Judging, punishing, exiling, executing, and look where it's—John! How are you, have you seen who's come back to Scetis?"

John, already heading for the church, had stopped to greet Poemen. Now his jaw dropped and his watery blue eyes rounded with astonishment. "Can it be...Is it possible...Zachary!"

"Yes, it's me," Zachary said. "I'm back, permanently, this time. I hope. God willing."

"I'm delighted to see you," John said with a warmth, a frankness, an utter lack of affectation that made Zachary ashamed of what he had feared from this interview. "Are you...I mean, who have you..."

"He's with me," Poemen said.

"So you've finally done it," John said, delighted.

"I don't think it's that big of a deal," Poemen said defensively. "As a hermit grows older…"

"Oh no," John said vehemently. "I see it as a step towards perfection."

Poemen shook his head. "A concession to human frailty."

"No, no!" John said earnestly. "I don't quite know how to say this without offending you, the last thing I want to do, and I certainly don't mean it in any derogatory sense, far from it, I've always regarded you as morally superior to me in every…"

Poemen sighed. "John, please, spare me the flattery and get to the point. Whatever it is, I can take it."

"You wouldn't take disciples because you were afraid."

Poemen stared at him in disbelief. "Me? Afraid?"

"I know it's hard to believe," John said, regretting his bluntness. "Because in every other way you're more fearless than any of us. But just in this one respect. You were afraid of the responsibility. You were afraid of making a mistake, of someone coming along and saying, "Oh yes, so-and-so, wasn't he with the Shepherd, and look how he's turned out…"

John's words were cut short, for his face was rudely thrust into the folds of Poemen's tunic as the Shepherd threw his arms around the little hermit and embraced him. "You're absolutely right! And I never really admitted it, even to myself." He turned his face towards Zachary. "It was a weird kind of pride— remember what I said about the Nile? Vice will always find a path. And convince you with flawless logic that it's really virtue. Thanks, John, your discernment is unsurpassed, as always."

"It was such a waste," John said once he had extricated himself from the embrace. "Not passing on all that you'd learned, all the good you could do for another. And," he went on, turning to Zachary, "let that be a warning to you, young man. Never to let him down. To be always worthy of him in word, thought and deed."

Zachary, awed by this new responsibility, could only nod and murmur that he would do everything in his power to achieve this. As he did so, Papnoute passed, surrounded by his disciples. For a second their eyes met and Zachary half-opened his mouth for a greeting. But Papnoute's gaze went right through him, Papnoute's face remained flint like in its expressionlessness. One of his disciples, bringing up the rear, flashed a surreptitious finger at Zachary and then the whole group was gone, swallowed in the stream of hermits exiting the refectory doors.

Zachary glanced at his two companions, but their faces expressed no awareness of what had happened. "We shouldn't be standing here talking," Poemen said. "We'll be late."

"So we will," John agreed, and without another word they headed in Papnoute's wake.

Chapter 29

Days passed, each, on the surface at least, hardly different from the one that preceded it. The heat decreased, the dry air cooled in the night. Hyenas howled from caves in the escarpment. And gradually, with a word here and another there, Poemen taught Zachary about prayer.

Prayer, he pointed out, meant different things for different people. For the layman, it usually meant asking for something for oneself. But prayer could not have this meaning for a hermit. A hermit should not want anything. The whole purpose of the ascetic life is to kill off all those wild and conflicting desires that continually plague one. Rather than strangle them one by one, you should cut off their common, single root by surrendering your will, your power to want anything at all. Then, your will becomes God's will. End of story.

Of course, in the nature of things, such a goal could hardly ever be achieved. In moments of crisis, our human frailty continues to call on God to get us out of the pits we dug for ourselves. But the hermit's attitude to such frailty should be zero tolerance. You had to approach as closely as you could to that goal of wantlessness, even while knowing you might never fully attain it.

Less reprehensible than praying for oneself was praying for others. Showing charity in word and deed, one could hardly avoid it in one's thoughts, too, wishing the best possible outcome for your neighbor. But either God willed that best outcome, or He did not. If He willed it, it was superfluous to pray for it. If He did not will it, it showed lack of piety to request it. So, in charity, one might pray God to grant something for someone else, but only with the preface, "If it be Thy will..."

But even this degree of intercessionary prayer was really only a concession to human frailty. Or worse, a hangover from pagan times, when people treated their gods as if they were puppets that anyone could manipulate. "I'll sacrifice a calf to you if you make my daughter fertile." With the implied threat, if you don't make her fertile, that's the last calf you'll be getting from me. No, the Almighty and Everlasting God was not something to be jerked this way and that by humans. He was what He was, He would do what He would do.

Really, Poemen told him, the only kind of asking prayer appropriate for hermits was that which is uttered when beset by temptation, when you fear your own unaided strength may not be enough to overcome it. Then, the request does not serve your own selfish desires. Rather, it falls into line with what God wills for you, for surely God wishes you to resist temptation. Then and only then, in such moments of inward turmoil, it is not merely permissible but essential to cry out with all the force in your soul. "O God come to my aid! O Lord make haste to help me!"

Of course there were prayers of gratitude for the grace and mercy of God in our daily lives. This was something, Poemen said, that he saw rather differently from some old men, in particular some priests, who laid emphasis on thanking God for particular mercies and at particular times and places. Rather, Poemen thought such gratitude should be ceaseless, should express itself not merely at every morsel of food or drop of drink that crossed one's lips, but at every breath one took. For after all, were it not for God's giving life in the first place, one would not exist, and if His will and if His love did not constantly sustain you, then you would surely perish.

With every breath you take, he told Zachary, you should give thanks to Him for allowing you to take it. Nor should you look on this as anything special, but rather a condition of being, a condition as natural and continuous as that of breathing itself. And not as some special department or type of prayer, rather as the ground on which all other forms of prayer were based. It was prayer of this kind, he believed, that the Apostle had in mind when he told us to "pray constantly."

Then, there was something that on the face of things might look similar to the prayer of gratitude: prayer as praise, prayer as worship. Such prayer would typically focus on some attribute of God—His power, His glory, His will, His mercy, and so on. Or on some scriptural episode, Moses in Egypt, Daniel in the lions' den, the Christ-Child in Mary's bosom, the scourging and the crowning with thorns. All very edifying. And nothing wrong with it, surely. But...

The "but," Poemen said, arose from the need to attach such prayers to concrete forms or incidents, specific examples of His mercy, particular Bible characters, whatever. Godly, for sure, but not God Himself. At best, mere attributes or manifestations of God, containing no more of His true being than a portrait or an image in a mirror contains the true being of a human person. You might just as well say of someone, "Oh, I've seen his footprints, his seal, his discarded tunic—I know him intimately!"

"But," Zachary said, "isn't that the best we can do? Doesn't Scripture say, 'No man living has seen God'?"

"That indeed is true," Poemen said, and added, grinning, "I've heard that somewhere, I don't remember where, there's a heretical sect that worships something called Noman, because Noman saw God before he died... But, in all seriousness, it's true that we can never apprehend God either through the senses or the intellect. Some have thought they could. But that's not just false, it's extremely dangerous—they lay themselves open to all kinds of diabolic illusions, one can go mad that way, as well as lose one's soul."

"I don't understand," Zachary said. "If it can't be done—"

"I never said it can't be done. I said it can't be done that way."

"Then how…"

"You're not ready yet," Poemen said abruptly.

"Then, when will I be ready?" Zachary asked, a trace of resentment in his voice, for several months had passed since his fateful meeting with Celia, and he felt he was not progressing as fast as he would have wished.

"When you no longer have that trace of resentment in your voice, among other things," Poemen said tartly.

Zachary recoiled in shock. He himself had been quite unaware of his tone, but he recognized the justice of Poemen's remark as soon as he heard it.

Poemen's wintry expression lightened suddenly. "Zachary, my son, I could explain it all to you easily—well, relatively easily—right now. And you're intelligent, you would grasp it easily, I'm sure. In your head. As an abstract concept. Where it would be totally useless to you—mental lumber, along with all the isosceles triangles and Ptolemaic epicycles and all the other intellectual junk I'm sure you've got stowed away in there somewhere. But I'm not teaching you ideas, Zachary. I'm trying to teach you how to live! What you need to know can be learned only through experience, and you're not adequately prepared for that experience, not yet."

"How will you know when I'm ready?"

"When you don't smell of the city any more. When your mind has stopped harking back to it, as it does whenever you're alone in your cell for more than an hour or two."

"How did you know that?" Zachary asked in wonder. "I never told you that."

"I know you didn't. That's part of the problem. I just guessed, and you just confirmed it. You'll be ready when you tell me all that's going on in your mind instead of leaving me to guess the bits you think do you the least credit. When you yourself know in your heart you're ready, and tell me so, and I can't trip you up. When this and when that. You can't rush these things. Just thinking you can shows you're not ready."

"I'm sorry," Zachary said sincerely, but feeling more than a little crestfallen. "I have a lot to learn."

Poemen patted his shoulder. "To know that is the beginning of wisdom. But above all, don't get discouraged. If I hold you back now, it's only so you can go farther in the future. I believe you can do it. I always have. But it won't be easy. It never is. Believe me."

The weeks passed, lengthened into months. There were times when Zachary felt he would go mad from the boredom of it, weaving in his cell, reading, reciting psalms, weaving, reading. People would come by to ask Poemen for a word, but usually the old man saw them in his own cell and he heard only the murmur of their voices. But occasionally, as on one chilly, overcast afternoon in late winter, a passing stranger would share their meal.

This time, it was a hermit from the Thebaid who had come to learn wisdom from the hermits of Scetis. He had just visited Arsenius. "I was shocked," he said between spoonfuls of lentil stew, which by now Zachary had learned to cook rather better than Poemen.

Poemen's eyebrows raised, but he continued to eat calmly and in silence.

"I had been told he was a great ascetic, with an austere way of life," the visitor went on in an aggrieved tone.

"That's right," Poemen said.

The visitor paused, put down his spoon and stared fixedly at his host. "Are you serious?"

"Of course."

"He has a BED," the visitor exclaimed indignantly, so upset he forgot to go on eating.

"Who doesn't?" Poemen inquired equably.

"I mean a BED bed!" the visitor exploded. "A thing with a frame, and a…a MATTRESS, if you please."

"Really."

"And the bed had a PILLOW on it! And he was wearing SANDALS, can you believe it?"

"It's winter," Poemen pointed out.

"But he's not even old!"

"His health's not very good."

"That doesn't mean he has to have his feet washed! Can you believe it? Right there in front of me, this old fellow supposed to be a brother but looks more like his slave to me gets down on the floor and WASHES HIS FEET!"

"Are you through with this, Father?" Zachary asked, firmly grasping the rim of the visitor's bowl, which could be emptied back into the stewpot once he'd left, heated through and used to eke out another day's supply.

"He…eh? What? No, I haven't finished." The visitor seized his spoon again as Zachary reluctantly relinquished the bowl. "And what's more," he went on, turning to Poemen, "he was drinking WINE!" Zachary congratulated himself on having kept their wine-jar out of sight. "What's your opinion of all that, eh?" the visitor demanded in a belligerent tone. "You don't think your austere Roman colleague is a bit of a fraud?"

Poemen's mouth was full, and he took his time chewing and swallowing before he replied. "Where are you from, originally?" he asked.

The visitor looked surprised. "Egypt, like you, what do you think? "

"Of what city, then?"

"No city," the visitor said, in a blustering voice in which pride and shame fought for dominance. "Country born and bred."

"And what was your trade back then?"

"I was a shepherd. What exactly is all this leading…?"

"That's a coinci…" Zachary began brightly, then clamped his mouth as Poemen flashed him a look.

Poemen smiled blandly. "Forgive me. I have a sincere interest in what leads people into the ascetic life. You must have had a hard time of it, then."

"You bet I had a hard time!"

"No beds there, huh?"

The visitor laughed contemptuously. "How would I have a bed, out there in the fields?"

"So how did you sleep?"

"How do you think? On the bare earth, that's how!"

"And not much in the way of food, I suppose. Let alone wine."

"I had dry bread," the visitor snorted. "Dry bread and water, and a few herbs when I could find any."

"And no baths in the village, eh?"

"Are you kidding? Yes, you can take it now," the visitor said, handing his empty bowl to Zachary. "When we got dirty, there was the river. That was it, summer or winter."

"Hm," Poemen said. He wiped his mouth meditatively, gave Zachary his bowl, and said, "All in all, how would you rate your life now? Harder, or easier than it was then,"

"Oh, easier." The visitor did not hesitate. "Much eas…" Then his voice tailed off. A clouded look of puzzlement appeared in his eyes. He as beginning to suspect where Poemen was leading him.

"You know what Arsenius was, before he came here," Poemen asked with a deceptive casualness.

"Dunno. Some kind of big bug in the capital?"

"He was the tutor of our Emperor Arcadius while he was growing up. He lived in the Imperial palace, he had slaves by the dozen to do his bidding. He slept on beds of swan's-down and was served the finest meats on platters of gold and silver. You and I," and Poemen leaned forward to transfix the visitor with his gaze, "could not even begin to imagine the luxury in which he lived. Now instead of a palace he has a miserable cell. Instead of his swan's-down mattress he has a wretched little paillasse on a cracked wooden frame. Instead of fine silken robes he wears the same dirty black tunic you and I do. The pillow, the wine, the sandals—yes, he pampers himself a little because, as I said, he came straight to this life from a life of luxury and I'm afraid his stomach's shot as a result of it. In other words, while you're better off than you ever were before, he's infinitely worse."

All the time Poemen was talking, Zachary was watching the visitor's face. He saw its expression change gradually as the speech progressed, becoming more drawn, more haggard, the corners of the mouth turning down in a wholly unconscious reflection of his feelings. As Poemen at last fell silent, the visitor slipped from his stool to the floor, first kneeling, then prostrating himself and clutching at Poemen's calves.

"Father! Forgive me! Forgive me for what I said."

"It's not me who should forgive you," Poemen said, nervously disengaging himself from the visitor's grasp, for such emotional exhibitions distressed him greatly. "You did nothing to offend me. Arsenius is the only one you might have offended. But it was a perfectly natural misunderstanding on your—"

"Then I should beg his pardon immediately," the visitor cried, leaping to his feet.

"Come back," Poemen called after him, "and say the twelve Psalms with us, if you..." His voice trailed off into silence, for all that was left of the visit was a swinging outer door and a cold blast of air that caused the smoldering cooking fire to fill the outer cell with swirling currents of smoke.

Zachary closed the door.

"You nearly blew my cover, back there," Poemen said.

"I'm sorry, I didn't think you'd mind him knowing you too were a..."

"I don't mind him knowing anything. But he'd have guessed right away what I was up to, if he'd known I'd had the same life as he had. I didn't want to accuse him, judge him—I just wanted to bring him to where he could see for himself how unjust he was being. He's a decent enough fellow, I don't doubt. A bit rough, but decent. I don't think he'll make that kind of mistake again." Poemen paused, then said reflectively, "He can't have much of a sense of smell, though."

Zachary, putting away cups and bowls, paused in his work. "Why not?"

"You've never been in Arsenius' cell, have you?"

"No, never."

"Well, you know the water we soak our palm fronds in. Know how often he changes it?" Zachary shook his head. "Once a year! Can you imagine what that smells like? I almost threw up, I said to him, "Arsenius, you don't think this is going a bit far?" He said, "Poemen, when I was in court I had all the perfumes of India and Arabia to feed my senses. I must learn to bear this foul odor as a penance for all the sensual pleasures I enjoyed." I said, "All right, but we weren't told to kill our bodies—just our passions." I don't think he got it, even then. I could have told him he was violating the Commandment just by inflicting that stink on his guests, but I didn't want to make him feel bad."

He paused for a moment, then said, "You know, I missed a trick there, not asking our friend what the place smelt like. If he'd gotten one whiff of that water, he wouldn't have reproached Arsenius for lack of austerity."

"We can ask him when he comes back," Zachary said.

"If he comes back," Poemen corrected him. "He's so embarrassed he'll spend about an hour apologizing, and it'll be so late by then, Arsenius will feel obliged to have him stay the night."

He was right, and they recited the twelve psalms of the evening office alone together, as they did most nights.

The months passed. The days lengthened imperceptibly. The summer heat, creeping northwards, invaded Scetis like a fifth element. And a traveling hermit from Antioch brought strange news.

Isidore and the Tall Brothers, driven from diocese to diocese by Theophilus' ceaseless propaganda, had finally wound up in Constantinople, where they had somehow managed to get the ear of the Empress Eudoxia. And now a special synod was being convened to try Theophilus for his crimes, and the Emperor himself had commanded Theophilus to appear before it.

Zachary's reaction to this reversal of fortune was one of frank pleasure. At last, justice could be done; the unrighteous would get their deserts. He felt surprise and disappointment when Poemen didn't see it the same way.

"But surely you of all people don't approve of what he did."

"Of course I don't," Poemen said curtly.

"Then you must agree, he deserves to be punished."

"I'm not sure that I agree that anyone deserves to be punished. I'm not even sure I know what 'deserves to be punished' means. Sin I can understand, and repentance, but these other things…" Poemen shook his head.

"But suppose there's sin and no repentance?" Though he would have been shocked to realize it, Zachary had developed an unconscious desire to, just once, come up with something Poemen had no answer for.

"That would be very sad."

"But one who won't repent should surely be punished."

"Would that make them repent?"

Zachary thought this over. "Well…maybe not. But they'd be sorry they'd done it, whatever it was."

"And that's repentance."

"Part of it, anyway."

"Speak from your own experience. Is that repentance?"

Zachary chewed his lower lip. "All right. There's more to it than that."

"Say what more there is."

"Well. You must truly hate what you did. And seek to make amends. To the extent that's possible." He thought hard. *Am I leaving anything out?* "Oh. And to genuinely intend not to sin again."

"Why?"

"I'm sorry, I don't quite…"

"Why should you intend not to sin again?"

"Because…well, like I said, because you hate what you did, and because you want to truly love the good."

Poemen cupped his hand round his ear. "Did I hear you right? Did you say, because you truly love the good, or, because you want to truly love the good?"

Zachary racked his memory. Already he had forgotten the exact words he had used. But obviously it was important, or Poemen wouldn't be making such a fuss about it. His original wording had sprung to his lips without thought. Now he tried to go back over it, to think what reason one might have to prefer one wording over the other.

"Because you want to truly love the good," he said at last.

Poemen beamed at him. "Excellent. You're getting there. Well, I think you're getting there. Make me sure, tell me why you made that choice."

"Because if you already truly loved the good, you wouldn't have sinned in the first place."

"Good. Go on."

"Because loving the good isn't just something you can step into, like a new suit of clothes."

"Better still…You'd be amazed, the number of people, not just seculars, some of our own too, who'll say, 'Oh dear, I've been a bad boy, but everything's fine now, I love the good.' What more need I say? Love of the good has to be learned. Just like anything else. Learned and earned."

"Earned?"

"Of course. Learning is never enough. You can learn and forget. Learn and distort. Learn and substitute. You earn something, once you've learned it, by living it, by acting it out until it becomes second nature to you. So the very best you can do, at this stage, even if you truly mean to amend your life, is want to love the good. Want it with all your mind and all your heart. You missed out one further thing."

"I did?" Zachary was agreeably surprised he had not missed more.

"Yes. If you already truly loved the good...you'd be perfect. And that doesn't come the morning after repentance, if indeed ever." Poemen ribbed his brow, he was afraid he was getting too wordy again. "How did we get into all this?"

"You asked why one should intend not to sin."

Poemen yawned. "Oh, that. So I did. But if we're not careful we'll get into all kinds of other stuff, and we have our daily bread to earn."

Zachary was not to be put off so easily. "We never finished with Theophilus, either. Or why punishment is wrong."

"Too bad," Poemen said, turning away.

"You wouldn't condemn him."

"Absolutely not. The Commandment forbids it."

"The Commandment tells you to love him. Do you love him?"

Poemen froze in midpace. "Ah," he said. He stood there for a moment, staring at Zachary with an expression Zachary could not read. "I would be happy," he said at last, "if I could just say yes to that. I know I am enjoined to, by Scripture. I accept that. I try to love him. I try to think, once he was an innocent child..."

"With pagan idols crashing to the ground wherever he went," Zachary put in.

"Yes," Poemen said, more sternly than Zachary had expected. "So you too have heard that nonsense, well just forget it, it's irrelevant to what I'm telling you now. Once even Theophilus was a child, happy in his innocence, running about. 'Unless you become as a little child...' Do you believe we are all children of God?"

"Of course."

"That though we may not literally be made in God's image, there is something of the divine in all of us?"

"Yes." Zachary sounded a little more doubtful this time.

"Well, then. That part of Theophilus I love, that's the best I can manage, so far, I'm afraid." Poemen fell silent, though he no longer showed any inclination to start work. "You know," he said after a few moments, "our paths have crossed twice, his and mine. The first time I tried to avoid him and the second I tried to outsmart him. Both successfully, I thought at the time. I think now I'm just beginning to see how far I am from perfection. You know what I should have tried to do? I should have tried to love him. Without qualification."

"Would it have made any difference?"

"To whom?" Poemen countered, quick as a flash. "To him, or to me?"

"To him."

Poemen considered. "Probably not. But to me...Yes, to me it would have made a difference. Zachary, I'm in your debt. You have taught me a lesson in humility. You may yet get to be an old man while you're still a young one."

"Then teach me true prayer," Zachary said quickly.

Poemen smiled, frowned, and scratched the back of his neck. "When you've stopped being bored," he said.

"Who said I'm bored?" Zachary was indignant. "I'm not in the least bored, I'm—"

Poemen cut him short. "Zachary, don't. Don't try to fool me about what you're feeling. You have a bad case of accidie. You've done a great job of hiding it from me, even from yourself, you're fighting it, you're holding your own...by a fingernail, right? But that won't do, will it? You know you can't beat it alone, but your pride won't let you admit that, even to yourself, still less to me, least of all to God...Don't think I don't know what it feels like. The minutes grinding by, slower and slower, you pray for any diversion, any distraction. An ant crawling across the floor would be better than nothing. See how you pounced on this news about Theophilus? Next thing you know you'll be asking everyone, has he left, has he got there yet, is he being tried, have they found him guilty? Will knowing any of that do your soul any good?"

Zachary, mute, shook his head.

"Why didn't you talk to me about what you were feeling?"

Zachary could not meet his gaze. "I...I was ashamed."

"Ashamed? Why?"

"I felt...I don't know. I must be weak or something. It's not as if I didn't know about it. I'd experienced it before, when I was here before. I thought with the experience and all, I ought to have been strong enough to overcome it."

His voice trailed off into silence. Poemen let the silence linger until it was almost painful, then he asked, "Do you still think you're ready for true prayer?"

"No."

"Good. We'll start work on the boredom tomorrow. You do realize, don't you, that this whole thing goes just as quickly or as slowly as you want it to go?"

"Yes," Zachary admitted ruefully. "I realize that now."

Derek Bickerton

Chapter 30

Ever since the Sabbath on which he had passed Zachary without speaking, Papnoute had made sure he avoided his former disciple. At first he had been troubled a little in case his attitude might be regarded as uncharitable. He had finally decided it was fully justified. After all, Zachary had deserted him without a word of apology or explanation. He had not even known whether Zachary was alive or dead until that moment when he had suddenly reappeared with—of all people!—Poemen.

At first, Papnoute had assumed that the juxtaposition of Poemen, Zachary and John was purely fortuitous. For all he knew then, Zachary had not returned permanently to Scetis, might merely be passing through or seeking counsel. But for all that hermits claimed to love silence and hate gossip, news traveled fast in Scetis. By sunset on the Lord's Day following that Sabbath, Papnoute had learned that Zachary was Poemen's disciple.

Papnoute was deeply shocked by this news. To him, it seemed like an insult, whether deliberate or not, on Poemen's part. Zachary had been Papnoute's disciple. And of course Papnoute would have taken him back, after a suitable period of supplication on Zachary's part. On probation, naturally, and under strict vigilance, to avoid backsliding. But Poemen—Poemen who had never taken a disciple of his own—had welcomed the renegade at first asking, unconditionally!

He had neither asked Papnoute's permission before doing this, nor his forgiveness afterwards. The insult was made worse, if that was possible, by Poemen's apparent unawareness that he had done anything wrong. More than once during the months that followed, Papnoute had been on the point of going out to reproach him, but had decided against it. It would be too demeaning to have to admit publicly that Zachary preferred Poemen to him. Moreover, he was not sure whether he could control his anger. If he failed to control his anger but Poemen controlled his, he would lose merit and Poemen would gain it—the offender would come off better than the victim. Which was intolerable. On the whole, it seemed better not to take the risk.

But the injustice was hard to swallow. It was not as if, in the years following his last angelic visitation, Papnoute had neglected any ascetic observances. Had he not fasted more, prayed harder, gone without sleep for longer and longer periods? Had he not reduced his water intake to a point where his desiccated flesh barely separated a parchment-like skin from the underlying bone? Had he not raised a whole generation of disciples in practices as austere as his own? Surely by now his merit should equal that of the most renowned men of Scetis. But if that were so, why had God inflicted this humiliation on him? Why had He allowed Poemen, of all people, to steal his disciple?

Above all, Papnoute needed reassurance. He needed to know that he had indeed made tangible steps towards perfection. Perhaps what had happened with Zachary was a test—a final test of his humility which, if he passed it, would admit him definitively to the pantheon of the blessed.

He began to pray again that an angel would visit him and clarify his situation.

Before, the angel had come in daylight, and Papnoute had supposed that, if his prayer was granted—and why shouldn't it be, if it had been, before?—he should expect a similar visit. He had forgotten that the angel always appeared when least expected.

So it was that, in the middle of a night of solitary vigil, he became aware that he was no longer alone. This time there was no imperious summons to the door, indeed no warning whatsoever of the angel's approach. Perhaps, despite all his efforts, sleep had momentarily overcome him, and the angel had profited from his moment of unconsciousness (it could have been no longer than that, he anxiously assured himself). Be that as it may, there the angel was, and there was no mistaking him. He even glowed faintly in the dark. But, he was not in a good mood.

"It doesn't improve your credit," the angel said sternly, with no other word of greeting, to keep calling me like this, just to satisfy your greed for information."

Awed though Papnoute was, he couldn't let this pass. "But it's been years since I called on you."

"Many hermits never call on me at all."

Papnoute bowed his head and did not answer the implied rebuke.

"Many hermits are quite content to do their best and wait for the Day of Judgement to see what rank they have attained."

"Forgive me," Papnoute murmured. "This is my only weakness. Other hermits may not call on you, but do they fast like I do, do they pray as constantly, do they…"

"Don't hide the beam in your own eye by plucking the motes from the eyes of others," the angel thundered.

Papnoute prostrated himself. The angel let him lie there for quite a while in silence, and then said, "Well, while I'm here, I suppose it's the same request as last time."

"If you would be so gracious," Papnoute whispered, his voice barely audible.

"And if so, how long before you start pestering me again?"

Papnoute gulped. "This is the last time. I swear it."

"You know we don't like swearing."

Papnoute stammered in his confusion. "I'm sorry. I don't...I mean I never normally swear, it's just that...I feel so nervous in your presence."

"I should hope so."

"I mean it. I really do."

"All right." The angel relented, unrolling his scroll. "Here it is... Papnoute, your merit now equals that of the flute-player in the temple of Isis at Terenuthis."

Papnoute, appalled, recoiled in horror. "Wh—what—?"

"You heard me."

"But that's impossible!" A flute-player! One whose foul, lascivious melodies incited others to lust, himself too probably, as if in that atmosphere anyone could escape it. And in a pagan temple! Not just an ordinary flute-player, that would have been bad enough, but a flute-player in a temple, one who took part in obscene and blasphemous ceremonies, a slave of Satan! It was unthinkable. "There must be some mistake."

"To err is human," the angel said. "We never make mistakes."

"Then you are a diabolic illusion," Papnoute exclaimed in what he genuinely believed was a flash of insight. Why hadn't he thought of that before, it was obvious once you thought of it. "Get thee behind me, Satan!"

"I've always thought that was a ridiculous expression," the angel said imperturbably. "The last place you'd want the Devil is behind you, where you can't see what he's getting up to. The correct expression is, "Back off, Satan!" Remember that in case you ever need it."

Papnoute was hoping the angel would disappear in a puff of smoke and a bad smell, as diabolic illusions were said to do. But the angel was still there.

"Prove to me you're not a diabolic illusion!"

"Force me to do that and you lose five years' progress," the angel countered sternly. "For lack of faith," he added. "Take the risk if you want to. Your choice entirely."

Papnoute made the sign of the cross at the angel. The angel smiled benignly and made the sign of the cross right back to him. "Bless you, too," he said.

Papnoute gave up. Incredibly, this had to be the real thing.

"What have I done wrong?" he asked, weeping.

"I'm not allowed to discuss that."

"What must I do to gain merit?"

"I thought I'd explained all that last time." the angel said wearily. "Our job is to give messages. We don't do spiritual counseling. But that's the least of your problems, you won't find anywhere with more qualified people than right here in Scetis," As Papnoute continued to weep, the angel took pity on him and said, "Anyway, aren't you jumping to conclusions? You know how it is, some seculars are a lot holier than some hermits. Your fellow may well be one of those."

"A temple flute-player?" Papnoute asked incredulously.

"Who knows? I've seen stranger things. And there's one thing you can say about the Kingdom. We're not snobbish."

"You know something I don't," Poemen hazarded.

"That's quite possible."

"Tell me what the flute-player did that was so wonderful."

The angel shook his head. "Sorry." Moments before he vanished, he added, "If you want to know that so badly, you'll just have to ask him yourself."

Chapter 31

"Kill the self," Poemen said, "and you will kill boredom."

He did not explain to Zachary what he meant by this. He left Zachary to think about it while he worked on his baskets, for he believed that insights that were not struggled for were hardly worth having. Then, when Zachary had made some headway on his own he might be given a further glimpse or two down the path. That way one didn't so much learn things as grow into them, by imperceptible degrees.

For Zachary came to realize, by stages so gradual he himself could not have told when the process was complete, that he became bored while sitting alone in his cell because his selfish nature had not yet entirely perished. If you say, "I am bored", what you are in fact saying is "I demand things to keep myself diverted." Simply denying yourself these diversions was futile. For every diversion you rejected, a new one popped up. Instead, you have to strike at the root, the love of self.

Who are you that you should feel entitled to diversions? You are nothing—a mote in the whirlwind of space and time. So how could it matter whether you are bored or not? What impudence, to call on the world to divert you!

And if that was hard to grasp, Poemen said, ask yourself whether an athlete in training for some important event worries because he is not being amused. Of course he doesn't. He's training. He expects it to be hard, boring, painful even. Or think of a man digging a well. Does he expect digging a well to be entertaining? Of course not, he needs the water. That's all he's thinking about, getting to the water. But suppose the water was the Water of Life?

The trouble with the contemplative life was that it didn't involve anything obvious in the way of action, like digging or running laps. When you thought of it you didn't naturally think in terms of work. And anything you didn't think of as work, you expected to be entertaining, to some degree. Well, contemplation was work. Hard work. Harder than training for a sport or digging ditches, because it was both—both training and work. You trained your soul to overcome temptation and you worked to achieve greater closeness to God.

Zachary didn't realize he had learned these lessons until sometime after he had learned them. How long, he wasn't sure. Well over a year had passed since his return to Scetis, and the skies had once more lost their brassy hardness. You felt a dry chill in the air even before sunset—nothing uncomfortable, rather a bracing, exhilarating feeling. And the quality of the light, its remote and utter purity, filled the heart with formless longings. Over their daily meal, Poemen asked out of the blue, "How long were you bored today?"

Zachary, taken by surprise, said, "I don't...I'm not sure...No wait! I wasn't bored! Today, I really wasn't bored!"

"Hm," was all Poemen said as he took another spoonful of beans.

"I really hadn't noticed," Zachary went on in the same excited tone, amazed at his discovery. "It...it simply never occurred to me. I just didn't think of it."

"Any more ways you could say that?" Poemen inquired drily.

"You're laughing at me," Zachary complained.

"Certainly not. Just trying to get you to speak less. Not that I'm any kind of example, I'm probably over-reacting. Well, how long since you felt bored?"

Zachary thought about that. "Maybe since yesterday...No. No, to tell you the truth, now I come to think of it, I wasn't bored yesterday, either. I don't think. I mean, I really don't remember."

"Hm," Poemen said again. There was silence while they both soaked up the bean-juice from their bowls with what was left of their daily bread ration. Then Poemen said, "do you remember any time you felt bored recently?"

Zachary shook his head.

"Then maybe it's time to start thinking about pure prayer."

Pure prayer, Poemen told him, was something paradoxical. People prided themselves on being rational creatures, on having powers of reason that exceeded those of the beasts. Powers that approximated, however remotely, to the higher reason of angels and of God Himself. So you might suppose that this power of reason was what would enable us to approach God most closely. How wrong you would be! Precisely because it was only the remotest shadow of divine wisdom, our reason could not hope to encompass the Deity.

Only through prayer could one approach God. But even then, it had to be prayer stripped of all its rational content, prayer that was a pure outpouring of love. Only a loving heart could grope through the darkness enshrouding Him from mortal eyes, darkness impenetrable to the endlessly-chattering, pride-soaked mind.

But how, exactly, was this done? Again, the process defied rational analysis, it could not be reduced to the simple either-ors, this-and-thats into which the human brain chopped all its experiences. Even the most learned and holiest of teachers could do little more than give a few pointers in the right direction.

First, one had to have solitude, silence, absence of any form of outside distraction. Though the work could be undertaken at any time, night was best—the darker and stiller the night, the more conducive to pure prayer. Poemen himself preferred the hours between midnight and dawn, but each one was free to choose the time and place that seemed most congenial.

Then, one had to shut down the logical, discursive voice in the mind that tried to weave everything into coherent patterns. Even when that voice was quieted, random ideas and images would continue to rise, just as fish rise sluggishly to the surface of a still pool. But those ideas and images would no longer be able to form themselves into the logismoi, those relentless trains of coherent and organized thought which gave you the illusion that you, rather than God, controlled your fate. Fragmented thoughts could more easily be driven down into the murk from which they came. What you did, you took a single word, the shorter and simpler the better, and repeated it over and over, focused on it until all else vanished.

It really didn't matter what word you chose, Poemen said. He himself set little store in the belief that words had magical powers, that they somehow controlled the things they represented. The form of the word mattered more than the meaning. Two syllables were better than three, one better than two. "Christ" was better than "Jesus", although "Jesus" was more popular among many hermits. "God" or "love" would do just as well. The word was only a means to an end.

That end was brought closer when the mind, emptied of all thought, clean and clear as a newly-swept room, relaxed and waited—waited to be possessed by God's presence.

But the work was not yet done. Two more things were needed.

The one who prayed, who had concentrated his mind into a single point of energy, had to reach out into the encompassing darkness in absolute love and submission to God.

And God, out of His infinite grace and mercy, had to enter and fill the vacant space that the one who prayed had created for him.

Whether he did that or not was His business, not that of the one who prayed or anyone else. There were hermits, Poemen said, who gave up if they didn't get quick results. That was arrogance and folly. You had to go on, patiently, without questioning, without protesting. Knowing it was not impossible that one might work a lifetime without success. Not that this was likely, Poemen hastened to add. But a possibility you could not rule out, because to be certain of success would be to doubt God's omnipotence.

"That will do for now," Poemen said. "I want you to start tonight, and tomorrow tell me all that happened, or what did not happen. Even if you had trouble with the first step. Especially if you had trouble with the first step. Remember that in this, we are all, me included, rank amateurs. There is no shame in failure. Rapid success would be much more worrisome." He seemed about to close their session, then he said, "But perhaps I've been too hasty. There is one more test you should pass before you begin. Because without absolute purity of heart, you cannot hope to achieve it. A while back, you remember, we talked about why one should intend not to sin. And I said I wouldn't get into it then, because it was part of a much larger question: why not do evil?"

There has to be a trick in this, Zachary thought. I*t's too obvious.* "Because God wills that we should not," he answered piously.

"I am here, God is a long way away. Or seems so. I would profit from this evil. Why not do it?"

"Because God will punish it throughout eternity."

"That thought does deter a lot of people. We are good because we fear the consequences of evil. Is that the best reason?"

"No.

"Name another."

"Because if we refrain from evil we will be seated at God's right hand and receive an everlasting crown in the Kingdom."

Poemen frowned. "To do good to obtain a reward. That implies that if there were no reward we would do evil, if we profited by it, right?"

Zachary could see no logical objection to this.

"Name me another reason."

Zachary hesitated. "You mean—to follow virtue only because you love it?"

"Better," Poemen said. Then, he leaned forward and gazed at his disciple with an intentness that was almost frightening. "Fine, in principle. But it's not principle we're talking about now. It's you, Zachary. Answer me and answer me with absolute truth. Do you reject evil because you fear punishment, because you hope for a reward, or because you truly love virtue?"

For a long time, Zachary didn't answer. He sensed from Poemen's manner that this was not some routine catechism but something far more important, perhaps a turning-point in his life.

Poemen spoke his unspoken thought: "It would be awfully easy to give the third answer, wouldn't it?"

"But I won't."

"Because it's not true?"

"Because I want to be sure first."

Poemen nodded, and composed himself as if for a long wait, should that be necessary. Zachary thought, *Can I truly acquit myself of cowardice, of fearing what may follow death, not knowing how in that hour I am to be judged? Of course not. Who can?* Yet it seemed to him despicable to act from fear of future pain. *And surely, too, God would not want this, given that His nature was as reported by His own Son. A God who loved his children was hard to reconcile with a God who used fear like a whip. And the Son surely knew His Father better than a bunch of Old Testament prophets,* he thought irreverently.

As for hope of heavenly reward, it surely could not be wrong to desire a closer union with the Divine than could be achieved in this life. Nor could it be wrong to ensure, insofar as one was able, that no sin committed in this life should prevent that union. But that desire, holy though it might be, still involved one's own personal satisfaction. In other words, concern for one's own salvation was, in the last analysis, a selfish concern. And had not Poemen taught him that in love of self lay the root of all evil? So should the desire for personal salvation serve as the driving force of one's actions?

Surely not.

But that was not the question.

The question was, was it the driving force of Zachary's actions?

He remembered how he had felt during his last meeting with Celia. How he had learned the true meaning of the phrase, "to hunger and thirst after righteousness." Could he not then claim quite honestly that he loved righteousness for its own sake?

"I think," he said cautiously, "I honestly think that I reject evil because I love good...That's not to say I achieve it, every day I fall short of what little good I can even imagine. But to the extent that I'm able, I don't think I do it out of fear, or hope of reward. Of course I could be deceived. I mean I may be deceiving myself. But I've looked as hard as I know how, and I think that's the truth."

"Thank you," Poemen said.

"Thank me? Why?"

"For giving such a thoughtful answer. For reassuring me I'm not hopelessly incompetent as a teacher, as I've always feared I'd be. It's one thing to throw off words of wisdom for casual inquirers, it's quite another to be responsible for someone else's spiritual welfare. But see how I'm still flattering myself? Pride, Zachary. See how it still finds ways? No, God and your own heart have done more than I ever could."

Zachary hardly knew how to respond to this. "Without you, Father, I could have done nothing, would have been nothing—"

"Let's cut out the mutual congratulations," Poemen said briskly. "Am I to take it then that if you suddenly discovered that there was no such thing as hell, no fire, no torment, no eternity of punishment, you would really continue to live as you do now?"

"I would try to do so."

"And if at the same time you discovered there was no God, no heaven, no reward whatsoever for your virtuousness?

"I would still try to do so."

Poemen stroked his chin reflectively. "I really believe you would. Happily, that's a difficulty that need never affect you."

But his words had brought back to Zachary the thought that had troubled him, on and off, ever since the death of Cosmas the Syrian—that there really was nothing, no hell, no heaven, no just and eternal God, nothing but atoms and the void. Suddenly, just when he felt safest, he was seized with a moral vertigo, a free fall into regions of inexpressible darkness and horror. Surely, even to entertain such a thought was the Unforgivable Sin, and he had committed it! Yet worse than this fear was the fear that the thought itself might, after all, reflect the truth.

"Did you ever hear of someone called Lucretius," he asked in a voice he could barely control.

"Yes, as a matter of fact, I have," Poemen said, starting in surprise at this sudden change of topic, and the change in his disciple's complexion that had accompanied it. "He wrote a book called 'On the Nature of Things', didn't he?"

Zachary gaped at him in amazement. "Do you know everything?" he asked.

Poemen burst out laughing. "Sorry to disillusion you. That was just one of the books my friend's grandfather sent to the country. I told you about that, didn't I?"

"No you did not."

"I did, too."

"No you didn't. If you had, I'd have remembered it. I've never forgotten a single thing you've told me."

Poemen looked at Zachary's flushed and earnest face, and felt more than a little awed by the responsibility. "I know I told somebody. Recently, too."

"Not me."

Poemen slapped his forehead. "You're right! I'm getting as bad as John. It was Arsenius. Anyway, that wasn't the point. The point is, I know the book.

So?"

"The book says," Zachary forced himself to say, "that there's nothing, nothing at all in the universe but atoms and the void."

"True. He said that, among other things."

Zachary stared at his teacher. How could the old man take such a statement so lightly? Shuddering, he said, "I think I…I almost believed it."

"You did?" Poemen's tone showed not a trace of surprise.

"But surely! Even to think a thing like that might be true! Can it be forgiven?"

"I don't see why not. It's not as if it could have hurt anyone but yourself. Unless you tried to spread the idea. Did you?"

Vehemently, Zachary shook his head.

"And do you still 'almost believe it'?"

There was a long silence. Then Zachary, trembling, said "I don't know."

"Of course you don't know," Poemen snapped. "You're only human— aren't you? I asked what you believed."

Zachary took a deep breath. "To be absolutely honest with you—"

"And with yourself!"

"I really don't know what I believe."

"But you came to Scetis."

"Yes, I did."

"To become a hermit."

"Yes."

"Without knowing whether you believed or not."

"Put that way," Zachary said ruefully, "it sounds ridiculous."

"You wanted to seek a God that you didn't even know whether He was there or not."

Zachary fell to his knees. "Forgive me! I should have told you that, right at the start. I tried to hide it. Even from myself. I was so ashamed. Afraid, too." He could not look at the old man.

"I don't think it's ridiculous," Poemen said. "In fact, I find it rather beautiful. What does Scripture say? "Lord, I believe—help Thou my unbelief!" Faith, even in the absence of faith." He tapped Zachary's shoulder. "Get up, my son, and let's take a good look at this Lucretius fellow. Nothing in the universe but atoms and the void, he said?"

Zachary nodded.

"He'd been everywhere and seen everything, of course, and that's how he knew."

Zachary smiled faintly. "I don't suppose so."

"Exactly. So what he believes is an act of faith, too."

"I suppose so."

"The plain fact of the matter," Poemen said, "is that we know nothing, or next to nothing, about the universe we inhabit, and what our limited little minds tell us, what in our arrogance we think we know, is probably quite wrong, too. So. Whatever we think about the universe is an act of faith, no more, no less. We can have faith in something, or we can have faith in nothing. I myself prefer to have faith in something. Especially when I have tested in my own life experience the practical consequences of having that faith, the love and mercy that can flow from it. By their fruits shall ye know them, it is written. I wish I'd known Lucretius. I'd like to have seen what fruits grew from his faith. Nothing much, I suspect, except the feeling that he was a mighty clever fellow for having found out something hidden from others."

He patted Zachary's shoulder, "Courage, my son! Everyone who's had that thought thinks he's the only person who's ever had it. But most of them have the sense not to go public with it. 'The fool said in his heart, there is no God." But I've already talked far too much for one day."

"So I'm not damned for all eternity," Zachary said with disbelief.

"For what? For thinking God might not exist? Did that thought lead you into sins you might not otherwise have committed?"

"I don't think so."

"Then forget it!" Poemen snapped his fingers. "There! It's gone! Along with all the other follies of your youth."

"Did I ever tell you about the time I performed a miracle?" Zachary asked.

Poemen stared at him, slowly shaking his head. "Zachary, you're too much! Just shut up for now, would you? Tell me another time….Really, is there any foolishness you haven't gotten into?"

"I doubt it", Zachary said ruefully.

Chapter 32

"Go ask him yourself."

For most people, that would have been a simple solution. For Papnoute, it posed all manner of problems, psychological as well as logistic.

Psychologically, he could not accept that any secular, let alone a pagan flute-player, could ever come near him as regards righteousness. So how could he bring himself to interrogate such a person about his supposed virtues? To even speak to him would be like admitting that they really might be comparable in merit.

He ran the further risk of discovering that the angel was not mistaken. Such a discovery would devastate him. He would be forced to admit that his years of deprivation had earned him nothing. He might just as well have used his energies in sinning.

As for logistics, it might seem that all he had to do was go to Terenuthis, locate the flute-player and interview him. But, in all his years in Scetis, Papnoute had never gone to Terenuthis. He didn't know the way, and was ashamed to have to ask. Even if he got there, how could he ask for a flute-player? People would ask him why. What could he tell them? A lie would lose him merit. The truth would make him look ridiculous.

For weeks, he agonized over it. His temper got worse. His disciples tiptoed around him as if on eggshells. He found it harder and harder not to yield to anger over the most trivial incidents. Gradually, he realized that if he didn't find out the truth, it would no longer be a question of relative merit. His very salvation would be in peril.

He confided in no one, not even his most trusted disciples. Early one morning, long before the sun rose, he crept from his cell, took a circuitous route to avoid other cells, and headed in an easterly direction, hoping that the quality of his intent would earn him at least a little divine direction. Indeed, a passing camel-driver indicated to him the path over the escarpment. By mid-day he was in the town.

For Papnoute, towns were a dim memory from his childhood. He was shocked by the sheer numbers of people, and even more so by the snatches of their conversation that he could not avoid overhearing. Ripe smells of meat simmering in rich sauces reached out to him from the kitchens of eating-houses, assaulting his chaste nostrils and causing his stomach to contract in a mixture of disgust and envy. Acid wine-smells leaked from the taverns, as did raucous laughter, shouted obscenities and other signs and sounds of drunken debauchery. The lascivious glances of women were not aimed at him in particular, but he could hardly fail to be aware of them, or to be outraged by their attire, clearly designed to incite lust in the beholder. He stumbled on, struggling without success to blind his eyes, deafen his ears, and deaden his nose to all that was happening round him.

Roaming aimlessly thus, unwilling to announce his business, he might have gone on wandering all day had not the unmistakable pylons of the temple of Isis loomed over him as he rounded a corner. A white-clad form stood taking the air in the temple entrance. A clean-shaven, sardonic face turned towards him, and a deep reverberant voice said, "Greetings, hairy servant of a different god."

"Get thee behind me, Satan!" Papnoute exclaimed automatically, forgetting the angel's superior version, before he had time to realize that he was endangering his most promising source of information.

Luckily, the priest was not easily deterred. "Harsh words," he said, a crinkle of amusement at the corners of his mouth. "Is that how your crucified leader told you to address perfect strangers?"

Papnoute gulped. "Well...as a m-m-matter of fact..." He would have cursed himself if cursing had been in his repertoire. Why did his adolescent stutter have to come back, just at this crucial moment?

"He didn't, did he?" the priest said, not unkindly.

"You startled me," Papnoute explained unconvincingly.

"I did? I'm sorry. I was just standing here." The crinkle spread into a broad grin. "Must be my face. Scary, huh?"

"No, no!" Papnoute protested. "I'm sorry, I didn't mean to of-f-f-end you..."

"Oh, you didn't, you didn't," the priest reassured him. "I hear far worse than that, daily, I promise you...Were you looking for something?" he asked, as Papnoute made so sign of moving on.

"No, er, I mean yes, actually. Do you have a f-f-f-f-, a f-f-f-, a f-f-f-f-f-f-"

"Take your time," the priest said. "I'm in no hurry."

"A f-f-flute-player here?"

"Indeed I do," the priest said, surprised. "But what on earth would you want with a flute-player? Not hoping to hire him away from me, surely? I've always understood you folks weren't into to musical accompaniment."

This of course was just the question Papnoute had feared. "Gu-gu-gu-God's business," he managed at last. It wasn't altogether a lie. Not to the extent that an angel was mixed up in it.

"Hm," the priest said, rocking on his heels, considering it. "If you folks intend to go that route…I told him when I hired him there wasn't much future in our end of the business. If you want him, go ahead. I wouldn't want to stand in his way. But I'm afraid he isn't here now." Reading Papnoute's expression, he said, "No, that's not a stall; he really isn't here."

"W-w-where is he?"

"Probably in the tavern two blocks from here, turn left and it's on your right. Or," he went on, perceiving Papnoute's reluctance, "he'll be back before dark; he's on again for the evening service. You're welcome to wait in the temple, if you'd prefer that."

Papnoute weighed the two impieties. Maybe the tavern was the lesser. "I'll look for him in the t-t-tavern, then."

"Suit yourself," the priest said with an amused shrug.

Papnoute found the tavern without difficulty. He hesitated before entering. Acrid smells greeted him, shouts and laughter. He was afraid. Of what, he couldn't be sure. Not so much of temptation as of being subject to abuse and ridicule. Yes, that was it! This was a world of which he knew nothing, where he could hardly fail to make himself the butt. His soul, used to respectful treatment, cringed at the thought of that.

First, he thought of waiting until the flute-player came out. Then he realized he had no way of identifying the man. Besides, the longer he stood there, the more curiosity he would arouse. Glancing furtively to right and left to make sure no hermit or other religious person was around, he plunged into the tavern.

It was quite full, but a few stools were vacant. Trying to make himself as small and unobtrusive as possible, he quickly sat down on one of them. Indeed, for a while no one paid him any attention. Then a youth with an impudent face, passing by with several jugs in his hands, called out, "Hey, you! Waddaya want?"

"Wine." What else could he say without drawing attention to himself?

"What kind?"

Papnoute's mind went blank. 'the-the-the…Ordinary wine. The cheapest."

The server laughed. "Mighta guessed! How much?"

Papnoute's mind stayed blank.

"Quarter? Half? Biggie?"

"Quarter," Papnoute gasped. Surely that would be the smallest, the last injurious to his merit. And, he reassured himself, he didn't actually have to drink it. Look at it just as his passport to the place.

"You're on," the youth cried, plunging off to serve other customers.

Slowly Papnoute relaxed, even risked glance around him. Most of the other customers were working class, to judge by their dress, with a sprinkling of women whose eyes he was careful not to catch. He tried to identify the flute-player, but since no one was carrying a flute, he failed.

What most disturbed him, he realized after a few moments, was the lack of stir his appearance had caused. He had expected, and feared, instant negative reactions from all the pagans and sinner with which such a place must be filled. Certainly there was no mistaking what he stood for, with his plain black tunic and unshod feet. But everyone, even the serving-boy, was behaving as if it was the most natural thing in the world for hermits to come in and order drinks. That, surely, spoke volumes for the moral standards of his colleagues.

The server, grinning impishly, came back with a small jar of wine and a smaller earthenware cup. Before he could rush off again, Papnoute, summoning all his courage, praying he would not stutter again, thrust into the boy's hands some copper coins he had had the forethought to bring with him, caught the receding arm just in time and said, "Can you tell me if the flute-player is here?"

This time the youth did seem surprised. He stopped dead, did an exaggerated double-take, as if he had no idea what Papnoute was talking about.

"The flute-player," Papnoute repeated, "from the t-t-t-temple." His stutter had betrayed him after all, on the very last word too.

"Oh," the boy said. "Oh, you mean D-d-d-d-arion. He's over th-th-th-ere." And with a whoop of derisive laughter he was off again.

Papnoute, his face flushed, kept his head low for a few moments, then peered cautiously at the one who had been pointed out to him. He saw a sharp-faced, intelligent-looking man in his mid-thirties, talking animatedly to a couple of men and a woman who screeched with laughter and slapped one another ever few seconds. He seemed to be telling a story, his hands sketching the action, his mobile features shifting as he expressed the emotions of the characters concerned. At last he paused, and his audience cheered their appreciation.

Now or never. Papnoute took advantage of their distraction to slip across the intervening space. Mastering his revulsion, he touched the flute-player lightly on the shoulder.

"Excuse me."

Darion looked around, startled.

"Can I…can I have a word with you?"

Darion did an exaggerated double-take, just like the serving-boy had done.

"You're the flute-player at the temple of Isis, aren't you?"

Darion blinked and said, "I have that honor...if you could call it that." Someone laughed.

"That's who I want...Could you, would you s-s-spare me a few m-m-moments? I p-p-p-p-promise it won't take long."

Darion rolled his eyes at the ceiling, shrugged, and rose slowly to his feet. "Excuse me, folks."

Papnoute had thought to take the man outside, but he suddenly realized that if he did, someone from Scetis might see them together and his reputation would be forever blighted. The lesser of the two evils seemed to be to stay right there. Luckily, there were still two empty stools at the table where his wine still sat untouched. He sat down.

Darion's gaze fixed on the wine and stayed there so pointedly that even Papnoute felt obliged to ask, "Would you...care for a drink?"

"Sure. But where's yours?"

Papnoute glanced at the single cup. "I don't d-d-drink."

"Then why order it?"

Once more Papnoute's mind went blank.

"I don't drink with people who don't drink with me," Darion said firmly.

"I..." Papnoute hesitated. "I want to ask you a few questions."

The flute-player's eyes went dark, he tipped backwards on his stool as if gathering momentum to throw himself on his interlocutor. But Papnoute had too little experience of the secular life to recognize such signs. "A few simple questions," he babbled on, "it won't take a—"

"Who are you?"

The words cut across him like a whiplash. He blinked, and said, "I'm a hermit. Just a hermit from Scetis."

"I can see that for myself," Darion said scornfully. "But just what gives you the right to come in here and start asking me questions?"

Papnoute opened his mouth, but no words came. What came, to his utter horror and mortification, were tears—hot, scalding tears of rage, frustration and despair. Burying his head in his hands, he passively awaited the scorn and contempt that must now be poured over him.

It was not. Insensibly, Darion relaxed, letting his arms fall loosely to his sides. "Sotas," he called, barely raising his voice. Across the room, in the middle of serving someone else, the boy stopped and came over immediately. "Sotas, fetch another cup, would you?"

The server hurried to obey. When the second cup was set before them, Darion, who had ignored the other's outburst, carefully shared the contents of the small jug between them. "Well, that won't go far," he said meditatively. "Sotas, fetch us another half."

"But I don't..."

"That's all right. This one's on me."

"I mean, I never..."

"Then it's about time you did," Darion said decisively. "I'm not answering questions from anyone who won't drink with me."

Papnoute shuddered. This was worse than he had expected, the man was an unregenerate sinner. The angel had made a terrible mistake. But he had come so far and if he gave up now he would spend the rest of his life wondering. Gritting his teeth, he took a sip and, almost gagging, swallowed it. That wasn't so bad, part of him said. Of course not, screamed another part, otherwise how could it drag people down into sin?

He pulled himself together. "Have you, have you ever, er, d-d-done anything virtuous?"

Darion thrust his head forward, squinting, as if to make sure he had heard right. "What is this?"

"No, please, listen to me," Papnoute said, at last getting the better of his stutter. "This is something that's very important for me. What great acts of holiness have you achieved in your life?

"Acts of holiness? Me?" Darion burst out laughing. Then he stopped abruptly, suspicion danced in his eyes again. "You better tell me what this is all about."

"I can't!"

"Course you can."

"No, really."

"Drink some more. That'll help."

Papnoute obeyed him. "I don't care what it is," Darion said, "I'm sure I'll have heard worse. And I don't talk, either. My criminal training."

Luckily, Papnoute didn't catch the last remark. He was thinking that, after all, the pagan was right. The wine did help. He felt the beginning of a warm glow spreading through his stomach.

"Well...the other day an angel visited me..."

Darion caught the eye of one of the men he had been sitting with and gave him a look that said plain enough even for Papnoute to read, just what kind of nut-case have I got myself stuck with? But the hermit was into it now, he pushed on doggedly, "And the angel told me, he said, my merit was no greater than that of the flute-player in the temple at Terenuthis..."

"You must have done something really awful, then."

This was not what Papnoute had expected. "Never!" he exclaimed indignantly, "my life has been of the purest, most ascetic."

"Doesn't make sense," Darion said. "Know what I was, before I came to the temple?"

Papnoute shook his head.

"I was a robber. A bandit. I even killed someone, once…Well, self-defense, I suppose…I never killed anyone in a robbery. That I know of. I mean, if they resisted…"

His voice tailed off. To hide his bewilderment, Papnoute lifted his cup, to find to his surprise that he had already emptied it. But he no sooner put it down than Darion refilled it from the larger jar that had by now appeared.

"No, you must have done something," Papnoute insisted. "Something that earned you merit. Think! Just think! Please!"

He was on the brink of tears again. Darion bit his knuckle and thought as hard as he could. "Well…"

"Yes! Yes! Go on!"

"I saved a virgin from rape."

"You did? Really?"

"Yeah, really. Actually I didn't intend to, not at first. It just kind of happened."

"But you saved her," Papnoute said eagerly, "you did save her."

"Sure."

"And you didn't afterwards…"

"What? Do her myself? What do you take me for?"

"Forgive me! I just wanted to make sure." Papnoute tried to imagine himself saving a virgin, from some lust-crazed beast, or beasts. His imagination, in overload, whited out. After a moment he asked hesitantly, "Anything else?"

"Yeah. There was something. I rescued a hermit."

"You did? How?"

"Oh, he was sick. Unconscious. Dying, I guess. Somewhere out in the interior desert. I had to carry him…oh, quite a way. Which would have been no problem if we'd had enough water. But that's all square, because if I hadn't had him with me, the Mazices would have killed me, like they killed my buddy. So no big deal."

"You risked your life?" Papnoute said in amazement. "Did you know him?"

"Course not."

"You risked your life for a total stranger?"

"What could I have done? Left the poor bastard for the vultures?"

Without thinking, Papnoute took another drink. It was surprising how much better he was feeling. Maybe the angel was right, after all. "There must have been other things, too."

Darion racked his brains. "Don't think so...No, wait! There was this woman I gave all my money to, once."

"As a gift?"

"Sort of. She was a victim of government oppression. It would take too long to go into now."

"And was it...a lot of money?"

"Upwards of three hundred solidi."

Papnoute's jaw dropped. It was more money than he had seen in a lifetime.

"Again, no big deal," Darion said airily. "It was all stolen anyway."

"And you asked for nothing in return?"

This time Darion did not get indignant. His eyes grew wistful, reminiscent. "No. Can't think why. Often wish I had. She was real good-looking, at that."

Papnoute resolutely ignored the implications of those last remarks. "So you've always kept yourself pure?"

"Certainly not," Darion exclaimed. "Just because twice I didn't take advantage...No, if they're willing and look cute, they're mine."

"But maybe you've fasted."

"What?" Darion's grin showed fierce white teeth. "Only when there was no food around. And then I made sure I made up for it, afterwards."

"Or kept vigil."

Darion made a rude noise with his lips.

"Or worn a hair shirt."

Darion rose to his feet. "Are you trying to be funny with me?"

"Then," Papnoute said desperately, "it must be your faith. Are you a Christian? If so, how could you work in that cauldron of abominations? What do you believe?"

"I believe...Take another drink of that and I'll tell you." Mutely, Papnoute obeyed. "I believe," Darion said, grinning, "for every drop of rain that falls, someone gets wet. I believe what goes around, comes around. I believe in this wine; it's good. I even believe in you. After all, I couldn't have invented you. You're too weird."

Papnoute sprang to his feet. He could endure this no longer. Oblivious to the remark flung after him—"You could at least have said thanks for the drink!"—he plunged towards the door of the tavern. A group of rough-looking men blocked his path. In his blind haste, he bumped one of them and a hand grabbed his arm. He turned, terrified, babbling apologies. Then, the words froze on his lips.

"So, you finally did take my advice," an all-too-familiar voice said.

The angel? Here? It wasn't possible! He must be hallucinating. Wrenching his arm free, he hurled himself into the street. In the fresh air, the bright afternoon sunlight, he turned suddenly dizzy. The street blurred, tilted. Its dusty surface seemed to be undulating like a snake. It was only by a supreme effort that he kept his balance.

With a shock of horror, he realized he must be drunk.

He, Papnoute, drunk! It was unthinkable. But more unthinkable still was the discovery that a licentious toper, an unrepentant sinner, a blackguard who scoffed at everything, believed in nothing, should be valued in Heaven as much as he, who had foregone all the pleasures of the world to ensure his salvation!

No. It must be a dream. He must still be in his cell, on his sheepskin bed, caught in one of those rare moments of unconsciousness that sleep—"the wicked servant," Arsenius called it, and how right he was!—had imposed on him. And Satan, replete with wicked tricks, had sent him this dream to torment him. Soon, soon, any moment now, he must wake up…

But he did not.

Derek Bickerton

Chapter 33

"I'm still having a little trouble," Zachary said.

It was far into the night, but where they were now, day and night had little meaning. They would pray alone, talk together, pray and meditate again as the spirit moved them, regardless of the hour. Only the dawn and evening prayers and the weekly synaxis served as their anchors in time. These they unfailingly observed, reciting the twelve psalms together at dawn and sunset, joining the others every sixth day. It was surprising to both of them how well their minds accorded, how when the one wished for guidance the other was always ready to provide it, how smoothly they moved back from converse to solitary prayer. I *should have taken a disciple before*, Poemen thought, *for surely the good it does to my soul equals or exceeds any I can do for his.*

At the same time, he realized he had been fortunate in his choice of Zachary—or rather, he corrected himself, the choice of providence, for he had simply taken the first candidate who offered himself. It was not just that he could feel Zachary growing in seriousness and strength as the days passed. One could recognize spiritual growth in another and still find the way they bit their nails, or slurped down their food, distasteful to live with. The true test of affinities between people comes when they have to live together constantly. Nothing Zachary did upset him. The relationship between them had grown so comfortable that it sometimes frightened him. Should he not pray for a more irritating disciple, the tolerance of whose habits would make him practice daily the essential virtue of humility?

It was not that he and Zachary were alike. The younger man lacked entirely the streak of impish humor that had somehow managed to survive within the calm and sweetness of Poemen's wisdom. Yet, being younger, Zachary had not yet developed the control over the passions that Poemen had. None of these differences, however, seemed to count. Poemen, who had never sired a child, felt all his unsatisfied fatherhood surfacing at last. Zachary, who had never really known his true father, moved without noticing it into the role of son.

"Trouble with what, Zachary?" Poemen asked.

"Keeping my mind fixed on something. Even if I'm just repeating a single word, like you told me to." He was frowning, looking intently at a spot just below and to the left of Poemen's face—not deliberately avoiding his mentor's gaze, but focused entirely on the problem before him. Poemen smiled inwardly, thinking, a couple of years ago he would have been equally focused on what to wear for a party, or how he could make more money. And even now he doesn't realize how much he's changed.

"That word sets off a thought in my mind, and that thought suggests another, and in no time I'm completely off course. It's as if I didn't have any control, as if my thoughts weren't mine, they had a life of their own."

"They do," Poemen assured him.

"What should I do?"

"It's hard. Because there's a very deep paradox in here. What we are trying to do, what this work is, in a sense, all about, is experiencing the oneness of everything, which is of course the oneness of God. But we're not built to do that. We're built to chop things up into little pieces, bits small enough for our limited understandings to grasp. You have to use little stratagems, to outwit yourself, as it were. Imagine, for instance, all your thoughts are cows in a field."

"Cows?" Zachary said, startled.

"Horses. If you prefer. Makes no difference, maybe horses are better, they're more restless beasts. So each thought is a horse. Tell it to lie down quietly and go to sleep. When all the horses are quiet, others will come in. Tell them too to lie down. Imagine them all, every last one, lying down, going to sleep. Now there's nothing moving in the field at all. And then…"

Poemen broke off abruptly. "Did you hear that?"

"What?"

"If you heard nothing, then these old ears are playing me tricks… Well, as I was saying, once they've quietened down—"

Now it was Zachary's turn to interrupt. "You mean a sound like somebody weeping?"

Both fell silent. The night, utterly dark, utterly still, was disturbed by a faint, tumultuous sound—a sobbing, a gasping, a sighing as if from some mourner totally possessed by grief. Poemen rose and flung open the door of the cell. At first he could see nothing, though the sound seemed louder.

"Whoever you are, come in and we will help you," he called out.

The sounds ceased abruptly.

They waited.

"Could it be a demon," Zachary asked, 'trying to—"

"Sh! Listen."

The sounds had begun again, although so muted Poemen thought for a moment that their maker was retreating. Then came a shuffle of feet in loose sand, and suddenly they both saw and recognized the figure coming reluctantly towards them.

Papnoute.

"Welcome, come in," Poemen said.

Papnoute would not meet his gaze. Rubbing his face with his sleeve, he stood at the edge of the pool of dim light cast by Poemen's lamp. "I have no right to disturb you," he muttered between sobs.

"You need none," Poemen said. "This door is open to all."

"Even at this hour?"

"At the hour of need, that can be any hour."

And as Papnoute still stood there, snuffling into his sleeve, Poemen stepped forward and, taking his arm, led him as one might lead a blind or infirm person, into the cell. Zachary closed the door behind them and reached for the flask of wine Poemen kept discreetly hidden behind the jars where their reeds soaked. Poemen gave him a sharp shake of the head and he desisted.

"Sit down," Poemen said, "and tell us all that is troubling you, and if we can help you in any way, be assured that we will."

"I...I just..."

Papnoute seemed unable to speak. Poemen patted his arm and said, "Take your time. We have the whole night."

"Does...does he have to be here?" Papnoute indicated Zachary with a jerk of his head.

"He's my son, Papnoute," Poemen said. "We share all our thoughts. If I tell you that whatever is said here will never be repeated, that goes for him too, right, Zachary?"

Zachary nodded. He knew at once the reason for Papnoute's reluctance—whatever he needed to say, he would prefer not to say it to the disciple who had deserted him. "I've learned obedience, Father," he said respectfully. "You did your best to teach it to me—no fault of yours if I was so slow to learn it. I was too young and foolish to appreciate you in those days."

Over Papnoute's shoulder he saw Poemen nodding approval of his words. "Very well, then," Papnoute sighed, and he began to tell them all that had happened to him, from the very first visit of the angel.

The story took a long time, for Papnoute would start to sob again and have to be reassured and comforted before he could continue. When he finally came to his adventures in Terenuthis, it was all Poemen could do to keep his composure. He could see it all too vividly—the sardonic priest, the impertinent waiter, the cynical ex-brigand, and poor Papnoute, caught in the middle of them, unable to understand half of what was going on. He let none of this show in his face, for when someone is in pain you must respect that—even if their suffering had been brought on by their own foolishness, it was no less real for that.

Finally, his ordeal over, Papnoute sat staring at them as a man found guilty stares at his judges, awaiting and dreading their sentence. "Where have I gone wrong?" he asked piteously.

"It's not for us to judge you," Poemen said.

"But the angel said, if I wanted spiritual counseling, this was the place for it, and now you're saying…"

"I'm not saying I won't give you advice," Poemen said. "For what that's worth, from one poor sinner to another. But I won't tell you what you did wrong, because you already know that."

Papnoute gazed at him, uncomprehending.

"Look into your heart," Poemen went on. "You were weeping, weren't you? A man doesn't weep for nothing. He weeps for compunction, because he has seen his own true nature, even if he doesn't want to admit it. Look into your heart and answer the question yourself."

"I…" Papnoute hesitated. "Is it, is it because this Darion—"

"The flute-player?"

"Is it because three times in his life he risked everything for total strangers? Is that why his merit equals mine?"

Poemen nodded. "You knew that without me telling you."

"And that what I did wrong was…well, never truly loving my neighbor as myself?"

Poemen remained silent.

"I never loved my neighbor as myself."

It was no longer a question, and it was followed by a torrent of weeping. Poemen leaned forward—their stools were only inches apart—and put his arms around Papnoute, hugging him and then patting and stroking his shoulders. Zachary had a sudden flash of memory—his mother giving birth to his youngest sister, and the midwife holding his mother, patting her, stroking her, in time with her convulsions, as she struggled to expel the child. Poemen's moves were just like those of the midwife, and that was only appropriate, for what was happening here was a spiritual birth. And like other births, it did not come without pain.

"I should have loved more," Papnoute said in a shaky voice, when his fit had finally subsided. "Fasted and prayed less, loved more."

Poemen nodded. "We were told to kill the passions, not the body," he said. "Asceticism is just a means to an end. If it becomes an end in itself…"

"It counts for nothing," Papnoute said bitterly.

"No," Poemen was quick to counter him. "No, that's going too far. Your intent was good. That has to count for something. You avoided sin..."

"Not pride!"

"Well, maybe not pride, but a lot of other sins. That counts for something too. And you learned to discipline yourself, too. That means your tools are sharp and well-oiled. Now you know how to use them. Nothing is lost. You still love God, don't you?"

Papnoute turned to him a face piteous in its misery. "How can I truly love God without loving my neighbors, since whatever I do unto the least of these..."

"You do it unto Him," Poemen completed, and Zachary saw that his face too was moist with tears. "Have courage, brother. The worst is over already. He who wishes to purify his faults, purifies them with tears, and he who wishes to acquire virtues, acquires them with tears. Truly, there is no other way than this."

"But the years," Papnoute protested, "the years I wasted, the years that are lost to me forever."

"By no means entirely wasted," Poemen assured him, "as I explained to you just now. But what of it? The past is past, it can't be remedied. Why agonize over it? Let the dead bury their dead. If you had repented, sincerely, as you have now, in the very last second of your life, you could still have been saved. And a single sincere penitent is worth a dozen of those who tiptoe through life, afraid to do anything, good, bad or indifferent, lest they blunder into something evil. So be of good heart, have courage, man!"

"Will you help me?" Papnoute asked.

I never expected to hear those words from you, Poemen thought. But he let no trace of that thought show in his expression. "Of course I will, and gladly."

"I can come to you?"

"At any time. Go back to your cell. Get some sleep, and come whenever you need to."

Papnoute, still weeping, clasped Poemen's hands. Embarrassed, Poemen pulled his hands away and clasped them firmly behind his back. "You don't have to thank me. I may very well be coming to you for help."

When Papnoute finally left, it was already beginning to be light. Zachary closed the door behind him and snuffed out the lamp to save on oil. Then he and Poemen looked at one another in silence for several minutes.

"Was that for real?" Zachary asked.

"Better believe it," Poemen said. "You don't see tears like that every day. I know. I've been through it. I think we may see some big changes in him...

Now, where had we got to?"

Zachary shook his head reluctantly. "We'll have to go back later to that. Right now it's time for matins."

"The Psalms. Yes of course. Remember which one we got to?"

"'Save me, o God, for the waters are come in unto my soul,' Father," Zachary said.

"I suppose I might as well give up asking you not to call me 'Father'," Poemen said resignedly. "Yes, number 69, and very appropriate too, for the waters are the waters of pride, and smugness, and self-satisfaction, and feeling ourselves superior to those who humbly seek our assistance. Do you appreciate the courage it took him to do that, after all these years?"

"Papnoute?"

"Who else? Very probably neither of us would have had that courage, and don't you ever forget that." Poemen fell to his knees. "Right, now, repeat with me: "I sink in deep mire, where there is no standing; I am come into deep waters, where the floods overflow me...""

Chapter 34

In silence. Theophilus and the guards descended the narrow, damp, winding, windowless and utterly dark staircase of the jail. The military commander preceded him, the guard who immediately followed (there was no room in the staircase for two to walk abreast) held over him the sputtering torch whose light, reflected from the slimy, faintly glistening walls, alone allowed them to descend. Their footsteps resounded hollowly in the silence, an irregular rhythm, and Theophilus felt the chill of the place penetrating his very bones. *This place must be below sea-level*, he thought, and he remembered tales of cells where the sea entered with every tide, forcing prisoners in them to stand on tiptoe to escape drowning, or scramble up the walls, clinging desperately to their own chains.

That could have been him.

But this jail was in Alexandria, not Constantinople. And though he still awoke occasionally with a palpitating heart, having dreamed that he was judged and condemned in the trial he had been summoned to, that trial had never taken place. The Sly Fox, even in the very jaws of the trap, had succeeded in turning the tables on his accusers. He had beguiled Empress Eudoxia, made a fool of Emperor Arcadius (*if nature had left room for any more moves in that direction*, he thought dryly), and hopelessly outwitted and outmaneuvered his enemy John Goldenmouth, calling in every marker accumulated over a lifetime of intrigue, spreading bribes with reckless abandon—how that had hurt, good money that could have raised a dozen new churches, but there was no remedy—so that in the end it was John who was tried and John who was expelled from the post that should be rights have belonged to Theophilus' protégé.

But Theophilus had been unable to savor his triumph, had had to flee, his life in danger yet again, this time from a Byzantine mob outraged by the indignities heaped on their beloved pastor John. And it still hurt him even more to think that what was perhaps the most masterful plot of his life had had to be aimed, not at making him (as he had dreamed) the most powerful prelate in Christendom, but merely at saving him from dethronement and probably things far worse (for men as powerful as he could not simply be dismissed, they had to broken, humiliated, made forever incapable of regaining that power).

Now, he was back in his own archdiocese, licking his wounds, repairing his power base. Would he get a second chance to achieve his goals? Could he take advantage of such a chance even if he got it? His body no longer responded as it had when the Anthropomorphites attacked him, or when he struck down that self-mutilated troublemaker Ammonius for his heresy. He was tiring, ageing fast.

And there was still one festering source of opposition in his domain that even he had never succeeded in overcoming.

Scetis.

There still burned in his memory that scene with Arsenius, years ago now yet as vivid as if it had happened yesterday. Arsenius, whom he had taken under his wing, helped into the ascetic way, and been repaid—how? He remembered his own innocent reaction when Arsenius had asked him, "If I ask you to do something, will you promise to do it?" "Of course," he had said, expecting some holy admonition, but instead Arsenius had said, "If you hear that Arsenius is anywhere..." and paused, while Theophilus waited, puzzled, but still not suspecting anything. Then the blow, the glacial rejection: "...don't go there." Not judgement, not condemnation, just an absolute severance that had left the archbishop speechless. And others from Scetis whom he had favored and helped in the past, Mother Theodora for instance, had turned on him too. He knew who was behind it all—Poemen, Moses and their friends, all of those holier-than-thou hypocrites who fancied themselves his moral superiors. As long as that nest of vipers was permitted to survive and spread its baneful influence, he could never be entirely safe. It had to be destroyed.

But how?

Charges of heresy? That would never work. He remembered that strange encounter with Poemen in the burning ruins of Nitria. They would accept whatever orthodoxy the church preached, not because they believed it, but because they didn't care, because they believed it was simply irrelevant to Christ's message.

Attack them as he had attacked Nitria? Drive them out of Egypt by force, as he had done with the followers of Origen? That had worked once, but look at the disasters it had brought in its train! A second time could be far worse. Scetis had always ranked above Nitria in terms of holiness, and without any heretical pretext he would be mad to attack it openly.

Luckily for Theophilus, there was a third way.

He had caught his first glimmer of it that very night, when the lame centurion had told him of threats against the Nitrians by desert dwellers. For a century or more, the hermits of Egypt had lived free of barbarian attacks. A mixture of respect and superstitious fear had kept the Mazices and Blemyes at a distance. That could change.

The military commander had reached the foot of the staircase. He stood to one side, allowing Theophilus, the guard with the torch and another man to stand in the mouth of a narrow passageway while a second guard, carrying keys, squeezed in front of them and preceded them to a massive, rusting iron door, which he opened.

Even with the torch casting its uneven glare, it was hard for Theophilus to see anything in the cell. It seemed at first sight to have no aperture other than the door, so that when that door was closed it must lie in impenetrable darkness. But the floor held faintly luminous encrustations of salt, so Theophilus' forecast had been correct: somewhere there must be a hole that allowed seawater to flow into the cell. Instinctively he glanced up the wall nearest him, but could not, in that uncertain light, determine where the high-tide mark was, or even if there was one. Then his eye was drawn to what at first he took for a bundle of rags on the floor, up against the furthest wall. But if it was just a bundle of rags, why did a long chain secure it to an iron ring set in the wall?

The commander stepped into the middle of the cell, followed by the fifth man. The commander spoke, in Latin: "Come on, we know you're awake." He had been in Egypt a mere three months and as far as Theophilus knew he didn't speak anything else. The fifth man, the interpreter, translated into Coptic. Theophilus chafed at the cumbersome procedure, for he could have interrogated the prisoner in Egyptian himself. But it was better for all concerned if he stayed in the background so that afterwards he could claim without total dishonesty that he had taken no part in the execution of the scheme he had planned. And anyway this commander was a Christian, not a follower of Mani or Arius but, just for once, a real orthodox Christian, who would do whatever Theophilus told him to, say whatever Theophilus told him to say, and (if the Prefect ever found out) tell him that military affairs were none of the Prefect's business.

The bundle of rags stirred and resolved itself into a figure, a crouching figure that moved on all fours, like an animal. And like an animal's was the howl of incoherent rage with which the prisoner greeted the commander's words. A pair of feral eyes, burning through a shapeless mass of dark hair, like an animal's pelt, went straight past the commander and fixed on Theophilus, as if the prisoner somehow knew that while the commander was his captor and jailer, it was Theophilus who held the key to his ultimate fate.

That gaze had made other man quail. It had daunted Zachary, in a desert tent, when its owner had demanded that he heal the blind girl. It had struck a chill into the heart even of Darion, when in the same tent, but in another part of the desert, he had been told how narrowly he had escaped death and how ruthlessly he would be disposed of if the Mazices caught him a second time. But Theophilus returned it without blinking, and not merely because it was now he and not the chief of the Mazices who held the power of life and death in his hands. No, each man had sensed immediately the nature of the other, and knew that at bottom they were the same: proud and reckless men who would go to any lengths to achieve their goals.

"Have you made your decision?" the commander asked, the interpreter translating.

Only a snarl of contempt came from the prisoner, as he gradually raised himself to an erect posture. *I hope they haven't driven him mad*, Theophilus thought with a sudden pang of apprehension. *If he's mad, then he's useless to me. I'll have to start all over, with some other tribe.*

"Do you remember the terms?" the commander asked.

The reply was equally unintelligible.

"If we set you free, you are to attack the desert settlement of Scetis and devastate it, killing any who resist you, driving out those who do not."

After the translation, there was a long pause. Finally the prisoner, in a harsh croak, asked, "For who is this? For you," glaring at the commander, "or for him?"

He was staring directly at Theophilus. No point in temporizing with a man of that kind. "For me," Theophilus said, without waiting for the interpreter to translate.

"Kill holy men…for a holy man?"

"Yes," Theophilus said, thankful that the commander spoke no Coptic and would not have to swallow such bluntness. "If it is necessary. Sometimes leaders have to punish their own kind. You are a leader. You understand that."

Again, the prisoner remained silent, for so long that Theophilus, shrugging his shoulder, gestured to the commander that they should leave. But as he did so, the prisoner spoke.

"Release all my people first."

Theophilus looked questioningly at the commander.

"What did he say?" the commander asked.

"He wants you to release his people. How many of them did you capture?"

"Twenty, thirty…what's the difference?"

"Release them, if that's his price."

The commander sneezed; the cold and damp of the cell were getting to him, too. Stifling a second sneeze, he said, "that's crazy."

"Why?"

"Then, we have no hold on him, he'll be gone and that's the last we'll see of him."

Of course, Theophilus thought. *I'm slipping. I should have thought of that immediately. Never be over-eager to achieve something, you'll make mistakes and it will slip through your fingers.* "Half now and half when he's done it?" he asked.

The commander made a wry face. "I suppose so."

Switching from Latin back to Coptic, Theophilus said "We will release half of the prisoners when you are released. The others we must keep until you have completed your mission. As hostages. You must understand why we have to do this."

"How do I know you will release them?" the prisoner asked.

Theophilus smiled, spread his hands. With this man he did not need to spell things out. The smile, the gesture said eloquently enough: What choice have you? You are our prisoner, stay that way if you want. You just have to trust us.

"Does he agree?" the prisoner asked, jerking his head at the commander.

No fool, this barbarian, Theophilus thought. *Knows the difference between clerical and military uniforms. Knows that even if I direct the operation, the army has its fingers on the triggers of power.* Quickly, he explained things to the commander, the commander nodded, agreed and was translated.

"I accept your terms," the prisoner said. "Your god is not my god."

The commander signaled to the guard with the keys. Theophilus had already turned to leave when the prisoner called out, "You! To your god—what will you say?"

Theophilus shuddered.

Derek Bickerton

Chapter 35

As they ate at the ninth hour one sultry afternoon, Zachary said to Poemen, "You know, there's something troubling me."

Since he did not immediately continue, Poemen said, "Go on, my son."

"Last time I mentioned it, you didn't want to talk about it."

"I didn't what?" Poemen said, setting down the bread he had been dipping in lentil-juice. "That's impossible."

Not wishing to contradict his mentor, Zachary remained silent.

"But I never, without fail, fail to respond whenever you bring something to me," Poemen complained. "No matter what it is."

"Then I'll have to tell you."

"Naturally,"

"It's been troubling me for years, on and off."

"Come on, son, spit it out!"

"It's…it's the miracle I performed."

"Oh," Poemen said. "That. I'm sorry. I'd forgotten about that. Yes, just that once, on that particular occasion, I had heard enough of your youthful follies. I didn't mean to bar the subject permanently. Far from it." He looked keenly at Zachary, who for the first time since beginning to speak of it allowed his eyes to meet those of his teacher. "The first thing to do is find out why it troubles you."

Zachary looked surprised. "Why wouldn't it? Look, even now, as far as you've brought me, and that's a long way, you'll have to admit, I'd never… never have the—the impertinence to even dream that I could work a miracle. I mean it's as far above me as…as…"

He was at a loss to find any adequate word of comparison. Poemen nodded, sympathetically. "I agree. So?"

"Well how much more so when I was hardly even a beginner," Zachary burst out, "and an ignorant and deluded one at that!"

"Who works miracles?" Poemen asked sharply.

"Why…why, saints, men of great holiness, men…"

"Men?"

Zachary fell silent.

"God works miracles," Poemen said with great firmness, "when He so desires, by His special grace. Men of holiness are only one of the means through which he works. Nothing could prevent God from using you in that way, if He so desired. Don't try to limit Him."

"But you have to admit, it's highly unlikely."

"I agree," Poemen said. "Highly unlikely." He picked up his bread and began to eat again.

"It was the work of demons, then," Zachary concluded. "That's what it was. It must have been. There's no other explanation. But why? What was the purpose of it? Just to fool me? To make me think I was far holier than I really was, to tempt me into the sin of pride, what?"

Poemen mopped up the last of the lentil-juice in his bowl and said

"A delicious stew, Zachary, you really excelled yourself today…Now, about demons. I suppose your miracle, which you haven't even described to me yet, had some kind of physical result. Well, no one can be sure of this, but I suspect demons, discarnate beings, can't have any direct effect on the physical world. They can fool us with illusions, creations of our own mind, and that's it. Oh, I know there are all these stories about hermits being beaten black and blue by them, but frankly I'm skeptical, would be even if I'd ever seen such bruises—which I haven't, by the way. I'd suspect the hermit had gotten into such a state wrestling with delusions he'd been throwing himself about and they were self-inflicted, though he might honestly not know that himself and draw what seemed a logical conclusion. So why don't you just tell me exactly what happened."

Zachary did so, starting with the arrival of the Mazices in the valley of the temple, describing the blind girl and what happened when he sought to heal her, and finishing with the humiliating details of his own gluttonous, drunken state at the barbarians' feast.

When he had finished, Poemen said, "I hate to disappoint you, Zachary, but at least this should set your mind at rest. There was no miracle."

Zachary starred at him. "But she was blind! I know she was blind. And then she could see!"

"No doubt," Poemen said. "Have you finished eating?"

"Yes…er…I mean no, no."

"Then eat, and listen." Poemen smiled. "There is a condition, far from rare in Egypt, called hysterical blindness. It seems to be caused by some conflict within the mind, or between the mind and forces outside of it. Possibly that is what struck the Apostle, Saul as he then was, on the road to Damascus."

"But he was struck blind by the Lord," Zachary exclaimed, genuinely shocked.

"Did I say he wasn't?" Poemen asked sharply.

"You said…you said it was a natural—"

"I have never understood," Poemen said in a weary voice, as if this was something he had often tried to explain but never succeeded, "why people suppose that God has to use supernatural means when perfectly natural means are available to Him. Anyway, it's irrelevant here, I'm not suggesting your girl's blindness was divinely ordained. More likely it came about through her intense desire for this boy and her parents' refusal to let her have him. Then, when she was blind, and her parents no longer raised any objection, he didn't want her. Now blindness like this, that has no physical cause, tends to go away of its own accord once the conditions that caused it are no longer present."

"And that just happened to coincide with my healing her," Zachary said incredulously.

"No, it probably preceded it." And Poemen picked up his bowl and placed it on top of Zachary's, which by now was also empty. Zachary remained speechless. "We'll never know for certain," Poemen went on, "but I strongly suspect that she had recovered her sight before you ever saw her. That would have put her in a very difficult position. If she simply said, "I'm not blind anymore", for no apparent reason, everyone would have thought she'd faked the whole thing. Her parents would have been extremely angry with her, and though I'm not familiar with their ways, I would imagine that parental discipline among the Mazices can take some pretty frightening forms. Then, you came along, and you were the perfect solution for her. The hermit cured me! The hermit cured me!" he exclaimed in a falsetto voice. "Just what everyone expected and hoped for, so she was home free."

It took Zachary a long moment to absorb this. Then he said, "thanks, Father. You don't know what relief I feel." Then a shadow crossed his face. "But you know—that stuff about Saul—I wouldn't say that to too many people round here, if I were you. They might misunderstand you."

"Wouldn't dream of it," Poemen said airily. "Age hasn't yet made me totally foolish...I hope."

Chapter 36

Zachary had not, until that moment, thought of his mentor as being of any particular age. Poemen's wiry body belied his years, and his mind, barring an occasional forgetfulness, seemed as sharp as ever. True, his face was lined, and when he did not smile it often had a tense, strained look; but that was true of many ascetics—Arsenius, for instance, who was decades younger in terms of years, if not of gravity. Now for the first time Zachary realized that their relationship, which had come to feel as natural as breathing, could not go on forever, and could indeed be terminated at very short notice. He felt a pang of apprehension, partly for his own sake—he would once again be alone, solely responsible for his own destiny—but mostly for Poemen. Over the years he had come to love the old man.

Because of this, he studied Poemen with greater care and watchfulness than before. He must notice any sign of weakness or sickness at its earliest occurrence, so that he could move to correct it, to the extent that this lay in his power. He must also watch what Poemen said. For some of the factors that made Poemen so good at counseling—his independence of mind, his indifference to society's conventions, his willingness to see things as they were, without counting the cost—were, if his exterior vigilance was relaxed, likely to plunge him into serious danger. That remark about Saul, for instance. He understood what Poemen meant, but Scetis had far too many people who would see only the surface of such remarks, who would construe them as rank heresy.

So it was that he became aware sooner than he would otherwise have done that all was not well with the Shepherd. He noticed it first when, a couple of days after they talked of his miracle, he had mentioned to Poemen how he now felt he had finally cleansed his heart of all the follies of the past. Not surprisingly, Poemen cautioned him against overconfidence: hermits were never as vulnerable as when they felt they had passed a milestone in their progress. They could now afford to relax, they might feel, but this was dangerous; rather their interior vigilance should be doubled, they should maintain unchanged, if not increase, their ascetic practices.

Sound stuff, doubtless, and yet it lacked something. It was couched in too vague and too general terms; it lacked the bite and spontaneity of Poemen's usual advice, directed always to precise and immediate needs of the other. Even Poemen's eyes had taken on a dull, abstracted look, very different from their normal quick, birdlike gaze.

"Something's troubling you," Zachary said.

"It's nothing. Don't bother yourself on my behalf."

But Zachary persisted, and Poemen finally agreed that his stomach had been troubling him, and let Zachary add some herbs, with supposedly purifying properties, to their regular diet of bread and vegetables.

These, however, seemed to have little effect, Poemen did indeed make efforts to look and sound his normal self. But to Zachary's heightened awareness, efforts were what they all too obviously were.

One evening, as they sat opposite one another, plaiting reeds into handles for the baskets stacked in a corner of the cell, Zachary saw, in the flickering light of the one lit oil-lamp, something he had not seen before. The mixed light and shade accentuated the ridges and hollows of Poemen's face in such a way that, for a moment, Zachary thought he was seeing not a face but a skull. Then the lamp burned suddenly clearer, and the illusion passed. But not before Zachary had been reminded of the long-dead monk whose body he had found in the valley of the temple.

He shuddered. At least the Shepherd would be spared that lonely end.

Then he noticed something else that, though it was less scary, disturbed him much more deeply. As each handle was completed, it would be put to one side, on a pile, ready to attach to a basket once the task was done. The two piles lay on the ground between them. Zachary had begun to wonder why Poemen's pile was so much smaller than his own when he saw what Poemen was doing.

He was continuing to weave the same handle.

By the time Zachary spotted it, the handle was so long that if a giant had carried it, the basket would still have dragged on the ground. Yet Poemen showed not the least awareness of this; he continued to plait, while the handle curled around his knees and feet like a serpent.

"Father," Zachary said quietly.

At first Poemen seemed not to hear him; he continued to weave, the only sound the scarcely-audible soft slithering of the reeds on one another. Zachary leaned forward and lightly touched Poemen's arm. Poemen started, blinked, his eyes momentarily out of focus. Zachary pointed mutely at the handle.

Instantly, Poemen was himself again. He chuckled drily, said, "Disgraceful, eh? And from someone who's always talking about vigilance, attention…What can we do with it, d'you think?"

"Nothing. If you cut it into the right lengths, the stuff will just unravel."

"If we had a sharp enough knife, we might…"

"We don't."

Poemen sighed. "Then I'll just have to unweave it and start over. Serves me right."

He began to do so, but Zachary wasn't going to leave it at that. "You're still troubled in your mind, aren't you?"

"What makes you think so?"

"Lots of things. For over a week you haven't been yourself. It's nothing physical or the herbs would have put it right. Nothing has happened in all that time that could have upset you." Zachary spread his hands. "The only solution left!"

Poemen sighed again, more deeply. "Just...random thoughts," he said after a long pause. "The fancies of an old man. Nothing I can't deal with."

Zachary looked hurt. "I thought it went both ways," he said reproachfully.

"What went both ways?"

"You and I. I tell you everything that's in my heart..." Poemen gave him a skeptical glance, and Zachary hurried on, "I do, I really do...I know I may not have done, at one time, but for several months...Everything! And I thought it was the same with you."

"It's not quite the same," Poemen said.

Zachary gazed at him questioningly but did not speak. "I'm your teacher," Poemen went on. "I need to know your thoughts, your emotions, because it's my duty and my responsibility to guide you towards perfection. Burdening you with my thoughts, my emotions will not help your soul grow, it will rather drag you back, move you further from perfection. That I do not want to happen. Ever."

Zachary hesitated. "With all due respect, Father, I think that...just this once...you're wrong."

He flinched slightly. Poemen would be well within his rights to reprimand him for insolence. But Poemen did not. "Explain," was all he said.

"If I take on the burden of your thoughts, I halve that burden. To do so is charity, so long as I can lift it. If I could not lift it, you would be right. But I think I am able to lift it, and I would far rather lift it and bear it, for the rest of my life, than allow you to remain in suffering. If I can indeed bear it, then my merit is increased rather than lessened, but that is not my reason for doing it. My reason is the Commandment. If the burden were mine, you would take half of it, and I would be glad of it. Can I do less than that and keep the Commandment?"

Poemen bowed his head. "You are right," he said. "My discernment failed me, but yours did not." A faint flicker of the old twinkle came back into his eye. "You have finally excelled your teacher."

Horrified, Zachary threw himself at Poemen's feet, scattering the remains of the giant handle Poemen had been unweaving. "Don't say that!" he cried. "Don't ever say that! Not even as a joke!"

"It wasn't a joke," Poemen said, gently pushing him away, gesturing for him to rise. "On this occasion you've certainly excelled me, and if you keep it up…"

"Father, how could I! You're a hundred times wiser and stronger than I could ever hope to be, and if…just one time…you're not quite yourself, that is nothing, that must happen, occasionally, as one ages, it has nothing at all to do with…"

"That's enough," Poemen said, a little more sharply than he had meant to, for he genuinely hated to hear praise of himself. "The very first day you came to me, I warned you I couldn't stand excessive displays of emotion. Just be quiet, and I'll tell you what you want to hear,"

Zachary obeyed. But Poemen did not speak immediately. He had laid aside his work, his gaze was now distant, turned inwards. *Having second thoughts?* Zachary wondered. He composed himself to wait in silence. If the old man confided in him, good; if he did not, good also. The obedience of disciple to teacher merely imaged the obedience of each of them to God's will.

Outside, in the darkness, a single hyena howled dismally, very far away.

"Have any of the brothers ever spoken to you about the devastation of Scetis?" Poemen asked at last.

Zachary shook his head. "Never. When did that happen?"

"It didn't. Not yet. But I'm afraid it will."

"Why?"

"Many reasons. There have been prophecies. One by Macarius, a long time ago, nobody took much notice, at the time. Others since. I began to be troubled by the thought of it quite a while ago, before the attack on Nitria. I fought it—successfully, I thought, at the time. I took it for just another form of accidie…Then, I think it was the night after we talked of your miracle…or maybe it was the night after that…Well, that's no matter. I had a dream."

Zachary almost gave a start of surprise. A dream? Poemen, the most rational, the least superstitious of hermits, had lost his composure because of a dream? He suppressed his reaction, so as not to put the old man out of countenance. But the effort was hardly needed, Poemen being so absorbed in his interior world that he would not have noticed any reaction from his disciple.

"A dream," he repeated. "The church burned. Hermits were slain. The desert ran red with blood." He paused, then half-smiled. "I know what you're thinking. His mind is going if he lets himself be troubled by a mere dream...I agree with you. I agree entirely. Truly prophetic dreams are rare, very rare. You remember the handful that came true, and forget the countless number that did not...Normally, I would have taken not the least notice of it. But normally... You know how it is, when you wake from a nightmare, what you feel most, right away, is relief. Relief that what you dreamed isn't true after all, that it was just a dream...Well, I never felt that. Quite the reverse. Each time I felt more and more depressed...And the worst thing of all," he continued, after another long pause, "is that my discernment has failed me in this. I cannot tell whether this is from God, or the Devil, or my own fancy." He brooded in silence a moment, then said, "I've had that dream twice, since then. I'd rather keep vigil throughout the night than dream it again."

Zachary sat there in mute confusion. He did not know what to say; anything he said beyond mere platitudes could only hurt or offend the old man. The silence dragged on, but it was not a silence of peace—rather one tense with unspoken thoughts. *Perhaps*, Zachary thought at last, *he could be reasoned out of it.*

"How could God will that Scetis be destroyed?" he demanded.

"Why shouldn't he?" Poemen asked reasonably.

"A place as holy as this!"

"Well, how holy is that, really? Everyone knows it's not like it was in the old days. And you remember when Anoub saw the hermit buggering the mad boy, how he did nothing because if God hadn't sent down his fire from heaven..." Zachary nodded. "Well, suppose God's fire had just been delayed a little."

Zachary looked sharply at Poemen to see if the old hermit was teasing him, as he sometimes did. But Poemen's face looked perfectly serious, perfectly composed. "When there are so many places so much worse?" Zachary cried. "Why Scetis? Why not Alexandria?"

Poemen shrugged. "Perhaps He doesn't will it, after all."

"Then, it can't happen, so forget about it."

"I wish it was as easy as that," Poemen said sadly. "Do you really suppose that everything that happens, happens because it's God's will?"

Zachary stared at him. "But it says in scripture...Not a sparrow shall fall..."

"And Jesus told us to obey the Commandment. Would he have bothered to do that, if we were obliged to obey it? Would there be any sin, or any virtue, it God had determined beforehand whether we were to be sinners, or virtuous?"

"But surely, if God knows everything—"

"Then, everything must have been decided in advance. Who will be saved, who won't, regardless."

Zachary gazed at his teacher, horror struck. He felt like one proceeding down a peaceful road when an earthquake strikes, and instead of solid ground before him there is suddenly a yawning chasm, impossible to plumb. At the very heart of his faith, suddenly there lay revealed to him this horrifying contradiction.

"These things! They can't...they can't both be true!"

"What can't?"

"That God foreknows everything but that we are free to do good or evil."

"Why can't they?"

Couldn't the old man see? Was he already losing his mind? "If one's true the other's false, it's obvious!"

"To us, perhaps," Poemen said with utter calm. "But that doesn't necessarily make it true." Then, he added, as if to himself, "they're all over the place, getting into our food, yet just when you need one you can't find any."

He was groping around on the floor round the earthenware pots in which their reeds stood soaking. What is he doing now, Zachary asked himself, he's really losing it, what am I to do to help him? Abruptly Poemen stood up, reached out a hand. Something black was crawling across his index finger.

"What's that?"

"An ant."

"Exactly. Do you suppose now that this ant, raised here and spending all its life in this desert, has any conception of...of, say...the ocean?"

Zachary shook his head.

"Good. As much as our mind exceeds that of this ant, so much, or far, far more, does God's mind exceed ours." And Poemen, with a quiet smile of satisfaction, extended his arm to the wall and allowed the ant to walk off into a cranny of it.

Zachary still wasn't quite sure he had it right. "You're saying that what— what seems a contradiction to our human mind...isn't really? Not in God's mind, as He sees things? How can you know that?"

"Zachary, Zachary," Poemen sighed, "haven't I taught you anything? All this Greek logic you learned at school! All very well in its way, mind you. Human intelligence is fine as long as it sticks to the things of this world. Beyond that, it's useless. Worse, it gets in your way, stops you from coming as close to God as you otherwise might."

"You have faith."

"I try to."

"Faith that somewhere, somehow, opposites are reconciled."

"I try to," Poemen repeated. "I don't always. Any honest person will admit to you that his faith has wavered, some time, somewhere. But, yes, in my heart I do believe that somehow that is true. That what we think we see so clearly with our intellect is merely the outward appearance of things."

Zachary tried to digest this thought. Part of his mind revolted against it, cried out that logic was not just a quirk of humans, that it was universal, infallible, irrefutable; another part admitted quietly that, yes, our minds were weak and finite things and to suppose that they could encompass the infinite mind of God was, as Poemen had suggested, more absurd than an ant imagining the ocean. While the two parts continued to struggle for precedence, he asked, "So, where does that leave Scetis?"

"I don't know."

"Should we flee from here, are you saying?"

Poemen looked shocked. "Certainly not! I came here to dedicate my life to God and if He chooses to take that life, so be it. I stay here."

"So," Zachary considered, "all these thoughts that you've been having, they won't help you to any decision. Change your course of action in any way."

"That's correct."

"Will they do your soul any good, do you suppose?"

Poemen shuddered. "Certainly not."

"Then fight them."

Poemen's head jerked back and he stared fixedly at his disciple. "Now you are the teacher and I the pupil, is that it?"

Instead of awe at his own rashness, Zachary felt himself filled with a sudden, new confidence. "No," he said, "I will always respect you and love you and all you have taught me. But it says in Matthew 23 that we should not call one another 'teacher', that we are all brothers, and have only one Teacher, which is Christ."

His words died into silence, and he gazed at Poemen, no longer so confident, struck with his own temerity. But the quality of the silence had changed, it was not filled with anxiety and tension as it had been before. Slowly a smile spread across Poemen's face. "I am rightly rebuked. From here on we are brothers, no more, no less. Give me a word, Zachary, for my salvation."

Zachary felt, not pride, but an awesome sense of responsibility. His mind went totally blank for a few seconds. Then, without any conscious decision, words sprang into his mouth. "If you leave food in a box, and never take it out, it will rot, and in time the box that contains it will rot, too."

Poemen nodded. "So, if my heart has thoughts that it won't act on, or can't act on, those thoughts will themselves go rotten and corrupt my heart. Thank you, Zachary. I am truly edified. With your help, I will drive out these thoughts. Will you pray with me?"

Chapter 37

A small cloud had formed on the southwestern horizon. It might have been a dust-storm raised by one of those turbulent updrafts of hot air that occasionally scourged the desert. The weather made such a possibility more likely—close and sultry, shapeless masses of cloud shifting behind the thin layer of dust-particles that veiled the sky. Somewhere, very far away, thunder muttered. But the sun still shone fitfully over the Wadi Al-Natrun, and gave fleeting gold touches to the distant cloud.

Had it been a dust-storm, it would have moved erratically. This cloud did not. Indeed, it did not seem to move at all. If you looked at it hard you might have convinced yourself that it was growing larger, or smaller—was approaching you or receding from you—but at that distance it was really impossible to tell.

The fat camel-driver to whom John the Dwarf sometimes sold baskets wasn't taking any chances. "Amoun!" he called out.

His companion, also astride a camel, was about twenty yards ahead of him, dozing in his saddle. The fat camel-driver had to call two or three times to get his attention.

"Amoun! Look over there."

Amoun stopped his mount—not without difficulty, for a camel, though not so hard to stop as a full-rigged ship before the wind, has a will of its own—and with their beasts almost side by side, the two men sat motionless, shading their eyes with their hands against the morning glare.

"Can't be what it looks like."

"Yes it can!"

"They daren't. This close to the settled lands."

The fat camel-driver shrugged.

"They'd be mad to. If the Romans are out there, they could cut 'em off."

Although neither of the men knew it, the Romans were out there. A small unit of speculatores, mounted, was on patrol several miles to the west of them. One galloped up to his commanding officer.

"Sir! Barbarians, sir!"

"I've seen 'em" the officer said.

"Permission to engage, sir!"

"Denied."

"Sir?" The soldier stared at his officer, uncomprehending.

"Have you counted 'em?"

"No, sir, but…"

"They outnumber us ten to one. Give the order to head due west." The commander turned away; as far as he was concerned, the interview had finished.

"But, sir…"

"Yes, Cletus?" The officer's tone was ominous.

The soldier went on, undeterred. "You're not sending anyone back to base, sir?"

"What for?"

"To alert the garrison, sir. Barbarian incursion."

"No," when the soldier still failed to ride off, risking punishment for mute insolence, the officer said, "we're to let them pass."

"But sir!"

"Orders. From above." The commander made a sour face. "I'm as pleased about them as you are. But that's how it is."

The soldier saluted, without irony. *Wonderful thing, discipline,* the officer thought. *About all that's left of the old Rome. Wonder how long that will last.*

"Oh, and Cletus."

"Sir!"

"You never saw any barbarians. Nor did I, nor did anyone else. Pass it along. That's an order, too."

Back in the wadi, the two Egyptian camel-drivers still sat watching the cloud. No question, now. It was getting bigger.

"Off!" the fat one exclaimed suddenly. "Run for cover!"

"But they'll get our camels!"

"Wanna try stopping 'em?"

Amoun was nobody's fool. The two of them scrambled off their mounts and ran. Cover? That was ridiculous. There was not as much as a blade of grass in sight, if you didn't count the shallow reed-grown pools over towards Scetis. These shimmered and undulated on the horizon; if the distance had been shorter, the two drivers could have submerged themselves, reeds up their nostrils, like the informer that Moses had hunted long ago. But the nearest pools were two miles or more away, they would never reach them before the Mazices arrived.

Over to their left, low ribs of rock thrust up through the bare sandy dirt. Only a few inches, but that would have to do. They threw themselves down, wriggled forwards, flattened themselves in the dust. "Don't move," the fat one said. "Whatever you do, don't move. Never mind the camels. We can always get more camels."

After a few minutes, they felt the ground under them begin to tremble.

They came, eighty to a hundred of them, tightly bunched but not tightly enough to get under one another's feet; riding their small, hardy, wiry little horses furiously, riding bolt upright, their eyes swiveling constantly from left to right as they rode; water-gourds slung on shoulders, long knives and scimitars at their sides. The dust they raised hung in a curtain behind them, dispersing slowly in the all-but-windless air. They rode straight past the camels, which were ambling slowly away, stopping to munch at the spiny, stunted growth that, here and there, had managed to find a foothold. The nearest of them passed within a couple of hundred feet of the drivers, but he did not see them, his eyes turned towards the horizon.

The leaders approached the marsh. On the moisture-firmed ground their horses' hooves no longer raised dust, but here and there tore up clods of dirt that flew through the air, sometimes striking the riders who followed. They took no notice but continued to ride, at the same furious, unvarying pace. Now they were in shallow water, the hooves flung out a fine spray. Water-drops flashed like jewels in the sunlight. Shrieking, a flock of water birds rose from the reeds, circled in a dark spiral, like smoke, and made off to the north, towards the Canopus and the Nile delta.

A dog—it could not have been the same dog that had sniffed around Moses' herb-garden early that sunny morning so many years before, but it could well have been one of that dog's descendants—broke, panicked, from the reeds as the horses bore down on it. The nearest horse swerved and its rider drew his scimitar. The dog increased its speed, yelping, but it could not outrun the horse. As its rider drew level, he dropped his arm, swinging the scimitar, and the dog's head, sliced loose from its neck, flew through the air, a few scattered drops of blood falling from it as it flew. Then the head splashed into a pool. Before the ripples from it had ceased to spread, the whole troop had passed, the only sound now the dull unbroken thunder of hooves, heading north-west, heading towards Scetis.

As they dwindled and vanished in the broken, shimmering light over the pools, the fat camel-driver rose slowly to his feet. Although he was not a Christian, he had seen plenty of Christians, and he made a fumbling motion with his right hand across his chest, as he had seen them do.

"May their God help them," he said.

Derek Bickerton

Chapter 38

It must have been around the fourth hour of the day when Zachary heard a distant shout and then, before he could even begin to question its source, the sound of running feet, approaching the cell. He dropped the mat he was weaving, but almost before he could stand, the outer door of the cell was thrown open and a hermit he hardly knew, whom he recognized only from having seen him at synaxis, thrust in his head.

Simultaneously, Poemen came through the inner door of the cell.

For a second the three men formed a silent tableau. The stranger was panting so violently he could hardly speak; sweat-moistened hair clung to his forehead, sweat rolled down his face. He hung with one hand on the doorpost and gasped, "Get out! Now!"

"This is our cell," Zachary began indignantly, "we..."

Poemen cut across him. "What is it? Speak, man!"

The man gasped, caught his breath. "Barbarians! Attacking us!"

"That's not possible," Zachary said. "They respect hermits."

"No more," the stranger choked out. "They're killing us!"

"Where?" Poemen demanded. "Which direction?" But he was too late, with a lurch the man had already torn himself from the doorway and was heading off at a staggering run, clutching his chest with one hand. Poemen's gaze went to the doorposts and the sand between them. Zachary, following that gaze, saw a red handprint on one of the doorposts and a small puddle of red beneath, soaking into the sand. He felt a sudden, visceral spasm of fear. He fought it down. Quickly he seized Poemen's arm and swung him towards the inner cell. With a strength he had not known the old man possessed, Poemen broke his grip.

"Father, get inside there, for the love of God..."

"Zachary, for the love of man, I'm going out," Poemen said.

"You're mad; they'll kill you; they..."

"If they're going to kill me," Poemen objected reasonably, "they'll kill me just as easily here. If I am going to die, let me at least die helping my neighbor. Besides, I've had my time. You haven't. You may stay here, if you wish."

"You think I'd leave you?" Zachary cried out.

"Do whatever you have to. You're free to choose."

"I'm coming with you."

"So be it. In that case, compose your soul and fix your mind on the Four Last Things."

Death, Judgement, Hell and Heaven. Those words, so fearful yet so familiar, had never impinged themselves on him as they did now. Even in the interior desert, where three times at least he had come to the very brink of death, he had not seen death as clearly as this. Twice, when hunger and exhaustion or sickness had brought him to that brink, he had been reduced to the level of an animal, able to think of nothing beyond his own physical survival. The third time, in his previous encounter with the Mazices, things had developed so fast and in such a bizarre manner he had hardly had time even to feel fear, let alone contemplate his last hour. Then, at other times, death had seemed infinitely far away—he was young, strong, healthy, his end might be inevitable but there were years ahead of him to prepare for it. And he had not then had his mind focused by long months of prayer, contemplation, ascetic training.

Was he ready to die? Was his soul prepared for judgement?

He did not know. He knew, in a sense, one could never be ready. He knew that even the holiest, when death came for them, had begged for more time to repent their sins. What could he offer beyond the intent of his heart? Oh God I tried. I tried quite hard, at times. Was that enough?

There was still time to make up for things. He could die a good death. He could redeem all the sins and follies of his life by the manner of his dying, by using his death to save the lives of his fellow-hermits.

They went out. It was late afternoon. The heat was stifling, even though there was no sun. The clouds, massed in a huge semicircle from north-east to south-west, had merged into a single looming wall of blackness. Lightning flickered above the horizon, and, well after it, there came the sullen rumble of thunder.

A mile away, John Colobos too had just come out of his burrow.

"Benjamin! Where's Arsenius? And Anoub?"

"I don't know. Aren't they in their cells?"

"No! I just…"

Looking over the Dwarf's shoulder, Benjamin saw a hermit running. Behind him, came a man on horseback. An arm whirled. Something flashed in the sunlight. The hermit screamed, fell. The horseman kept on going, vanished behind a row of cells. Benjamin wrapped both arms around John and swung him off his feet.

John squealed. "Help! Put me down!"

"Just what I'm going to do," Benjamin said, heading for John's burrow.

"I have to go to the church! I have to be with the others! Put me down!"

"No way. I'm not the stuff martyrs are made off. And as long as I'm around, you're not going to be, either." Benjamin's feet found the top of John's ladder; he swung John, still struggling and protesting, over one shoulder—the poor fellow, after a lifetime's fasting, weighed hardly more than a feather—and began to descend. Because his back was turned, he did not see Arsenius.

Arsenius watched the two of them disappear. He stood for a moment, deep in thought, then turned and entered his own cell, coming out moments later with a roll of mats under one arm. He walked to the hole unseen by those below, hoisted up the ladder, threw it across the top of the hole to support the mats, spread the mats across the ladder, scooped up handfuls of sand and sprinkled them carefully over the mats. He could hear screaming somewhere in the distance and at various points around him black-clad figures were running aimlessly. He did not allow any of this to distract him, that part of his mind not needed to direct his actions was already engaged in running over his past life, balancing his account—years of courtly luxury against years of abstinence, actions driven by pride and self-righteousness against actions driven by humility and love. He worked slowly and carefully, as if he had all the time in the world. When he was done he stood back and surveyed his handiwork. It wouldn't survive close scrutiny (he had felt obliged to leave holes, he wasn't sure how long two people could survive down there if he blocked off their air) but with any luck, close scrutiny was something it wouldn't get.

He began to walk briskly towards the church, from which the first sluggish coils of smoke were just beginning to rise. As he walked, he continued his self-assessment. Alas, there was still too much to regret. It had taken him too long to shake off the coils of the world. He had had all too little time in which to learn humility and love. God, if I am spared, he prayed, help me to keep my feet on Your path, and if it pleases You to take me, take into account the sincerity of my intent.

Halfway to the church a barbarian horseman, swerving suddenly from behind an outcrop of rock, rode straight at him. He had no time to dodge, barely time to throw up an arm in front of his face before the horseman knocked him down and rode over him. A flying hoof struck his head. Everything went black.

Up ahead of him, Poemen and Zachary were running now. Their tunics were drenched in sweat, but they did not even notice the discomfort. They had seen the smoke, seen that it was coming not just from the church but from the bakery, the refectory, several of the cells that were close by. *Nitria all over again*, Poemen thought, a spasm of nausea churning his stomach. The sacred books would be burning, here as well as there. But this time there was no centurion to discipline the troops, no Archbishop to control the operation. This was the hour of slaughter. Although he knew his end might be only moments away, neither the thought of his own soul nor the chances of its salvation had entered his mind even for a second. He was totally focused on stopping or at least limiting the killing.

"Look," he said. "There's Moses."

Serenely indifferent to the chaos surrounding him, the Robber, in his priestly robes, was advancing at a fast but steady pace, coming at an angle that would cross their path and heading, not towards the church, but towards the cemetery. For there, at the summit of its low hill, beneath the stone cross crowning that hill, as if that cross alone offered protection, a cluster of several dozen hermits had gathered. Had they been the remnants of an army, it wouldn't have been a bad place to make a stand. But they were not an army, and soon now the horsemen who were coursing the plain in pursuit of fleeing hermits would tire of that and come after them.

Zachary saw shapeless heaps of black scattered around the church and the refectory. Bodies of hermits. A thick layer of oily smoke lay over the church and the buildings surrounding it; the smoke scarcely moved in the windless air, it spread westward in a slow ooze as the fire beneath generated more and more of it. To his nostrils came the acrid smell of burning and beneath it another, sicklier smell, the smell of burning flesh. His mind reeled at the pointless savagery of it all. But he no longer felt fear. He had ceased to be concerned about his own fate. He had composed his mind as best he could, and if his account was negative, so be it. Not my will, he repeated to himself as he ran, but Thy will, Lord. He was with Poemen and Moses, and they would see it through to the end—Poemen and Moses, men whose merit outshone his as the sun outshines the moon. He could hardly die in better company.

Lightning flashed, much nearer now. Zachary found himself counting automatically, as he had done as a child. Between six and seven, the thunder spoke. Much nearer this time. Briefly the thought flashed into his mind, *Is God sending the storm as our deliverance? If so, why so late?* Quickly he extinguished it. *You're in His hands now, Zachary,* he told himself. *Not my will, Thy will. And into Thy hands I commend my spirit.*

Moses had seen them. He stopped, and they caught up with him.

"I hope you're ready for your last hour," he said.

"I've been ready for a long time," Poemen said.

"In my case, the means is appropriate."

"How so?"

"Those that live by the sword shall perish by the sword."

"Come on!" Poemen said. "It's so long since you lived by the sword, you've forgotten how."

"Makes no difference," Moses said gloomily. "Sooner or later, your sins catch up with you."

They reached the cemetery. So far, its scattered headstones and uneven ground had deterred the Mazices from riding in on the huddled mass of hermits at the foot of the cross. The risk of one's mount stumbling and breaking a leg was too great, at least for as long as there were hermits easier to reach. But, even as they climbed the low hill, a scream came from the further side of it, and the huddled mass churned like milk in a pail, sending up confused, answering cries.

"This is it," Moses said, plunging forwards, with Poemen and Zachary in his wake, into the crowd. Some were praying with arms uplifted, some had fallen to their knees, others struggled to push their way to the less vulnerable center of the mass. Towering over them, Moses saw what had happened.

A single horsemen had ridden up between the stones. It was the chief of the Mazices, the man Theophilus had addressed in the underground dungeon. He crouched on his horse, red-eyed, screaming incoherently, spittle flying from his lips. His scimitar, waved aloft, streamed blood. Under the hooves of his rearing horse lay a broken, black-clad body. The thunder came again, without visible flash this time, and scattered raindrops, heavy as coins, began to fall. The barbarian leader put down his head and charged at the shrinking, reeling mass before him. The scimitar whirled. Another hermit fell.

"He's insane," Moses muttered as if to himself as he shouldered his way to the other side of the crowd. "Gone mad with the lust of killing. I've seen it happen."

Poemen was behind Moses, right in front of Zachary. He stopped, and suddenly, unbelievably, his voice burst out singing:

Yea, though I walk through the valley of the shadow of death,

I will fear no evil.

For Thou art with me,

Thy rod and Thy staff, they comfort me.

He was singing the Twenty-Third Psalm, and at the sound of his voice, loud and clear, without the least tremor of age, the turmoil around him gradually stilled, and, haltingly, one after another, other hermits took up the psalm. Recoiling from its charge, the horse pawed the ground, and its rider stared disbelievingly at the hermits who had all turned now to confront him, and whose voices swelled every second more loudly.

Perhaps, he had expected them to break and flee so he could hunt them down one after another. He perched on the prancing horse for a moment, indecisive; then he rode forward again. Moses pushed aside the last couple of hermits and confronted him. There was a moment of absolute stillness, and then the barbarian screamed in Coptic, "Bow down!"

Moses stood immoveable. A half-smile flickered over his somber features. Behind him, the singing rose:

...surely goodness and mercy shall follow me

All the days of my life;

And I will dwell in the house of the Lord forever.

"Bless you," Moses said, "in the name of the Father, the..."

"Bow down!" The barbarian screamed. "Fear me!"

"I fear no man, living or dead," Moses said.

The barbarian reared and struck. Blood flew out in a great geyser from Moses' throat, staining the white robes, splashing the ground at the feet of the nearer hermits, who backed off, horror struck. The tall black figure toppled slowly, like a tree that at first tilts only slightly from the killing stroke and then slowly accelerates towards the ground. The barbarian slashed wildly at the falling body, screaming in his own language, incomprehensibly. The horse, nervous now, reared and rocked back and forth as its rider continued to hack at the now prostrate corpse that had been Moses the Robber.

And, towards them walked Poemen.

Zachary caught his tunic, pulled, and got a grip on him under the arms.

"Let me go," Poemen said between his teeth, "I know what I'm doing." He pushed past the last of the hermits, through rain that was beginning to fall faster now, into the narrow space between them and the chief of the Mazices. As he did so, Zachary swung around in front of him, his back to the barbarian.

"No...you...don't," he said, astonished that he, by far the younger and stronger, had to push with all his might to stop the Shepherd's advance. "You're not going to die. I am. I'm ready. I'm next. Stand back."

Into Poemen's mind, from days long ago in the Thebaid, poured sudden memories of the wrestling tricks he had had to learn when the other children tried to bully him for his love of books. His right leg went between Zachary's legs as he suddenly and simultaneously yielded to Zachary's force and pivoted on his left leg. Zachary, off balance, lost his grip. He tried to regain it but his hands and Poemen's arms were slippery from the rain. He pitched forward, and Poemen caught him and threw him among the other hermits. He fell headlong. Someone's foot stuck him, inadvertently but violently, just above the ear. He blacked out for several seconds. When he came round, groggy, shocked and disoriented, he was under people's feet. He struggled to rise. By the time he stood upright, it was all over.

Poemen walked slowly, firmly towards the barbarian. The horse, more and more skittish, started to back up. The barbarian controlled it, but barely, and screamed:

"Bow down!"

Poemen kept walking.

"Fear me!"

Poemen stopped and lifted his right hand with its index finger extended skywards, at the cloud looming over them so close it seemed about to burst on their heads—not that he thought God was up there (God was everywhere), but because the barbarian probably did.

"No," he cried in a stentorian voice. "Fear Him!"

Derek Bickerton

Chapter 39

As to what happened then, you could get any number of stories. Almost as many stories as there were survivors. Some said that the lightning-flash scored a direct hit on the barbarian's sword. Others said, no, it hit the barbarian himself, God's judgement slew the infidel in that very instant. Others again believed that lightning struck the cross, or was really some distance away, up on the escarpment, and that it was the Arm of God that smote the barbarian, through some supernatural agency, or by itself, an actual physical arm that had come out of the cloud. One or two swore they'd actually seen it. It was huge, they said. No one would ever know for sure where the bolt had actually struck.

What most accounts agreed on was that the barbarian had forced his horse forwards, swung up his scimitar and brought it down in a blow that, if it had fallen where it was intended to fall—between Poemen's left shoulder and neck—it would have split the hermit to the waistline. But it did not. Something, somehow (no one would ever agree on exactly what—the horse, the lightning, superstitious terror, divine intervention) turned the blade a fraction in the last fraction of a second so that it struck a sideways, glancing blow. The barbarian let loose a shriek of rage, raising the blade to strike again as Poemen fell.

And then came the thunder.

Deafening, within two seconds of the flash, almost directly overhead. And the horse, panicking, reared on its hind legs, reared high, flinging its rider from its back. The barbarian turned over once in midair and then his head struck the edge of a tombstone with a sound like someone hitting a watermelon with a club. His body went limp. His brains spilled over the stone.

Somewhere a voice screamed "Alleluia!"

Zachary staggered to his feet. The rain was now falling with a violence and intensity seldom seen in the desert; it sluiced the blood from the fallen bodies and washed it away in the sand, it washed the smear of white and grey matter from the tombstone's face. As if through a dense curtain, Zachary saw Poemen, motionless on the ground, and beyond, the bodies of Moses and the other slain hermits. Over to their right he saw the frantic horse and the dead barbarian, and beyond them...

The singing had stopped. All you could hear was the whinnying of the barbarian's horse and the ceaseless roar of the rain. And in that rain the surviving hermits stood transfixed, water pouring down their white faces and running from the hems of their soaked black tunics to the ground. Prior to that moment, their gaze had been focused on Poemen and the barbarian chief, and they had not even noticed the row of horsemen, a dozen or more of them, who had silently approached and now sat motionless astride their beasts, in a rough semi-circle, twenty yards away, confronting them.

For a long moment, neither group moved, neither group uttered a sound. The sky had turned so dark it was as if a premature night had fallen. Zachary knew with a sudden flash of insight that the hermits behind him were about to break and run for it and that if they did the barbarians would come swarming in to avenge their fallen chief. Lord help them, Christ preserve them, he prayed, and then into his mind there came a small clear voice: *Follow the Shepherd.*

And immediately he took up Poemen's psalm again from the beginning, singing out wildly and at the top of his voice:

The Lord is my shepherd, I shall not want;
He maketh me to lie down in green pastures;
He leadeth me beside still waters...

Lightning flashed, revealing a rigid mass of hermits, shoulder to shoulder, pallid faces transfigured in a kind of ecstasy as they joined Zachary in the psalm; then they were plunged again into darkness, but the singing went on.

The horsemen hesitated, looked at one another, exchanged a few muttered words, then three of them rode slowly forward.

The singing faltered. Zachary felt the backward surge of the crowd suck at him, as a wave sucks back one who strives to emerge from the sea. Frantically, he gestured to them to stay calm, hold their place.

The three barbarians stopped. Two of them dismounted; lifted the chief's body and laid it across the shoulders of the third rider's horse. The two men remounted, one rode up to the chief's horse and cut its throat. All three rode slowly back to their companions, who turned, one after another, and moved away in the steadily-falling rain. As they passed the church, one of them broke into a wild, ululating lament, and the others joined him.

Zachary ran to where Poemen had fallen. He bent his cheek to the old hermit's lips, but felt no breath. Others were crowding round him, he heard a babble of voices but could make no sense of it. The rain began to slacken. Thunder rumbled, moving further off. He spoke, but Poemen did not answer. It was inconceivable that the Shepherd should have lost his life even in the moment of deliverance. It wasn't really happening, it had all been an evil dream. Someone took him by the shoulder and was pulling at him but he flung the hand away, his own hand groping for a pulse in the birds-claw wrist—

Poemen's eyes were closed, but the eyelids stirred, as if the eyes beneath them had moved as they sometimes do in sleep. Zachary couldn't tell whether it was real, or just his imagination, avid for the least sign of life. He called out the Shepherd's name. And the body began to tremble, as if with extreme cold.

"Take this, lay it over him," a voice said.

Zachary turned; the hermit who had touched him was Papnoute. To his utter astonishment, Papnoute, naked but for a cloth about his loins, was holding out his own tunic. That's soaking wet, that won't do him any good, Zachary was on the brink of saying, but he collected himself in time, thanked Papnoute, and spread it over Poemen's body—it could hardly make him wetter than he already was. Someone else spoke behind him.

"I just got here, what happened?"

It was Arsenius, the left side of his face swollen and discolored by a huge bruise that leaked blood from its lower edge.

Briefly, Zachary told him.

"Is he alive?"

"I'm not sure. I think so, barely."

"We must do something for him immediately."

"Yes, but what?"

"We daren't move him, it might kill him. But we can't leave him here in the wet like this, either. Perhaps if we used our tunics we could make some kind of sling for him and carry him like that. There's still the problem of how to lift him without hurting him, though."

Someone coughed. "May I make a suggestion," Papnoute said softly.

"Go ahead."

"Take three tunics. Lay them on the ground, side by side. Someone lift up his legs while someone else slides the end one under him. Do the same again with his head and shoulders. Then four people lift him while someone slides the third tunic under his middle part. That way you move him as little as possible."

Arsenius considered a moment. "Well, let's try it. Carefully, though. No telling how badly he's hurt." He and Zachary took off their tunics, took Papnoute's tunic from Poemen's body and laid them down as Papnoute had suggested.

"Where are we taking him?" Papnoute asked

"It's too far to his cell, isn't it?"

"Much too far."

"The church, then."

"It's burning."

"Not anymore."

It was true. The rain had put out the flames. The wooden beams, or what was left of them, sent up wisps of smoke as the rain shrank to a slow drip. Six of them lifted Poemen on their improvised stretcher and carried him down the slope. Thunder rumbled far off around the horizon like heavy wagons over cobblestones. A fugitive beam of sunlight split the clouds and vanished as abruptly as it had appeared.

"There are benches over there that haven't burned," Arsenius said, taking charge of the situation. "Bring a couple. Lay him down on them, gently, gently now...That's it. We've got to get dry clothes for him somehow. Get some wood—That beam that's hanging down there. Can you reach it?"

"A fire? In the church?" someone asked in tones of horror.

"I think there's been one here already," Arsenius said, with the nearest thing to a smile anyone could remember seeing on his face as he gestured up at the half-burned beams, etched against the sky, that were all that was left of the roof. "In any case, it's for a work of mercy. Get it going and we'll dry out the tunics for him."

Within minutes a fire was blazing on the floor of the church. Zachary dried his tunic before the fire, then carried it back to the improvised bed. Poemen lay there naked, they had cut his clothes away from under him and his body was exposed in all its frailty.

From the time Poemen broke away from him until that moment, Zachary had been in shock. As long as there were practical things to do, doing those things had allowed him to function. But, when he saw the helpless, pitiful body of his friend and mentor, the horror of it hit him with overwhelming force. He fell to his knees by the improvised bed and buried his head in his hands; his chest convulsed with dry, racking sobs. His guilt was intolerable. How could he not have held him back! How when he was young and strong and the old man so weak! Why could he not have held on a moment longer?

No one paid any attention to him. Everyone else was busy about their own affairs. The chaos in the church gradually organized itself. Papnoute and Arsenius were conferring about treatment. Nothing could really be done, they agreed. Something inside him might have broken, but none of them had medical skills, either to diagnose or to heal. Keep him warm, quiet, give him wine if he could take it, water if not, a moist cloth held to his lips if he could not take water, and pray. Mostly pray. God alone would decide whether he lived or died.

Elsewhere, hermits were bringing in the bodies of the slain and laying them before the altar. Others shed all their eremitic decorum; men who, fearful of the demon of fornication, had refrained from touching one another for countless years now embraced, weeping, overcome with joy that their friend, disciple or mentor had survived. More and more hermits kept straggling in from the furthest parts of Scetis, drawn, in time of trouble, automatically to their place of worship.

"You were there," Arsenius said. "Why do you think they stopped killing?"

I'm not sure," Papnoute answered. "They're strange people. More like animals than people. They don't think like you and me."

"We're all children of God," Arsenius said sternly. "Wayward children, some of us, but His children nonetheless. Could He have touched their hearts, do you suppose, in some way?"

Papnoute did not think it likely.

"What happened, exactly, after their chief was killed?"

"Their horsemen surrounded us..." well, that was what it had felt like "...and then we started singing again."

"All of you? Or just one of you?"

"One of us, and then the rest joined in."

"You know which one that was?"

"It was Zachary."

"Hm," Arsenius said thoughtfully, but without too much surprise. "I'll remember that. And then?"

"Then, they took their chief and left."

"You know what I think?" Arsenius said. "They're a superstitious lot. They believe we have powers. They must have thought we'd killed their chief by magic or something. That maybe the singing was part of it, you'd strike all of them dead too if they attacked you. At least they weren't ready to take the chance. If you'd shown the least sign of weakness, they'd have known it wasn't true, and your lives wouldn't have been worth—" and he snapped his fingers. "I think if Zachary hadn't..."

Someone touched Arsenius' sleeve; he broke off. "What is it?"

"We're holding a service. For the dead. And to give thanks for the living."

"Quite right too."

"But there's a problem."

"Really."

"We don't have a priest anymore."

"That's true," Arsenius admitted. "Moses is dead, God rest his soul. But what has that to do with me?"

"We want you to conduct the service."

A look of genuine horror crossed Arsenius' face. "Me? No! I'm not worthy. There are dozens here more worthy..."

"You have the strength and the knowledge to lead us," a firm new voice announced, "You have the experience..."

It was Mother Theodora. "What's that got to do with it?" Arsenius asked. "Anyway, I was just an overpaid schoolteacher. "It's ridiculous, I'm not even one of the old men, I'm still a disciple." And at that, Arsenius broke off, threw up his arms and called, at the top of his voice, "John! Is John Colobos here?"

"Here I am!" a voice piped from the back of the church, and the diminutive hermit was pushed and pulled through the crowd until he was face to face with Arsenius and Theodora.

"John, praise to God you're alive," Arsenius said. "Have you heard this nonsense they're talking, they want me to be substitute priest, me, when there's you who've been here from the beginning, and..."

"No," John said decisively.

"You're the obvious..."

"No. How could I conduct a service, my memory's gone..."

"You got it back."

"Not completely, by any means..."

"Serapion!" someone shouted.

"Serapion was killed by the barbarians, his soul's with the All-Highest!"

"Papnoute," one of Papnoute's disciples called out. But Papnoute had somehow managed to disappear.

"John, John!" other voices called, drowning out all the alternatives. Arsenius, towering over his mentor, placed his hands on John's shoulders.

"John, the three of you, you, Moses and Poemen, were the holiest men in Scetis, the men who followed most closely in the path of their Savior. Moses is dead, Poemen may be also. That leaves you. And you are chosen by public acclamation. In your humility, please accept that choice."

John bowed his head, and moved slowly and hesitantly to the altar, the others surging after him, standing in absolute silence while he spoke:

"Brethren, dear friends in God. You know with what reluctance I accept this office, temporary though it be. You have required it of me despite all my infirmities, so I ask you in turn to bear with me and to help me out when my tongue falters. We have not two but three services to perform here today, a service for the souls of our beloved companions who are no longer with us, a service of prayer that, if God wills it, those of us who were wounded, and most especially our beloved Poemen, may recover their strength, and a service of gratitude for God for sparing those of us who are left to pray for those souls. The first must come first, as our sorrow for those we have lost must, in all charity, exceed any joy that we feel at our own deliverance; it must take precedence even over our prayers for our injured comrades, since their fate lies in God's hands not ours. Later on, I shall want to say a few words about those who now, most surely, sit close to the throne of the Almighty, and if any of you should wish to join in this, I welcome you to do so. But first, it is fitting we begin with a psalm, Psalm 46, which we will sing responsively."

And John sang, "God is our refuge and strength."

And the congregation answered, "A very present help in trouble."

And John: "therefore will we not fear, though the earth be moved."

And the congregation: "And though the hills be carried into the midst of the sea..."

The sun had set before the services ended. It had burst through the clouds quite early in the afternoon, and burned down through the charred and shattered rafters of the church onto the bare heads of the assembled hermits. Now they could return to their cells, those who still had cells to return to. They dispersed slowly, talking in low voices. What would they do now? Many were for leaving, going to Palestine or Upper Egypt; others were determined to stay at all costs, Most of them filed past the improvised bed where Poemen still hovered between life and death, to express their hope for his recovery and to murmur a few words of condolence to Zachary, who throughout the services had remained at Poemen's side. John, preoccupied now with his new duties, was one of the last.

"Please accept my humblest apologies," he said.

"Whatever for?"

"For not being there to stand by you all."

"My fault entirely," Benjamin, behind him, put in.

"John, we're just glad you weren't there."

"I will stay with you and Poemen, tonight," John said.

"You don't have to."

"I want to. We can take turns watching, if one of us gets sleepy."

"I'll stay too," Benjamin said. "Keep you company."

Zachary looked at him in genuine respect, for he knew that keeping vigil wasn't Benjamin's style. "Thanks, Benjamin," he said sincerely. "I really appreciate that."

Finally, when the church had emptied, Papnoute came.

"I was there, you know." he said.

"Where?"

"At the cross."

"I know you were."

"But I did nothing," Papnoute said in a voice of bitter self-reproach. "I could have helped, but I did nothing."

"I did nothing. I let go of him."

"But you tried. I was afraid. Not of dying itself, but of dying before I was through repenting. And afterwards you started the psalm again. I cannot tell you how edified I was by that."

Zachary felt tears beginning to prickle against his eyeballs. To hear this, from the man who had treated him with such coldness and severity in his first year in Scetis! Overwhelmed, he tried to speak, but Papnoute interrupted him.

"You'll be cold tonight."

Zachary had totally forgotten that he was still almost naked, his tunic spread over Poemen's body.

"You have a spare tunic in your cell?"

"Yes, but…"

"Stay here with him and I'll fetch it for you. Your sheepskin, too, and John's and Benjamin's, you'll all need something to rest on."

"But," Zachary objected, 'that must be a good five miles, to my cell, John's, back here, then…"

Papnoute shrugged, said, "It's nothing," and turned before Zachary could speak again.

Zachary watched him go, and suddenly tears began to pour from his eyes. He had not wept for Moses, he had not even wept for Poemen, but somehow this simple act of kindness and humility touched some spring in his heart that unlocked all the grief that had filled it to bursting point—grief for Moses and Poemen, most of all, but beyond that grief for himself and all the sins and omissions of his past, for his father, for Celia, for Leila, for all those who wittingly or unwittingly he had injured.

As the tears flowed, John and Benjamin turned tactfully away from him, and John offered up a silent prayer of gratitude that he had been freed of his unholy desire for the younger man. He had questioned himself often on this, over the last few years. Was it merely because Zachary had grown older, had lost some of the handsomeness he previously possessed? No, he could answer honestly, that had nothing to do with it. Desires of that kind were long past, for him. He loved Zachary, indeed, but as a brother. He had not failed to notice, too, that the change in Zachary's looks was not the only change that had taken place in him. There was a sureness, a maturity about him that he had never had either in that first year or even when he returned to the desert. *God be praised,* John thought. *He has truly grown in wisdom and discretion—maybe there's hope for Scetis yet, if not the place itself, then all that it has striven to stand for.*

At last, Zachary's weeping ceased. He sat up and looked about him, rose and bent over Poemen's face. The old shepherd was breathing softly, almost imperceptibly, his soul still wandering in some no-man's-land between this world and the next. The three men silently watched him, while above them, beyond the roof of the devastated church, one after another the stars began to appear. *Funny,* John thought, *how you never actually see one come out—it's not there, then suddenly it's there. But that's an illusion, of course, because they're really there all the time. Like all true things of heaven, the mists of the world may often hide them from us. But for ever and ever, there they really are.*

If you enjoyed *The City and the Desert* consider the first part in the Commandment Trilogy, *The Desert and the City*

Among the dunes and in the full glare of the desert sun, young Zachary finds that the madness, the politics, and the appetites which we all try to escape from, dwell deep within each and every one of us.

Late in the 4th century AD, the young Greek man abandons his family's home in Alexandria with its wealth, comfort, and a promising future with a beautiful girl betrothed to him, to venture out into the desert to prove the earnestness of his Christian faith among the fascinating mix of misfits who have chosen to pursue a Christ-centered life.

There, among the hermits, he earns crusts of bread, calloused hands, and the derision of the older adepts. Unfortunately, before coming to the conclusion that his romanticized idea of giving away his wealth to pursue the ascetic life was not as simple as he originally thought, he finds himself as part of a fanatical mob bent on smashing a pagan temple and burning Ptolemy's famed library and all of its collected wisdom.

and the second part in the Commandment Trilogy, *In the Heart of the Country*

Zachary, the failed hermit, begins to expiate his sins in the interior desert of fourth-century Egypt. This second part links his story with that of Leila, the peasant girl whom the bandit Darion saved from rape at the hands of his gang. While Zachary goes through a series of bizarre experiences in a lost desert oasis, Leila travels to the White Monastery, ruled by the ruthless Shenoute, where instead of the holy calm she expected she finds only lesbian practices and spiteful intrigue. When Zachary falls mortally ill he is rescued by an unexpected savior, and recovers to find himself a peasant in the Nile valley. There he meets Leila, who has been expelled from the White Monastery, and slowly, cautiously, almost unwillingly these two "Casualties of the Life", as they call themselves, begin to fall in love.

Once again, with exemplary research and evocative writing, Derek Bickerton brings to life an exotic but little-known period of history, and sheds a unique light on the early development of Christianity-both its good and its bad sides.

About the Author

Derek Bickerton (d. 2018) was an English-born American linguist and academic who was Professor Emeritus at the University of Hawaii in Manoa. He is the author of numerous academic works as well as the renown novelist of the Commandment Trilogy. A poet extraordinaire, he wrote extensively on the richness of life and the mysteries of death. He is survived by his wife, Yvonne.

If you enjoyed *The City and the Desert,* consider these other fine books from Aignos Publishing, an imprint of Savant Books and Publications:

The Dark Side of Sunshine by Paul Guzzo
Cazadores de Libros Perdidos by German William Cabasssa Barber [Spanish]
The Desert and the City by Derek Bickerton
The Overnight Family Man by Paul Guzzo
There is No Cholera in Zimbabwe by Zachary M. Oliver
John Doe by Buz Sawyers
The Piano Tuner's Wife by Jean Yamasaki Toyama
An Aura of Greatness: Reflections on Governor John A. Burns by Brendan P. Burns
Polonio Pass by Doc Krinberg
Iwana by Alvaro Leiva
University and King by Jeffrey Ryan Long
The Surreal Adventures of Dr. Mingus by Jesus Richard Felix Rodriguez
Letters by Buz Sawyers
In the Heart of the Country by Derek Bickerton
El Camino De Regreso by Maricruz Acuna [Spanish]
Prepositions by Jean Yamasaki Toyama
Deep Slumber of Dogs by Doc Krinberg
Saddam's Parrot by Jim Currie
Beneath Them by Natalie Roers
Chang the Magic Cat by A. G. Hayes
Illegal by E. M. Duesel
Island Wildlife: Exiles, Expats and Exotic Others by Robert Friedman
The Winter Spider by Doc Krinberg
The Princess in My Head by J. G. Matheny
Comic Crusaders by Richard Rose
I'll Remember by Clif Mc Crady
Critical Writing: Stories as Phenomena by Jamie Dela Cruz Ed.D.
The Edge of Madness by Raymond Gaynor
'Til Then Our Written Love Will Have to Do by Cheryl L. Woods

Ainos Publishing at www.savantbooksandpublications.com

Derek Bickerton

and these other fine books from Savant Books and Publications

Essay, Essay, Essay by Yasuo Kobachi
Aloha from Coffee Island by Walter Miyanari
Footprints, Smiles and Little White Lies by Daniel S. Janik
The Illustrated Middle Earth by Daniel S. Janik
Last and Final Harvest by Daniel S. Janik
A Whale's Tale by Daniel S. Janik
Tropic of California by R. Page Kaufman
Tropic of California (the companion music CD) by R. Page Kaufman
The Village Curtain by Tony Tame
Dare to Love in Oz by William Maltese
The Interzone by Tatsuyuki Kobayashi
Today I Am a Man by Larry Rodness
The Bahrain Conspiracy by Bentley Gates
Called Home by Gloria Schumann
First Breath edited by Z. M. Oliver
The Jumper Chronicles by W. C. Peever
William Maltese's Flicker by William Maltese
My Unborn Child by Orest Stocco
Last Song of the Whales by Four Arrows
Perilous Panacea by Ronald Klueh
Falling but Fulfilled by Zachary M. Oliver
Mythical Voyage by Robin Ymer
Hello, Norma Jean by Sue Dolleris
Charlie No Face by David B. Seaburn
Number One Bestseller by Brian Morley
My Two Wives and Three Husbands by S. Stanley Gordon
In Dire Straits by Jim Currie
Wretched Land by Mila Komarnisky
Who's Killing All the Lawyers? by A. G. Hayes
Ammon's Horn by G. Amati
Wavelengths edited by Zachary M. Oliver
Communion by Jean Blasiar and Jonathan Marcantoni
The Oil Man by Leon Puissegur
Random Views of Asia from the Mid-Pacific by William E. Sharp
The Isla Vista Crucible by Reilly Ridgell
Blood Money by Scott Mastro
In the Himalayan Nights by Anoop Chandola
On My Behalf by Helen Doan
Chimney Bluffs by David B. Seaburn
The Loons by Sue Dolleris
The Judas List by A. G. Hayes
Path of the Templar—Book 2 of The Jumper Chronicles by W. C. Peever
The Desperate Cycle by Tony Tame
Shutterbug by Buz Sawyer
Blessed are the Peacekeepers by Tom Donnelly and Mike Munger
Bellwether Messages edited by D. S. Janik
The Turtle Dances by Daniel S. Janik
The Lazarus Conspiracies by Richard Rose
Purple Haze by George B. Hudson

Imminent Danger by A. G. Hayes
Lullaby Moon (CD) by Malia Elliott of Leon & Malia
Volutions edited by Suzanne Langford
In the Eyes of the Son by Hans Brinckmann
The Hanging of Dr. Hanson by Bentley Gates
Flight of Destiny by Francis Powell
Elaine of Corbenic by Tima Z. Newman
Ballerina Birdies by Marina Yamamoto
More More Time by David B. Seabird
Crazy Like Me by Erin Lee
Cleopatra Unconquered by Helen R. Davis
Valedictory by Daniel Scott
The Chemical Factor by A. G. Hayes
Quantum Death by A. G. Hayes
Running from the Pack edited by Helen R. Davis
Big Heaven by Charlotte Hebert
Captain Riddle's Treasure by GV Rama Rao
All Things Await by Seth Clabough
Tsunami Libido by Cate Burns
Finding Kate by A. G. Hayes
The Adventures of Purple Head, Buddha Monkey and... by Erik Bracht
In the Shadows of My Mind by Andrew Massie
The Gumshoe by Richard Rose
Cereus by Z. Roux
Shadow and Light edited by Helen R. Davis
The Solar Triangle by A. G. Hayes
A Real Daughter by Lynne McKelvey
StoryTeller by Nicholas Bylotas
Bo Henry at Three Forks by Daniel D. Bradford
One Night in Bangkok by Keith Rees
Kindred edited by Doc Krinberg
Cleopatra Victorious by Helen R. Davis
Navel of the Sea by Elizabeth McKague
68 Via Condotti: Book One - Eternity Ltd by A. G. Hayes
Critical Writing: Stories as Phonomena by Jamie Dela Cruz
Truth and Tell Travel the Solar System by Helen R. Davis
The COMPLETE Koski & Falk by A. G. Hayes
*Leon & Malia's Island Music (*CD) by Leon & Malia
Aloha La'a Kea (Sacred Light of Love) edited by Uhene
Hawaii Kids' Music Vol I by Leon & Malia

Coming soon:

Honeymoon Forever by R. Page Kaufman
A Gathering of Poets edited by Dorothy Winslow Wright
Hawaii Kids' Music Vol II by Leon & Malia

http://www.savantbooksandpublications.com

www.ingramcontent.com/pod-product-compliance
Lightning Source LLC
Chambersburg PA
CBHW051240260626
47162CB00002B/527